Girls'
Night In

Girls' Night In

Edited by Jessica Adams,
Chris Manby, Fiona Walker

HarperCollins*Publishers*

HarperCollins*Publishers*
77–85 Fulham Palace Road,
Hammersmith, London W6 8JB
www.**fire**and**water**.com

A Paperback Original 2000
1 3 5 7 9 8 6 4 2

A catalogue record for this book
is available from the British Library

ISBN 0 00 651485 5

Set in Minion by
Rowland Phototypesetting Ltd,
Bury St Edmunds, Suffolk

Printed and bound in Great Britain by
Clays Ltd, St Ives plc

Contents

Introduction

It's difficult to see what devastatingly handsome men, heart-breakingly wet tissues and the odd glass of Cava have in common with a school in Rwanda and a playground in Kosovo. But here, in this glorious book, you have it.

This book was the brainchild of writing friends Chris Manby, Jessica Adams and Fiona Walker. Meeting up for drinks one night, they talked about the host of young women whose unique brand of fiction currently top the book charts, and decided to bring all that talent together in one book for one terrific cause. Scribbling ideas on napkins, they were determined from the outset to create a book that raises spirits as well as funds. Within twenty-four hours, this unique collection was born.

The approaching deadline saw stories flying across the internet and writers who had previously been head to head in the book charts asking each other for advice. Of course, there were a few obligatory girls' nights out to discuss narrative structure over a glass or two as well! With best-selling authors from the UK, Ireland, America and Australia donating their stories free of charge, the generosity and enthusiasm of all involved has been extraordinary.

One pound from every copy of *Girls Night In* goes towards War Child's Safe Play Programme in the Balkans and an educational programme in Rwanda. In Kosovo, thousands of children have been left without anywhere to play, have fun, or have a normal childhood. In Rwanda most girls have no access to education. So thanks for buying this book – you've just helped these children, have a great night in on me.

Why War Child Are Great:

Since it was founded in 1993, War Child has alleviated the suffering of tens of thousands of children throughout the World. Providing mobile bakeries and supplying insulin to stricken warzones, the charity directs aid where it's needed most. But they do not disappear when the guns have stopped shooting and the fires have died down. They are also instrumental in healing the psychological damage caused to children by their experiences of war.

The money raised from this book will fund two essential projects:

The Safe Play Areas Programme runs throughout the Balkans on land cleared of mines, unexploded bombs and rubble. War Child builds playgrounds where children of all ethnic backgrounds can play without fear, encouraging them to make friends and build bridges for the future.

In Rwanda, girls rarely have the opportunity to be educated into their teens – in fact as few as 8% complete primary school and are able to go on to secondary school. In partnership with Girls' Night In, War Child will fund essential improvements to a girls' school near

Kigali, ensuring that a greater number of young girls are given the opportunities taken for granted throughout the West.

Acknowledgements

by Jessica Adams, Chris Manby and Fiona Walker

There may be a certain nobility in being an unsung hero, but we would prefer to get the biggest sound system available, dig out our Bananarama puff-balls and yodel 'Really Saying Something' to the rafters to emphasize how many people have worked their socks, shoes and toe-nail polish off to make this book happen. They all deserve a long, sustained high C, high 5 and high kick of thanks.

The twenty-eight other authors who donated their wonderful stories free of charge are all stars. We'll remain eternally grateful to each and every one for pooling so much talent, so many contacts and so much time. A special mention has to go to Freya North and Karen Moline, who by serendipitous luck were in the same bar on the night that we thought this idea up and who immediately agreed to be involved. Their enthusiasm gave us the extra momentum needed to start the ball rolling. As for our networker and naughty-quote doyenne, Jane Owen, thanks for pulling strings and pitching treatments all over the BBC. And, for making our girls' nights out such fun, raised glasses go to honorary Lit Girls – Jenny Frielich, Julie Wright and Joanne Finnie.

We were very lucky to land Jonathan Lloyd from Curtis Brown as our agent on this project – it was worth getting him out of bed at an ungodly hour in Australia to make him say yes. To Jonathan, Tara Wynne and Carol Jackson, a huge vote of thanks.

There was only ever one publisher for *Girls' Night In*. HarperCollins' enthusiasm was matchless from the start, and their cross-departmental input, understanding and energy has been phenomenal. The Hammersmith Massive is a huge, friendly posse and the fact that its Lit Home-girl, Rachel Hore, agreed to take on thirty-one mistresses of the pen is worthy of a bravery award and a diploma in diplomacy. Huge thanks to her, to Yvette Cowles, Fiona McIntosh, Claire Round, Jennifer Parr, Georgina Hawtrey-Woore and to the unflappable Anne O'Brien (no more one-eared Easter bunnies after this, we hope). Also hip-hop-hoorays to Martin Palmer, Jane Harris, Karen Davies and Katherine Ball who have secured all those orders which mean more money to build playgrounds and dormitories.

In Australia, we would also like to thank Julie 'Jewels' Gibbs and Fiona Inglis, who have helped create Stage Two – a new version of this amazing book, to be published on the other side of the world this year.

Liz Sich and Melody Odusanya at Colman Getty PR deserve a song all to themselves for juggling so many author contacts, differing schedules and delicate egos to come up with a sensational media campaign.

ACKNOWLEDGEMENTS

In the hero stakes, they don't come better-qualified than the ultimate T, D and H Neil Morrisey, whose work with War Child extends far beyond the usual celebrity endorsement. He gets our big love ballad.

And the song we'll sing loudest goes to those for whom this book is only a small step on a long mission. When Jessica first walked into War Child's London office, she knew it was somewhere special. Piles of diabetic supplies were on the floor next to telephones, and sacks of sleeping bags stood next to the kettle. It was clearly a hands-on aid organization, and it still is. Thanks to Heather, James, Johnnie, Nicky, Sue, Anne-Marie and especially Lynne Kuschel, who has been War Child's right-hand woman on this book. Thanks too, to Bill Leeson, War Child's co-founder, for his vision.

Girls' Night In

In 1991, Freya North gave up a PhD in Art History to devote herself to her first novel, though it necessitated four years of demoralising temping jobs and the turning of deaf ears to parents pleading with her 'to get a proper job'. In 1995, Freya landed top agent Jonathan Lloyd by sending him a page of completely fabricated reviews; 5 publishers entered a bidding war for her work. A three-book deal for a 6-figure sum was the result and William Heinemann published *Sally* in 1996 to great acclaim. A bestseller a year has followed since with *Chloë*, *Polly* and *Cat*. Set around the Tour de France, the research for *Cat* took Freya deep down to the secrets behind the lycra. 'You wouldn't believe what the riders do with bananas,' she marvels.

In and Out

Freya North

'Lady – is your nose itching?'

Finty McKenzie took the palm of her hand from the tip of her nose, where it had been doing all manner of pressing, rotating and jiggling, and looked up. Locating the owner of the husky mid-Atlantic drawl, he who had posed the question, she alighted on an elderly man, clad in plaid.

'You got an itchy nose, huh?' he pressed, not waiting for an answer. 'Honey! Doncha know? You're gonna kiss a fool!'

The exclamation mark soared instantly from floor to ceiling of the plush hotel bar, but it was the word 'fool' which reverberated; the 'f' having been expelled from teeth and lips like a bad taste, the 'l' lingering on a very spiked tongue tip. The aged American chuckled extravagantly (because he knew what he was talking about), Finty whooped with sudden laughter (because she hadn't a clue what he was talking about), but Brett, the man sitting next to her, he who had been bedding her these past three months, gave no hint of reaction.

To prove a point, but not quite sure what, or to

whom, Finty affectionately kissed Brett in front of the American. This served to make the man guffaw so heartily that a fit of coughing befell him and expedited his exit from the bar.

'What a character!' Finty laughed.

'Shoot me when I get like that,' Brett said measuredly. Immediately, Finty experienced a quite violent reaction which she had come to term 'a moment'. She'd never had one until she'd met Brett. Every so often, something he would say or do would, for a moment, alarm her so severely that it would course through her blood like acid. The searing horror came as much from self-disgust that she could be with such a man, as from his crime itself. However. Here she still is. These were but moments. And she wasn't sure from where they originated. Head or heart. And which should rule which? These were but moments. Wasn't she just looking for things to throw at the relationship? She'd scold herself for sabotaging something that might well be very good indeed. More tolerance, that's what's needed. But from him or her? She had justified the thinly veiled racist comment he had once made as but a momentary aberration. And he'd only been joking, of course, when he'd asked her to make his bed the morning after they'd first slept together there. And he had a migraine that night he left her stranded in Soho in the early hours. It had been OK. She'd found a cab almost immediately, just a street or three away. And Brett had phoned the next day to explain that he suffered from migraines. That they made him do strange things. Like leave people in the centre of the city at an unseemly hour. Of course, of course. All forgiven.

'Brett gives *me* a fucking migraine,' Sally said, peering into the oven and wondering if it was the slightly grimy door that made the Marks & Spencer luxury cheese puffs look golden or if they were indeed ready. 'How long?'

'Three months, must be,' said Chloë distractedly, rocking against the radiator as if forgetting how hot it was each time her bottom met it.

Sally stared at her. 'The cheese puffs,' she said with theatrical kindness, raising an eyebrow at Polly and fixing Chloë with a look of exaggerated pity.

'Oh, *them*,' said Chloë in a bid to patronize Sally for ranking cheese puffs higher in the grand scheme of things than Finty and Brett, 'almost eight minutes.'

'But they look ready,' Sally protested, saliva shooting around her jaw and her stomach reminding her that crisps and a pot of coleslaw at lunch had not hit the spot.

'You leave them be for another four minutes,' Polly warned, brandishing the empty carton for emphasis and opening a bag of hand-cooked vegetable crisps in a futile bid to lure Sally away from the oven. 'Here. And wine while you wait. It's my bloody oven.'

It was Polly's turn to host the Gathering. Though, as hostess, her responsibilities were minimal apart from ensuring that ready-made luxuries were in the oven, that the corkscrew was foolproof and that any live-in lovers had been banished. The Gathering was a monthly institution, founded instinctively three years ago when all four girls found themselves dumped and depressed and desperate to do voodoo. They had convened with a need to exhaust their repertory of expletives, to drink much vodka and perform a cleansing ritual Chloë had read about which entailed the burning of a bunch of sage and much chanting. The swearing and the smoke from the sage gave them giggles, they soon found themselves quite drunk on spirits bottled and natural, and their sense of personal justice and order in the world was restored. Where their hearts had hurt at the beginning of the evening, now their sides ached from laughter. They decreed that such a restorative tonic should not be restricted to times of crisis but should become a mainstay of every month. Raucous in Richmond at Polly's place or dancing in Dean Street until the proprietor told them to leave; chilling out at Chloë's or conversing animatedly at a Conran restaurant; a few sniffs rapidly devolving into mass sobbing at a chick-flick at the Leicester Square Odeon, or getting stoned and saying not a lot at Sally's. Wherever they were, their sense of togetherness could make a month make sense. In or out, they'd shake it all about, kiss each other liberally at home time and look forward immensely to the next gathering.

'I think I'm planning my life, and doing the things I'm doing, safe in the knowledge that I can always Workshop-Through-It at our Gathering,' Polly had once said, to much nodding all round. Which was why

Finty's absence was so unfathomable. Rather insulting. Just a little worrying, too.

'Don't like,' said Chloë, wrinkling her nose.

'I'll have yours, then,' said Sally, fanning her mouth and eyeing Chloë's cheesy puff.

'*Brett*,' Chloë said. 'Don't like *him*.'

'You've only met him once,' Polly protested.

'As have you,' said Chloë, 'and did you like him?'

Polly gave Chloë a swift smile of defeat. 'No.'

'Ditto,' said Sally who'd burnt the roof of her mouth but couldn't possibly admit to it and therefore took another cheesy puff. 'I don't like what he's doing to her.'

'Do you mean that he's taking her away from us?' Polly, who feared this to be the case, asked.

'No,' Sally said, 'not that. More, I feel that he's detrimental to her self-confidence; which is why she jumps to his beck and call.'

'Forsaking us for him,' said Polly.

'Yes,' Sally clarified, 'but I can't believe it's because she deems him preferable, nor that she's taking advantage of us.'

'I think he's a harmless creep,' said Chloë, 'way *way* out of Finty's league. I think she'll figure that out soon enough. When the novelty of new sex abates.'

The three women fell silent.

'However, I, for one, cannot believe that sex with him can make up for his questionable personality,' Chloë continued, 'nor for it taking precedence over the Gathering.'

The three women fell silent.

Was their concern for their friend's welfare with this man? Or that they rued the fact that their hitherto sacred coven might be fallible? An era ending? If they conceded that this was the case, weren't they investing a harmless creep with more power than they felt he warranted?

'My point is,' Sally said, using her hands for emphasis to prevent herself from succumbing to a fourth cheesy puff, 'Finty should be here, not there. I think it's indicative of a floundering relationship that she isn't. It's only one night a month. She has a duty. I mean, when have any of us ever rejected a Gathering?'

'You did, you old tart!' Polly cajoled. 'When you first started seeing Richard. When he was going to seduce you with his culinary skills.'

'Yes,' Sally said patiently, 'but he did. And then I married the man.' She peered into Polly's fridge and brought out reduced fat guacamole and humous. 'See me now – banning husband from home on a monthly basis – grounds for divorce, surely! Mind you, if he ever objected – well, grounds for divorce, surely.'

'Oh God!' Chloë exclaimed. 'Please don't let Finty marry Brett!'

The girls made noises and gesticulations of a mass vomiting session and then giggled guiltily. Perhaps Finty really was in love with the man. Perhaps he was a really lovely chap who wasn't very confident in company. Or merely had an awkward manner, rather than no manners at all, which is what they all suspected. Perhaps he was to be on the scene for months, even years. He would remain great gossip fodder – as long as Finty remained oblivious to the fact. Suddenly, along with the vegetable crisps and rather luminous guacamole, the three women also passed around a smile steeped in slight suspicion and discomfort. It occurred to them that perhaps their own partners had been the subjects of such unfavourable scrutiny. Maybe still were. No. Surely not. Richard was such great company. William was sensitive. Max always had them laughing. And the fundamental difference was that these three men were openly at ease with their respective partners and her friends. Whereas Brett had stiffened when Finty had kissed him in front of them and he'd squirmed when Sally had burped, when Polly had sworn, when Chloë had touched his knee in a bid to extend welcome, to establish familiarity.

'Where was he taking her anyway?' Chloë asked, uncorking a bottle of Semillon and giving Polly the thumbs up at the bumper bag of oven chips held aloft for their approval. 'Where have they gone that could possibly be preferable to oven chips, low fat dips and our delectable company?' She burped under her breath, as demurely as she could. Sally responded with one that made the rafters tremble.

Peanuts. Finty detested peanuts. She hated the taste and she couldn't abide the smell. And now Brett reeked of peanuts. But more loathsome than this was what he was doing to them. He was snatching little handfuls by contorting his fingers over the bowl like the hands of an Action Man doll. He was then bouncing his clutch up and down in his palm as if panning for gold, before pushing his whole hand against his mouth. His trousers. He was wiping his fingers over his trousers, leaving salt there, before doing Action Man Hands and reaching for the bowl again.

This is nuts. This is crazy. I want Marks & Spencer finger-food.

'How about sashimi?' Brett suggested. 'There's a place near here. We use it for business lunches. They know me.' For Finty, who'd never ordered anything medium rare in her life, let alone raw, the thought of it turned her stomach at a slightly faster rotation than the peanuts. 'Stop rubbing your nose,' Brett said, irritation in his voice manifest in the way he swirled the ice around his glass. 'Go and blow it, for God's sake.'

Ladies Toilets. Haven. Peace and camaraderie. Hair products and perfume and mints laid out by the basins. An attendant handing out paper towels and a part-of-the-job smile behind sad (part of the job) eyes. Finty locks herself in a cubicle and sits there awhile. Her nose itches but there's nothing to blow. She pulls the chain though there is nothing to flush. She washes her hands automatically and checks her reflection. If there's sadness behind the toilet-attendant's eyes, Finty's gaze is underscored with a flatness. It shouldn't be so. She should be having a wonderful time. She's on a date. Being wined and dined. Whined at and to dine on foodstuffs she doesn't like. But there'll be sex too. That's to look forward to. Though she'll close her eyes and conjure Brad Pitt.

'Gorgeous skirt!' marvels a stranger.

'Thanks!' Finty replies, all smiles.

'Nice bloke too,' says the stranger's friend, 'but doesn't he like his peanuts!'

'Yeah!' says Finty, wondering why she's lacing her voice with a hasty approximation of affection, or possessiveness; and suddenly craving her own girlfriends desperately.

Must call them. Just to say hullo.

The entrance to the bar is the foyer of the hotel and, though Finty has both battery and strong signal on her mobile phone, she eschews privacy, opting for the payphone.

'Hullo?' Polly answers, with a voice suggesting outrage that there is such an intrusion on a night when she's gathered her soul mates around her.

'Hey!' says Finty with commendable bounce.

'Finty!' Polly shrieks and suddenly the phone has been given to Sally, then Chloë, before all three attempt to listen and chat en masse. Finty says something about peanuts and her nose and an old man clad in plaid. But the girls are too eager to tell her that she should be there with them, on the third bottle of wine, now called vino-darling, with her stomach full of fancy morsels.

'I'd better go,' says Finty all breezy, 'I'll speak to you tomorrow. Have fun.'

'We are!' they sing. 'We are!'

Finty replaced the receiver and rested her head against the side of the booth momentarily before quite literally pulling herself together.

'Young lady!' It was the elderly American gentleman. 'Your nose still itching?' Finty smiled and shook her head. 'So you wised up and dumped the guy?' Finty smiled and shook her head. 'Steak!' The man proclaimed, 'I'm going out to get me a steak. Aberdeen. Angus. Horse. I got to have steak – why don't you join me?' Finty smiled and shook her head. 'More nutritious than peanuts,' he said. Giving Finty a shrug and a wink, he had the doorman summon a taxi. Comforted that he knew about the peanuts, Finty returned to the bar.

'It's half-eight and she's phoned,' Chloë assesses.

'Wonder why?' Sally contemplates.

'Hmm,' Polly ponders, offering more wine and oven chips.

'Any ketchup?' Sally asks. Polly shakes her head and begs forgiveness.

'Did Finty say where she was?' Chloë asks. Polly shakes her head. The three of them had forgotten to ask. Unforgivable.

On approaching Brett, who was very obviously cleaning his teeth with his tongue, Finty was pleased to see the peanut bowl had gone. But it was returned, replenished, just as soon as she sat down. Brett winked at the waitress. And then he winked at his girlfriend. His Action Man hand reached for the peanuts. Finty diverted her gaze for fear of hitting him and scanned the bar with a half-smile fixed to her face. She tuned in to the sounds surrounding her. Animated chatter. Music. Bursts of laughter. Clink and clank of glasses and china and ice. Brett munching peanuts, rubbing his salty fingers on his trouser legs. Her involuntary sigh was loud, but the silence between Brett and her was louder. Sally, Chloë and Polly had each, at some point, marvelled to Finty how wonderful silence between partners could be. Chloë had termed it 'the ultimate in communication'. Polly had defined it 'proof of compatibility'. Sally had proclaimed it 'a seal of safety'. For Finty, it was as uncomfortable as the fake smile she was forcing upon her lips.

It's not even a loaded silence – of things left unsaid, or wounds being licked or issues being brooded over, Finty realized, *it's the result of there being very little to say. Soon enough he'll say, 'Another drink? Shall we eat?' and after that, sex and sleep.*

'Another drink?' asked Brett, 'or shall we go and eat?'

'What's your favourite colour?' Finty asked him, turning her body towards him, making an effort and really wanting to know.

'What?' Brett replied, because he really didn't understand the question. He frowned at Finty and winked

13

at the waitress who sauntered over with notepad and attitude.

'Film!' Finty tried. 'What's your favourite film?'

'Another G and T?' Brett asked her, now perplexed to the point of irritation.

'Never heard of that one!' Finty said lightly, nodding at the waitress to affirm her drink.

'I'm going to the bog,' Brett said with fatigue, as if to suggest it was a place far preferable to Finty's company and Top Ten questionnaire.

'Desert Island Discs?' she implored in vain as he rose and left.

What are mine this week? She pondered, enjoying how impossible it was to select only eight pieces of music. And then it struck her that she would really rather be on a desert island with no music at all than with Brett, even if he placed the world's jukebox at her disposal. She glanced around the room. A couple, much her own age, sat locked in each other's company; no limbs touching, just engrossed, obviously stimulated, undoubtedly in love. Near to them, a group of four women. A gathering, a girls' night out – replete with the essential alternation between whispering, giggling and shrieking 'No! Oh my God!' Their conversation was shared naturally, their laughter and interaction unforced and obviously highly cherished. Finty didn't want to be on a desert island; she didn't want to be in the West End. She wanted, desperately, to be in Richmond. The waitress arrived with the replenished drinks. Finty glanced at her watch. It was gone half nine.

'Do you think we could have some more peanuts?' Finty asked. 'A large bowl?'

'No!' Polly laughed.

'Oh my God!' Sally shrieked, hiding behind her hands.

'Oh yes indeed!' Chloë confirmed. 'And I'll tell you something for free, it was weird at first – but bloody amazing before long.'

'You old slapper!' Polly said, clapping.

'Sexual deviant, more like!' Sally laughed.

'I'm a bit pissed I think,' said Chloë, theatrically forlorn.

'You'd have to have been,' Polly snorted, 'to have done *that*!'

'Better have some more vino-darling,' Sally said, all doctor-like. 'Here's to you, you dirty, dirty girl!' The three women raised their glasses and drank.

There was signal and battery on Finty's mobile phone but again she went to the payphone in the foyer.

'Lady! Let me guess, you're calling for the rescue services!' the now familiar American voice called softly to her as she was about to drop coins in the slot. Finty turned and regarded him quizzically. 'Hey! You could have the fire brigade drench him with water, the police lock him up, or an ambulance take him away to a very special hospital.'

'Look,' Finty remonstrated, though it was against her better judgement, 'he's my boyfriend. You're offending me.'

'No,' said the man, 'I'm not offending you. Unnerving you, maybe. Offending you – no. I just had a terrible steak. I left most of it and, for some goddamn reason, a large tip too. I'm going to my room. Come use the phone from there.'

Finty didn't think twice about following him into the elevator. But she did think of Brett. Fleetingly. And then she remembered the peanuts and the waitresses to whom he could wink, and she knew he'd be OK. For the meantime, at least.

'I'm Finty,' she introduced herself before disembarking the lift on the sixth floor.

'And I'm George,' the American said. They shook hands and he led the way to his room.

Rooms. The American had a suite.

'Are you drunk?' he asked.

'No,' Finty rued.

'Hungry?'

'No.'

'Want to make that call?'

'Please.'

'Would you like a gin and tonic? And some room service?'

'Yes please.'

'Dial 9 for an outside line.'

'Thank you.'

'Hullo?' Polly answers the phone. Finty can hear singing in the background. She knows it is Chloë doing her

16

Gloria Gaynor. She can almost see Sally collapsed in a fit of giggles on the couch. She can envisage Polly sitting cross-legged on the floor with the telephone crooked under her chin while she rolls a joint.

'It's me again.'

'Finty!' Polly trills. Suddenly, the other two join her in a wonderful, if dissonant, chorus of 'Finty McKenzie! Finty McKenzie!' The volume is such that Finty holds the receiver away from her ear and the cacophony wafts into the room much to the delight of George.

'Are you having a lovely time with Brat?' Polly asks while Chloë in the background hisses, 'Brett! It's Brett.'

'I'm not with him any more,' Finty says. 'I'm with George, in his hotel room.'

There is silence. She hears Polly repeat her last sentence verbatim, but with dramatic full stops between each word, to the other two.

'Who the fuck is George?' she can hear Sally gasp.

'Where the fuck is the hotel?' she can hear Chloë implore.

'Are you OK?' Polly says, suddenly sounding sober.

'Ish,' says Finty. 'Can you come and get me?'

Sally, Polly and Chloë stare at each other. They are in Richmond. Not so much drunk as utterly sozzled and somewhat stoned to boot. They have a friend in need holed up in a hotel room with a man called George and a boyfriend called Brett in the bar beneath. The information is too much to digest, let alone act upon.

'Finty,' says Polly.

'George,' says Sally.

'We need a cab,' says Chloë.

Finty replaced the receiver and became engrossed immediately in the chintz of the curtains because it seemed like a safe place to be; lost in the swirls and details of something other than her own life. She was vaguely aware of someone unfolding her clenched fist and placing a glass in her hand, a plate on her knee; of someone stroking her hair and patting her shoulder. When the hand was removed, her shoulder felt chill and so she reached for the hand and placed it back there. She hadn't the energy to swallow down the lump in her throat, or the wherewithal to prevent a large fat tear glazing and stinging her eye before oozing itself out to splat against the glass in her hand. The noise brought her back to the present.

'Spoiled,' she said quietly.

'Hey,' said an American voice soothingly.

'But I *have*,' she shrugged, as if it was a fait accompli. 'I've spoiled his evening, your evening, their evening. And my own.'

'Horse shit!' George protested. 'And bullshit!'

'But the Gathering,' Finty stressed, 'it's sacred. I turned it down for a man with a penchant for peanuts and the ability to make my nose itch.'

'Well, hon,' George said after a thoughtful slurp at his glass, 'I guess you won't be doing that again.'

* * *

'A Man Called George!' Sally proclaimed to the concierge, giving the counter an authoritative tap. 'Please.'

The concierge bestowed upon her a look of great distaste, followed by a withering glance at Polly and Chloë who were sniggering behind the faux fig tree in the foyer.

'George Who?'

'He's expecting us,' said Sally, refusing to drop eye contact.

'He's American,' Chloë added helpfully.

'And he's wearing plaid,' Polly announced as some kind of open-sesame password.

'Hi, I'm George,' says George, 'and she's in there.'

'Hullo, George,' Sally says, eyes agoggle at his unexpectedly advanced years.

'Hullo, George,' says Chloë, eyes agoggle at the extent of his plaid-clad attire.

'Hullo, George,' says Polly, eyes agoggle at the opulence of his suite.

'Hi, ladies,' says George, 'she's in there. She's expecting you.'

'Finty!' the girls cry with love and sympathy, rushing to embrace their friend.

'Finty!' they marvel, looking around and spying two bottles of unopened champagne on ice and platters boasting crustless sandwiches and miniature pastries.

'Girls' Night In,' Finty says, very matter-of-fact. 'George says we should gather here.'

They all look at George. He reminds Sally of her late grandfather. Polly thinks he must be a fairy godfather and then she thinks she must have had one joint too many. Chloë wonders fleetingly what on earth they are doing here in the sumptuous suite of a kindly stranger at gone 10 p.m. Finty wonders where on earth to start.

'It all began when my nose started to itch,' she tells Sally, Chloë and Polly who are gathered about her, wide-eyed and jaws dropped as if teacher is about to tell a story.

'Champagne?' George suggests, dimming the lights, opening a bottle and pouring four glasses.

'Aren't you joining us?' Sally asks.

George looks rather taken aback, and clasps his hand to his heart for emphasis. 'God no! It's a Gathering. Out of bounds. Girls only. Anyway, I have business to attend to.'

And he leaves. He leaves them in one of the rooms of his suite, furnished with champagne and sandwiches. And pastries. And warmth. He leaves the girls, who are now giggling, wrapped around each other on a capacious settee. He has work to do.

The bar is still full and Brett is exactly where George last saw him and where Finty left him over an hour ago. Not that he seems to have realized. His winks at the waitress have provided fast-track service for his gin and tonic to have been frequently replenished. He's thought only fleetingly of Finty because, in the three months they've been together, he's only ever thought fleetingly of Finty anyway.

'Peanut?' George asks.

'Why not,' Brett responds.

'Some advice?' George asks.

'Why not,' Brett responds.

'Don't date women with itchy noses,' George says, with a slap to Brett's shoulder blades, 'they're not your type.'

Jenny Colgan was born in 1972 in Ayrshire. After graduating from Edinburgh University, she worked for six years in the health service, moonlighting as a cartoonist and a stand-up comic. Film rights for her bestselling first novel, *Amanda's Wedding*, have been sold to Warner Bros. Jenny now lives in the City of London, and has recently completed a second novel, *Talking to Addison*.

Dougie, Spoons and the Solarium Aquarium

Jenny Colgan

Doug's toes popped into life like little exclamation marks hanging over the end of the bed, and he rubbed his sticky eyes and tried not to catch the gunk in his stubble. He let out a groan as last night crept back into his head. How had it ended again? Not well. He spooled it through his mind. OK. He met a pretty girl in a nightclub, they'd danced, grinning foolishly at each other because it was too loud to talk, they'd come back here, they'd drunk whisky, they'd skirted the whole snogging issue by talking drivel about his record collection for hours, then he'd finally managed to snog her. That much he was sure of. More than snogged her? He turned his head, and his face crinkled at an opened condom packet. Huh. He had definitely more than snogged her. So *why* the sense of utter foreboding?

She – Chloë, that was her name – was a dental assistant, which sounded revolting to him, but he'd liked her, definitely liked her – absolutely – wasn't sweetly asleep and facing him on the pillow ... Just in case he'd gone blind, he stuck out his hand and patted all around the bed and under the mattress. Nope. She was a thin girl, but not Flat Stanley.

Tentatively he sat up and stared round his twelve-by-twelve room. The cupboard was a possibility, but an unlikely one. It struck him what was wrong. She was gone, but her clothes were strewn all over the floor. Therefore, unless she was flapping along a mile away in an enormously long shirt and clown shoes, it meant that, well, it had happened again . . .

'CHLOË?' he shouted, hoping vainly that he might be able to do this without having to get out of bed and touch the icy floor. This didn't feel like summer at all, as per bloody Doncaster usual.

'CHLOË?' There was no response. Sighing, he pulled the duvet round himself and landed heavily on the floor, then performed a speedy duvet-to-dressing-gown manoeuvre which didn't involve exposing his entire naked body to the elements at any one time. He opened the door, but couldn't see her on the landing.

Sighing again, he picked up her bra and used it as a glove puppet.

'CHLOË! 'E 'ees 'olding me 'ostage! Save me! Save me!'

'I'm out here, you twat.' The voice sounded hostile.

Doug went out to the landing, but it still seemed empty.

'Ah – good one.'

'Up *here*.'

Chloë, entirely nude, was crouched trembling on top of the old wardrobe that stood in the hall to contain shit he hadn't got round to throwing out yet. Doug stared at her.

'Hello again. Ehm, is this a sexual thing, or are you just a really fanatical duster?'

'Is it gone?' growled Chloë.

'Would you like some breakfast? I'll make you break-fast-in-wardrobe if you like.'

'IS IT GONE?'

'Not exactly,' said Doug, talking Fluffy out of his dressing-gown pocket.

Chloë screamed her head off.

'You know,' said Doug patiently, 'he's only a very baby python.'

Chloë continued to scream. Doug considered the situation.

'I don't suppose there's any point asking you for your phone number, is there?'

'Eek! Eek! Eek!'

Doug left the house for work eating a slice of toast and giving bits to Fluffy.

'Why can't we meet a nice girl, eh, Fluff? I mean, we're nice guys, aren't we?'

He turned into the road.

'Hmm. I hope she doesn't want to use the bathroom. I forgot to mention we had your dad staying for the weekend.'

From inside the house came the sound of glass breaking. 'Eek! Eek! Eek!'

Doug and his fat friend Spoons had set up the Solarium Aquarium with the money Spoons got when his dad was hiding it from his dodgy road-haulage business. The Solarium had been Spoons' idea: 'People can come in, get all their reptile needs and a suntan at the same time – and it rhymes! Brilliant, eh?'

Doug took care of the reptile end, and didn't quite share Spoons' vision. He personally wouldn't mind lying down completely naked and defenceless amidst lots of writhing dangerous things, but lots of people, apparently, did. The solarium wasn't going too well at all, although it did mean Spoons got to be bright orange at all times. This didn't help his pulling tactics though, as being fat, snaky and bright orange isn't actually that much more attractive than, say, just being fat and snaky. Doug, being tallish, and ruggedish, was a bit of a looker for a herpetologist, and supplied much of Spoons' fantasy requirements.

'Tops?' asked Spoons avidly.

'Yes,' said Doug.

'Fingers?'

'Yup.'

'You did it?'

'Yes, yes, yes.'

'And you're miserable?'

'Spoons, I'm a sensitive guy, OK? Maybe I'm just looking for that little bit more.'

'What, like up the bum?'

'I just don't understand it. Every time I meet a nice girl she goes screaming in the opposite direction.'

'Yeh, that happens to me too.'

'*After* she's met Fluffy. But I'm just ... I just need to meet a girl who shares my interests, you know what I mean.'

'If I met a girl who shared my interests,' reflected Spoons gloomily, 'we'd just wank all the time. I'd never see her.'

Suddenly, outside the shop, loud yells were heard and there came the sound of a car crashing. The shop bell tinkled. Spoons and Doug looked at each other and raised their eyebrows.

Into the shop strode a dramatically beautiful woman, all shiny black hair and slashed red lipstick. She was wearing a long, expensive and unnecessarily fiddly coat which looked designer. However, none of these things screamed attention to themselves *quite* as much as the eight-foot boa constrictor draped round her neck like a – ahem – boa.

'What a beauty!' said Doug and Spoons both at once.

'Thank you,' said the woman, flushing.

'We meant the boa,' said Spoons.

'I know,' said the woman.

Spoons nudged Douglas unnecessarily hard.

'Get off with her!' he whispered loudly.

'Can I help you, madam?' said Doug, gulping.

'It's Jumbo,' she said. 'We're new in town. I've come to buy him everything he needs – no expense spared.

Also, do you know of anywhere I could get a fake sun-tan around here?'

Doug and Spoons' eyes grew as round as a cross-section of the rare Australian ring snake.

Her name was Maia, and she had been brought up in Indonesia. She took to the Fluffster immediately, coiling him round her little fingers like a rope trick. The Fluffster, however, didn't take to Jumbo AT ALL and scuttled back to the safety of Doug's inner pocket after realizing he was – at this age at least – being pretty comprehensively out-snaked.

Maia was a primary school teacher, but had had to leave her last school after an incident she didn't seem to want to talk about too much; although now, six to eight weeks on, there were still definite signs of distension in Jumbo's belly.

Doug was in love.

'Would you, ahem . . .'

Maia had wandered out of the solarium covered only in a very slinky towel and Jumbo, which reminded Doug all too pleasantly of Nastassja Kinski. Spoons was gulping and quietly trying to stop hyperventilating in the background.

'Yes?' she purred.

Doug sighed. Asking girls out wasn't normally one of his problems. It was usually about the six-hour mark that his troubles started . . . but this one had him floored.

'I mean, if you're new in town . . .'

It occurred to him for a second that Doncaster probably didn't have a great deal to offer somebody this exotic. Maia, however, smiled widely.

'Oh, could you show me around? Do you know any good chip shops?'

Behind him, Spoons made a high-pitched whining sound.

Doug wandered up on time to Harry Ramsden's. Jumbo appeared to have a long piece of leather string coming out of his mouth attached to another woman's hand. She looked a bit shellshocked, and Maia appeared to be giving her two hundred pounds.

'Just two,' she said to the shocked waiter as they swept into the restaurant. 'Jumbo's already eaten.'

Maia launched ahead, just as Doug noticed Chloë getting up to leave with a clutch of squealing girlfriends. She raised her eyebrows at him.

'Playing with the big boys now, I see.'

He stopped.

'Look, Chloë, I'm sorry about the other night . . .'

'Oh, don't worry about it at all. I'm clearly just not slimy enough for you.'

'Snakes aren't slime – Oh, forget it. And I am sorry.' He'd forgotten how pretty she was. She looked like a dancer, even just pulling her coat on.

'Well, if I ever start up a tarantula collection, I'll ring you.'

'Douglas! Our table's ready!'

Chloë smiled and walked out of the restaurant, giving him an extremely wide berth.

'Spoons, please, just stop panting like a dog. You're steaming up the cases.'

'I just . . . Oh, *please* tell me. *Please.*'

'There's nothing to tell. We talked a lot about snakes and the shop. Entirely, in fact, about snakes and the shop. She's thinking about opening up a branch in Melton Mowbray.'

'That's brilliant! Global entrepreneurs, definitely. Er . . . were you feeling her up whilst you were doing it?'

'*No.* To be honest, I wouldn't have felt entirely secure *vis-à-vis* Jumbo and my right hand.'

'What – you mean you didn't score?'

'Nope.'

Spoons slumped.

'Fuck! Dougie, *I* could have taken her out and managed that.'

'I'm just . . . I mean, she's everything I've ever wanted – she's bright, she's beautiful, she loves members of the reptile family . . .'

'She tans . . .'

'She tans . . .'

'And the problem is, exactly?'

The bell tinkled. Maia stalked in looking like a Bond girl in a tight red leather jacket, Jumbo practically caressing her left breast. She looked breathtaking.

'Darling, which football team do you support?'

'Ehm, Newcastle. Why?'

'I thought so . . .' Maia drew a team strip and two tickets out of her bag. 'And here – I bought an extra sock and cut the foot off so that Fluffy can wear a strip too.'

Doug reached out his hand and held Spoons up before he fainted.

'Where's the office? I'll go and put it there for you, and you can try it on when you're not scooping out gecko poo.'

'Ehm, uhm, it's through the back . . .'

She sashayed off and vanished.

'If I were you I'd take one of those little garter snakes over there and use it as a WEDDING RING,' predicted Spoons.

'I would too,' said Mr Nebbington, who came in every day to stare at the animals in a vaguely disconcerting way for hours on end.

Fluffy popped out of Doug's pocket. He was obviously just looking around – but it looked weirdly like he was shaking his head, that was all.

'What's she doing in the office?' asked Spoons, fifteen minutes later. 'Maybe she stripped naked and is rolling herself in butter and Smarties,' he added thoughtfully.

'Hmm,' said Doug, and went through to have a look. Maia and Jumbo were hunched over what looked like a huge pile of files. He cleared his throat, and she straightened up guiltily.

'What are you doing?'

'Ehm ... actually, I was looking for a catalogue. I, ehm, want to buy Jumbo a little cowboy hat.'

'Are you sure that's wise?'

She shrugged. 'Well, he ate the beret.'

Doug looked back at the papers. 'I'm not sure ...'

'No, definitely not – Ooh, look! My shoelace is untied!'

Before Doug had a moment to think, she stretched fully over from the waist, bending away from him. Her skirt hitched up and up ...

Doug shook his head. His life didn't usually feel much like a porn film. He had, in fact, not quite believed that woman actually ever behaved like this. But the fact was, unless she was wearing a very bizarrely patterned pair of knickers, Maia didn't have any pants on. He wondered briefly if she'd possibly just forgotten, but his reliable trouser snake rather thought otherwise.

She turned her head up to him coquettishly from somewhere near the floor.

'Will I get to see you tonight?'

'Uh-huh-huh huh, ehm, ra*ther*!'

He watched a part of her beginning with 'b' sashay out the door. And, sadly, it wasn't her brain.

The problem, thought Doug to himself as he put on his tie, was ... could this maybe be perhaps just a little *too* perfect? It was like ordering a pizza and getting a five-course banquet delivered to your door, made up of all your favourite foods – say, in Doug's case, five different types of pizza. He wasn't quite sure what he'd done to deserve it.

'So did you think up the solarium idea all by yourself?'

'No, that was Spoons. He thought it would be good 'cause it rhymed.'

'Wow. How did he raise the internal necessary backing capital ... er, I mean, you know, the cash to buy the shop and stuff?'

They were sitting in a Café Flo. The management had found them a whole private section, which seemed amazing. Well, he assumed it was the management. Certainly the room had got up and walked out en masse.

'Wouldn't you rather talk about something else?' said Doug. 'Like – I don't know ... what's your favourite film?'

'*Anaconda*,' she said firmly. 'Waiter, has your kitchen got rats?'

'Of *course* not, madame!'

'Shame. Anyway, back to Spoons ...'

Still, she seemed keen enough to come back to his flat. And she was wearing a spray on dress, which on another woman might have looked a bit tarty, but on Maia looked – well, high-class expensive-hotel tarty.

Doug grinned at his trusty wardrobe as he made coffee. He didn't think they'd be needing that tonight.

Sure enough, when he returned, Maia stood in his bedroom, completely naked, except for the omnipresent Jumbo. Doug nearly dropped the coffee. He wished

Spoons were here – not joining in, just to see it for one second and then have to go home again. She was magnificent.

'Do you know what really turns me on?' she purred.

'I would guess that would be snakes,' said Doug.

'No!' She caught hold of his tie and pulled him slowly towards her. He felt unbelievably turned on, even with the knowledge that, if he so wished, Jumbo could bite off his head like a cocktail cherry.

'Money.'

'Money? I thought you were a primary school teacher.'

'I want you to talk money to me, Dougie. It really turns me on.'

'Ehm, God, I don't know . . . florin?'

She pulled him closer and kissed him hard on the lips, till he thought the top of his head was going to explode.

'Tell me . . . tell me how much money the shop makes.'

'What? I don't underst – Jesus!'

She was on her knees and had unbuttoned his trousers.

'Tell me, Dougie . . .'

'Oh God, don't stop that.'

'I will if you don't –'

'Three thousand a week give or take . . . oooh.'

'Yes, yes . . .'

Doug had his eyes tightly shut now. His mind was being blown, amongst other things.

'And how much of that do you pay in VAT?'

'What!? No, no, *please* don't stop.'

'How much do you pay in VAT?'

'Oh . . . my . . . God.'

'How MUCH?'

'Nothing. NOTHING! NOTHING! Ahhhhhh . . .'

'A *honey* trap?' said Spoons, eating a honey doughnut at the same time and seemingly unable to distinguish between the two.

'I think you're going to get nicked. I'm really sorry, Spoons.'

'It's my dad's fault. Those bloody lorries.' He sighed. 'Undercover. Who would have thought the Inland Revenue would be so *thorough*?'

'I know. She took us in, right enough.'

'I mean, where the hell did they find a woman who loved snakes and suntans and chips and Newcastle United and who would fancy you as well? Must have taken them *ages*.'

'No, Spoons, you see . . .'

The door swung open, tinging loudly. Maia and Jumbo stood there with four menacing-looking men in pinstriped suits with briefcases strapped to their wrists.

'It's all through the back,' she announced. 'Take it down.'

She faced the boys.

'No hard feelings. It's just business.'

They stared at her.

'So, I mean ... where did you get Jumbo?' asked Doug.

'His real name's Mambo. He's professionally under-cover too. Oh and there's ...'

She nudged Jumbo/Mambo, and the snake lifted its huge flat head. There was a clicking, whirring noise.

'... a miniature camera implanted in his head. Pain-less, I assure you. But extremely useful.'

Doug shook his head in disbelief.

'Well, for what it's worth, you really convinced us you loved that snake.'

'Thank you,' she said. 'Just doing my job. Really, when I'm not working, they make me want to vomit, scream, run away and burst into tears.'

Spoons, who hadn't been listening, nudged Doug hard.

'Doug ... does this mean you're not going out with her any more?'

Doug clasped him on the shoulder.

'Yes, Spoons. Yes, it does.'

'Ehm ... can I go out with her then?'

'Spoons, she's going to put you in prison.'

'Yeh, but when I come out, maybe?'

'Spoons, she's not really who she says she is.'

'I don't care,' said Spoons miserably.

'We'll talk about it,' said Maia crisply. 'Perhaps over forms 11a-95c. See how co-operative we both can be.'

Spoons was beaming as she led him off into the unmarked vehicle.

* * *

'Hello, snaky man.' Chloë was walking down the street carrying two bags of shopping with her hair in little bunches and her summer sandals on. Doug felt his heart lurch.

'Hello there. Ehm ... you know, I'm not really involved in that line of work these days.'

'Oh really?' she said, putting the shopping bags down.

'No, I kind of ... gave it up. I think in future I'm going to stick to the more rectangular animals.'

She nodded. 'What, like bears and stuff?'

'Bears, maybe ... anything with right-angles. Giraffes, stuff like that.'

'Huh.'

They looked at each other for a bit.

'So do you ...?'

'Well, maybe ...'

They both spoke at once, then smiled foolishly at each other.

'Yeah, all right,' said Chloë.

Later, walking away, Doug patted his pocket.

'Don't worry, Fluffster. I'm sure she'll come round sooner or later ...'

Fiona Walker is thirty-one years old and alternates life between homes in North London and the Cotswolds. Unable to stick to a nine-to-five job, she started her first novel at the age of twenty-one, and has written five best sellers to date. Her unique blend of modern romance, comedy and no-holds-barred sex has earned her the reputation as 'Jilly Cooper for Generation X'. A regular contributor to newspapers and magazines, Fiona is frequently in demand to comment on women and love. She and her long-term partner Jon will be marrying in 2001.

The Power of Two

Fiona Walker

'Al Matthews *is* PR, darling,' Sly winked, dragging out his Edinburgh brogue for emphasis. 'He is absolutely *the* man to boost your image. Look at Red and Slim.'

'Pul-lease,' I laughed. Last year's pop sensation Ruby 'Red' Richmond had been supposedly in lurve with cult actor Slim Tim Gorman for several weeks and pictures of them looking sickeningly couply were splashed all over the tabloids. Everyone knew it was a publicity stunt. Ruby was far too anorexic to kiss anything but bathroom fittings and Slim Tim was a coke addict who snorted Colombia's finest from the cistern lids of the best clubs in town. Come to think of it, they were as well matched as Armitage and Shanks. Clever old Al Matthews. And they said he was losing his Midas touch.

'Word on the street is that PR pairings are *the* thing when it comes to dating,' Sly persisted, flattening himself back on the sofa as my fat old terrier, Carrot, flumped from one cushion to another in search of buried crumbs. 'Meeting your lover at the Priory Clinic is *very* last year. Everyone's getting together through the Alchemist these days.'

'I don't need another relationship right now – fake or otherwise,' I sighed, reaching for my coffee. 'I prefer life away from the spotlight.'

He looked as though I'd said I'd be perfectly content wing-walking nude over the Gobi. 'Smack, darling, you're *festering*. You're just this far away from appearing in one of those ghastly where-are-they-now shows.' He pinched his fingers together and then narrowed his eyes as he spotted a chipped nail from fighting his way through my overgrown front gate.

'My name is Sadie, not Smack,' I reminded him gently. 'No one's called me Smack for months. People around here have no idea who Smack was.'

'Precisely my point!' he bashed his hand down on a cushion, propelling Carrot on to my lap. 'You need to get back into the scene, go to some lovely parties, buy some new frocks. Look at you, you're so *gorgeous*. You're sitting in the middle of this – this isolated *tip*, accumulating cobwebs like Miss Haversham. And what is *that*?' He spotted what appeared to be a sleeping woolly mammoth in the corner of the room.

'Carrot's bed,' I explained sadly. 'It's a pile of gorilla suits Bill was going to use in the Christmas special before it was scrapped.'

Admittedly, the cottage wasn't looking its best. It was as dusty as a moth's wing and three days of constant rain had left mud trodden all over the bare elm floorboards. When we'd bought the place six months ago, Bill and I had planned to scour antique shops and European flea markets for furniture. But I had no desire to shop now that I was alone and broke.

Sly shuddered, doubly determined to make his journey into the wilderness worthwhile. 'It's time you cashed in, darling. Since he left you, Bill's press has been so absolutely diabolical that he'll never work in the UK again. You know the deal. As your agent, it's my *duty* to get you out of this depression. I'm going to call the Alchemist straight away.' He delved in his Prada courier bag for his mobile. 'Face it, Smack – I mean, Sadie, darling – you're up to your silicones in debt. You'll lose this place soon. And Bill needs – *Ah, hello, Al. Sly Preston here – the sly guy with the eye for to-die-for stars, remember?*' Sly had been spending too much time in Hollywood lately. '*Now I am going to say one word and I guarantee you'll pass out with happiness. Smack!*'

I pulled a face at Carrot as Sly started discussing me with the Svengali of the tabloids, a man who could give so much spin to a fading star that the Sun lit up.

'Yes, that's right. Bill Roth's ex, as in "Smack my bitch up",' Sly was purring into his phone. 'Mmm, co-hosted *Loved Up*, yes – now on NBC with Ash Numan. Not a patch on Smack. No, she still looks great. Suicide attempts?' He looked at me in shock. 'Not as far as I know. Oh, I see, that's *good* press, is it? Maybe it can be arranged. Lunch? Let's gaze at our windows as Chekhov said.' He peered at his electronic diary.

I closed my eyes. 'Smack my bitch up.' Oh Bill, if only they'd really known you, your adoring public. If only they'd seen the private side I saw, the gentle humorist, the philosopher, the lover who took all night to satisfy me even though it no longer gave him pleasure.

In the six months since I'd been gone, London had turned its restaurant tables. I hadn't even heard of the Michelin-starred Course in which we met Al Matthews. It was a predictable minimalist hush of rich, celeb-spotting diners, and to my horror I seemed to be the star attraction.

As expressionless waiters glided around on invisible tracks tending to our every whim, I studied Al over a Zen flower arrangement. He was known as the Alchemist, not just because he could turn base metal into gold, but because it was rumoured he knew precisely the right measure of drugs to keep most of his burnt-out celebrity clients partying late into the night. Yet he wasn't quite the designer-suited automaton I remembered from endless parties with Bill. He was more self-effacing with very clever blue eyes. It was a calculated front, I realized, guaranteed to charm and disarm. It irritated me to find him so likeable. There was no denying his guile.

'Now, sorry to go through the obvious, but I want to get my facts straight,' he smiled easily. 'You exploded into the spotlight because you were Bill Roth's girl-friend, right?'

'Well, yes –' I started.

'Not at *all*,' Sly cut across me archly. 'Smack – or rather Sadie, was a serious broadcaster in her own right before Bill head-hunted her from GLR to become the female voice in his radio zoo crew. She also co-produced many of his television shows.'

'I can see why Roth brought you into the equation,' Al Matthews was looking at me thoughtfully, assessing the damage, the raw materials still available now that I had been robbed of my greatest asset, a celebrity relationship. 'And you co-hosted all three series of *Loved Up*, as well as fronting commercials, writing several columns and continuing to work on radio?' He sounded as though he was drafting my press release.

I nodded, not trusting myself to speak. *Loved Up* had, in fact, been my idea. Not that I had ever leaked that, not even when Bill had broken his UK contract after three hit series and taken the ten-million viewer TV show to America with an ultra-famous new co-host. He was Hollywood A-list now, whereas I was credit card black-list and only remembered as his long suffering side-kick, the Ernie to his Eric, the Little to his Larging-it success.

'The ad campaign for Tsar Vodka alone netted Smack a cool two million,' Sly boasted, having set it up. 'And let's not forget that she came in third in *MX* magazine's Sexiest Women on Earth pole only last year.'

'Just before Bill ran away with Ash Numan, who incidentally came in at number two,' I muttered. 'He would have tried for the chart topper, but boning Lara Croft might lead to electrocution, not to mention the constant threat of a T Rex attack.'

Al hid a smile. I know my loudmouth Essex raver

attitude irritates some people, but he seemed to like it which surprised me, given that he was so posh.

'Sadie's strength is in cutting-edge journalism,' Sly clearly didn't trust me to sell myself. 'Her party column made cult reading.'

'So did your credit card bills by all accounts,' Al glanced at his notes. 'And a black Amex card has a very good cutting edge.'

'There's only one Bill I still owe,' I hissed, deciding I didn't like him after all. 'Contrary to what you may have read in the papers, I did not take cocaine, or shop like it was going out of fashion, nor did I have personality and eating disorders.'

'So set the record straight,' Al creased his forehead. 'You can write, we know that; you're clever as well as beautiful. I know you won't kiss-and-tell but why not get a book deal? The syndication rights alone could earn you –'

'The story's not for sale,' I snapped. 'Like Sly says, I just want to be seen at a few parties, show the world I'm over it, raise my profile.' I knew I sounded like I was having my teeth pulled, and Sly kept kicking me under the table, which didn't help. I stared at Al's curious asymmetric face with its crown of wild curls. For someone that repackaged people for a living, it seemed odd that he cared so little about his own image.

Al was watching my reactions carefully. 'What good will appearing on a minor star's arm do you at this stage? You're not a bimbo.' He sounded strangely sad.

'Anyone would think you were trying to do yourself

out of a job here, Al,' Sly laughed nervously, knowing that if I hooked up with the right cheque-mate he stood to cash in on a small fortune, and not just in money. 'You're crying out for someone like Sadie. What's the problem?'

'I just want to make sure she's ready,' Al cocked his head, clever blue eyes seeming to strip my face of its skin. 'Once bitten, twice camera-shy, after all.' It wasn't the voice of a therapist, just a businessman who wanted to protect his investments and avoid messy mergers. It was common knowledge that Al's sham get-togethers were starting to irritate the tabloids.

'I'm ready,' I shrugged far from enthusiastically. 'I need the money.'

His eyes didn't leave mine. 'I wish I could be so sure that's all you're after.'

I stared back at him and instantly knew that he had rumbled me. I wanted to run back to my cottage. I wanted to bury my face in Carrot's neck until the bailiffs arrived to throw us out. But Al Matthews said no more; he simply nodded at me and looked away. He seemed weary and surprisingly indifferent. I followed his gaze around the Course dining room, totally alienated from all the little power-hunches over power lunches taking place all around us. I half suspected that if I suggested Al and I slope out for a quiet pint he'd be game on, but Sly was calling the shots and picking up the Bill today.

'You heard her, damn it, she *says* she's ready,' he was almost off his chair with excitement. 'Tell us who you have in mind. Sadie won't let you down, we promise.'

Sighing, Al delved into a slimline briefcase to pull out several folders. 'Next week is the Sound Awards, followed almost immediately by Elvis James' annual ball, the Duke of Suffolk charity gala and then Red and Slim's wedding. I am responsible for the smooth-running of all four events, and a big part of that is making sure the guest lists are topped up with newsworthy stars and their, er, partners.' He fanned the files out in front of him and looked up at me tiredly. 'Take your pick.'

I couldn't focus as I glanced at the names and faces swimming in front of me – druggy teenage pin-ups, fading comics, drunken footballers and wife-beating celebrity chefs all in need of an image boost. What did it matter? They were all in the same boat. I picked one at random. 'Have him washed and dressed and brought to my hotel in a limousine an hour before the party,' I joked feebly.

Al slid a finger beneath his collar and cleared his throat. 'Are you sure?' Again, his eyes seemed to bore into my soul.

'She's sure,' Sly grabbed the file and looked at it. 'Oh yes, he's *gorgeous*. Shame about the paedophile rumours. The papers will write anything these days.'

A week later and the papers were all writing that I was dating the Premier League's top striker. We had been seen at several parties together, plus shopping at

Brown's, lunching in Paris and out walking Carrot in Hyde Park. That annoyed me – I didn't want Carrot exploited, but I was determined to be a consummate professional. I wanted to get this over with as quickly as possible.

I wasn't yet headline news, but I was back on the Tiffany chain gang. The phone in my hotel suite rang constantly, mostly calls from Al who was picking up my bills and making sure I gave good quote.

'The *Mirror* want an exclusive. Your new-found love with Vizza, how he saved you from near-suicide. They're offering good money.'

'I won't talk about Bill,' I threatened. We argued about it endlessly, but I always got my way. He was annoyingly fascinated by our break-up.

Of course, I couldn't stop the press from writing about Bill anyway. Stories of my new romance had stirred up the whole love rat thing again, as I'd known they would. His name took another knocking as the nation was reminded how he'd dumped the pocket Venus for the six-foot Amazon to further his career over the Pond. The mud didn't reach him in the States, but it was looking more and more unlikely that he'd be popping back to see his old ma in Guildford in the near future.

'It's what you wanted, isn't it, Sadie?' Al laughed cynically. 'Revenge?'

Knowing he couldn't have been more wrong, I didn't answer. Something about Al got under my skin, struck me as odd. He seemed almost as reluctant to be in this business as I was. If it weren't for his reputation, I'd say he hated it.

My 'relationship' with Vizza lasted just over a fortnight, and Al gave me a week off for good behaviour while Vizza revelled in increasingly outlandish exclusives, revealing his broken heart. Yeah. Like he knew how it felt – not.

I installed satellite in my cottage, courtesy of the *Mirror* exclusive. Together, Carrot and I watched primetime television from America in the UK early hours. Night after night, I studied Ash Numan's face, wondering how one woman could be so flawless. Watching Bill made me cry. He was back to his old form, just like the early days, almost deranged with energy and anger, not the self-satisfied overweight smug-bugger he'd latterly become in the UK series. Christ, he was operating. He was cruel and funny and sexy. I couldn't take my eyes from the screen.

To my amazement Vizza called several times a day, sometimes in tears, begging me in his broken English to reconsider 'our love'. What love? He'd barely talked to me. Admittedly he'd tried to kiss me, but he'd also tried to kiss two members of a boy band in Kabaret, and Frankie Dettori at a sports charity dinner. At least Bill had been discreet.

Al phoned me on Sunday to demand I buy the *News* and read a feature they'd cobbled together about me in the light of my latest doomed love affair. I snorted with laughter as it talked of my 'inexplicable, compelling, dangerous sex appeal', which brought grown men to their knees. If only they could see me now, schlepping around in shorts and wellies, eating ice cream at two in the morning as I watched Bill on television. The gap between truth and tabloid had never been greater. The plan was starting to work.

'It's time for the big guns,' Al told me. 'Are you sure you're ready?'

'I'm sure,' I insisted, knowing that I had no choice now that the ball was rolling.

Soon afterwards, I was officially the love of George Brian's life. George was a tricky one. He was far more persistent than camp, confused Vizza, and he treated me as little different from a hired escort. Al had to repeatedly warn him off and remind him that it was just publicity.

'I can fight my own battles,' I told him, but he still appeared at most of the parties we went to, like a discreet bodyguard. To be honest, it was good to have someone to talk to – George communicated only in grunts. But the more I talked to Al, the more I realized that he resented saving celebrities from their own excesses.

'Take George,' he sighed, pointing out my supposed faithful new boyfriend slipping his hotel key card to a teenage model at a film premiere. 'He thinks his fame makes him invincible. That's my fault. I expect Bill was like that too, wasn't he?'

I ignored the question and made Al go and discreetly fetch George's key while I resumed my duties at his side, acting the adoring girlfriend, jokily deflecting journalists' questions about marriage and babies.

George Brian was far hotter property than Vizza, a big-name actor with a long criminal record. As his girlfriend, I was instantly headline news, and the press swarmed all over me. My hotel was besieged, my face was everywhere, and Sly delightedly reported that offers of work were now flooding in.

'You are so, so lucky going out with lovely George,' he giggled. 'Tell me, are the rumours true? Does he have a tattoo on it?'

'I wouldn't know – it's strictly business,' I snapped, although fighting him off was getting harder and harder. If only Bill had been so keen.

Despite my resilience, I couldn't take George for long. After a month, my body was black and blue from being felt up; I hated his stale breath and stupidity. George wanted me to join him on location in Italy, but I'd had enough and called time, asking Al if he could set me up with someone less demanding.

To my alarm, the once-ambitious Alchemist refused, saying that we needed to cool my hot date image. 'You've amazed me, Sadie. The press love you. You have the X factor they can't get enough of. But you can go it alone now.'

Much as I wanted to stay at home and watch *Loved Up*, I knew I was too close to my goal to give up. 'I have to do one more. Just one more.'

'They'll cotton on to the fact that you just date my clients,' he argued. 'We've gone far enough. Vizza's been transferred for five million; George has scotched the date rape rumours. You've got a column, a potential chat show and a new radio contract. It's worked. Don't be greedy. The press might well turn against you if you carry on.'

'Just one more,' I pleaded. 'You have a list of clients as long as your arm who could use my help. I have credibility and you need that.'

'Are you doing this for yourself or for me?' he laughed, giving in. Why did he suddenly keep reminding me of Bill?

My cottage was being made-over by a woman's magazine, so I stayed in London and gave away the endless roses Vizza sent me to local hospitals. By the end of the week, the wards of UCH looked like marquees at Chelsea Flower Show and the papers went into over-drive as I was spotted coming out of The Ivy with new young pop heat throb, Mac Savage. I strongly suspected that Al had only paired us up because Smack and Mac looked great linked in print. He was getting dangerously cynical.

Mac was sweet. Young, excited, hampered by a huge crush but far too shy to try it on. Best of all, he was a huge fan of Bill's. He even sat up yawning in my hotel suite, drinking Sprite from the mini-bar as he watched *Loved Up* on NBC and agreed that Bill had got his old spirit back. But then he blew it by asking me to seduce him.

'Bill was mad to dump you for that fake monster. You're so beautiful.'

I cried for hours. Poor Mac tried to understand, doling out tissues and joking that he'd been using Kleenex himself all week, but to mop up something far less delicate than my tears. He even said he loved me. Shit, I felt bad about that one.

Al was livid.

'You weren't supposed to sleep with him!' he complained when the papers were full of long-lens photographs of Mac leaving my hotel at dawn, looking rumpled and stubbly and devastatingly handsome.

'I didn't. We watched television,' I sighed. 'I thought this was precisely the sort of press you wanted. This is what you hired me for.'

'I didn't hire you,' he sighed. 'You employed me. I used to be quite good. And I don't want to make you look cheap. This story just makes you look cheap, Sadie.'

'I am cheap,' I muttered. 'Now it's out in the open.'

You see, the press had finally turned against me big time on this one. 'Sadie the Heartbreaker' ran the by-lines, 'Was Roth Right To Leave Her?' 'Mac and Smack the Bitch Uptown.' Sympathy for Bill was creeping into the alliterative, double-entendre prose. Rumours abounded that I had always been a serial tart, that Bill Roth had been at the end of his tether when he left me, that I was the reason his shows had started to suffer in the UK. The public was ready to forgive Bill at last; they wanted their big, loud, angry star back on home turf. It had done Mac no harm either, although Al was lampooned.

'You've totally discredited my work,' he fumed. 'My name's all over this.' It was true. The Mac thing was one set-up too much for the press and the long-prepared features about the Alchemist ran side-by-side with the latest Smack story. To say I'd blown his cover was an understatement – I'd napalmed his roof.

'You knew what you were letting yourself in for when you agreed to help me,' I said quietly, wishing it didn't make me feel quite so bad.

Darling Mac had sent a box of chocolates around to the hotel that morning with the note: *Mine's a soft centre, but please take it because you're eating me up already.* I looked at it for a long time, listening to Al's breathing on the other end of the phone.

'I know why you've done this, Sadie,' he said finally. 'And I hope it works, because you've not only burned my boats, you've burned your own too, and it takes a hell of a long time to swim to a desert island.'

I closed my eyes. He'd guessed at that first ever lunch. That's why he'd been so reluctant to agree to do this stupid dating thing. I still had no idea why he'd said yes.

'I think,' his voice shook, 'that we can help each other out here.'

'I'm sorry, Al,' I sighed. 'If I do employ you, then I'm afraid you're fired.'

'Wait! I have to ask you something,' he pleaded.

'Forget it,' I hung up on him, wishing I cared less, that the Alchemist had been a vulture after all, not the wise owl I'd grown to like.

* * *

I cried all the way home on the train, hours and hours of sliding past blurred green fields. My heart was hanging like a small corpse in my chest, wrenched from its strings. I wrote a letter to Mac to apologize for my behaviour. I knew his soft centre would harden up and go stale sooner or later – they all did – but I hoped that he got lucky.

Despite the dark glasses, I was still recognized constantly, which almost finished me off. I was sure my tear-stained autographs would make a mint in years to come if I finally committed the ultimate publicity stunt by committing suicide. I guessed that was what Al would want. It would make great press; at least three of his clients would have more column inches than the Coliseum in coming weeks and the posthumous biography would sell shed-loads, so Sly would be happy too. He'd always wanted to write and he was the only person besides Bill who knew the entire truth.

Back at my made-over, disgustingly twee cottage, I ignored the Al's increasingly irate answer phone messages and cuddled Carrot to my chest as I counted.

Seventy-eight sleeping pills. More than enough. But I knew I couldn't do it. Not while Bill's future lay in my hands.

Al turned up on my doorstep the next morning, armed with his slimline briefcase, like an estate agent arriving for a valuation. His wild curls had been slicked back and his blue eyes burnt with furious determination.

'I've brought you a file in the hope that you will

consider one last job,' he handed it over and looked around. 'Nice place.'

It looked disgusting, Colefax and Fowlered to within one inch of its sixteenth-century life with swags, stipples, indoor water features, distressed furniture and a distraught owner looking like sin from a sleepless night. It only took a moment for Al's professional cool to crack. Underneath, he was jumpy and nervous.

'OK, it's awful,' he admitted. 'I'm sorry. The magazine promised the best interior designers. We'll sue.'

'Thanks, but I have no interest in designer libels. And I appreciate you bringing this, but I told you, you're fired.' I threw the file on the dresser and waited for him to leave.

'I drove all the way from London,' he stayed put in my doorway. 'I brought you this too.' He fished a slim-line orchid out of the case, looking embarrassed. 'It reminded me of you,' he cleared his throat. 'Fragile and rare, and desired by too many people for its own safety.'

I looked at it for a long time and felt the sun flooding through the open front door on to my face. It gave Al an ill-deserved halo as he stood in front of me.

'I understand all your cuttings now,' he said, his face a dark silhouetted shadow. 'What interviewers meant when they wrote about your old-fashioned star quality, about how dangerous you are, how irresistible.' He looked at me curiously. 'I hope Bill knows how lucky he is.'

'What do you mean?' Cornered, I pretended not to understand.

'You hate the limelight, don't you?' his shadow moved, blinding me with sun. 'That's why you seemed so reluctant to go back into the public eye when I first met you, why you insisted on taking the fast-track to feature-spreads. You were doing it for love. Not revenge, nor self-glory. Love. Call Bill now,' he offered me his mobile. 'Call him. Tell him it's worked. That it's time to come home.'

'No,' I turned the flower around in my hands, voice choked.

He waited until a tear splashed on the cellophane before he spoke. 'Your relationship hasn't ended at all, has it, Sadie? It's simply on hold until Bill's career picks up. He staged that scandalous defection with Ash Numan to further his American interests with your support. He knew that if you went on a celebrity date-fest a few months later, you'd create enough personal publicity to negate all his love-rat bad press over here. That's why you waited a dignified amount of time after your "messy" bust-up and then approached me. You agreed to turn yourself into a media whore so that he'll receive a hero's welcome when he comes back. You did all this for him, didn't you?'

Stifling a sob, I pressed the back of my hand to my mouth. 'Yes.'

Al whistled quietly, almost incandescent with anger. 'What a sacrifice you made, Sadie. First he's a rat, now you're the bitch. First he's a tired shock-jock-turned-TV-star who's lost his edge, now he's Britain's lost misunderstood bovver-boy everyone wants to come home. Nice one, Smack – the ultimate publicity stunt. Clever old Sadie and Bill. The press will go wild when you two finally get it back together. No wonder my career's up in smoke. You made me look like an amateur, didn't you?'

'Faking a break up is no worse than faking relationships to get your clients in the headlines,' I howled. 'You do it all the time.'

'And I did it once too often with you, didn't I?' he laughed. 'Why couldn't I say no to you? Why?'

I couldn't answer that one.

'So now that you've more or less wrecked my career, why refuse to call Bill home for the romantic reunion?' His eyes blazed furiously. 'At least give me the satisfaction of knowing that I helped *Loved Up*'s young dream team get back together.'

'No! He needs more time,' I sobbed. 'He's not ready to come back yet.'

Then Al whistled again as the irony fist hit him in the face at last.

'Oh Jesus. Oh poor Sadie,' he shook his head, laughing bitterly. 'It hasn't worked, has it? You did all this for love and now you find out that he no longer needs you. He *likes* it in the States. He likes working with Ash – might be in love with her even. Is that it? Now he can bring her back here with him whenever he wants to and you've got zip-all except a zipped lip. He's used you just like you've used me. Well, I hope you're taking a cut, because I'm just taking a stab in the back here.'

'It's not like that,' I muttered tearfully.

But Al wasn't listening. He grabbed my hand and pulled it away from my face, blue eyes digging around for my tarnished soul. 'You have to help me out here, Sadie. Can't you see, I need you even if Bill doesn't?'

Ducking my head away from the shafts of sunlight, I looked into those curious, quirky blue eyes and fell in. I fell so deeply that the blood rushed to my head, the oxygen was punched from my lungs and my vision tunnelled until all I could see was blue, blue, blue. Christ, it was like coming home.

'What do you want me to do?' I tried to blink, to look away, but I couldn't.

'Save me,' he breathed, his mouth so close to mine that I could feel his breath on my lip, as warm and sweet as a patisserie. 'Save me like you saved Bill.'

Frantically shaking off his gaze, I turned away. I knew what I had to do. Sadie the sacrificial lamb had one more task. It was about time she performed a striptease and showed off her mutton.

'You'd better sit down,' I closed the door behind him and whistled Carrot from the sofa. 'There's something I should show you.'

Feeling charred with self-hatred, I went back to the dresser and pulled out a drawer. It was cram-full with airmail envelopes. Letters from Bill, increasingly desperate, telling me how much he missed me, how lonely he was and how much Ash got on his nerves. They asked me how things were going, why I wouldn't return his calls, when he could come home. The last few letters were the most heartbreaking, saying that he realized I no longer wanted to help him, that he could understand why, but begging me to reconsider.

Al read them in silence. When he finally looked up, his blue eyes were bewildered. 'Why, Sadie?'

I scrunched my eyes tight shut. 'Can't you see? I don't *want* him to come back to me, Al. I set him free. I did this so that he'd stop relying on me.'

I could hear his sharp intake of breath. 'You went through all this to what – to *chuck* him? Jesus, Sadie! I mean, I know you've done his career no end of good, but wasn't this all a bit elaborate, not to mention hurtful?'

'You have no idea!' I leapt up furiously, snatching the letters back. 'Bill and I had an agreement from the start. Our relationship was always a sham – not the sort that lasts a few weeks or months like the ones you set up, but one that has lasted for years and years, one that almost destroyed me. You see, I committed the ultimate sin by believing the hype and starting to love him for real. I know him better than anyone; I think he's wonderful and talented and warm and funny, but he could never love me in return, not in the way I wanted. God knows, he's tried. Yes, I'm "chucking" him, if you want to put it that way. I'm chucking him because sooner or later, he'll realize that he can live without me and he'll move on, find real love – one that matters. I *had* to hurt him to do this. It was the only way short of – short of –' I stopped myself short, knowing I'd said enough.

Al was mute with surprise.

'Now you have your story,' I opened the door. 'Go and tell that to your tabloid friends. It'll save your credibility, after all. Tell them Smack the Bitch dumped Bill Roth by sending him away to America to get famous there – she even paid Ash Numan to pretend to love him, which is why she's boracic. You can't make me look cheaper than I already do. Now fuck off and sell the story. If you want to double-up your PR while you're at it, I'll happily pose with a box of tissues. I'm sure one of your clients manufactures them. Why waste the opportunity to product place?'

'This isn't what I wanted, Sadie,' he pleaded. 'I don't need this.'

'Well, it's all you're getting,' I screamed, pushing him outside.

Carrot was old and rheumatic, but he always rose to the occasion. Al left the cottage with a small terrier attached to one leg, gnawing frantically.

When I finally heard his car engine roar away, I turned back to the dresser and spotted the file that he'd left. To my amazement, it contained a large photograph of just one man. Al Matthews, PR Guru, smiled at the camera with his lop-sided could-be-beautiful face and dishevelled comb-me-with-your-fingers hair. That, it seemed, was the final favour he'd come here to beg. Al wanted me to fake-date *him*.

It suddenly made such horrible sense that I started to laugh. He was caught up in his own spin and it had started to snowball. The press no longer trusted him. They didn't like the sham relationships, the client incest, or the manipulation. He'd had his fifteen minutes cubed and was now too famous to get away with a career as a Svengali. A future in panel shows or politics beckoned. And now that he'd been hoist by his own PR petard, he had to make himself even more notorious, more famous to survive and prosper. In his eyes, that meant hooking up with the most talked-about bitch in the country right now.

All he'd wanted was to trawl me around a few parties. Instead I'd told him my darkest secret. Shit.

I waited all week for the story to break. I bought the papers each day, scoured them obsessively. They reported that George Brian was now dating Ruby Red after her dramatic no-show at her wedding earlier in the year (yes, gratuitous photo of me at non-wedding). They reported that Mac's Number One single 'Older Woman' had turned platinum (cue another photo of me), that Vizza was hotly tipped for Sports Celebrity of the Year and believed to be seeing a Spice Girl whose solo career had bombed (small shot of her, huge one of me). There was nothing about Bill. The letters kept flooding in from America, but I had stopped opening them. They hurt too much.

In anticipation of the hacks calling, I'd changed my telephone number and only passed it on to the select few I trusted. After a full fortnight, when I'd just started to believe I was safe and that Al had gone to live in an ashram, Sly called. It was early morning and I'd been up all night bingeing on ice cream.

'What *have* you done?' he screamed. 'The *News* has dedicated three pages to it. The photo of me is *awful.*'

My face drained of colour and I fought to breathe as I dashed to the hall where the papers were waiting in a soggy pile. What had Al told them? How could he possibly know Sly was involved?

But the story that unfolded with more puns in bold italic than ever disgraced a *Carry On* script wasn't Al's. It was Bill's.

'Loved Up Star Comes Out' ran the headline. 'Bill tells how love for gay agent ruined life with sexy Smack.'

Bill told his story with the minimum of sentiment, outlining how his feelings for me had changed over the years, how he grew to rely on me as a sister, a mentor, and a therapist, but no longer as a lover. He told the nation how he clung to me even though I wanted to leave, how he begged me to stay, threatened suicide and even once locked me in our London flat for several days. He named Sly as his lover of close to five years, a man who had stood by him with unending patience and support. He spared himself no embarrassment as he finally exposed the true nature of our relationship and set me free. Christ, he was brave.

It was just after dawn, but the press had already started to gather outside. I ignored the knocks on the door and let Carrot bark himself hoarse as I hid from them all and took the phone off the hook. I'd been through it all before and wearily prepared for the long siege. 'Cross your legs, Carrot, mate.'

It was only when I hear a familiar voice yelling

through the letterbox that I opened the door a crack. Al burst inside, looking unshaven and exhausted.

'Why didn't you tell me he was gay?' he demanded.

'It was none of your business.'

We both jumped as a flash at the window almost blinded us. I closed the curtains on the photographer and buried my forehead in their dusty folds. 'Coming out will probably destroy Bill's career.'

'No it won't,' Al shook his head. 'He'll have to cling on to the sides of the boat for a while but he'll weather the storm. Look at Elton John, Michael Barrymore, Rupert Everett. They all came out and survived. Bill could see it was time. All he needed was good advice and a hand to hold.'

'How do you know?'

'I didn't get these red eyes from staying up partying,' he muttered, sagging down on the sofa. 'I've just got off a plane from California. Bill had no idea how much you've been suffering. Typical starry attitude, only thinking about himself. Still, he's a nice enough bloke. He'd just had lousy PR management, that's all.'

'You went to see him?' I was appalled. 'Christ, you're a bloody hyena, aren't you? Is there no bone you won't pick for your pound of flesh?'

'I gave him good advice, Sadie,' he sighed, looking even more tired. 'I thought that at least I could do one decent thing before I quit to prove I haven't been in the wrong career all these years.'

'But why Bill?'

'For you, of course,' he walked to the dresser where

his 'file' still lay under a pile of unopened mail. 'I hoped you might reconsider my final offer?'

I looked at the photograph and laughed. 'You must be joking! I couldn't fake another love affair. Can't you see what a mess that would make?'

'I don't want to fake it, Sadie. I never did. Like I just said, I quit PR.' Al was opening the most recent of Bill's letters. '*Sadie darling, he still won't go away. Christ, he's persistent. He says he loves you and says I have to set you free –*'

'Give that here,' I snatched it away and started to read. I'd trust Bill with my life – after all I'd trusted him with my love life for years. He'd clearly confided in Al a great deal. They had talked for hours, discussing the nature of fame, the way it destroys, creates untruths, damages souls. Bill liked Al, was clearly smitten, and even had the nerve to be irritated with me for using him. '*He's very like you, Sadie darling. He fell into this twinkly world by accident. Give him a chance. Don't let me down – now I'm allowed to be camp at long last, I simply must wear a ridiculous Versace suit to the wedding.*'

'Oh God, Bill, you daft bugger. Why wait so long?' I put the letter down with a sob and looked at Al's sad, dishevelled face. 'You don't want to fake it?'

He shook his head, cupping my face in his hands. 'I want the real thing, far away from the public eye. Just you and me and normality.'

'Oh God, that sounds good – a forever of normality,' I bit my lip, diving into his eyes again and swimming around for joy before splashing my way tearfully towards the most wonderful of long kisses.

'There's only one problem, Al,' I realized as I re-surfaced for air. 'Half the country's press are camped outside this house right now and they know we're in here.'

'So?' He laughed. 'Let's give them something to write about before we disappear forever. Where's your suit-case? Does Carrot need anything packing? Some food and her bed, maybe.'

Now that gave me an idea . . .

As we tanked along to M20, laughing our heads off, we heard the first reports of our extraordinary exit from my cottage on *Radio 5 Live*.

'The couple are believed to have left Smack's house dressed in gorilla suits. Most of the tabloids have already put this down to a publicity stunt after Bill Roth's extraordinary confessions in today's *News*. Editors say that the Alchemist has stretched his credibility too far this time.'

'Welcome to incredibility,' I laughed.

'Incredible,' Al stretched across to kiss me as we queued for the Channel Tunnel. 'We're the first celeb-rity couple who got together to escape the limelight completely. Where do you fancy going? I hear the South of France is lovely at this time of year.'

'Too many stars.' I wrinkled my nose. 'How about Belgium?'

'Well, the chocolate's nice,' he nodded. 'And we

could afford to rent a little farmhouse somewhere remote.'

'Perfect,' I sighed, leaning back and tickling Carrot's nose. 'What will we do there?'

'I rather thought,' he chewed his lip and glanced at me guiltily, 'that we could set up a super-discreet retreat for harassed celebrities?'

I started to giggle in England, and I was still laughing when we got to France.

Since she was first published in 1995 Marian Keyes has become a publishing phenomenon. Her four novels, *Watermelon, Lucy Sullivan is Getting Married, Rachel's Holiday* and *Last Chance Saloon* have become international bestsellers and have sold almost 2 million copies worldwide. She is published in several languages, the most unlikely of which are Japanese and Hebrew. Her fifth novel *Sushi for Beginners* will be published in Autumn 2000.

She lives in Dublin with her husband and is addicted to handbags, shoes and white Magnums.

The Truth is Out There

Marian Keyes

Los Angeles International Airport: teeming with passengers, arrivals, film stars, illegal immigrants, a dazed English girl called Ros and, of course, the odd alien or two freshly landed from another planet. Well, only one alien, actually. A small, yellow, transparent creature who liked to be called Bib. His name was actually Ozymandmandyprandialsink, but Bib was just much more *him*, he felt. Bib was in Los Angeles by accident – he'd stolen a craft and gone on a little joyride, only planning to go as far as planet Zephir. Or planet Kyton, at the most. But they'd been repairing the super-galaxy-freeway and diverting everyone and somehow he'd lost his way and ended up in this place.

Ros Little hadn't landed from another planet, she just felt like she had. The twelve-hour flight from Heathrow, the eight-hour time difference and the terrible row she'd had the night before she'd left all conspired to make her feel like she was having a psychotic episode. Her body was telling her it should be the middle of the night, her heart was telling her her life was over, but the brazen mid-afternoon Californian sun dazzled and scorched regardless.

As Ros dragged her suitcase through the crowds and the drenching humidity towards the taxi-rank, she was stopped in her tracks by a woman's shriek.

'It's an alien!' the helmet-haired, leisure-suited matron yelled, jabbing a finger at something only she could see. 'Oh my Lord, look, just right there, it's a little yellow alien.'

How very Californian, Ros thought wearily. Her first mad person and she wasn't even out of the airport yet. In other circumstances she'd have been thrilled.

Hastily Bib assumed invisibility. That was close! But he had to get out of here because he knew bits and pieces about planet earth – he'd been forced to study it in 'Primitive Cultures' class. On the rare occasions he'd bothered to go to school. Apparently, Los Angeles was alien-spotting central and the place would be over-run with X-Filers in a matter of minutes.

Looking around anxiously, he saw a small girl-type creature clambering into a taxi. Excellent. His getaway car. Just before Ros slammed the door he managed to slip in beside her unnoticed, and the taxi pulled away from the crowd of people gathered around the hysterical matron.

'But, Myrna, aliens ain't yellow, they're green, everyone knows that,' was the last thing that Ros heard, as they skidded away from the kerb.

With heartfelt relief, Ros collapsed on to the air-conditioned seat – then froze. She'd just got a proper look at her cabbie. She'd been too distracted by Myrna and her antics to notice that he was a six foot six, three hundred pound, shaven-headed man with an eight-inch scar down the back of his scalp.

It got worse. He spoke.

'I'm Tyrone,' he volunteered.

You're scary, Ros thought, then nervously told him her name.

'This your first visit to LA?' Tyrone asked.

'Yes,' Ros and Bib answered simultaneously, and Tyrone looked nervously over his shoulder. He could have sworn he'd heard a second voice, an unearthly cracked rasp. Clenching his hands on the wheel, he hoped to hell that he wasn't having an acid flashback. It had been so long since he'd had one, he'd thought he'd finally grown out of them.

When the cab finally negotiated its way out of LAX, Los Angeles looked so like, well, *itself* that Ros could hardly believe it was real – blue skies, palm trees, buildings undulating in the ninety-degree haze, blonde women with unfeasibly large breasts. But as they passed by gun-shops, 24-hour hardware stores, adobe-style motels offering waterbeds and adult movies, and enough orthodontists to service the whole of England, Ros just couldn't get excited. 'It's raining in London,' she tried to cheer herself up, but nothing doing.

To show willing she pressed her nose against the glass. Bib didn't, but only because he didn't have a nose. He was enjoying himself immensely and thoroughly liked the look of this place. Especially those

71

girl-type creatures with the yellow hair and the excess of frontage. Hubba *hubba*.

Tyrone whistled when he drew up outside Ros's hotel. 'Class act,' he said in admiration. 'You loaded, right?'

'Wrong,' Ros corrected, hastily. She'd been warned that Americans expected lots of tips. If Tyrone thought she was flush she'd have to tip accordingly. 'My job's paying for this. If it was me, I'd probably be staying in one of those dreadful motels with the water-beds.'

'So, you cheap, huh?'

'Not cheap,' Ros said huffily. 'But I'm saving up. Or at least I was, until last night . . .'

For a moment terrible sadness hung in the air and both Bib and Tyrone looked at Ros with compassionate interest laced with a hungry curiosity. But she wasn't telling. She just bit her lip and hid her small pale face behind her curly brown hair.

Cute, Bib and Tyrone both realized in a flash of synchronicity. She's cute. Not enough happy vibes from her though, Tyrone felt. And she's not quite yellow-looking enough for my liking, Bib added. But she's *cute*, they nodded in unconscious but undeniable male bonding.

So cute, in fact, that Tyrone hefted her suitcase as far the front desk and – unheard of, this – waved away a tip.

'Maaan,' Tyrone thought, as he lumbered back to the car. 'What is *wrong* with you?'

After the glaring mid-afternoon heat, it took a

moment in the cool shade of the lobby for Bib's vision to adjust enough to see that the hotel clerk who was checking Ros in was that Brad Pitt actor person.

What had gone wrong? Surely Brad Pitt had a very successful career in the earth movies. Why had he down-graded himself to working in a hotel, nice as it seemed? And why wasn't Ros collapsed in a heap on the floor? Bib knew for a fact that Brad Pitt had that effect on girl-types. But just then Brad Pitt shoved his hair back off his face and Bib realized that the man wasn't quite Brad Pitt. He was *almost* Brad Pitt, but something was slightly wrong. Maybe his eyes were too close together or his cheekbones weren't quite high enough, but other than his skin having the correct degree of orangeness, something was off.

Before Bib had time to adjust to this, he saw another earth movie star march up and disappear with Ros's suitcase. Tom Cruise, that was his name. And he really *was* Tom Cruise, Bib was certain of it. Short enough to be, Bib chortled to himself smugly. (Bib prided himself on his height, he went down very well with the females on his own planet, all two foot eight of him.)

The would-be Brad Pitt handed over keys to Ros and said, 'We've toadally given you an ocean-front room, it's rilly, like, awesome.' Invisible, but earnest, Bib smiled and nodded at Ros hopefully. This was bound to cheer her up. I mean, an ocean-front room that was rilly, like awesome? What could be nicer?

But Ros could only nod miserably. And just as she turned away from the desk Bib watched her dig her nails into her palms and add casually, 'Um, were there any messages for me?' While Brad Pitt scanned the computer screen, Bib realized that if he had breath he would have been holding it. Brad eventually looked up and with a blinding smile said, 'No, *ma'am*!'

Bib wasn't too hot on reading people's minds – he'd been 'borrowing' spacecraft and taking them out for a bit of exercise during Psychic lessons – but the emotion coming off Ros was so acute that even he was able to tune in to it. The lack of phone call was bad, he realized. It was very bad. Deeply subdued, Bib trotted after Ros to the lift, where someone who looked like Ben Affleck's older, uglier brother pressed the lift button for them.

Bib was very keen to get a look at their room and he was half impressed, half disappointed. It was very, *tasteful*, he supposed the word was. He'd have quite liked a water-bed and adult movies himself, but he had to say he was impressed with the enormous blond and white room. And the bathroom was good – blue and white and chrome. With interest he watched Ros do a furtive over-her-shoulder glance and quickly gather up the free shower cap, body lotion, shampoo, sewing kit, emery board, cotton buds and soap and shove them in her handbag. Somehow he got the impression that she wasn't what you might call a seasoned traveller.

A gentle knock on the door had her zipping her bag in a panic. 'Come in,' she called and Tom Cruise, all smiles and cutesy charm was there with her case. He was so courteous and took such a long time to leave that Bib began to bristle possessively. *Back off, she's not interested*, he wanted to tell Tom. Who'd turned out not to be Tom at all. He only looked like Tom when he was doing the smile, which had faded the longer he'd fussed and fiddled in the room. At the exact moment that Bib realized why Tom was lingering, so did Ros. A frantic rummage in her bag and she'd found a dollar (and spilled the sewing kit on to the floor in the process). Tom looked at the note in his hand, then looked back at Ros. Funny, he didn't seem pleased and Bib cursed his own perpetual skintness. 'Two?' Ros said nervously to Tom. 'Three?' They eventually settled on five and instantly Tom's cheesy, mile-wide smile was back on track.

No sooner had Tom sloped off to extort money from someone else than the silence in the room was shattered. The phone! It was ringing! Ros closed her eyes and Bib knew she was thanking that thing they called God. As for himself he found he was levitating with relief. Ros flung herself and surfed the bed until she reached the phone. 'Hello,' she croaked, and Bib watched with a benign smile. He almost felt tearful. But anxiety manifested itself as he watched Ros's face – she didn't look pleased. In fact she looked bitterly disappointed.

'Oh, Lenny,' she said. 'It's you.'

'Don't sound so happy!' Bib heard Lenny complain. 'I set my clock for two in the morning to make sure my favourite employee has arrived safely on her first trip in her new position, and what do I get? "Oh Lenny, it's you"!'

'Sorry, Lenny,' Ros said abjectly. 'I was kind of hoping it might be Michael.'

'Had another row, did you?' Lenny didn't sound very sympathetic. 'Take my advice, Ros, and lose him. You're on the fast-track to success here and he's holding you back and sapping your confidence. This is your first opportunity to really prove yourself; it could be the start of something great!'

'Could be the *end* of something great, you mean,' Ros said, quietly.

'He's not the only bloke in the world,' Lenny said cheerfully.

'He is to me.'

'Please yourself, but remember, you're a professional now,' Lenny warned. 'You've three days in LA so put a smile on your face and knock 'em dead, kiddo.'

Ros hung up and remained slumped on the bed. Bib watched in alarm as all the life – and there hadn't been much to begin with – drained out of her. For a full half-hour she lay unmoving, while Bib hopped from pad to pad – all six of them – as he tried to think of something that would make her happy. Eventually she moved. He watched her pawing the bed with her hand, then she did a few, half-hearted, lying-down bounces. With great effort of will, Bib summoned his mind-reading skills. *Jumping on the bed.* Apparently she liked jumping on beds when she went to new places. She and Michael always did it. Well, in the absence of Michael, she'd just have to make do with a good-looking – even if he did say so himself – two-foot eight, six-legged, custard-yellow life-form from planet Duch. *Come on*, he willed. *Up we get.* And took her hands, though she couldn't feel them. To Ros's astonishment, she found herself clambering to her feet. Then doing a few gentle knee-bends, then bouncing up and down a little, then flicking her feet behind her, then propelling herself ceiling-wards. All the while Bib nodded unseen encouragement. *Attagirl*, he thought, when she laughed. *Cute* laugh. Giggly, but not daft-sounding.

Ros wondered what she was doing. Her life was over, yet she was jumping on a bed. She was even enjoying herself, how weird was that?

Now you must eat something, Bib planted in her head. *I know how you humans need your regular fuel. Strikes me as a very inefficient way of surviving, but I don't make the rules.*

'I couldn't,' Ros sighed.

You must.

'OK, then,' she grumbled, and took a Snickers from the mini-bar.

I meant something a bit more nutritious than that, actually.

But Ros didn't answer. She was climbing, fully dressed, into bed and in a matter of seconds fell asleep, the half-eaten Snickers beside her on the pillow.

While Ros slept, Bib watched telly with the sound turned off and kept guard over her. He couldn't figure himself out – his time here was limited, they could find the space-craft at any time so he should be out there cruising, checking out the females, having a good time at somewhere called the Viper Room. Owned by one Johnny Depp, who modelled himself on Bib, no doubt about it. But instead he wanted to remain here with Ros.

She woke at 4 a.m, bolt upright from jetlag and heartbreak. He hated to see her pain, but this time he was powerless to help her. He managed to tune into her wavelength slightly, picking up bits and pieces. There had been a frenzied screaming match with the Michael person, the night before she'd left. Apparently, he hadn't wanted her to come on this trip. Selfish, he'd called her, that she cared more about her job than she did about him. And Ros had flung back that *he* was the selfish one, trying to make her choose between him and her job. By all accounts it had been the worst row they'd ever had and it showed every sign of being their last.

Human males, Bib sighed. Cavemen, that's what they were, with their fragile egos and sense of competition. Why couldn't they rejoice in the success of their females? As for Bib, he loved a strong, successful woman. It meant he didn't have to work and – Oi! What was Ros doing, trying to lift that heavy case on her own? She'll hurt herself!

Puffing and panting, Ros and Bib maneovured her case on to the bed and when she opened it and started sifting through the clothes she'd brought, Bib realized just how distraught she must have been when she'd packed. Earth still had those quaint, old-fashioned things called seasons and, even though the temperature in LA was in the nineties, Ros had brought clothes appropriate for spring, autumn and winter, as well as summer. A furry hat – why on earth had she brought that? And four pairs of pyjamas? For a three-day trip? And now what was she doing?

From a snarl of tights, Ros was tenderly retrieving a photograph. With her small hand she smoothed out the bends and wrinkles and gazed lovingly at it. Bib ambled over for a look – and recoiled in fright. He was never intimidated by other men but he had no choice but to admit that the bloke in the photo was very – and upsettingly – handsome. Not pristine perfect like the wannabe Brads and Toms but rougher and sexier looking. He looked like the kind of bloke who owned a power screwdriver, who could put up shelves, who could stand around an open car-bonnet with six other men and say with authority, 'No, mate, it's the alternator, I'm telling ya.' This, Bib deduced with a nervous swallow, must be Michael.

He had dark, messy curly hair, an unshaven chin and his attractiveness was in no way marred by the small chip from one of his front teeth. The photo had obviously been taken outdoors because a hank of curls had blown across his forehead and half into one of his eyes. Something about the angle of his head and the reluctance of his smile indicated that Michael had been turning away when Ros had clicked the shutter. *Real men don't pose for pictures*, his attitude said. Instantly Bib was mortified by his own eagerness to say 'Cheese' at any given opportunity. But could he help it if he was astonishingly photogenic?

For a long, long time Ros stared at Michael's image. When she eventually, reluctantly put the photo down, Bib was appalled to see a single tear glide down her cheek. He rushed to comfort her, but fell back when he realized there was no need because she was getting ready to go to work. Her heart was breaking – he could *feel* it – but her sense of duty was still intact. His admiration for her grew even more.

Luckily, in amongst all the other stuff she'd brought, Ros had managed to pack a pale grey suit and by the time she was ready to leave for her 8 a.m. meeting she looked extremely convincing. Of course Bib realized she *felt* like a total fraud, certain she'd be denounced by the Los Angeles company as a charlatan the minute they clapped eyes on her, but apparently that was par for the course in people who'd recently been promoted. It would pass after a while.

Because of her lack of confidence, Bib decided he'd better go with her. So off they went in a taxi to Danger-Chem's headquarters at Wilshire Boulevard, where Ros was ushered into a conference room full of orange men with big, white teeth. They all squashed Ros's little hand in their huge, meaty, manicured ones and claimed to be, 'trully, trully delighted,' to meet her. Bib 'trully, trully' resented the time they spent pawing her and managed to trip one of them. And not just any of them, but their *leader* – Bib knew he was the leader because he had the orangest face.

Then Bib perked up – a couple of girls had just arrived into the meeting! Initially, he'd thought they were aliens too, although he couldn't quite place where they might be from. With their unnaturally elongated, skeletal limbs and eyes so wide-spaced that they were almost on the sides of their heads, they had the look of the females from planet Pfeiff. But when he tried speaking to them in that language (he only knew a couple of phrases – 'Your place or mine?' and 'If I said you had a beautiful body would you hold it against me?') they remained blankly unresponsive. One of them was called Tiffany and the other was called Shannen and they both had the yellow-haired, yellow-skinned look he usually found so attractive in a girl-type. Although, perhaps not as much as he once had.

The meeting went well and the orange men and yellow girls listened to Ros as she outlined a proposal to buy products from them. When they said the price she was offering was too low she was able to stop her voice from shaking and reel off prices from many of their competitors, all of them lower. Bib was bursting with pride.

When they stopped for lunch, Bib watched with interest as Tiffany used her fork to skate a purple-red leaf of radicchio around her place. Sometimes she picked it up on her fork and let it hover in the general vicinity of her mouth, before putting it back down on her plate. She was *miming*, he realized. And that wasn't right. He switched his attention to Shannen. She was putting the radicchio on her fork and sometimes she was putting some into her mouth. He decided he preferred her. So when she said, 'Gotta use the rest-room,' Bib was out of his seat in a flash after her.

He'd really have resented being called a peeping Tom. An opportunist, he preferred to think of himself. An alien who knew how to make the most of life's chances. And being invisible.

But how strange. He'd followed Shannen into the cubicle and she seemed to be ill. No, no, wait – she was *making* herself ill. Sticking her fingers down her throat. Now she was brushing her teeth. Now she was renewing her lipstick. And she seemed happy! He'd always regarded himself as a man of the universe, but this was one of the strangest things he'd ever seen.

'I should be nominated for an Oscar,' Ros thought, as she shook her last hand of the day. She'd given the performance of a lifetime around that conference table. But she tried to take pride that she *had* done it. Between jetlag and her lead-heavy unhappiness over Michael she was surprised she'd even managed to get dressed that morning, never mind discuss fixed costs and large order discounts.

However, when she got back to her hotel, she insisted on shattering her fragile good humour by asking a not-quite-right Ralph Fiennes if anyone had phoned for her. Ralph shook his head. 'Are you sure?' she asked, wearing her desperation like a neon sign. But unfortunately, Ralph was very sure.

Trying to stick herself back together, Ros stumbled towards her room, where no force in the universe – not even one from Planet Duch – could have stopped her from ringing Michael.

'I'm sorry,' she said, as soon as he picked up the phone. 'Were you asleep?'

'No,' Michael said, and Ros's weary spirits rallied with hope. If he was awake at two in the morning, he couldn't be too happy, now could he?

'I miss you,' she said, so quietly she barely heard herself.

'Come home, then.'

'I'll be back on Friday.'

'No, come home now.'

'I can't,' she said gently. 'I've got meetings.'

'Meetings,' he said bitterly. 'You've changed.'

As Ros tried to find the right words to fix things, she wondered why it was always an insult to tell someone that they'd changed.

'When I first met you,' he accused, 'you were straight up. Now look at you, with your flashy promotion.'

He couldn't help it, Ros thought. Too much had changed too quickly. In just over eighteen months she'd worked her way up from answering phones, to being a supervisor, to assisting the production manager, to assisting the chairman, to becoming vice-production manager. None of it was her fault – she'd always thought she was as thick as two short planks. She'd been *happy* to think that. How was she to know that she had a natural grasp of figures and an innate sense of management? She had bloody Lenny to thank for 'discovering' her, and she could have done without it. Everything had been fine – better than fine – with Michael until she'd started her career ascent.

'Why is my job such a problem?' she asked, for the umpteenth time.

'My job!' Michael said hotly. 'My job, my job – you love saying it, don't you?'

'I don't! You have a job too.'

'Mending photocopiers isn't quite the same as being a vice-production manager.' Michael fell into tense silence.

'I can't do it,' he finally said. 'I can't be with a woman who earns more than me.'

'But it'll be our money.'

'What if we have kids? You expect me to be a stay-at-home househusband sap? I won't do it, babes,' he said, tightly. 'I'm not that kind of bloke.' She heard anger in his voice and terrible stubbornness.

But I'm good at my job, she thought, and felt a panicky desperation. She didn't want to give it up. But more than her job, she wanted Michael to accept her. Fully.

'Why can't you be proud of me?' She squeezed the words out.

'Because it's not right. And you want to come to your senses, you're no good on your own, you need me. Think about it!'

With that, he crashed the phone down. Instantly she picked it up to ring him back, then found herself slowly putting it back down. There was nothing to be gained by ringing him because he wasn't going to change his mind. They'd had so many fights, and he hadn't budged an inch. So what was the choice? She loved him. Since she'd met him three years ago, she'd been convinced he was The One and that her time in the wilderness was over. They'd planned to get married next year, they'd even set up a 'Meringue Frock' account – how could she say goodbye to all that? The obvious thing was to give up her job. But that felt so wrong. Oughtn't Michael to love her as she was? Shouldn't he be proud of her talents and skills, instead of being threatened by them? And if she gave in now what would the rest of their lives together be like?

But if she didn't give in . . . ? She'd be alone. All alone. How was she going to cope? Because Michael was right, she had very little confidence.

For some minutes she sat abjectly by the phone, turning a biro over and over, as she pondered the lonely existence that awaited her. All she could see ahead of her was a life where she jumped on hotel beds by herself. The bleakness almost overwhelmed her. *But just a minute*, she found herself thinking, her hand stopping its incessant rotation of the biro – she'd managed to get all the way from Hounslow to Los Angeles without Michael's help. *And* she'd managed to get a taxi to and from work. Had even held her own in a meeting.

To her great surprise she found that she didn't feel so bad. Obviously, she felt awful. Frightened, heartbroken, sick and lonely. But she didn't feel completely suicidal, and that came as something of a shock. She was so used to hearing Michael telling her that she was a disaster area without him that she hadn't questioned it lately . . .

How about that? She remained on the bed, and her gaze was drawn to the window. In all the trauma, she'd forgotten about her 'toadally awesome' ocean view and it couldn't have been more beautiful – Santa Monica beach, the evening sun turning the sea into a silver-pink sheet, the sand rose-coloured and powdery. Along the boardwalk, gorgeous Angelenos skated and cycled. A sleek couple whizzed by on a tandem, their no-doubt perfect baby in a yellow buggy attached to the back of the bike. He looked like a little emperor. Another tall, slender couple roller-bladed by, both sunglassed and disc-manned to the max. Hand-in-hand, they glided past gracefully, their movements a ballet of perfect synchronization.

'Fall,' Bib wished fiercely. 'Go on, trip. Skin your evenly-tanned knees. Fall flat on your remodelled faces.' He had hoped it might cheer Ros up. But, alas, it was not to be, and on the couple glided.

Ros watched them go, gripped by a bittersweet melancholy. And then to her astonishment, she found herself deciding that she was going to try roller-blading herself. Why not? It was only six-thirty and there was a place right next to the hotel that rented out roller-blades.

Hardly believing what she was doing she changed into leggings, ran from her room and in five minutes was strapping herself into a pair of blades. Tentatively, she pushed herself a short distance along the boardwalk. 'Gosh, I'm quite good at this,' she realized in amazement.

* * *

Bib held onto Ros's hand as she awkwardly skidded back and forth. It had been a huge struggle to convince her to get out here. And she was *hopeless*. If he hadn't been holding on to her hand, she'd be flat on her bum. Yet, her ungainly vulnerability made her even more endearing to him.

Bib had followed the evening's events with avid interest. He'd been appalled by Michael's macho attitude, the cheek of the bloke! He'd longed to snatch the phone from Ros and tell Michael in no uncertain terms how fabulous Ros was, how she'd terrified a roomful of powerful orange men. Then when Michael hung up on Ros, Bib used every ounce of will he could muster to stop Ros from ringing him back. He worked desperately hard at reminding Ros how wonderfully she'd coped since she'd arrived in this strange threatening city, even though it was so obvious, she should know it herself –

'Careful, careful!' he silently urged, squeezing his eyes shut in alarm, as Ros nearly went flying into a woman who was holding on to a small boy on a bike.

'Sorry,' Ros gasped. 'I'm just learning.'

''S'OK,' the little boy said. 'Me too. My name's Tod and that's my mom, Bethany. She's teaching me to ride my bike.'

Bethany was in the unfortunate position of having to hold tightly on to the back of Tod's bike and run as fast as Tod cycled. Bib eyed Bethany with sympathetic understanding because he was in the unfortunate position of having to run as fast as Ros was roller-blading. Which got faster and faster as her confidence grew.

'Wheeeeeh!' Ros shrieked, as she sped a good four yards, before losing Bib and coming a cropper.

When she returned the skates to the hire office, her knees were bruised but her eyes were a-sparkle. 'I had a lovely time,' she laughingly announced. Then she sprinted joyously across the sand to the hotel, Bib puffing anxiously behind her, tangling himself in his six legs as he tried to keep up.

She woke in the middle of the night, the exhilaration and joy of the night before dissipated and gone. She felt cold, old, afraid, lonely. She wouldn't be able to cope without Michael, she didn't want a life without him.

But then she remembered the roller-blading. She wasn't normally adventurous, usually needing Michael with her before trying new things. Yet she'd done that all on her own and it was a comfort of sorts.

'I am a woman who roller-blades alone,' she repeated to herself until she managed to get back to sleep.

Then she woke up, got dressed and went to work, vaguely aware that there was a new steadiness about her, a growing strength.

When she returned from her day's work, exhausted but proud from holding her own as they inched their way tortuously towards a deal, she bumped into Brad Pitt in the hotel lobby. From the look of things he was just knocking off work.

'Did you have a good day?' he enquired.

Ros nodded politely.

'So, what kind of business are you in?' Brad asked.

Ros considered. She always found this awkward. How exactly did you explain that you worked for a company that made portaloos? A very successful company that made portaloos, mind.

'We, um, take care of people,' she said. Well, why shouldn't she be coy? Americans were the ones who called loos *rest-rooms*, for goodness sakes!

'D'ya take care of people on a movie set?' Brad never missed an opportunity. The door to his career could open absolutely anywhere – there was the time he'd seen the director of *Buffy the Vampire Slayer* in his chiropodist's waiting room, or the occasion he'd crashed into the back of Aaron Spelling's Beemer – so he was always prepared.

'Actually, we have,' Ros said with confidence.

Quick as a flash, Brad's lightbulb smile burst on to his face and he swooped closer. 'Hey, I'm Bryce,' he murmured. 'Would you do me the honour of having a drink with me this evening?'

A good-looking man had invited her for a drink! What a shame that nothing would cheer her up ever again. Because if anything would do the trick, this would. But even as a refusal was forming in her mouth, Ros found herself pausing. Wouldn't it be better than sitting alone in her room waiting for the phone to ring?

'OK,' she said wanly.

Bryce looked surprised, women were usually delighted to spend time with him. Then he clicked his fingers. 'Oh, I get it. You're English, right? You kinda got that Merchant-Ivory repressed thing going on. Love it! Meet me in the lobby at six-thirty.' And smoothing his hair, he was gone.

In her room, Ros checked the phone, picked it up, trembled with the effort of not dialling Michael's number and frogmarched herself into the shower. America, the land of opportunity. She should at least try, after all Bryce really was gorgeous.

From the jumble of clothes thrown on the bed she managed to make herself presentable. A short – but not too short – black dress, a pair of high – but not too high – black sandals. But as she watched herself in the mirror, it was like seeing a stranger. Who was this single girl who was going out on a date with a man who wasn't Michael?

When the lift doors parted, Bryce was loitering in the lobby, sunbleached hair gleaming on to his golden forehead, white teeth exploding into a flashgun smile. Ros's spirits inched upwards. Maybe things weren't so bad. On the way to his car, she noticed Bryce patting his hair in the window as he passed by, then pretended she hadn't.

The bar was low-lit and quiet. 'So as we can really, like, *talk*,' Bryce said with a smile that promised good things, and the mercury level of Ros's mood began its upward climb again. As soon as they'd ordered their drinks, Bryce started the promised talk.

'. . . and then I got the part as the shop clerk in *Clueless*. They toadally cut it, right, but the director said I was great, really great. It was a truly great performance, I gave and gave until it hurt, but the god-damn editor was, like, toadally on my case . . .'

Ros nodded sympathetically.

'. . . of course, I should have got the Joseph Fiennes part in *Shakespeare in Love*. It was mine, they even toadally told my agent, but on-set politics, it's a toadal bitch, right?'

Ros nodded again. Despite Bryce's many tales of woe, his smile glittered and flashed. But as his litany of bad-luck continued, Ros began to notice that he didn't ever make eye-contact with her. Yet the intimate smiles continued anyway. Eventually, wondering if he was coming on to some girl behind her, Ros looked over her shoulder. And saw a mirror. Ah, that explained everything. Bryce was flirting with his favorite person. Himself.

On and on he droned. Great performances he nearly gave. Evil directors, cruel editors, leading men who had it in for him because they were threatened by his talent and looks.

'Hey, I've done enough talking about me.' He finally paused for breath. 'What do *you* think of me?'

Ros could hardly speak for depression. With Bryce she felt more alone than she had on her own.

'Would you mind terribly if I left? Only I'm ever so sleepy. Must be jetlag.'

'We've hardly been here thirty minutes,' Bryce objected. 'I'm just warming up.'

To her dismay, Bryce offered to see her back to the hotel. And up to her room. At her bedroom door she realized he was about to try and kiss her. She braced herself – she didn't have the the energy to resist him. He looked deep into her eyes and trailed a gentle finger along her cheek. Despite him being the world's most boring man, Ros couldn't help a leap of interest. After all, he was *so* handsome. Slowly Bryce lowered his perfect lips to hers, then paused.

'What are you doing?' Ros whispered.

'Close-up,' Bryce whispered back. 'A three second close-up of my face before the camera cuts to the clinch.'

'Oh for goodness sake!' Ros shoved the key in the lock, twirled into her room and slammed the door.

'Hey,' Bryce was muffled but unbowed. 'You ballsy English girls, toadally like a Judi Dench thing! Y'ever met her? I just thought with you both being English . . .'

'Go away,' she said, her voice trembling from unshed tears. This was the worst that Ros had felt. Wretched. Absolutely wretched. Was this all she had to look forward to? Boring, self-obsessed narcissists?

Bib had been against the idea of a drink with Bryce from the word go. He just hated those men that thought they could fell women with one devastating smile. He'd tried to warn Ros that Bryce was nothing but a big, pink girl's blouse, but she wouldn't listen and – *now* what was going on? Someone was outside their room, pounding and demanding to be let in. It was a man's voice – perhaps it was Bryce back to try his luck again?

'Open the bloody door!' A voice ordered, and as Bib watched in astonishment, Ros moved like a sleepwalker and flung the door wide. A man stood there. A man that Bib recognized. But he wasn't any of the would-be film stars, he was . . .

'Michael!'

Though it killed him to do it, Bib had to admit that Michael was looking good. With his messy curly hair, rumpled denim shirt and intense male presence he made all the wannabe Toms and Brads look prissy and preened.

'Can I come in?' Michael's voice was clipped.

'Yes.' Ros's looked like she was going to faint.

'What are you doing here?' she asked as Michael marched into the room.

'I wanted to kiss you,' he announced and with that he pulled Ros to his broad hard chest and kissed her with such lingering intimacy that Bib felt ill.

Finally he let Ros go and announced into her upturned face, 'I've come to get this sorted, babes. You and me and this job lark.'

'You flew here?' Ros asked, dazedly.

'Yeah. 'Course.'

Hmmm, Bib thought. Hasn't got much of a sense of humour, has he? Most normal people would have said something like, 'No, I hopped on one leg, all six thousand miles of it.'

'I can't believe it.' Ros was a picture of wonder. 'We're skint but you've travelled halfway around the world to save our relationship. This is the most romantic thing that's ever happened to me.' And Bib had to admit that Michael did cut a very Heathcliffish figure as he strode about the room, looking moody and passionate.

Bad-tempered, actually, Bib concluded.

'You come home with me now,' Michael urged. 'You knock the job on the head, we get married and we live happy ever after! You and me are meant to be together. We were terriff until you got that promotion, it was only then that things went pear-shaped.'

With his words, the joyous expression on Ros's face inched away and was replaced by an agony of confusion.

'Come on,' Michael sounded impatient. 'Get packing. I've got you a seat on my flight back.'

But Ros looked paralysed with indecision. She leaned against a wall and made no move and the atmosphere built and built until the room was thick with it. Bib was bathed in sweat. And he didn't even have perspiration glands.

Don't do it, he begged, desperately. *You don't have to. If he loved you he wouldn't ask you to make this choice.*

To his horror he watched Ros fetch her pyjamas from under her pillow and slowly fold them.

'Where's your suitcase?' Michael asked. 'I'll help you.'

Ros pointed and then began scooping her toiletries off the dressing table and into a bag. Next, she opened the wardrobe and took out the couple of things that she'd hung up. It seemed to Bib that her movements were becoming faster and more sure, so in frantic panic, he summoned every ounce of energy and will that he possessed and zapped her with them.

You don't need this man, he told Ros. *You don't need any man who treats you like a possession with no mind or life of your own. You're beautiful, you're clever, you're sweet. You'll meet someone else, who accepts you for all that you are. In fact, if you're prepared to be open-minded and don't mind mixed-species relationships, I myself am happy to volunteer for the position . . .* He stopped himself. Now was not the time to be side-tracked.

'I'll fetch your stuff from the bathroom,' Michael announced, already briskly en route.

Then Ros opened her mouth to speak and Bib prayed for her words to be the right ones.

'No,' she said and Bib reeled with relief.

'No,' Ros repeated. 'Leave it. I can't come tonight. I've got a meeting tomorrow.'

'I know that, babes,' Michael said tightly, as if he was struggling to keep his temper. 'That's what I mean, I want you come with me *now*.'

'Don't make me do this.' Misery was stamped all over Ros's face.

'It's make-your-mind-up time.' Michael's expression was hard. 'Me or the job.'

A long nerve-shredding pause followed, until Ros once again said, 'No, Michael, I'm not leaving.'

Michael's face twisted with bitter disbelief. 'I didn't know you loved the job that much.'

'I don't,' Ros insisted. 'This isn't about the job.'

Michael looked scornful and Ros continued, 'If you love someone, you allow them to change. If marriage is for life, I'm going to be a very different person in ten, twenty, thirty years' time. How're you going to cope with that, Mikey?'

'But I love you,' he insisted.

'Not enough, you don't,' she said, sadly.

For a moment he looked stunned, then flipped to anger. 'You don't love me.'

'Yes, I do. You've no idea how much.' Her voice was quiet and firm. 'But I am who I am.'

'Since when?' Michael couldn't hide his surprise.

'I don't know.' She also sounded surprised. 'Since I came here, perhaps.'

'Is this something to do with Lenny? Are you having it off with him?'

Ros's incredulous laugh said it all.

'So have I got this right?' Michael was sulky and resentful. 'You're not coming home with me.'

'I've a job to do,' Ros said in a low voice. 'I fly home tomorrow night.'

'Don't expect me to be waiting for you, then.'

And with the same macho swagger that, despite everything, Bib admired, Michael swung from the room. The door slammed behind him, silence hummed, and then – who could blame her, Bib thought sympathetically – Ros burst into tears.

No more Michael. The thought was almost unbearable. She lay on the bed and remembered how his hair felt, so rough, yet so surprisingly silky. She'd never feel it again. Imagine that, never, *ever* again. She could smell him now, as if he was actually in the room, the curious combination of sweetness and muskiness that was uniquely Michael's. She'd miss it so much. As she'd miss the verbal shorthand they had with each other, where they didn't have to finish sentences or even words because they knew each other so well. She'd have to find someone else to grow old with. It was all over, she was certain of it. There would be no more rows, no further attempts to change the other's mind.

They'd had so many angry, bitter fights, but what was in the air was the stillness of grief. The calmness when everything is lost. She'd moved beyond the turbulence of rage and fury into the still static waters of no return.

What would she do with the rest of her life, she asked herself. How was she going to fill in all the time between now and the time she died?

Roller-blade, planted itself in her head. Immediately she told herself not to be so ridiculous. How could she go roller-blading?

But why not? What else was she going to do until bedtime, and despite all the events of the evening it was only still eight-thirty. She pulled on her leggings even though they had a tear on one knee and ran across the sand. She was surprised to find how uplifted she was by whizzing back and forth at high speed on her skates. It had something to do with pride in what a good roller-blader she was – she really was excellent, considering this was only her second time doing it. Her sense of balance was especially wonderful.

The little boy Tod who had been there the previous

night was there again, with his long-suffering mother Bethany. Bethany was red-faced and breathless from having to run and hold on to Tod while he cycled up and down the same six yards of boardwalk and Ros gave her a sympathetic smile.

Then Ros went back to her room and against all expectations managed to sleep. When morning came she woke up and went to work, where, with a deftness that left the Los Angeles company reeling in shock, negotiated a thirty per cent discount when she'd only ever planned to ask for twenty. Blowing smoke from her imaginary gun, she gave them such firm handshakes that they all winced, then she swanned back to the hotel to pack. Successful mission or what?

Bib was in agony. What was he going to do? Was he going to back to England with Ros, or home to his own planet? Though he'd grown very fond – too fond – of Ros, he had a feeling that somehow he just wasn't her type and that revealing himself, in all his glorious custard-yellowness, would be a very, very bad idea. It killed him not to be able to. In just over two days he'd fallen in love with her.

But would she be OK? She *thought* she was OK, but what would happen when he left her and there was no one to shore up her confidence? Would she go back to Michael? Because that wouldn't do. That wouldn't do *at all*.

He worried and fretted uncharacteristically. And the answer came to him on the evening of the last day. Ros had a couple of hours to kill before her night-flight, so instead of moping in her room, she ran to the board-walk for one last roller-blading session. Bib didn't have anything to do with it – she decided all on her own. He'd have preferred a few quiet moments with her, actually, instead of trundling alongside her trying to keep up as she whizzed up and down, laughing with pleasure.

Bethany and Tod were there again. Time after time, Bethany ran behind the bike, holding tightly as Tod pedalled a few yards. Back and forth on the same strip of boardwalk they travelled, until, unexpectedly, Beth-any let go and Tod careened away. When he realized that he was cycling alone, with no one to support him, he wobbled briefly, before righting himself. 'I'm doing it on my own,' he screamed with exhilaration. 'Look, Mom, it's just me.'

'It's all a question of confidence,' Bethany smiled at Ros.

'I suppose it is,' Ros agreed, as she freewheeled grace-fully. Then crashed into a jogger.

As Bib helped her to her feet, he was undergoing a realization. *Of course*, he suddenly understood. He'd been Ros's training wheels, and without her knowing anything about it, he'd given her confidence – confi-dence to do her job in a strange city, confidence to break free from a bullying man. And just as Tod no longer needed his mother to hold his bike, Ros no longer needed Bib. She was doing it for real now, he could feel it. From her performance in her final meeting to deciding to go roller-blading without any prompting from Bib, there was a strength and a confidence about her that was wholly convincing.

He was happy for her. He really was. But, there was no getting away from the fact that the time had come for him to leave her. Bib wondered what the strange sensation in his chest was and it took a moment or two for him to realize that it was his heart breaking for the very first time.

LA airport was aswarm with people, more than just the usual crowd of passengers.

'Alien-spotters,' the check-in girl informed Ros. 'Apparently a little yellow man was spotted here a few days ago.'

'Aliens!' Ros thought, looking around scornfully at the over-excited and fervent crowd who were laden with geiger-counters and metal-detectors. 'Honestly! What are these people *like*?'

As Ros strapped herself in her airline seat, she had no idea that her plane was being watched intently by a yard-high, yellow life-form who was struggling to hold back tears. 'Big boys don't cry,' Bib admonished himself, as he watched Ros's plane taxi along the runway until it was almost out of sight. In the distance he watched it angle itself towards the sky, and suddenly become ludicrously light and airborne. He watched until it became a dot in the blueness, then traipsed back through the hordes of people keen to make his acquaintance to where he'd hidden his own craft. Time to go home.

Ros's plane landed on a breezy English summer's day, ferrying her back to her Michael-free life. As the whining engines wound down, she tried to swallow away the sweet, hard stone of sadness in her chest.

But, even as she felt the loss, she knew she was going to be fine. In the midst of the grief, at the eye of the storm, was the certainty that she was going to cope with this. She was alone and it was OK. And something else was with her – a firm conviction, an unshakeable faith in the fact that she wouldn't be alone for the rest of her life. It didn't make sense because she was now a single girl, but she had a strange warm sensation of being loved. She felt surrounded and carried by it. Empowered by it.

Gathering her bag and book, slipping on her shoes, she shuffled down the aisle towards the door. As she came down the plane's steps she inhaled the mild English day, so different from the thick hot Los Angeles air. Then she took a moment to stand on the runway and look around at the vast sky, curving over and dwarfing the airport, stretching away forever. And this she knew to be true – that somewhere out there was a man who would love her for what she was. She didn't know how or why she was so certain. But she was.

Before getting on the bus to take her to the terminal, she paused and did one last scan of the great blue yonder. Yes, no doubt about it, she could feel it in her gut. As surely as the sun will rise in the morning, he's out there. Somewhere . . .

Lisa Jewell is thirty-two years old and lives in North London with her brand-spanking-new husband and their cat. She used to be a secretary until redundancy, a bet and a book deal took her away from all that and she is now a full-time writer. Her first novel, *Ralph's Party*, was the bestselling debut novel of 1999 and her second novel *Thirtynothing* is published in September 2000.

Rudy

Lisa Jewell

Rudy brushes up the nap of his tan suede desert boots with an old toothbrush. He picks a bit of dried food off his grey T-shirt and checks the fly on his beige brushed-cotton combat trousers. Turning towards the mirror, he hooks his shiny conker-coloured hair over his ears and pushes his fringe out of his face. His top lip curls itself up over his teeth to allow for a tooth inspection and he's ready to go.

He moves through his sparsely furnished flat, dominated by his collection of guitars, displayed on stands: two Fenders, a twelve-string, two acoustics and a bass. He pulls the door closed behind him and takes the narrow stairway that separates his hallway from the kebab shop upstairs. He has to walk sideways because his feet are too big for the steps. Mojo, his dog, follows closely behind, his claws tapping on the bare floorboards.

On the street outside, he puts his hand to his eyes, shielding them from the sunshine. He doesn't get any daylight in his flat and the sudden burst of light brings tears to his eyes. He doesn't own any sunglasses, because he always loses them.

Rudy is on his way to Parliament Hill. Even though it's a mile and a half away, he's going to walk. Rudy walks everywhere. He doesn't believe in cars, he hates London Transport and the thought of negotiating a spindly little push-bike through the ruthless streets of London makes him break out in a sweat. He'll get in a cab if someone else orders it and he'll accept a lift if someone offers it, but otherwise, Rudy walks.

Rudy is what you might call non-conformist. Rudy hasn't got a job. He busks on the Underground, he signs on, the state pays his rent. He hasn't got a girlfriend. He sleeps with a girl called Maria nearly every other night, but he won't call her his girlfriend. He doesn't watch the telly, he doesn't read the papers, he doesn't read books, he refuses to buy CDs. He's a vegetarian and he lives over a kebab shop. He breaks the rules. Even the shape of his body, the size of his feet, the length of his fingers are non-conformist.

He's tall, very tall, about six-foot-three, with thick, unruly hair that he keeps tucked behind his ears. It's thinning a bit on top, but unless he's sitting down or with someone taller than him (unlikely), that remains his secret. He has his father's Italian features – thick eyebrows, an expressive mouth and very, very long eyelashes. That's the first thing that most women ever say to him: 'God, your eyelashes are *so* long.'

Very embarrassing.

He keeps himself in fairly good condition, washes his hair every morning, shaves every day, buys himself clothes occasionally, nice clothes, tactile clothes, chunky hand-knitted jumpers, moleskin trousers, huge desert boots for his size elevens, a big cashmere overcoat. It's all second-hand of course, he couldn't afford to buy nice stuff like that *new*. But when you know which shops to go to, when you know exactly what you're looking for, it's amazing what you can pick up for next to nothing.

Rudy's thirty-three years old and he's never had to work in an office, answer a phone or write a memo. He's never experienced that moment of ultimate flatness when you open your payslip and find that your boss *hasn't* given you a surprise pay rise, that your tax code *hasn't* changed overnight and that the accounts department *hasn't* cocked up and given you too much money by mistake. He's never had to wake up before ten o'clock or stay late or go to an office party. He only wears ties for weddings and funerals and he gets his hair cut whenever he feels like it. He can take his dog to work and have his lunch whenever he wants and for as long he likes. He doesn't have to be nice to anyone he doesn't like (except the police when they come to move him along every now and then) and he doesn't have to go on training courses or learn a company mission statement. He doesn't have to pretend to be ill if he wants to stay at home and watch television and he doesn't panic if someone in his department gets a better car than him. And best of all, better than anything else, he doesn't have to pay those thieving bastards at the IR a single penny of his hard-earned cash. In fact, the only thing he has in common with someone who works in an office is that if he wants to smoke a fag he has to go outside.

He lights a cigarette now, a slim white Craven 'A'. He lights it with a lighter shaped like a pistol, which Maria gave him for his birthday, and smokes it as he walks.

The sun-baked August streets of Kentish Town are thronging with fantastic women in fantastic clothes: midriff tops, halternecks, hotpants and skimpy sundresses. They are patchworks of honey, gold and strawberry pink skin. Some are rake-thin, some are muscular, some are flabby and some are curvy. They are all absolutely beautiful. He could fall in love with every one of them.

Rudy can feel his libido rising as he walks.

In the park, Rudy picks up a reasonable looking stick – about a foot long with a good wide berth and no sharp bits – and tosses it skywards. It spirals across the horizon a few times before coming to a halt underneath a bouffant horse chestnut. Mojo is there almost before it's landed, skidding to a halt and having to retrace his steps a little. He locks his powerful jaws round the stick and brings it back to Rudy.

'Good boy . . . good boy.' Rudy buries his fingers into the warm ruff of thick hair under Mojo's chin and gives him a good tickle. He picks up the stick from where the dog left it at his feet and throws it again. He watches the huge animal gallop off into the distance for a while and then turns his gaze to the bench at the foot of the hill. Is she there? He tucks his hands into his pockets and starts the steep walk back down towards the bench. There is someone sitting there, hard to tell even if it's a man or a woman from this distance. His pace quickens. Mojo appears at his side and joins him as he walks purposefully downhill, his rubber-soled suede boots squeaking against the greasy tarmac path underfoot.

A shape emerges from the undefined blob sitting on the bench. It has bare shoulders and brown hair. Could be. Could be her. The hair is long – yes, it is definitely her – and is held back with a black plastic claw-type-thing – reminds Rudy of an eagle's foot. He loves that thing.

She turns briefly to watch a hyperactive Highland terrier tear past in pursuit of a pigeon. Her nose, in profile, is perfectly straight, like it's been hand-finished with a plane. Her mouth is turned up ever so slightly into a small smile and she's wearing that dress again. That dress that Rudy loves so much. It's a sort of crushed velvet and tie-dyed about ten different shades of claret and bottle green. It has very thin shoulder straps and, as witnessed on the one occasion that Rudy has seen her walking, a skirt of the perfect weight and shape to be easily inflated by the slightest gust of wind, revealing an extra inch or two of her lovely legs. There's no wind today, though. It's bright and still and excitingly warm, no clouds in the sky at all, save for a few smudges to the east that look like they've been left there by grubby-fingered children. Parliament Hill is as busy as you'd expect it to be on the warmest day of the year

– there are people everywhere, stretched out on the grass, semi-clothed and sunbathing.

Rudy approaches the bench and considers his next move. Where to sit? Right here at the furthest edge of the bench, away from her? Towards the middle, closer to her, but still leaving her 'personal space' uncroached upon? Or should he just take his chances and plonk himself down there at her side? His breathing becomes hard and heavy as he tries to scrape together the nerve to sit down. In and out. In and out. In and out. Just do it, just do it, just ... bloody ... well ... do ... it. His breath by now is audible and the girl turns to meet his eye. She looks uncomfortable. Fuck. He lets his breath go, takes the other end of the bench and pulls a battered old paperback from the inside pocket of his jacket. Doesn't know what it is. Some old shit that Maria lent him a couple of years ago. 'Oh, you'll love it. It's so funny and so observant about *men* and *life* and *relationships*. You must read it.' So he'd just smiled and said thanks and tucked it into the bowels of his overcoat thinking, 'How many years do I have to know you, Maria, before you'll understand that I don't like reading, I don't like books, I don't like words, I don't like other people's thoughts in my head – how many books are you going to lend me before you realize that I'm just not interested?' But then he'd noticed that it was written by the same guy who wrote the book that the girl in the Velvet Dress was reading. So last week he'd pulled the book out of his pocket and he'd started reading it. And it was quite funny, he supposed.

About a man who runs a record shop in North London who's useless in relationships. It might have reminded him of himself if he had a job or if he ever actually had any relationships.

Rudy opens the book and then inexplicably clears his throat rather loudly, as if trying to attract someone's attention. The girl cocks her head a little in his direction and Rudy decides to turn the throat-clear into a full-on coughing fit. The girl turns away and immerses herself visibly deeper into the book on her lap. So, no sympathy, thinks Rudy. Hmmm . . . interesting. Very interesting. Not even a flicker of concern. She's either a heartless bitch or she's just very shy. Rudy decides to go with the 'very shy' option. It fits in better with his overall fantasy of her. If she turned out to be a heartless bitch, then he'd just have been wasting his time every Saturday morning for the past six weeks.

That was when she'd first appeared – six weeks ago – from nowhere and straight into his life, just like that. The first time he'd seen her he was walking so fast that all he could make out was a blur of crushed velvet and shiny hair. The second time, he'd passed her slowly enough to distinguish a perfect nose and a paperback novel. The third week, he'd approached her from behind and been enchanted by the plastic claw holding her hair back from her face, its talons digging brutally into the thickness of her hair. By the fourth week he'd got up the nerve to sit on the bench with her, but had stood up again after less than a minute and continued on his way. It was last week that he'd had the brainwave about the book. It gave him something to do while he sat here, something to quell the awkwardness and embarrassment of the situation.

The girl in the Velvet Dress looks away from her book very briefly and smiles ever so slightly at Mojo, who's eyeing her dolefully from where he's stretched out under the bench.

Rudy smiles to himself. Nothing warms Rudy to a stranger more quickly than a flattering remark or an affectionate attitude towards his dog. This girl on the bench, she'd given Mojo a nice look the first time she'd seen him, too, that same half-smile she'd used just now when the Highland terrier had run past her. She obviously likes dogs, which is good. Which is vital, in fact. I mean, Mojo is his best friend. Now, if she liked Muddy Waters and B. B. King and could play a bit of flamenco guitar as well, then she might just turn out to be his perfect woman.

Not that he'll ever find out. Of course not. He isn't going to *talk* to her or anything. He never does. Because the woman with the Velvet Dress and the Hair Claw isn't the first woman that Rudy has shared a bench with on Parliament Hill. Oh no. This year there's been the woman with the Blue Nail Polish and Jaunty Hat and before that the woman with the Pink Nose Stud and the Pigskin Rucksack and then the woman with the Raffia Bag and the Diamante Hair Grips, the one with the Dangly Earrings and the Snakeskin Shoes and the one with the Ethnic Ankle Bracelet and the Big Silver Rings. Rudy likes accessories. Not for himself, but on women. He loves them. Women can hide behind clothes, behind fashion, but it's through accessories that women give themselves away.

So – what does Rudy know about this stranger, about the girl in the Velvet Dress?

She's single, that's for sure. They all are, all these girls in the park. Of course they are. Why on earth would they be sitting alone in the park on a Saturday afternoon if they had someone to be with?

The velvet tells Rudy that she's sensuous, receptive to textures, likes a bit of luxury in her life. He imagines her to be the type of woman who might stop at a posh Belgian chocolate shop on her way home from work and ask for just one Champagne Truffle, gift-wrapped in a tiny little box. No wolfed down Mars Bars for this girl, no KitKat on the way to work, Twix bar in her office drawer or gobbled Cadbury's Wispa when she thought no one was looking. Just a brief moment of pure luxury.

He imagines her taking her chocolate home, all aquiver with excitement and then making herself a proper cup of tea, in a pot, with leaves.

He imagines her with a cat, a Persian, maybe, or a Ragdoll. Something with luxuriant fur. She probably buys him a piece of cod every now and then, or poaches a chicken breast for him, in milk.

The dress would have been a treat, too. Something she'd seen in a shop window, fallen in love with, saved up for for weeks. It would have been tissue-wrapped and handed to her in a shiny paper bag with rope handles. She still keeps the bag, in the back of her wardrobe. A souvenir of a perfect moment.

The girl in the Velvet Dress slips her finger between the next two pages of her book and chuckles almost imperceptibly under her breath at something she's just read. She turns the page over and sighs contentedly.

Rudy clears his throat again and eyes her surreptitiously. Were you watching, you might think that he's about to talk to her, that he's getting up the nerve. But you'd be wrong. Rudy doesn't need to talk to her, he doesn't need to get to know her – he already knows so much. He's never spoken to any of the women. That would just spoil everything. He prefers getting to know women without having to talk to them. That way he doesn't have to find out that they're thick, or bitchy, or boring, or silly, or shallow, or that they have a horrible accent or an ugly voice, or that they just really don't want to talk to him. At all. Better just not to try. Better just to sit here on the bench and breathe them in, work them out from the telltale clues they subconsciously leave all over the place. The body language, the jewellery, the book, the *accessories*. The way they react to Mojo, the way they react to him, the way they react to the weather and to things going on around them. Bitten nails or long nails, short hair or long hair, clean shoes or scruffy shoes – you could learn more about a person's levels of self-esteem looking at signs like that than you could in a whole year of psychotherapy. Probably.

But what about affection, you might ask, what about

contact, what about *sex*? The thing is, you see, Rudy doesn't actually *need* any physical contact with his bench women. He has Maria for that sort of thing, the barmaid at the Lady Somerset. Naughty little Maria with her uplift bra and her thick lipstick and her tiny little buttocks and lethal hipbones that protrude like shark fins from either side of her abdomen. She's half his size all over, and at least ten years older than him. She's on for anything, any time. She isn't interested in chat or love or going out or anything. She just likes coming back to his flat after the pub closes and crawling all over his big long body for as long as he'll let her. She's great. But she's nowhere near his ideal woman. She's way too thin, for a start. But she gives him exactly what he needs and in a funny sort of way, he loves her for it.

The girl in the Velvet Dress looks at her watch (plain, leather strap, looks like she's had it for years), folds down the corner of her page, closes it and slips it in to her bag (drawstring-top leather duffel). She stands up, hitches the bag on to her shoulder and turns to leave.

And then something unbelievable happens. She stops, turns around and looks at Rudy. She stares at him for what feels like at least ten minutes and then opens her lips, very slowly. Her cheeks starts reddening and she begins twisting her hands together self-consciously.

She smiles. 'Bye,' she says. She sticks one hand up at him, stiffly, palm-first, and begins walking away.

'Yeah,' mutters Rudy, sitting bolt upright, dropping his book at his feet and, a few seconds too late, 'yeah – see you.' She's already halfway into the distance. 'See you.'

He watches her amble down the hill, her hands in her pockets, her head downcast.

Jesus.

Jesus Christ.

What was that? What the fuck was that?

Rudy leans down to pick up his book, his head swimming. She spoke to him. The girl in the Velvet Dress spoke to him. She said 'bye'. What does it mean? What does she want?

He frowns and tucks the book back into his inside pocket. Why did she speak to him?

And then a terrible realization dawns upon him. She's been coming here on purpose just to see him! Every week, the same bench, the same time. It's obvious. She's . . . she's . . . stalking him. He's being stalked by a mad, obsessive, lonely, unloved, unhinged woman. Oh Jesus!

He stands up quickly and looks around him, making sure she's no longer in sight. She isn't.

'Come on, boy.' He slaps his thigh and Mojo joins him as he begins to walk back down the hill.

Rudy needs a drink now. His hands are shaking slightly and a light film of sweat clings to his brow. His pace quickens as he hurries down the tarmac path, towards Highgate Road, towards the Lady Somerset, looking over his shoulder every now and then as he walks.

Stella Duffy was born in London and grew up in New Zealand. She has written two novels published by Sceptre – *Singling Out the Couples* and *Eating Cake*, and four crime novels, *Calendar Girl*, *Wavewalker*, *Beneath The Blonde* and *Fresh Flesh*, all published by Serpent's Tail. *Singling Out The Couples* has been optioned for a feature film. She has written sixteen short stories, several articles, a short play for *Steam Industry*, a dance-theatre piece for *Gay Sweatshop* and two one-woman shows. Stella is also an actor, comedy improviser and presenter. She lives in Brixton with her girlfriend and a very hopeful future.

A Swimmer's Tale

Stella Duffy

I have come here to escape. To forget about the love that never was. (Not true of course, but right now, I would prefer the never was.) I can bear never was far more easily than never will again. Less present pain in return for denying earlier pleasure. I am raw and can no longer imagine what the earlier pleasure might have been. It is all hurt, all loss. And still there is no word, no sign, from you. I am melodrama abandonment, but find no enjoyment in my over-the-top. I've always placed far too much hope in the possibility of eternal clairvoyance for lovers. The possibility of love for lovers.

Girlfriends and boyfriends and ex-lovers and maybe-lovers and concerned mother smiles have all offered helpful advice. The same helpful advice. I was counselled warm beaches, hot sun, hotter bodies. I was counselled sun and sea and surf and alcohol and illicit drugs if at all possible and beyond that, over and above the hedonism of sinning skin, I was counselled hedonism of the flesh. Let them get in. Anyone, anyflesh, anyman, anywoman. Just let someone in, not too deep, but far enough, fill enough of that aching gap and then you

117

won't notice it quite so much. The pain, the loss, the yawning void of the full urn on my mantelpiece. (You'd think after almost a year I'd have done something with it, scattered them somewhere, for God's sake. My friends think it's time I did something with it. They're quite possibly right. Their rightness is why I'm here.)

My friends think it's high time I did something with you. But I'm still waiting for a sign, a smile, a cool breeze in the middle of the night from a draft-proofed double-glazed window. You promised you'd let me know it was all right. I'm still waiting. How hard can it be for you to break back through? Is your love really so held by traditional physics? Where's the quantum leap of desire you promised me? I'm looking for miracles and seeing darkness magnified through tears. I'm looking for hope and losing you to black holes.

The obvious correctness of my friends' and family's suggestions though, is why I'm here now, why I'm by the sea. Come to find myself again. (They actually meant come to lose you for the first time, come to let you go, though no one had the guts to say so.) I think perhaps I was supposed to try Barbadian lust, Bondi bonding, cruise the cruisers and find one for me. (Maybe not the latter, even my most desperate mates don't think seventy-year-old rich Americans are my type.) Instead I have chosen Wales. Anglesea. Peninsula insular. Like me. Like I've become. I used to be the outgoing one of our pairing, the loud one. There seems little point now. Without my other there is nothing for my shadow to fall against. I find I am undefined.

You found me too loud always. In bed, in bath, in Bath. In hotels especially. Too thin walls letting through my too loud desire. You tried to hush me, shut me up. You tried to shut me. Impossible. I blossomed open, time-lapse photography fast, when I met you. And stayed that way – it's why daily life scrapes against my open flesh now – I do not know how to close up again. Not since you. You loved to go away, summer killed you in London and you made a motorway maid of me too. We found the finest – and grottiest – hotels in the land, and the so many others. As long as they were within the reach of the sea, or sunshine, or just a running tap if that was all we could manage. You needed water and I needed you. Need you.

At first I thought this was a mistake. There was too much of a sense that you might be round the next corner, hiding in the headway. I kidded myself for a whole half a day that we had arranged for you to meet me later. I do not like to dine alone. It takes no time at all to eat a three-course meal by myself and even the best intentioned kitchen staff cannot maintain the pace when there is no knife-and-fork banter to fill up the clock space necessary for perfectly sautéed meat. You did not come to the table. I offered your glass to Elijah, but he wasn't thirsty either. I drank it myself instead. I have drunk alone far too many of the bottles I used to share with you. It's one way to get to sleep. It's the only way to get to sleep. Which is still infinitely preferable to waking up.

Milos. Cycladian sea island. Circadian rhythms shot to fuck by the fuck shooting through me to you and back again. We are on a tourist boat charting the island circumference. You marvel at my bravery as I dive into cliché-clear waters. I marvel at your bravery as you dive into me. I swim beneath the sea and look up to you, magnified by the depths of sea-through ocean. You are an amplified version and the water might be sea, might be me. My love/lust/lost-in-you tears make you huge. You fill the space of my vision. You fill the space of me.

The first night here it rained seven hours solid. Howling rain pelted by a broken wind against my window. I knew how it felt. I lay awake as I do so often now, waiting for you. Wondering if here you might be able to find me again. I worry that you are lost out there, elemental soul beating against closed doors unable to worm-hole your way through to me. And then too, I worry that there's nothing to worry about. That there is none of you left. That the reason you have not managed the Cathy/Heathcliff reunion we promised each other is because there is nothing to reunite. I am real, corporeal. You are not. I should hope that your present nothingness is the truth, hope for your sake that you aren't wandering the darkness trying to find me. Should, don't. My grief is still selfish enough to deny you a peaceful nothing. I just want to touch you again. (And even when I say that, I know it's not true. One touch would never be enough. I would keep you with me forever.) Your departure has made a genie-keeper

of me. I'd lock you back in that urn quick as kiss you.
I'd lock you back in my flesh quick as love you. Love
you quick again.

Sydney sunshine. You and I and the antipodean sky, lost
in the sharp blue, astounded by the fierceness of the sun,
astonished that while it burnt my skin, you burnt my lips
more, branded ourselves with each other. My body was
made to hold yours. There were wonders to see and you
ignored them to look at me. We were not good tourists,
I could send home no postcards of the fine sights they
offered us, I had no 'wish you were here' when I was with
you. Your topography was more than enough.

There is a man here, also alone. I think the breakfast
waitress would like us to talk to each other. I think she
is more interested in the morning ease of having to
clear just the one table, than the possibility that this
man and I might find conversation possible. We don't
talk, but I do begin to watch him. He eats toast and
marmalade, no butter, as you did. But his toast is
cut into quarters, eaten carefully, he does not crush a
slice in half as you did and finish one piece in three
mouthfuls. He seems to have more time than you did.
I'd steal it from him if I could, give you his time. Your
death has made a murderer of me. The man is slow
and deliberate. Every morning he sets out, walks the
mud flats of the shallow tide. He has binoculars and
telescope. It is a wet summer, he watches shore birds,
writes them down in a notebook. At least that's what

I imagine he's doing – sighting, writing. As if simply seeing is enough. He does not need to touch as well. It's a skill I would do well to learn.

Hot Paris summer. All the Parisians have left, abandoning their over-heated city to we foolish tourists. You and I are over-heated and weighed down with shopping and crowded by jostling Italian school children. We fight on the Metro, an argument about nothing, escalating to everything. It is not unusual for us to fight and even so, every time we do, I think it means the end. Still I cannot stop myself. Run up the stairs and into the sweltering city and far from you. Will not back down, don't remember where this began, probably don't care, and yet am so caught up in the emotion, the wave of your fury and my anger, that I have no way of coming back to you. You come back to me instead, remind me that however much I hate you, you are going nowhere without me. That I can push you away as much as I want, beat you off with my violent words, but you're not leaving. I glare at you and refuse to admit my relief, my gratitude at your astonishing staying-power. It's impressive. And I do believe you. Believe I cannot push you away. That night we lay in a hot bed, desultory ceiling fan stirring humid air around our dark-painted room, sticky skin making the slow approach, remembering who we are because we are with each other. And I did believe you when you said I couldn't send you away. You were right, of course, it wasn't me who sent you. It was summer.

On the third morning the sun was shining when I awoke. I was surprised by the brighter light through the heavy curtains. Did not understand the faint ease of spirit, tried to banish the half-smile playing with my features, but it wouldn't leave my face. It was late when I woke, two solo wine bottles conspiring in my hot, heavy slumber. I'd missed breakfast, missed the man with his carefully quartered toast. I dressed without showering first – you'd have been appalled – pulled on yesterday's tired clothes, dragged my matted hair back into a careless ponytail. There was a new urgency, I didn't know why or what for, I did know I'd better get out there and use it before my inebriate brain woke up properly and grief lethargy hit again.

The sun was hot on my covered arms, your old jumper that I've been wearing half the time for most of a year was not meant for summer, not even British summer. I pulled the sleeves up to my elbows and looked at my pale arms, thin since you. Bony fingers reaching out for a hand to hold. I stopped on the road above the shore and saw the man, his telescope trained on a rock far out, exposed by the low tide, I saw wheeling dots around the rock, no doubt he saw and knew his prey, jotted notes on salt-damp paper, categorized, called and caught. He watched the birds for an hour or so, I watched him for almost as long.

It was peaceful and warm, not enough tourists had lasted the wet week for the remaining few to disturb me over much. Those who had stayed were families with too many small children and too few large bank balances to move on to the next place the sun might be. The shore was blessedly free of hand-holding couples who might have rubbed sea-salt in my fresh wounds. It is close to a year, I know, but the wounds are as fresh as the day you made them, ripping yourself away from my grasp. They stay fresh, I like them that way. I understand them that way.

The man began to pack up his equipment and I quickly moved on, up the hill, beyond the headland where the wind is fresher and cooler. I did not want him to see me watching. He might equate distraction with interest, and I can no longer manage polite conversation. Strangers are not usually equipped to deal with unexpected tears. I never used to cope so well either. Now the salt-flow is my norm. You always preferred sea water to fresh. How nice to know I am still pleasing you. (I would rather not please you.)

Venice. They all said not to go in summer. They were right. Would have been all right if we had been tourists, clammy bodies cramming St Mark's Square, over-flowing flesh flooding into the Lido overflow. But we were not tourists you and I. I had not travelled to the lagoon to marvel at Tintoretto or applaud the bravery of the Guggenheim collection. Instead I took a hotel room-bound long weekend to marvel at the delicate flesh tones of you, to applaud the priceless modern collection, astonishing bravery of spirit, the audacity and shock that was only you. Your body offered to me on cool white sheets, your self laid out with room service care, the touch and taste of you making a bland white bread of their coffee, biscotti, bruchetta, prosecco, proscutio, prandial-offered prospect. Childhood-myth and long awaited Venice lay before me, open plate, offered wide. I closed the shutters on the grounded visitors of the grand vista, Grand Canal, you were all the view I needed. I toured you that weekend. Unlikely rest weekend away, I went home exhausted and thin. Who could ask for more?

Since then I have been offered another chance to view you, laid out on equally cool white sheets. They said it might have helped. But I wasn't interested in making it better. They could not make you better, you were my very best, so why bother? I closed the wide eye-shutters on their kind offer. Some sights should remain unseen wonders; wonder-full, awe-full. Awful.

You and I swimming. You have always swum further, faster, deeper than me. I would struggle to keep up, against the current, against the waves, against my grain. I am really a land person, understand dirt, rocks, hills, mountains, prefer my horizon bordered with recognizable jigsaw edge pieces. You like a long straight line of water against the sky, would swim far out until I was left behind, bobbing in the shallows, straining salt-splashed eyes for your return. No change there then. But I always enjoyed the intensity of your enjoyment, happily lay hours on the beach, leathering my skin as you watered your parched soul, several summers of block-buster reading discarded for the better-seller option of reviewing you.

Fifth morning and I found myself watching the man again. This time from my bedroom window, wet day, no sleep, no energy to make the dressed politeness of dining-room breakfast, I sipped already cold tea with UHT milk and couldn't taste the difference anyway. He walked through the morning drizzle, apparently untouched by the disgruntled irritation of bed and breakfasters all along the coast, their one-week-a-year panic settling and sending out just-suppressed fury, a heavy wave of pissed-off mist lining the damp shore. It seemed though that perhaps this was just what the man wanted. Empty coastline, morning haze, ugly mud-flats of low tide exposing the bird breakfast smorgasbord. Like him, you wouldn't have cared about the weather, might even have welcomed the rain, clearing the sea for your endeavours alone. But you wouldn't have seen his sights. Your eye would have been trained on the fuzzy horizon, the thin grey line blurred by the cool land and the warm rain. You would have walked right past him, run even, to get into the water, drench your skin in its welcoming cold. But I watched him searching carefully, patiently training his eye on something too far to touch, too wild to get close, yet there. Within his sights. Watching and noting and writing down the real.

And then I found I'd been watching the man for three hours. He'd been watching the birds for three hours. It was almost midday, the clouds began to clear and the beach-bound families re-found their summer resolve – we will play on the beaches, come rain or shine. The shine finally came and so did they, deserting the indoor shopping malls for the outdoor version. The bird man turned away. Clearly needed fewer people for his telescopic foray. It seemed that perhaps no people might suit him better. Made sense to me. And I began to think about what he was looking at, that he seemed to have made it his job to view what was actually there.

When they told me what had happened, it was impossible to believe. Not that I chose not to believe, or couldn't understand, simply too far-fetched for truth. We'd talked about it. Late-night lover conversations, 'How will I survive without you?', 'You won't ever have to.' 'I'm never leaving you.' 'I'm never leaving you.' 'If anything ever happens to me I'll come back.' 'Promise?' 'Promise.' But it wasn't something else that happened to you. Not something outside, beyond our control, no freak accident, creeping disease that took you. They told me that you took yourself, the creeping disease of accidental freak. You should have come to find me, confided in me. You should have cooled yourself swimming in me, but while I could always lose myself in you, soothe myself in you, it seems the reverse was not true. In summer, in London, sweltering city of land-locked people and grid-locked cars, you could find no water-marked horizon to cool yourself, so you swam out into the sky instead. Diving towards a sharp line horizon that could not be real, swimming yourself to the same place.

And it seems I've been doing the same. Training my telescopic eye on the not-there. Scanning impossible horizons for a blessed untruth, notebook and pen poised to record the self-created hope.

The next day, a solid night's sleep for the first time in nearly a year, and again I am up before the sun has made it through the thick morning drizzle. My bags are packed, my room tidied, and I'm on the shore before all the other visitors who have learned to wait until at least five hours of daylight has burnt away the rain. I carry you to the shore as you sometimes tried to carry me. Picking me up and stumbling a few feet to dump me in the water, both of us tumbling in the waves and each other. I carry the full urn and take this chance to look at you, really see what is here, not my dream of you. The truth is that you are ashes. That is all you are. And ashes cannot come back to me.

I can see the bird man, maybe three hundred feet away, his telescope trained on the high cliff to our right. The breakfast waitress told me he had hoped to sight a pair of gannets this week, that someone had told him they had been seen around here recently, staying on too long into summer, a special treat for the watcher. She told me gannets mate for life. It's a nice idea, but I don't know much about birds, don't care much about birds. It turns out the hope of flight was your thing, not mine. The man raises a hand to wave to me, after all, we've seen each other every morning, every day, for almost a week now. But I don't respond. I have a job to do. Something real of my own to view. I have the truth of you to concentrate on.

The water is warmer than I had expected. I walk out to almost waist deep. There is very light rain, a thin horizon of pale grey, the certainty of bright sunshine in another hour or so. I'm training my vision only on what is here, now. I'm holding the urn that is holding you and walking out to do the right thing.

Mid-summer, warm water, me flesh, you ashes. Mid-summer, warm water, me here, you gone. Mid-water, hot summer, you're gone, I'm here. Mid-me, then mid-you, scatter the summer of you in the warm water around me. Swimming with summer you in the warm water, scattering around the swimming me. Me swimming in you, in letting go, leaving you, swimming around, scattering in me. You and me and summer water, the warmth of the waves and a thin grey horizon that is growing stronger with the hotter sun, bluer as the bright light burns off the misty grey. I am letting you go. Like the bird man, I will concentrate only on what I can see. Breathe in deep only what I can see. Breathe in. I can see you. Sea me. We too are warm. We two are warm.

Later, the bird man, unfortunately not much of a swimmer himself, said it had certainly looked as if the woman knew where she was swimming to.

Isabel Wolff was born in Warwickshire and read English at Cambridge. She is the author of two bestselling romantic comedies, *The Trials of Tiffany Trott* and *The Making of Minty Malone*. Her freelance articles have appeared in many national newspapers, she writes a column for *P-S* magazine and reviews the papers for *Breakfast News* on BBC1. She lives in London and is *not* a Friend of the Royal Academy.

Post Haste

Isabel Wolff

He was certainly clever, Jane thought as she pulled navy mascara through her pale lashes. Oh yes, she thought as she appraised her reflection, Gerald was clever all right. That's what she liked about him. That's what had drawn her to him that Saturday afternoon three months ago. In the Friends Room at the Royal Academy. In the queue for coffee. That's how they'd met. They'd both reached for the cream jug at precisely the same second. And they'd laughed, then blushed, then politely murmured, 'after you', and then he'd suddenly looked her in the eye and said, 'Don't you find early Kandinsky a little ... jejune?' Jane had been too taken aback to reply straight away. And too busy surveying this strange man who was now calmly whitening her Kenco as though they'd known each other for years.

'Jejune? Well ...' she gave an amused little shrug, 'I'm not sure I know what that means.'

He dropped first one pale brown sugar lump into his coffee, and then another.

'It comes from the Latin, *jejunus*,' he explained as he began stirring vigorously. 'Meaning fasting.'

131

'Fasting?'

'Insubstantial. Intellectually thin. Feeble,' he added, confidently. He chinked the spoon three times on the rim of the cup then said, 'Would you like to sit down?'

Jane had smiled her assent and followed him to the black leather sofa by the door. She'd heard about this, she reflected with wry amusement. The Friends Room was a notorious pickup place. Everyone knew that. And this, she presumed, was a pick-up. Really! she'd thought. What a *nerve*. And then she'd remembered that that was precisely why she'd joined. The man was still talking about Kandinsky – 'Middle period ... Cubism ... superior to Picasso ... Klimt ...' – and as he did so Jane had sat there half smiling, and nodding politely while she discreetly took him in. Bookish. That was it. Owlish, even. He looked a bit like Stanley Spencer. Round, horn-rimmed specs. A mop of thick brown hair. Small features which seemed to crowd into the centre of a soft, round face. Not a handsome face she'd thought with a pang. No. Not handsome at all. But not hideous either, she reflected judiciously, and at this she'd felt a sudden rush of hope. She'd casually let her gaze drop a little to scrutinize his physique. He wasn't slim. Nor was he fat. He wasn't tall. But his shoulders were broad. Chunky. That's what he was. And smartly-dressed, in a navy blazer and grey casuals. A chunky, well-spoken forty-something man. Single, she presumed.

'Do you come here ... ?' she began, then stopped herself just in time. 'I mean, have you been a Friend

of the RA long?' The man sipped his coffee, then lowered his cup.

'Years,' he replied. 'I'm a friend of the Warburg too.
And the Tate.' At this Jane had felt something within
her stir. Oh yes. She *adored* clever men . . .

. . . Jane dabbed on a smidgen of blusher, drew a
brush through her short blonde hair, then sprayed a
mist of 'Allure' on to her lightly powdered throat. She
looked at her watch. Ten to seven. As usual, she was
going to be late. She was always late for Gerald. She
knew it didn't do to be prompt. Usually, it was a question of five or six minutes. Sometimes, when she was
feeling more confident, she might be eight minutes late,
or even ten. For Jane had been playing Gerald carefully,
like an angler with a large trout. Tickling him. Taking
her time. Doing nothing to startle or rush him. Because
Gerald was clearly not the kind of man who could be
rushed. She walked slowly downstairs, took a final check
in the hall mirror, then picked up her bag and stepped
outside. She thought of the cultural evening which lay
ahead. There'd been so many since she met Gerald.
They'd been to *King Lear* at the Barbican, and Edward
Lear at the Tate. They'd been to Hodgkin at the Hay-
ward and Shostakovich at the Festival Hall. They'd seen
Pinter at the Almeida, and Ballet Rambert at Sadler's
Wells. And she was beginning to think that, after three
months, it was time that he . . . Yes, it was time.

Jane's heart began to pound a little as she turned
into Kentish Town Road. Tonight was the night that
she was going to move things on. Give him a gentle

prod. After all, he'd already agreed that they had lots in common. Like her, he loved the opera – he went to Glyndebourne every year. Jane had a sudden, happy vision of them there, sitting side by side on a mohair rug, laughing, and sipping champagne. Gerald liked the theatre too, and films, as long as they were of the high-brow kind. And concerts of course. He went to lots of those. And he was passionate about the visual arts. Oh yes they had so much in common she told herself again as she entered Kentish Town tube. Naturally there were some differences. For example, Gerald was brilliant at maths and she . . . but then everyone had agreed that the O-level questions had been particularly tough ones that year. But Gerald was a genius at maths. He had a double first in it from Oxford. One of his favourite hobbies, he told her, was 'thinking about the universe'. Another thing they didn't have in common – television. He didn't have one; 'Nothing to watch!' he'd say. But Jane worked in TV. As a freelance producer. Another point of departure – he was a humanist, and Jane was a Catholic. A half-hearted one, admittedly, but she knew she could never give it up. It was ineradicable. It ran through her like the lettering in a stick of seaside rock. But Gerald was devout in his unbelief – evangeli-cal almost. 'Look, *I know* for a fact that God does NOT exist,' he'd announce, pushing his glasses up his nose. 'Absolutely not. No way!' This slightly dismayed Jane, who thought there was an outside chance He might. But then you can't expect to have *everything* in common with your potential partner, can you, she told herself philosophically as she slipped her ticket into the automatic gate. And Gerald was interested in her. That was clear. She knew this because after each date, he would phone her the following morning, without fail, and say, 'Well, Jane, go and get your diary.' And they'd pencil in the next time – usually four or five days hence.

Jane always left it to Gerald to phone her. She knew that that was best. And though not naturally manipulative, she felt her coy caution was paying off. Because he'd started to call her when he was away, on business, for his bank. He'd rung twice from Glasgow and once, even, from Paris. At this she'd been quietly thrilled. And as they'd chatted she'd imagined him standing at a window overlooking the Place Vendôme with the Seine glinting in the autumn sun. Oh yes, he's keen all right, she'd thought as she stepped on to the train. And that's why he was taking his time. But now she felt like applying just a *little* pressure to the button marked 'FF'.

Gerald was forty-five. Ten years older than Jane. He didn't talk much about his past. Jane knew only that he'd been divorced for eight years (high time he took the plunge again then!) and that he regarded his ex-wife, Susie, as a 'moron'. This had dismayed Jane a little. She'd felt her heart sink when he'd said that to her, over dinner, on their second date. She'd looked at him slightly reproachfully and gently murmured, 'Oh Gerald.' Then he'd guiltily explained that he'd left Susie because though she was 'absolutely gorgeous', she was 'thick'. And it had surprised Jane that Gerald had been married to someone gorgeous as he wasn't exactly gorgeous himself. But on the other hand, yes, on the other hand ... on the other hand, he was rich.

For her part Jane strenuously avoided talking about herself, though sometimes Gerald would probe. She rather liked it when he got a little bit inquisitive like this, but took care to keep her replies breezy and light.

'Oh well,' she'd say airily, 'I suppose I've just never met the right one ... you've just got to get it right, haven't you?' she'd add. She never admitted that if she ever, *ever* laid eyes on her ex, Philip, again she'd probably fell him with one smart blow from her bag. 'Oh yes,' she'd go on, with a regretful little smile, 'it's just got to be *right.*'

As the train rattled southwards Jane checked her make-up once more, pushed her hair behind one ear, and removed a piece of fluff from the velvet lapel of her coat. They were going to the opera – to see *Hansel and Gretel* at the Coliseum. As always, she'd got the tickets, and he'd take her for dinner afterwards. 'I'll take care of the entertainment,' she joked at the start, 'and you can be in charge of catering.' And though she knew he earned a fortune, she was always careful to pay her way. Jane stepped on to the escalator at Leicester Square and floated up, and out. Through St Martin's Court, then sharp right, and now she could see the opera house, and the crowd hurrying up the steps. And there was Gerald. By the box office. Waiting. She spotted him before he saw her and was pleased to see that he looked slightly concerned.

'Sorry I'm late,' she breathed as she proffered her

cold cheek for him to kiss. 'The phone just wouldn't stop ringing – couldn't get away!' This wasn't so much a white lie, as a flashing fluorescent pink and green one. No one had rung her at all. She glanced at Gerald's suit – a Prince of Wales check. He looked good in it, and though he was far from handsome, at least he always looked smart. She dropped her coat off quickly, as the two-minute bell began to clang. Underneath her coat she was wearing a pale blue cashmere cardigan and a short, bronze-coloured velvet skirt. She smiled at Gerald, ran a manicured hand through her hair, then they made their way upstairs to the front of the dress circle.

'I love this,' she thought as they took their seats and the house lights dimmed. 'I love this moment when the curtain goes up and the hush comes down, and I'm cocooned in the darkness with him.' Convinced that her right profile was more attractive, she always tried to sit on Gerald's left. She crossed her legs, aware that he could hear the gentle rasp of expensive tights. She hoped too that he'd notice the soft gleam of her velvet skirt as it stretched across her thighs, and inhale the warm, vanillery sweetness of her scent. 'Tonight,' she thought as the music swelled. 'Tonight, maybe. Tonight.' Sometimes, when they went to the theatre, she'd place her right elbow on his armrest. And if he did the same, with his left arm, then they could feel each other's bodies rise and fall. Up and down. Up and down. Then one of them would shift.

In the interval, Gerald was in raptures: 'Post-

Romanticism ... Wagnerian harmony ... folkloric melodies ... Richard Strauss *very* keen ...' Jane listened with a warm glow inside as she sipped her red wine, happy to be with this clever man; happy, happy, *except*... At dinner, afterwards, she decided that she'd drop a gentle hint. But Gerald was still waxing lyrical about nineteenth-century music. But then, as the waiter brought coffee, there was a moment when their eyes met, across the table, in sudden silence. Courage surged through Jane's veins with the white Bordeaux.

'Gerald ...' she began carefully. 'Gerald, there's something I ...'

'Schoenberg!' he exclaimed.

'What?'

'Sorry. Schoenberg. At the Barbican. I've just remembered,' he said. 'Next Thursday. Shall we go?'

'What? Oh. Yes. Yes,' she agreed. 'Schoenberg would be great.'

'You were going to say something,' he apologized. 'So sorry. Do go on.'

'Was I?' she said, vaguely. 'Oh, it was nothing important. Er ... I was just going to ask you whether you were keen on Liszt?'

Afterwards, as always, Gerald walked Jane to the tube. He always walked her to the tube, before getting a cab himself to his mews house in Earl's Court. They'd stroll along, side by side, Gerald walking on the outside of the pavement because he was always very 'correct'.

'Another wonderful evening,' he said happily, as she rummaged in her bag for her pass. 'Another splendid evening. Splendid. What fun.' He kissed her on the cheek. 'Schoenberg,' he repeated cheerfully. 'I'll call you tomorrow, Jane. Bye.'

'Bye,' she replied with a watery smile as he turned away. On the train, she avoided looking at the infatuated young couple sitting opposite her, their limbs entwined, like rope. And though Jane could always keep a stiff upper lip, her lower one was giving her trouble. So she breathed deeply – in and out – and held her book up in front of her face. Leaving Kentish Town tube she stared down, hard, at the paving stones as she walked along. Then she arrived at her flat, closed the front door, shouted 'Jesus *CHRIST*!!!' and burst into tears.

The next day, after lunch, the phone rang.

'Jane. It's Gerald. How are you?'

'I'm . . . confused,' she replied, before she could stop herself. Oh God. Oh *God*. Too late.

'Confused?' he repeated. 'About what?'

'About you, Gerald,' she said quietly.

'Oh. Oh dear. Why?'

'Well . . . *because* . . .' she went on, inhaling slowly, '. . . I've been seeing you for three and a half months now – and you haven't even held my *hand*!' There. It was said. She had knocked a hole in the dam and now the water was going to pour through.

'Ah . . .' he began awkwardly.

'I just don't know what you want.'

'What I want? Er . . . ah . . .' he stuttered. 'Well . . . well . . . this is most surprising,' he expostulated, recovering now. 'Yes! This really is a *most* surprising conversation.' Jane took a deep breath.

'Well I find it surprising', she went on calmly, 'that you keep asking me out, but never do anything.'

'Do anything?'

'We go on all these dates,' she added wearily, 'week after week after week, and you don't even, you don't even . . . Look, it's no good if you're going to be shy.'

'Shy?' Gerald exclaimed indignantly. 'Shy? I'm not shy!'

'Aren't you?'

'No!'

'Well, you are with *me*,' she replied.

'Am I?'

'Yes. Though you weren't to begin with. When you picked me up at the RA.'

'I didn't "pick you up",' he said wonderingly. 'I was just making conversation. Being polite.'

'Oh. Well then why did you ask me out after that? And why did you *keep* on asking me out? That's my problem, Gerald. I don't understand what you want.'

'Oh. I see.'

'I assumed you were interested in . . . you know . . .' she sighed. 'In getting to know me better.'

'Well, I was. I mean, I *am*,' he corrected himself.

'But I think you know me quite well by now, Gerald. And to be honest I've been finding your 33 r.p.m. approach a little . . .' – she avoided saying 'frustrating' – 'slow.'

'Ah. I *see*. Well Jane, this really is a *most* surprising

conversation,' he said again, now sounding almost amused. 'My dear, I simply didn't realize you felt like this,' he added. 'I . . . I . . .' Words eluded him. 'But now I know what I have to do!' he suddenly exclaimed. 'Yes! I know what I have to do. And I'm going to *do* it!'

By now Jane regretted her emotional candour. She felt her insides twist and coil.

'Yes,' he went on, excitedly now. 'I know what I've got to do and next time I see you, I'm going to hold your hand!'

'Look, Gerald,' she said wearily. 'You don't have to do anything you don't want to do . . .'

'Oh, but I do!'

'All I'm saying,' she added patiently, 'is that I'd just like to know whether you see our friendship as just, well . . . friendship?'

'Well, we do have to be friends first,' he said. 'That's very important. I mean I was friends with my last girl-friend for a year before we . . .'

'A *year*?' she repeated. Good God!

'. . . but now I know how you feel I'm going to . . . well,' he concluded darkly, 'I know *exactly* what I'm going to do.'

Jane replaced the receiver with a leaden heart. Having a conversation with Gerald about whether or not he was going to hold her hand was not quite what she'd had in mind. She just wanted him to do it. She'd been wanting him to do it for weeks. She just wanted him to quietly take hold of her hand, at some suitable moment, and hold it in both of his. But there'd been nothing. Not so much as a touch. Just these endless cultural excursions in which they sat side by side, like intimate strangers, barely brushing sleeves. She'd sometimes wondered if he was gay.

'He *isn't* gay,' she reassured herself again, as she headed down Harley Street later that day. 'He's just a bit awkward with women. Very brainy men often are. But at least now, he knows how I feel. I can't let it go on for too long.' She went upstairs to Dr Sharp's waiting room. Dr Sharp was her gynaecologist. Jane was too embarrassed to take 'those' sorts of problems to her GP because he was an old family friend. Dr Sharp's name suited her, Jane thought, as she lay back on the examination table, staring at her stirruped feet.

'It's probably candidiasis,' she said, briskly. Well, I *have* been candid recently, Jane thought.

'Commonly known as thrush,' Dr Sharp went on as she prodded Jane's nether regions with a latex-gloved hand. 'A bit itchy, are we?'

'Yes.'

'Had sex recently?'

'No,' said Jane ruefully.

'Ever had it before? Thrush, I mean, not sex.'

Jane shook her head.

'However,' said Dr Sharp, judiciously, as she picked up a swab, 'it *could* be bacterial vaginosis. I'll just . . .' Jane winced, '. . . get it looked at. It's called *Gardnerella vaginalis*, if you want the Latin name.' Jane rather liked that. It sounded like a type of clematis.

'Gardnerella's often linked to anxiety,' Dr Sharp explained as Jane pulled up her tights. 'But it's nothing to worry about,' she added. 'And it's easy to treat. I'll write to you with the results.'

On Tuesday, Jane received a letter from Dr Sharp informing her that she had a simple case of thrush, and that it would clear up in no time with the enclosed prescription. On her way to meet Gerald at Frederick's that Thursday Jane took it to a nearby chemist's.

'Do read the instructions carefully,' advised the pharmacist as Jane slipped the slim package into her bag. Then she made her way to the restaurant, breathing deeply. She and Gerald weren't going to the Schoenberg. They were just going to have dinner, and talk. And though Jane was glad she'd cleared the air, she felt like Gary Cooper in *High Noon*. She'd dressed carefully. Nothing too sexy. Just a smart grey Jasper Conran dress. She opened the door and there was Gerald, sitting on a dark blue sofa by the bar. Jane had imagined he'd be looking nervous. But he wasn't. He was all smiles.

'Our table's not going to be ready for fifteen minutes,' he explained, as he got to his feet. 'Would you like a drink?'

'Yes please,' she said as the waiter took her coat. 'I'd like a glass of white wine.' Gerald gave her order to the waiter, and sat down. Then he looked at Jane, cocked his head to one side, and patted the sofa in a flirtatious way. Jane felt her entrails begin to knot. She sat down at the other end of the sofa and put her bag in the space in between. Now Gerald was just looking at her, smiling, knowingly. She found herself wishing he'd stop.

'Have you had a busy day?' she asked. He nodded. She sipped her glass of wine nervously while he talked about some merger he'd been doing.

'And have *you* had a good day?' he enquired with an amused smirk, as though there were some secret between them.

'Er, yes,' she said, 'I did,' and she babbled on about a project she was taking to Channel 4 about men who have plastic surgery. And all the while she spoke Gerald sat with his body turned right in towards her, one eyebrow raised, smiling.

'You see, the proportion of men having plastic surgery has gone up hugely in the past ten years,' she explained. 'In fact it's gone up by 20 per cent and many of the men who have it say they're doing it to please their wives or girlfriends so I talked to the commissioning editor at Channel 4 – he's very nice by the way – about maybe a three-part series in which –'

Suddenly, Gerald's hand shot out and his chubby fingers clamped themselves round hers. I have been hoist with my own petard, Jane thought, as her face began to flame.

'Gerald . . .' she began. 'Gerald, when I said . . .'

'You're right, Jane,' he interrupted, oblivious to her polite resistance. 'It's *high* time I held your hand and may I say . . .' he gave it a squeeze – 'what a charming hand it is.' Jane wished she could return the compliment but his own hand felt clammy and hot. He was still smiling at her. She felt her bowels shrink as he now interlocked his short, thick fingers with her own.

'Look, Gerald . . . this wasn't quite what I meant, I . . .' But he continued to hang on to her as though she were about to run away. And then, to her horror, he began to incline his face towards hers . . .

'Another drink, madame?' It was the waiter. Thank *God*!

'Oh yes, yes, please, yes,' she said. But, despite the presence of the waiter, Gerald continued to paw her with his broad, damp hand.

'Please, Gerald,' she said softly, aware that they were beginning to attract strange looks.

'Do you know what I'm going to do now, Jane?' he whispered, hoarsely, as he shuffled along the sofa towards her.

'No,' she said truthfully. Oh God.

'I'm going to *kiss* you!'

'No, Gerald, please don't,' said Jane. 'Not here. It really isn't the right place, I . . .'

'Ah*aaaa*!' he was grinning now. 'You're embarrassed,' he announced triumphantly. 'You're discomforted. You are – might I add – discom*bob*ulated even! But I don't care, I'm going to ki –'

'Sir!' It was the waiter again. Thank God. Jane wanted to kiss *him*. 'Your table's ready now. Please follow me.'

Jane was overwhelmed by feelings of relief as she sat down opposite Gerald – with the table a buffer in between. Furthermore he could hardly grope her whilst wielding a knife and fork. She swallowed the rest of her wine, too quickly. Gerald was talking about T. S. Eliot.

'I *really* want to get into the *Waste Land*,' he announced, pushing his glasses up his nose. 'Can you recommend a good critical guide?'

'Er, well, I think the Helen Gardner's the classic one,' she said. 'It's called *The Art of T. S. Eliot*, I remember reading it at college it's . . . oh, thanks –' the waiter was refilling her glass. Gerald looked at him as he did so, indicated Jane with a flourish of his right hand, and said, in a theatrical whisper, 'Don't you think she's *gorgeous?*!'

'Gerald, really . . . !'

'Yes, sir,' said the waiter politely. And as he retreated Gerald reached across the table and grabbed Jane's hand again. I have only myself to blame, she thought bitterly, as she felt a little pool of sweat start to collect in the runnel above her upper lip.

'You're embarrassed!' he said again, gleefully. 'Aren't you? Ha!' There was a faint layer of steam on his glasses. He leant forwards across the table and grabbed her hand again, and she wanted to shout, 'No, Gerald! No, Gerald! *Down!*' But now he was forced to let go again as their plates of sea-bass arrived. Jane found it hard to eat, so she drank instead. By the time the bill came, she'd had the best part of a bottle.

'Cab . . .' she mumbled as they collected their coats. 'Need a cab . . .'

'We certainly do,' said Gerald, with a smirk. 'My place or yours?' he added with a knowing grin.

'What? Look, sorry . . . I've had too much . . . drink. G'ld. Iss been . . . great . . . but . . . Oh God . . . gotta go *home*.' They walked out on to Upper Street, and Jane flung out her right arm as an amber light came into view.

'Thanks, G'ld,' she mumbled. 'S'great. See . . . soon.' She offered him her cheek, but instead he gripped her by the shoulders and clamped his soft, rubbery lips on to hers.

'Helen G'dner,' she called out of the open window as the cab pulled away, '*Art of Teeyessel't*. Faber. C'n lend it to you if y' like.' Gerald stood there, for a moment, a lonely figure. Then he waved once and turned away.

He didn't phone the next day. Jane didn't mind – she was too hungover to talk. But by Saturday her searing headache had gone, leaving just a vague fog. She called Gerald's house, but his answerphone was on. 'He'll ring,' she said to herself. But he didn't. He didn't ring on the Saturday, or the Sunday. Nor did he return any of her calls. On the Monday she was feeling neglected and wondering what to do when she suddenly remembered her prescription. She opened the packet. Inside was something that looked like a torpedo, and a small tube of white cream. What on earth were you meant to do with it? She'd never used this stuff before. Unusually, there were no instructions. So she rang Dr Sharp.

'I'm afraid Dr Sharp's away until Wednesday,' said the assistant. 'If it's not an urgent matter I suggest you write.' So Jane got out her pad and wrote, 'Dear Dr

Sharp, by an unusual oversight my packet of thrush treatment came without any instructions. Please could you tell me whether that white torpedo thing is a pessary or a suppository? How far up should it go? And can the accompanying cream be applied directly into the vagina or not?' There, that should do it, she thought. Then she picked up the phone, and dialled.

'Gerald, it's Jane. How are you?' There was a momentary silence at the other end.

'I'm fine,' he said cautiously. 'But I'm ... busy.'

'Oh,' she said, and was surprised at how disappointed she suddenly felt. 'Well, maybe we can get together when you're not so busy,' she went on quickly. 'There's a new production of *Rosenkavalier* opening at the Opera House – shall I get tickets?'

'No,' he said, curtly. 'No thanks.'

Jane felt her face begin to flame.

'I thought you liked Richard Strauss,' she said.

'I do.'

'Don't you want to see it then?'

'Yes. But not with you.'

'Oh.' Jane felt her knees begin to shake. 'May I ask why?'

'Look ... let's just call it a day, shall we?' said Gerald, irritably. 'There's really not much point.'

'I see,' she said. Her hand shook. 'Or rather, I don't really see at all. In fact I find your present attitude rather strange. Are you cross?' she added gently, backtracking a little. 'Because I pushed things along a bit?'

'No,' he said. 'Not at all. But I just ...' he sighed.

'I've just decided that I don't think I could feel really
. . . *passionate* about you.'

'Oh. Well . . . don't you find me attractive?' she
enquired, fatally, her heart banging in her chest.

'Um. No,' he said brusquely. 'I don't.'

'Oh. Well then . . .' she said. 'That's fine. Although
it's a *bit* of a surprise. After your bizarre behaviour in
Frederick's. But thank you for making it so clear,
Gerald. Thank you *very* much indeed. Good bye.' She
put the phone down, then shouted, 'WAN-KER!!!'
What a *creep*! What an effing *weirdo*! What a – Christ
she'd never be able to show her face in Frederick's
again! She went into the kitchen to make herself a cup
of coffee. How dare he, she said to herself as she
slammed the cupboard door shut. How *dare* he say that
to her after asking her out for three months. How
DARE he say that to her after slobbering over her in
public like that. Jane went to her writing desk and
opened her pad. Right. He was going to get it now.
'*Quite* unnecessary candour . . .' she scribbled. '. . . *total*
lack of chivalry . . . *embarrassing* performance in Frederick's . . . behaviour *flatly* contradictory . . . not *exactly*
God's gift . . . *no* wish to meet again . . . Good*bye*!' Jane
re-read it with immense satisfaction, addressed it to
Gerald's office, then rushed straight out to the letter
box, and posted it with the note to Dr Sharp.

'I am SO glad I did that,' she said to herself as she
got the tube to Channel 4 the next day. 'Bloody weirdo.
Dysfunctional bastard. He'll be livid, but he won't write
back.'

Two days later Jane heard the clatter of the letter box and the soft fall of envelopes on to the mat. There were three – a couple of bills, and a reply from Dr Sharp. Jane opened the oyster-coloured envelope. Puzzlement furrowed her brow. 'Dear Jane,' Dr Sharp had written. 'I do hope your thrush has now cleared up with the treatment I prescribed. I was rather surprised to receive the enclosed' – it was Jane's letter to Gerald – 'which you seem to have sent me in error – easily done when one's in a rush. But I enclose it now, in case it's important. Yours ever, Janet Sharp.'

Cathy Kelly is the author of three novels – *Never Too Late, She's the One* and *Woman to Woman* – all No.1 bestsellers in Britain and Ireland. She is a journalist for the *Sunday World* newspaper in Dublin and lives in County Wicklow, where she is currently working on a new novel, *Someone Like You*, to be published by HarperCollins in autumn 2000.

Cassandra

Cathy Kelly

Cassandra always had a very complicated private life. Like, incredibly complicated. We're talking about the sort of relationship twists that would make an episode of *Dallas* look straightforward. All of which was a million miles away from my personal life, I might add. I am Ms Sensible to Cassandra's Femme Fatale of Upper Posset.

That's where we both come from, by the way. Upper Posset. A small town, no, make that a village, in Surrey, so small that it's not really on the map. But if it ever does get on the map, it'll be because of Cassandra.

We met as gangly five-year-olds in junior infants. To be accurate, I was a gangly five-year-old and Cassandra was a serious contender for the Miss Pears' Soap contest. Blonde ringlets, blue eyes the colour of holiday-brochure swimming pools, and endearing dimples. Naturally, she's lost the ringlets now and has gone for the sort of sleek crop with razored edges that you see in the trendier hairdressing magazines. She gets it cut in Trevor Sorbie and, needless to say, she doesn't have to wait three months for an appointment, either.

153

Cassandra keeps telling me I should do something different with my hair, which is exactly the same as it was
when we first met twenty-three years ago, but I've got
used to having it long and loose. I'm not cut out to be
chic and, besides, long hair hides a multitude of sins.

'Molly, curls are so nineties,' Cassandra says, trying
to be helpful. 'The bed-head look would be so you.
Look what it's done for Drew Barrymore.'

Personally, I can't see me in the bed-head – you
know, the short, messy, just-out-from-under-the-duvet
look. You need cheekbones and blow-job lips to carry
that off. I'd just look as if I'd spent the night sleeping
in a cardboard box in a C & A doorway. Cassandra
could wear it, though. She's stunning. Doesn't need to
wear make-up, although she loves MAC and looks
totally amazing when she does that heavy kohl thing
which makes her resemble a *Vogue* cover girl when the
Millennium/Barbarella vibe was hot.

So where was I? Oh yeah, the reason I'm telling you
this story. You see, it was Cassandra's personal life that
got me into this mess in the first place. Cassandra and
a man, to be exact. She was always the one with more
boyfriends than you could shake a stick at.

During our college years, she had a string of besotted
men hanging around her. I know, it's weird that we
went to the same college but I had my heart set on
journalism in Cardiff and when Cassandra thought
about it, she decided not to bother applying for that
drama course and went for journalism too. I was a bit
surprised because she'd never been too keen on writing

but you see, Cassandra is so good with people that she's a natural at journalism. She's got that charm thing. People just like her and want to talk to her. Being glamorous and wearing sexy clothes helps, or so my mother says a bit snidely. (Mum and Cassandra have never seen eye to eye. They haven't talked since Cassandra ended up going to our graduation dance with Ted. He'd been my date originally but there'd been a bit of a mix-up and I was quite happy going with Cassandra's younger brother Mitch, who was good fun when he wasn't bitching about his sister.)

She and I shared a flat in college and spent lots of time working on assignments together. Cassandra is very clever but she loved talking to me about my opinion. She's got an incredible mind, really.

That time we had to write an in-depth piece about the UN and she'd been too hungover to do much research in the library, well, all I had to do was sketch in the briefest idea of the whole thing and she went on to get an A+ for it. The tutor loved my point about how giving humanitarian aid made the wealthy West feel better about itself, although he said it was a bit derivative and sounded as if I was using other people's ideas. Men were a problem for both of us during those wonderful student days. Well, they were a problem for me because I never had one, while Cassandra's problem was getting rid of them when she was bored.

She likes to be a free spirit: 'Can't stand long-term relationships,' she always said, usually after she had to dump some guy who'd been getting annoying. It was incredible the way men became so boring once they'd gone out with Cassandra for a few weeks. She loved partying and they couldn't always keep up, especially close to exam time.

'God, they're all so thick,' she groaned one December night when she was racing out to an Arts student bash and I was planning to stay home studying. 'Can I borrow your notes tomorrow?' she asked, heavily mascara'd eyes on the mirror as she adjusted the straps on her Wonderbra. 'It's our duty to show these brain-dead males how clever we are and how we don't have to spend the entire month at home poring over the books.'

There was a bit of trouble when three of her exes joined forces and sent this horrible note around campus about her, saying she was a one-woman demolition squad who ate men for breakfast, or something nasty like that. It was terrible. I'd thought they'd been lovely guys, particularly Steve, whom I'd sort of fancied myself until he clapped eyes on Cassandra. That was the one negative thing about being best friends with Cassandra: once a guy saw her, I hadn't a chance. Not that I minded, or anything. Cassandra was special, as her dad used to tell her all the time. We couldn't all be like that.

'Beauty's a curse, Molly,' she insisted. 'Everybody wants a piece of you. They don't treat you like a person but like a beautiful object. You're lucky not to have this problem, you don't know how I envy you.'

She was right, poor love. Everybody did want a piece of her. I tried to help out when I could. One time, I had to keep her current boyfriend in the kitchen so she could sneak an old flame out of the bedroom. Which is, incidentally, a bit like what's just happened.

I'm deputy features editor on *Your Kind of Woman* (YKOW) which is a middle-of-the-road women's magazine. We both started working there on a college work placement scheme. I'd actually applied for a job on YKOW and Cassandra had applied for a job on the *Independent*. When she didn't get in there, it was sheer coincidence that they had a second student vacancy in YKOW. We both stayed a year and nobody was more amazed than me when I was offered a full-time job. I mean, me, not Cassandra. Startled and thrilled, I did once pluck up the courage to ask Madeleine, the editor, why they'd hired me. I never really understood her answer: 'Because we want someone with originality and talent, who doesn't need to rip off other people's ideas,' she said.

That's Cassandra to a T, and she's gorgeous too, which was always useful in our business. Not that I need a brown paper bag over my head at all times, but I'm not a patch on Cassandra with her feline beauty.

'Mol, you're one of a kind; quirky, fun ... er, and you've got a great personality,' she says to me when I'm feeling insecure about my looks. That was the nice thing about Cassandra, I always thought. She's truly beautiful but she never made me feel insecure. Instead, she bolstered my confidence and used to help me buy clothes. I'm hopeless at fashion and she's like Rachel from *Friends*: clothes are her hobby and *Elle* is her bible.

She had a positive fetish about making me wear fleecy tops. Dunno why – she never wears them herself. Prefers stuff from Morgan. But Cassandra reckons I'm a fleecy-top-and-denims sort of girl. We make an odd combination: her in head-to-toe second-skin garments with Gucci shoes (her father does spoil her with an allowance), me in baggy stuff that wouldn't look out of place down on the farm. In our flat – didn't I mention that? We were still sharing, this time in a two-bedroomed shoe-box in Clapham – Cassandra had to have the bigger bedroom so she'd have somewhere for her two clothes rails. Every penny of her wages went on clothes and there were weeks when I don't know how we paid the rent because she'd blown her cheque on 'an adorable pair of boots, Moll. I simply had to have them!'·

She used to march into my office – I always felt bad that I had a tiny office with a window and she was stuck out in the freelance Siberia where everyone shared desks in that horrible hot-desking system – and beg me to borrow the fashion editor's Karen Millen discount card for her. (She and the fashion editor had this hate:hate thing going on, so she couldn't possibly ask herself.) Even though I felt guilty about going behind the fashion ed's back, I could never say no. Cassandra looked perfect in Karen Millen. Nobody could wear those cobwebby, beaded dresses like she did. She was wearing one at the magazine's birthday party when she met the publisher, Tony Milano, which was where the trouble started. Tony's in his forties and isn't bad-looking, in an Italian wide-boy sort of way. Not Cassandra's type, mind you. But she fell for him big time.

I don't see the attraction myself. Tony may have three homes, four sports cars and several offshore accounts, but he also has three chins and no sense of style. Oh yeah, and a wife. That was the real problem. Cassandra didn't see it as much of a problem, but I did. Still, there's no talking to her when she's in love. I didn't think she was in love to be honest, but once Tony had whisked her off to St Lucia for a week and given her a Rolex, well, she never stopped talking about him. (That was only a month after the party. Normally when people say Tony's a fast worker, I think they're referring to his prowess as a businessman.)

'He says I'm not to wear the Rolex to the office,' she swooned in our messy sitting room, trying on lots of different outfits to see which ones had the shortest sleeves and would therefore reveal the most expanse of slender, tanned, Rolex-encrusted wrist. 'But nobody will notice, will they, Moll?'

I said that I thought they might but Cassandra was determined to have her own way and anyway, I was busy trying to organize an interview with Neil Morten, this gorgeous young rock musician who'd just been on the cover of Q, so I left her alone. Big mistake.

Two weeks after Cassandra had got the Rolex, the editor called me into her office at lunchtime and launched into this speech about how I was a talented journalist but as naïve as hell and needed to cop on pronto or I'd end up in serious trouble thanks to that 'scheming bitch of a friend of yours. Who isn't much of a friend, if you really want to know,' Madeleine finished up.

I goggled at her. 'You mean Cassandra?' I said, startled.

'Jesus, Molly, will you ever wake up?' screamed Madeleine. 'Of course I mean Cassandra. She rides around on your coat-tails, steals all your ideas, does her best to get your job when your back is turned and is now ruining your career thanks to her affair with the publisher.'

I goggled a bit more. I wanted to get her to explain but I couldn't, could I? I mean, Cassandra was my best friend. She'd been my best friend for years, since we'd been five. She cared for me and we'd done everything together. It was my job to stand up for her, like I'd been doing for years. I couldn't stop now.

'I think that's most unfair, Madeleine,' I said pointedly. 'She's my best friend and I can't listen to you say terrible things about her –'

'Have it your way,' Madeleine interrupted wearily and went back to her cottage cheese and crispbread. Everyone in the magazine was always on a diet except me. I am 'sickeningly thin', as Cassandra puts it, and can consume vast quantities of just about anything I like and not put on weight.

I went home early because I felt unsettled and also because the next day I was bringing Neil Morten to The Ivy for lunch to interview him and I wanted to be prepared. I mean, I know it was a bit daft to bother putting on fake tan and applying all-night conditioner just for an interview with a guy who is so devastatingly handsome he could probably date all the current Miss World hopefuls. But you know, a girl can dream. I'd invested in this soft-as-kitten-fur vermilion cashmere cardigan that made my hair look dark and lustrous, and even gave me a bit of cleavage because it was so clingy. But when I went looking for it the next morning, the cardigan had disappeared from my drawer, along with my new feather necklace and the gel-filled bra which was the only item of lingerie I'd ever owned that made me look bigger than a 32A.

'Sorry, Moll, knew you wouldn't mind me whipping these,' went the note scrawled in Cassandra's trademark gold handwriting. I did mind but there was no point crying over spilt milk. It'd have to be my boring old black suit. Again. I tried not to think about Cassandra as I sat in the taxi on the way to The Ivy. It was uncanny how people had loved her to bits in college and how everyone at work disliked her. Well, not everybody liked her in college, but most people did, surely? So why did Madeleine and the fashion editor and, actually, most of the rest of the YKOW staff loathe her and slam their office doors when she strode along the corridors in the mood to chat? And what exactly had Madeleine been trying to warn me about?

Neil Morten was just as gorgeous as he looked on the cover of both Q and his new album. Tall, lanky, with straw-coloured hair, blond stubble, greeny-grey eyes like Pernod with water added, and this sweet, almost anxious smile that lit up his face. In the flesh, he was even better than I'd expected and we just . . . well, this is going to sound stupid, but we got on like a house on fire. Most of the time you interview famous people and they talk to you as if you're a tape recorder without a real person attached. They emote, get all their charming little anecdotes out, tell you how much they loved working on the album/movie/soap show and then they're gone. You're a part of the process and they don't really notice you as a member of the same species, never mind as a proper human being. But Neil talked to me as if we were on a date and as if he'd seriously consider going out with me. He was funny, charming and very normal. By dessert, we were finishing each other's sentences and talking so fast we were running out of breath. The interview hadn't even happened. It was simply two people talking nineteen to the dozen, laughing and smiling, falling in love, practically. I was, anyway. Falling in love.

He had this spiky blond hair that stood up but one bit defied the gel and drooped over his left eye. I had to stop myself from leaning over the table and pushing it back tenderly. Did you ever feel like that about someone: that you can't help wanting to touch them? He must have felt the same, I thought ecstatically, because he stroked my hand across the pristine tablecloth with his long, guitar-player's fingers. We'd gone through a bottle of wine and four brandies and were thinking about wandering off to a little pub somewhere to actually do some interviewing when it happened.

This blonde woman marched into the restaurant and, after a consultation with the maître d', marched over to our table. She looked vaguely familiar and because she was one of those elegant women who shop in Jaeger and have diamond rings the size of gobstoppers, I assumed she was somebody semi-famous whom I had written about in our gossip pages.

'Are you Molly O'Rourke?' she said between clenched, beautifully-polished teeth.

Despite having the best part of three glasses of wine and two giant brandies inside me, I instinctively knew something was wrong. So did Neil. He leaned towards me protectively, but wasn't fast enough for Ms Jaeger.

'You bitch!' she howled. 'You've been having an affair with my husband and you don't even have the shame to pretend to be someone else when you ring up. I'll see you out of your job, you cow! The magazine belongs to me, not Tony Milano. And he's out on his ear, too!'

With that, Mrs Milano leaned over and belted me. Thank God she got me with the hand without the diamond rings or I'd be in serious trouble, I can tell you. Not that a black eye isn't serious trouble, but it's marginally better than having your eyebrow painfully removed by a massive diamond with no anaesthetic. Luckily, the maître d' calmly escorted her out before she could black the other eye and before Neil could throw our untouched glasses of water over her. He was white with rage.

'It's Cassandra,' I managed to say in shock. 'My flatmate Cassandra is having an affair and it must be with that woman's husband. Mrs Milano.' I shook my head in bewilderment. 'I can't imagine why she thought it was me.'

With Neil hugging me and petting my battered face, we made it home to my apartment, where he put ice on my eye and fed me hot chocolate all afternoon. I explained a bit about Cassandra and Neil became quite grim the more I explained. It did make sense of what Madeleine had been trying to tell me. And when I rang Madeleine she explained in greater detail.

'Tony Milano' – she said his name as if she was spitting simultaneously – 'talked to me about firing you to give Cassandra your job. She's using him to crawl up the career ladder and she doesn't care who she walks over to get to the top, including you, Molly. I'm sorry. I know you think she's your friend, but she isn't. She's also wrong about Tony. His wife's family own the magazines and without her, he's got nothing. I can't imagine how she thought Tony was having an affair with you, though.'

Neil was in the kitchen draining pasta when Cassandra walked in, wearing my new cashmere cardigan and with a self-satisfied expression on her beautiful face. She got a fit of the giggles when she saw me with my rapidly blackening eye. 'You poor thing,' she said, stuffing a tissue into her mouth to stop herself laughing.

She did a double take when Neil came out of the

kitchen with the pasta in one hand. He really was amaz-ing-looking, and famous too. Cassandra's expression changed in deference to both his fame and his gorgeous-ness. Off went her giggly face and on went the Athena the Huntress expression she adopts when she sees a man she likes: her mouth curves up into this wicked smile and her eyes glint with an arch look that says, 'You'd never believe how sexy I am, much sexier than the lump of a girl you're with now.' It always worked. Until this occasion. Neil didn't look impressed.

In fact, he looked angry and contemptuous.

'Molly has a black eye because your lover's wife hit her in The Ivy.'

'I rather thought she'd been hit in the eye,' quipped Cassandra, obviously wrong-footed about the way this conversation was going. Under normal circumstances, the object of her affection would be gazing mistily at her, not staring at her harshly and being nasty.

'Why do you think this man's wife thought Molly was having an affair with him?' Neil asked coldly.

Cassandra tittered, a sound which had never sounded irritating to me until that precise moment. 'It's silly,' she said, turning to me. 'Sorry, old thing, but when I rang his house looking for Tony and he wasn't there, I said I was you.' She must have noticed my eyes widen so she rushed on. 'Their housekeeper is some stupid Puerto Rican or something and she can barely speak English, so I didn't think it'd matter. It was like our code. You do understand, Moll, don't you?' she wheedled.

'Could it be that this mistaken-identity prank was part of a plot to help you get Molly sacked so that you could get her job?' Neil asked.

He'd grasped the whole idea so quickly. No wonder he was a multi-millionaire songwriter. Brains as well as beauty.

'Don't be silly. That was nothing to do with it,' Cassandra said crossly. 'Tony would give me a job anytime I wanted. I said I was Molly because if his wife ever met her, there's no way she'd think Tony was seriously contemplating an affair with her. She's far too dull for him. It was the perfect alibi.'

'I happen to think Molly's very beautiful,' Neil said softly, looking at me. 'I like the natural look as opposed to the done-up-like-a-dog's-dinner look.' He cast those Pernod-with-water eyes over Cassandra in a manner which left her in no doubt that she was the dog's dinner in question.

She quivered indignantly. 'It hardly matters any more.'

'Just one thing, Cassandra,' I said, speaking for the first time. 'I'm afraid you miscalculated with Tony. He can't give you a job. In fact, I daresay he'll be looking for the Rolex back when his wife throws him out. You see,' I paused, amazed to find that I was enjoying this, 'he's not the real boss of the magazine. His wife is. The publishing empire belongs to her family and Tony is utterly replaceable. I've told Madeleine the whole story and she's told his wife. Mrs Soon-To-Be-Ex-Milano was most apologetic about the black eye. But I rather think you've lost your job. You and Tony can visit the job centre together.'

Cassandra's mouth hung open, giving both of us a good view of her expensive dental work. 'You're joking,' she gasped. 'He promised . . .'

She babbled away to herself in shock and I looked at her, wondering how I could have possibly spent twenty-three years of my life standing up for a woman who rode roughshod over me in her stilettos. She stole my men, my ideas, my self-confidence and had tried to steal my job. The real Cassandra was revealed to me after years of blinding myself to her true character. It was like scales falling from my eyes, which is how Neil puts it. The true Cassandra was a nasty piece of work and it must have been some flaw in my own character that kept me in thrall to her for so long. Perhaps I needed her in my life for contrast, a contrast between the difficult times (the Cassandra years) and the wonderful years (right now with Neil).

I haven't seen Cassandra for months. She keeps phoning me at work but I don't return her calls very often. Not surprisingly, she got fired from YKOW and she's now freelancing for the *Tree Surgeon's Gazette*, desperately trying to get a foot in the door of women's magazine journalism again. Mind you, Tony Milano's wife has put the word out on Cassandra, so it's doubtful she'll ever get another job in our tight-knit little industry. She's also desperate to get invited to our house. Neil and I are living in a lovely old townhouse in

Islington and despite having the builders in all the time, building the recording studio downstairs and renovating the nursery upstairs – yes, you've guessed it: the baby's due in March and Neil is over the moon – we're getting a reputation for throwing wonderful parties. The *Daily Mail* called us London's newest power couple. That's because I've been made editor of *Uber-Babe*, the latest magazine in our publishing empire. Between that and the parties with the rock-star guest list, we're embarrassingly trendy. Cassandra is hysterical to come to one of our parties but Neil refuses to have her in the house. I do feel sorry for her. Sort of.

Jane Owen tried a variety of different jobs before taking up writing: horse riding instructress, special effects make-up artist, photographer, party organizer, casting agent, music business press and promotion, band management, TV presenter and even recorded a single with Dave Stewart which, fortunately for music lovers, never saw the light of day. Her first novel, *Camden Girls*, was published by Penguin in the UK and has been translated into several languages. She has recently finished her second, *Take Me To Your Dealer*, and also a play, *The Angelraven*, which was commissioned by Brennan Street. In 1998 she ran, as leader of the Right To Party, in the local council elections and this year toyed with the idea of running for Mayor of London. In the end she decided against it on the grounds that it would interfere with her social life. She lives in Chalk Farm with a bearded collie called Bafta and divides her time between writing, horse riding and going out a lot.

Access All Areas

Jane Owen

Thursday morning

36 Marlboro Lights, 9 Becks, 12 vodka and Red Bull, half an E, countless spliffs and two illicit snogs with stripper dressed (originally) as traffic warden. V. good.

Woke up in position of prayer by bed. Had momentary, and horrible, thought: could be end result of some dreadful sex game with Him (of all people) but deduce from tights still twisted round ankles and three-inch Manolo spike heel pressed into left buttock, that probably passed out in this position whilst trying to get undressed. Face glued to duvet at strange and uncomfortable angle. Seems slept with mouth open and dribbled a lot.

Staggered downstairs to get coffee and dirty looks from extremely displeased Him. Can't remember exactly what happened last night but am in no doubt that He will remind me, many, many times, before day is over. Something to do with partially clothed traffic warden and bottle of olive oil, the fancy stuff with the leaves and twigs etc if memory can be relied upon at all. Probably wouldn't have been so bad if had actually been part of birthday group, not just unknown couple at next table, but didn't ask the Himbo to put Self on table and simulate oral sex. Well, not in so many words. Just seemed much better idea (at time) than dinner with Him and discussion of Lycos versus Alta Vista. Especially as spent first fifteen minutes of that particular conversation thinking we were talking about obscure Greek islands and next year's holiday and trying to prepare excuse not to go well in advance.

Thursday night

2 bottles Chardonnay, 15 Marlboro Lights, several spliffs, two Caramacs and a Toblerone. Not v. good.

Oh God. Having cooked, actually *cooked*, not even gone to M&S, *and* done best Stepford Wife impression all night, just as He's beginning to take stupid disapproving look off His stupid face, phone rings. 'Ignore it,' he says. Tried but then Best Friend starts babbling into ansafone about access all areas and aftershow end-of-tour party for some band on Friday night. Lunge for phone to shut Best Friend up before smoke starts coming out of His ears and nearly break big toe by stubbing it, hard, on stupid coffee table as Best Friend witters on and on about drop-dead gorgeous singers in leather trousers. It's not fair! Want to go! But already had two nights out with girls this week and suspect one more would come under 'pushing my luck'. Still, at least it's exercise.

Sneak upstairs early and pretend to fall into deep sleep bordering on unconsciousness moment head hits pillow.

Friday morning

Woke up with His face inches away. Thought He was having nasty stroke and screamed but apparently was supposed to be sexy smile. After breakfast (coffee and cigarette), check e-mail. Best Friend has e-mailed all details of tonight's shindig and whilst pretending to sleep last night, devised cunning plan which intend to put into action soon as possible. Best Friend No. 2 has also e-mailed. She's being sorely tempted by some young stud and at same time is convinced her Significant Other is already shagging some other bird. Or is she just doing that to justify her own lustful thoughts? Personal opinion is that once you start screwing around, relationship's all over bar the shouting and lord knows there'll probably be a shit load of that hitting the fan. If you love someone, you don't *want* to sleep with anyone else. Don't suppose it's much help but e-mail it anyway.

Make more coffee and initiate plan. Suggest we invite all His boring friends round tonight for Trivial Pursuits which is about their level. He leaps at chance. Phase One completed. Now must go round Safeways buying crips and disps. Please God He doesn't want to come. People might think we're a couple.

Friday evening

So far, plan running like clockwork. Whilst smoking spliff in bath, Best Friend phoned dead on cue, in floods of tears and spoke to Him, begging for Self to go over and offer comfort and consolation. He, of course, couldn't possibly refuse a maiden in such distress but has consolation prize of party with His own friends. How fortuitous. Meanwhile, got changed in bedroom and if all goes well, alleged minicab should arrive at same moment oven timer rings in exactly forty-two seconds, thereby allowing mad dash out of front door before anyone notices short sparkly dress with all the accessories and comments on its inappropriateness for consoling broken hearted Best Friend.

Saturday evening

47 Marlboro Lights, 7½ bottles champagne, 6 large tequila slammers, gramme and a half cocaine (approx), one pop-star. VVV GOOD!

Oh my God! OH MY GOD! Can't believe it happened! Can't believe did that! Never mind got away with it! Oh my God!

Escape plan worked a treat. Best Friend nearly blew it by arriving in stretched black Mercedes with tinted windows rather than usual dodgy Toyota minicab with fake fur seat covers but Him so busy retrieving assorted vol au vents from oven, didn't notice as whisked off to Wembley Arena in such decadent style. Limo, and champagne therein, provided by Best Friend's latest squeeze along with shiny laminate passes to hang round neck allowing Access All Areas. Now there's a thing. Still not entirely sure who band is but never really had finger on pulse of rock and roll world. Assuming it's got one.

Decided to pass on support band and avail Self of free champers in hostility, sorry, hospitality, while Best Friend simpered and batted eyelashes at new squeeze. And she's not even a natural blonde! Sneaked off to loo for quick snort. Whilst in cubicle, hear someone next door doing exactly same thing and leave cubicle just in time to see legendary rock and roll DJ wiping evidence from under her nose. Well well. DJ hurriedly replaces mirrored sunglasses (can see why she wears them) and exits with embarrassed smile. Upon leaving, think must've turned left instead of right cos got completely bloody lost. Endless tunnels with door after identical bloody door. Panic starts rising as starting to realize could be lost walking the tunnels of Wembley for years, a waif-like wraith doomed to such eternity for an exit. Start walking as fast as heels will allow, teeter round corner and walk straight into best looking man ever seen in life. Drop handbag, spill contents, and watch speechless as he drops to knees to pick it all up for me.

Can't speak in presence of such beauty. Tall, sexy, longish black hair, blue blue blue eyes and that mouth oh God that mouth. While you're down there . . .

Adonis called away by some bloke with clipboard and am alone in corridor again. Find way back to hostility room just in time. Band about to go on and guests being escorted to Press pit in front of stage. Darkened arena hot and sweaty and packed full of long haired people in denim and tour T-shirts dating back to the eighties. Still have slight feeling that most of audience need to get out more and then bang! Lights go up, sound roars out, energy level surges and wham bam thank you ma'am, there in the follow spot it's the man on his knees! Can't believe made such crass remark to such famous Rock God and mentally kick Self, hard, on both shins. Watch spellbound as Rock God struts, rocks, snakes hips and then swaggers down catwalk towards Press pit and winks at Self. Best Friend insane with jealousy. Band quite probably brilliant but could only watch while Rock God strutted his funky stuff, gleaming with sweat which found strangely attractive, and eight thousand punters cheered and screamed. Seemed to be over much too soon even with three encores. Could've sworn Rock God winked again but decide not to make too much of it.

Start to make way backstage again and, as house lights come up, am amazed to see floor littered with notes, phone numbers, hotel room keys and underwear, all hurled at Rock God. Personally can't see him coming out to pick up all these offers but suppose a girl can dream. On to party. By now, high as kite. More champagne in limo accompanied by non-stop lecture from Best Friend on the art of pulling pop stars. Party all set down Mexico way, somewhere in W9. Tequila slammer girls, Mariachi bands, enchiladas, whole crates of Dos Equis and a llama all squashed into a large courtyard and two rehearsal rooms. Rock God arrives with band and entourage and is immediately swamped by people including hundreds and hundreds of absolutely gorgeous girls. Soon realized hopelessness of Best Friend's plan. Just catch his eye, she said. Yeah right. Only if he plucks it out and throws it to me. Don't feel can compete with such well made-up determination and all that silicone and hit tequila slammers with vengeance. Best Friend said he kept looking over but doubted it personally and then he was gone. Bugger. Where's that tequila-girl?

Left party around half-two. Decided to leave Best Friend dirty dancing with new squeeze and find taxi. I wish she'd wear underwear if she's going to dance like that. As left building, immediately set upon by two brick shithouse-type males with ear pieces who picked Self up and started carrying Self towards large black coach despite loud protestations and before know it, am inside with Rock God himself. Told him what thought of being kidnapped in this undignified fashion in no uncertain terms. Well, should've done. Actually just stood there with mouth open wondering how long before knees gave out while Rock God apologized for the indignity inflicted on Self and pointed out that he had in fact been waiting out here for Self for nearly two hours and how about some champagne? V. hard to resist. Would've been churlish, nay rude, to refuse.

Desperately want to say something witty, sexy, cool but can hardly pronounce own name when he asks. Just stand there like an idiot and stare at what is quite possibly most beautiful man ever met. Ever. World starts to swirl and for one awful moment think might be falling in love but turns out to be bus leaving car park. Hardly time to finish champagne before arrive at posh hotel in Holland Park.

Managed to make complete prat of Self in corridor when mistake naff *trompe l'oeil* on wall for real doorway and walk straight into it. The wall that is. Rock God's suite is monument to excess. Lots of bouquets and fruit baskets and champagne wrapped in cellophane sent by music biz luminaries (well, their secretaries anyway) as befits star of his status not to mention the multi-patterned multi-coloured multi-textured decor: all silk drapes and curtain poles, squashy sofas and gilded coffee tables, obligatory huge ugly lamps on occasional tables all round room and *the* most enormous four-poster bed ever seen. Throw Self on it with such enthusiasm bounce straight back off and on to floor. Fortunately Rock God seems to think all this clumsiness is cute and endearing as he opens bubbly, rolls joint and chops out line of coke. Never seen man do more than one thing at a time before and am well impressed. And then he kissed me. Whoa!!

Next thing, clothes flying round room, we're on bed, on balcony, in shower, discovering new uses for soft fruit, washing it off with champagne, tying each other to bed with stockings, bent over sofa, rolling around on carpet and back on bed for grand finale. It was, without shadow of doubt, the most spine-tingling toe-nibbling nipple-licking back-bending heart-pounding groin-straining sweat-dripping arse-slapping neck-biting mouth-watering face-sucking back-scratching lip-smacking sex ever had in entire life.

Afterwards, opened another bottle of Bolly and talked for ages. As sun came up over London, sat on balcony to finish bubbly. Could hardly believe it. In fact, so gob-smacked, had to drag Rock God back to bed just to make sure. Second time around, took it much more slowly. *Much* more. So slowly, hardly moving at all, locked together at groin and mouth, never taking eyes off each other. Sexy motherfucker. Finally fell asleep all tangled up in his arms and legs.

Woke around eleven. Major panic. Rock God lying on top and sleeping. Men always seem to weigh so much more, had trouble pushing him off. Ran round room like startled deer trying to find all of clothes, including both shoes not to mention untie stockings from bedpost. Rock God offers to order breakfast but demand taxi. Seems didn't mention fact that had boyfriend, well long term partner and co-mortgagee probably more accurate description, and now Rock God getting all hurt and injured. Well really! Now *screaming* for taxi, not choice of Continental or Full English. Nasty feeling am in big big trouble. Not v. good.

Hotel reception full of rich American tourists who stare open mouthed at sight of Self still in what is quite obviously last night's frock and some seriously laddered stockings. Race straight out and into waiting cab. Thank God brought sunglasses. Look at voicemail on mobile. Seems Himself's been phoning every forty minutes. Oops. Maybe shouldn't go straight home. Head for Best Friend's house instead.

Best Friend is both curious and furious. Says she was worried. Yeah right. Last time saw her she was doing fair impression of a contortionist on the dance floor. Now seems to have come over all moral. Still, at least when He phoned, Best Friend had presence of mind to invent story involving Self, her, and bottle of tequila and apparently He is under totally erroneous impression that Self is passed out in spare room right now. Now lecture is over, Best Friend wants all gory details. Tell her to put kettle on while jump in shower. Next time He phones, pretend to be all fuzzy round edges and promise to come home soonest.

And here I am. What was it said to Best Friend No. 2? If you shag someone else, you're obviously not in love. And did. Shag someone else. And then some. So obviously am not. And if not in love, what the hell am doing here? Not only that, have promised to go to Cornwall with Him to watch sodding eclipse. Can't wait. All those hours, trapped in car in traffic jam that goes all way back to sodding court of King Arthur, just so can stand on overcrowded beach with thousands of strangers, not to mention regional news crews with their sun guns and their over enthusiastic cub reporters, and watch sky get dark. Well hold fucking front page. Still, anything for quiet life. Oh God. Can hear Him coming back with takeaway. Better go and watch *Casualty* with Him. Am in enough trouble already. Anyway, hangover wearing off and huge curry in front of telly seems like fab idea. Maybe a bottle of wine . . .

Sunday Morning

2 bottles wine, half bottle Baileys, 17 Marlboro Lights, eighth skunk weed.

Not really enough to constitute major hangover but think it's bit of a rollover hangover. Spent last night trying to avoid physical contact with Him on grounds that every nerve end in body is hurting following alleged tequila binge but still have to sit through *Casualty* and although know full well blood and guts not real, scenes of multiple car crash have stomach churning. Or maybe that was guilt. Do feel very guilty. Mainly cos don't feel guilty. Not about shagging Rock God. Heavens no. One of best experiences in life. Feel guilty that can't talk to Him about it. Whole dissatisfaction thing, not shagging. But then think, don't really give a toss. Have been rerunning edited highlights of night of passion with Rock God in mind over and over and over again and now whole episode tinged with unreality. Still can't believe really did that. Maybe didn't. Wouldn't want to 'fess up to something only imagined.

Woke up to find Him whimpering for sex so decided, in interests of domestic harmony, to lie back and think of Rock God. No sooner has He started, He's pulling out and shouting rubbish about feeling something inside Self. Like what, exactly? His car keys? But no, He's totally convinced felt something on the end of his knob. More than I did. Eventually makes connection between alien object and possible infidelity at which point decide must retaliate (attack being best form of defence) by joining in and being mortally offended by implication that might have strayed off straight and narrow. How dare He! Twist this immediately into sick of not being trusted, His insane jealousy, etc etc etc and storm off to have bath. Still not entirely sure what he's talking about.

Lay in bath and watched fish swimming around fake Rolex put in tank last Christmas. Feel slightly envious of their short-term memory. Sometimes think forgetting things three seconds after they happen might not be so bad. Noticed sunshine coming through Venetian blind and how shadow on wall resembles bars. Hrrrmmm. Start having wash, bit absent mindedly, still thinking things over again and again and then realize insides are falling out. Reach between legs and, as horror rapidly turns to disbelief, find something emerging from nether regions: something soft, slippery, slightly squishy, oozing out of Self. For a moment thoughts of divine retribution and the actual existence of some angry god leapt into head but dismissed stupid notion immediately and then whatever it was floated to surface and lay there, semi-submerged, like some soapy jellyfish. Hardly daring to breathe, picked it up with extreme caution. A condom. A condom! The Rock God's condom! Oh my God! So much for safe sex! And what am supposed to do with it now? Send it back? I believe this is yours? Lovely night – you forgot this? Or just keep it to show grandchildren in next millennium. Well, Granny had her wild moments when she was young you know. Had to laugh. And then had to laugh even louder as everything fell into place. So *that's* what He felt with his willy. And then had to endure ten minute torrent of abuse from Self on just exactly how sad a man has to be to try and trick his beloved with such a stupid, obviously made up story. Had to laugh like a drain now really. Poor bastard. Almost feel quite sorry for Him. But the condom ... When finally stopped laughing, made mental note to Self: next time decide to shag pop star, don't let him fall asleep inside you.

Wendy Holden, 34, spent fourteen years as a journalist before turning to full-time novel-writing. Her first book, *Simply Divine* (Headline, £5.99), a send-up of glossy magazines and ghastly celebrity socialites, was inspired by her experiences as deputy editor of society glossy *Tatler*; her second *Bad Heir Day* (just published in paperback by Headline, £5.99) is about downtrodden nannies, pushy parents and social climbers from hell.

The E-male of the Species

Wendy Holden

The e-mail pinged on to Georgie's screen. 'It's. So. Hot – J x.'

Georgie looked at it, disappointed. Three words. Hardly worth opening the damn thing really. That was the trouble with e mail. They were the electronic equivalent of hearing the letterbox go and rushing to the door to find a flier for Salmonella Pizza and something from the Inland Revenue. A let-down, basically. All gong and no dinner.

But Jenny wasn't wrong. It was boiling. The office air-conditioning faithfully echoed the hysterical lurches of the weather – but, unfortunately, several lurches behind. Today's blistering indoor temperatures, apparently meant to address the cold snap of last week, had in fact coincided with the third day of blue skies, blazing sunshine and parks full of sunbathing office workers at lunchtime. The summer had started with a vengeance.

Georgie, restless with the heat, looked round the perspiring office. The telephones beeping and chirruping like parakeets in the jungle only added to the tropical effect. Everyone from the subs to the editor's secretary looked distinctly moist under the armpits. In the case of the editor's secretary, however, this was nothing out of the ordinary; apparently oblivious to the great strides forward made in the field of anti-perspirant technology, Moira had a faint odour of Camembert about her even in the depths of winter.

Opposite Georgie, Jenny, reaching over for her ringing telephone, certainly seemed to be suffering. Her face was flushed and there was sweat on her upper lip, as well as tiny bristles of hair. Why the hell, Georgie wondered, didn't Jenny wax it? No wonder she never got anywhere with men. Her clothes, too, were hardly a come-on. Which reminded her . . .

'Effing hell.' Georgie stabbed furiously at her keyboard. 'Literally. My "f" key's stuck again. Bugger it. Just as I've got four hundred words to write about the style of Ffion Jenkins.'

But Jenny wasn't listening. She was gawping into space, as indeed, Georgie realized, she had been since putting the receiver down. Something momentous had clearly occurred; something, Georgie guessed, Jenny didn't want the rest of the notoriously nosy features desk to know about. Discreet whispering, however, was out of the question; two bulky computer screens blocked the space between them. Only by leaning over so far she practically fell out of her chair could Georgie see her colleague at all.

Georgie had long decided on e-mail as being the only way to communicate. Not that Jenny's were anywhere as amusing as her own of course. But then, not everyone had her abilities; this was why Jenny was merely a commissioning editor for the paper's features pages and Georgie their star writer. Meaning that, while Jenny spent her days writing pleading letters requesting face-time with various celebrities of the moment, Georgie actually got to go and interview them, got to go clacking in her Jimmy Choos into everywhere from the Savoy to the Metropolitan Hotel, zooming up in the lift to the marble bathrooms and crystal caviar-holders of the hotel's most expensive apartments. It was Georgie's boast that she'd seen more Presidential Suites than Bill Clinton. Such boasts, as well as vast quantities of free cosmetics and (thanks to her other role as the paper's fashion writer) clothes and trips to the Paris shows, had made her less than popular in the office. Which is why she tolerated Jenny. If only for intelligence/gossip-gathering purposes, one needed an office friend, even if it was a tragic single thirtysomething who advertised in lonely hearts columns for love.

'My blind date! Jx', Jenny pinged back a few minutes later in reply to Georgie's enquiring e-mail. *Blind date*. Georgie tried to shoo away the pitying smile that wanted to play about her lips. Not because she wished to spare Jenny's feelings particularly. No, it was entirely because her pathetic campaign to find a man was too amusing to run the risk of not hearing about it any more.

'The one you wrote to of the Lonely Hearts ad? Gx' It was difficult to suppress a snigger.

'That's right. We're meeting tonight. Jx'

'Any idea what he looks like? You haven't met him

before, have you? How will you know it's him? Gx.' It was annoying, this kiss. But Jenny always did it – just how desperate for affection was she? Leaving it off in reply seemed unfriendly; again, Georgie risked not hearing the full story of her catastrophic love life.

'No but will recognize by what he has on. Jx'

'What's that? Cravat and blazer? Gx' It was below the belt, Georgie knew, but the 'lonely soldier' of Jenny's last encounter, far from being the gym-hardened SAS officer she had imagined, turned out to be a retired colonel from Andover with a cravat, blazer and walrus moustache. Although one would have thought the latter suited Jenny to a T. Bending slightly to the side, Georgie could see her colleague's reddening face as she read the message.

'No. Socks with Scottie dogs on. Jx'

Some things couldn't be confined to e-mail; certainly not one with no effing facility. Georgie leaned sideways in her chair and stared at Jenny, her eyes wide with scorn. '*Scottie Dog Socks*? You are joking?' she repeated loudly.

Three desks down, the features assistant looked up with interest. Georgie scowled at her before renewing the assault on Jenny. 'How the hell will you see them anyway?' she demanded. 'Will he be wearing shorts?'

Jenny's heat-flushed face flushed deeper as she tapped furiously.

'He'll be sitting down with his socks clearly visible, he says. It's all very well for you to laugh. You've got a boyfriend. Jx'

'Of sorts. Gx' Georgie pressed Send with a twist of the lips. Yes, she had Tim, which in the great scheme of things was good. But he was also a penniless freelance writer (bad); whose ambition, if so it could be called, lagged several miles behind her own (bad). Yet he was handsome (good) – he had stood out a mile amid the greasy hacks at the newspaper Christmas party they had met at (good, if not difficult) – even though his dress sense left a lot to be desired (bad). Added to which, they weren't having much sex at the moment (bad), but then, they weren't having rows either (good). You had to see someone to have rows with them; Tim had been out every evening for the past week at least.

'Where are you meeting him? Gx'

'Odeon Leicester Square and then Pizza Express. Jx'

Georgie smirked as she typed a reply. The light fantastic it wasn't. She was annoyed, however, at a faint pang of what felt suspiciously like envy. It would be fun to have a flirt, although obviously not with a man with naff socks. But it was summer and the sap had risen, even if Tim had not. The particular sap in her life had still been in bed as she had left for work – stayed up all night to write a piece, apparently. Well, tough luck, thought Georgie. He should be more organized. It would serve him right if she met someone else.

'Got some clean knickers in your bag? Gx'

The answer pinged on to Georgie's screen.

'Congratulations. Thought that piece you wrote about men being terrible dancers was hilarious. Wondered if you were thinking of the school disco!'

Georgie stared. What was Jenny talking about? The piece in question had appeared in the paper several weeks ago. It had been good, of course – declared one of Georgie's best by the editor himself, in fact. But Jenny had been at Roedean, an institution whose knees-ups Georgie imagined to be something along the lines of the ball scene in *My Fair Lady*. What did *she* know about the exhibition of uncoordinated stomping and snogging otherwise known as the Elmhurst school disco?

Georgie read the rest of the message. 'You probably don't remember me – David (Dave) Anderton (Elmhurst School)?'

The 2000 volts that suddenly shot through Georgie had nothing to do with the tangle of dangerous-looking computer wires at her feet. Did she remember David (Dave) Anderton? Was the Pope Catholic, roses red, violets blue and hopeless teenage crushes the most keenly felt of all? Yes, she remembered David (Dave) Anderton, even though ten years lay between now and her final lustful glance at him at sixth-form speech day. She had not seen him – or anyone else from school – since.

Ping. 'I'd rather not discuss my underwear, thanks. Jx'

Georgie grinned, aware that although her mind was no longer on her colleague, it was very much on underwear. Dave Anderton's underwear. Not that she had ever got to see it. The affair that had raged in Georgie's head throughout the two years of Elmhurst sixth form had never been consummated; Dave Anderton had been oblivious to the love that had burned in her bosom. The love that had dared not speak its name for fear of repudiation. For then Georgie had been Georgina, a lumpen, swotty, tongue-tied creature neither male nor female, but something that wore glasses. She blushed at the memory.

Ten years ago. Years during which she had worked hard not only to beat the competition and become top women's feature writer on a successful newspaper, but to become slim, tanned and polished as well. From the doughty Georgina, she had become the skittish Georgie. Two sizes smaller than her sixth-form self, blonder (thanks to Stefano and his nifty way with tinfoil), taller (various hands from Office to Jimmy Choo) and bluer of eye (tinted contact lenses, the glasses having been long since ceremonially stamped on with a steel Gucci heel). If only Dave Anderton could see her now.

Tossing back her hair and pouting at the computer screen, Georgie pressed Reply and typed that of course she remembered him, wasn't it a small world, she was surprised he remembered her after so long, she was so plain, so boring . . .

Her heart pounded as she pressed the Send key. It would be fun to meet up. See him again. More to the point, see him see her again. Watch him take in the slender figure, the plunging cleavage, the glossy hair she had never had at school. Replace the memory of her on the netball court in a hideously unflattering pleated gym skirt with the sight of her in fishnets, in a bottom-skimming skirt designed to show off legs half the width of the ones he had last seen.

Ping. 'What are you grinning at? Jx'

Georgie realized she had never entirely stopped wondering what might have been between them. The memory of what had been between Dave Anderton and Susan Stringer, the glamorous, bronze-limbed hockey captain, however, still rankled.

'Something naughty. Gx'

The ball was now in Dave Anderton's court, it was up to him to reply.

'Have fun with Scottie Dog Socks,' Georgie called loudly as the office was emptying. She grinned as Jenny, en route to the lifts, threw her a furious look. Georgie shut down her machine with a rare feeling of regret. No more e-mails today. But no doubt there would be developments tomorrow.

'Earth move? Gx'. Georgie had returned to the office in a completely different mood than she had left it the night before. If Tim's eventual arrival home at half-past twelve last night had been irritating, his claim to be researching a feature whose content he could not reveal, because Georgie worked for a rival newspaper, had been infuriating. 'If it wasn't obvious no one would touch you with a bloody bargepole,' she had spluttered, 'I'd almost think you were having an affair.'

But Georgie had more important matters to consider this morning. Such as the devastating lack of communication from Dave Anderton in her mailbox. Aptly enough, considering how she felt, her 'f' key was finally back in action.

'It was OK. Jx'

Looking across at her, Georgie was gratified to see that Jenny was as red as a Mon Rouge lipstick. The date had obviously been a disaster – presumably there had been so little to talk about that Jenny and Scottie Dog Socks had ended up discussing the number of regional branches on the back of the Pizza Express menu.

Georgie shivered. The air-conditioning had finally caught up with the weather; walking into the office had been like opening the deep freeze. Moira's perspiration stains, however, were intact. *Damn* Dave, Georgie thought, savagely typing the opening sentence of a piece the fashion editor had rushed over and demanded almost as soon as Georgie had sat down. The feature would eventually be billed as a directional think-piece critically examining a staple of the contemporary wardrobe; for the moment, however, it bore the headline Georgie had been given: 'Leather jackets. Yes or no. By five o'clock'.

Why hadn't he replied? It was almost embarrassing how disappointed she felt.

Ping. 'I don't remember that but it was ten years ago! D.'

Georgie's brain, occupied as it had been on the Big Double Or Single-Breasted Fastening Debate, suddenly raced. He had replied. She stared, frantically dividing the message into good and bad points. Ten years ago – bad. It made them both sound ancient. But he didn't remember her being fat and boring, which was definitely good.

Ping. 'Conference in five minutes. Don't forget. Jx'

Damn. Five – no, four now – minutes to get ready for the morning features meeting. Georgie flicked frantically through the newspapers, ripping out pages wildly as half-formed ideas struck her. She'd hone them in the meeting, there'd be plenty of time if she positioned herself far enough away from the Editor so she could go last with her suggestions – and show him a bit of leg to soften him up . . .

'What was the matter with you in conference?' Jenny asked, as she and Georgie headed for the shops at lunchtime. 'You barely said a word. Even when the ed raved about that piece you did on beards being the new black, you hardly seemed to notice.'

'That's because I'm rather preoccupied at the moment,' Georgie declared. 'An old flame from school has got back in touch with me.'

'Really? Why?'

A wave of irritation went through Georgie. When push came to shove (and she sincerely hoped that it would), Georgie had no idea why Dave had got back in touch. Call it Fate, call it unfinished business, call it a bit of fun. Jenny, naturally, would have no idea about the latter. In reply, she shurgged theatrically.

Jenny looked doubtfully at Georgie. 'Maybe he's seen you in the paper recently? There've been some pretty good pictures of you, after all.'

The suggestion hit Georgie like a high-speed train. *Of course* that was it. Perhaps he had seen the current, sleeker, go-faster, Mark II version of Georgie Lee, doing one of her regular 'how to get the look' stunts for the paper's features pages. The most recent one tied in with a new series of vintage episodes of *The Avengers*; Georgie had, even if she thought so herself, looked stunning in a tight black rubber suit and killer heels. Even if she hadn't been able to walk for days afterwards and her intestines still ached.

As Jenny headed for the M&S sandwich counter, Georgie continued down the High Street, her head buzzing with new possibilities. If that was the reason – and how could it not be? – then it was better than she could have hoped. She and Dave could go ahead and have a fully-fledged cyberfling. One heard about e-mail romances. Making passes at each other over the Net would be the perfect way to pass the summer. Not for nothing was her service provider *excite.co.uk*.

Georgie smoothed her thin magenta cardigan over her bony hips and smiled to herself. She had destroyed all the photographic evidence she knew existed of her size sixteen adolescence, but there was, she realized with mounting excitement, only one way to lay the ghost that lurked in Dave Anderton's mind. Lay *him*.

'Are you living in London? Gx' There. She'd dithered about it, but finally dared to add a kiss.

Ping. 'Freezywater. D.'

Georgie swallowed. *Freezywater.* Where the hell was that? Still, at least he was keen, if cool (no kiss), but then, that was probably Freezywater for you. He replied immediately; at this rate, thought Georgie, excitedly, they'd be having a naughty lunch *tomorrow*. Or even naughtier drinks. She imagined him, Dave Anderton, taller, thinner, more distinguished-looking than when she had last seen him, but with the same grin, that same flash of wicked white teeth, that same blond fringe.

'What's Freezywater like? Not sure where it is – sorry. Gx'

Jenny had, Georgie now noticed, returned to her desk after lunch with a number of distinctly racy-looking carrier bags. Scottie Dog Socks must be still around then. Giving it one last go, no doubt, Georgie thought contemptuously. But beggars like Jenny couldn't be choosers.

'Been exercising the plastic have we? Seeing SDS tonight? Gx' Georgie felt irritated as Jenny went purple. What the hell was the matter with her? At the moment, she was flushing more than a Royal Opera House loo in the interval.

Ping. 'In Hertfordshire. It's great. There's a good golf course nearby and the social life is excellent – the local Rotarians are a crazy bunch of guys! D.'

Georgie wasn't quite sure what she made of this. Once upon a time, Dave Anderton had been all but a deity. The school football, cricket and rugby captain, he had smoked behind the bike sheds and had sex in music cupboards or, at least, so everyone had heard. The first pupil to have a car, he regularly thrilled the rest of the sixth form by performing handbrake turns in the car park at lunchtime and thrilled them further by smashing the headmaster's wing mirror. Things had evidently changed since then. And who the hell was *we*? Girlfriend?

'I never asked you – did you get married? Any kids? Gx' It was her fifth draft of the enquiry and sounded, she thought, as breezy as an e-mail could. She pressed Send and sat back, exhausted with the effort. It was all so much more complicated than she had thought. She hadn't imagined e-flirting to be the equivalent of grand-master chess. Every syllable pored over, every comma checked for its interpretative possibilities: far from being the cyber-highroad to untrammeled lust, their exchanges had been so chaste they made Jane Austen look like Jackie Collins.

There was no reply to this for the rest of the afternoon. I've put him on the spot, Georgie thought, panicking and wishing she hadn't.

'How was it? Gx'

Obviously good, Georgie observed, irritably. There was a definite sparkle about Jenny this morning. That was a new, more flattering skirt she had on, her white shirt, reflecting more light to her face, made her skin look less muddy. One of Georgie's own tricks, of course, obviously copied, as were those high heels to make Jenny's stubby little legs look longer. Imitation, Georgie consoled herself, was the sincerest form of flattery, though watching the usually flat-soled Jenny wobble into the office as if she were on stilts had made Georgie hope it might be the sincerest form of flattening as well.

Sadly Jenny hadn't fallen over, but the possibility had been almost amusing enough to make up for there being no message from Dave Anderton.

Ping. 'Fine thanks. Jx'

Oh, she wasn't getting away with this, thought Georgie. Not with that 'I-had-great-sex-last-night' aura about her. Scottie Dog Socks was obviously good at *something*.

'Where did you go? Gx'

Ping. 'R. K. Stanley. That bangers-and-mash restaurant. Jx'

'Never been there. Think Tim has though. Not my type of thing. Gx'

Jenny blushed violently again. For Christ's sake, thought Georgie. It was like working with a nun in a sex shop.

Ping. 'Yes, Morag and I got married three years ago. She's a policewoman. No children though – Morag can't have them, unfortunately. But we're very happy with the cats. D.'

At lunchtime, Georgie walked round the shops in a daze. Dave Anderton was married to a policewoman called Morag. And he had cats. No wonder he was feeling frisky – there was something definitely weary about that 'got married three years ago'. And then the death blow, delivered with devastating timing – 'she's a policewoman'. Know what I mean? the line had silently added. Georgie grinned to herself as she fingered the crotch of a lace-trimmed pair of knickers.

* * *

Steady now, Georgie told herself, as she returned ten minutes early from her lunch-hour. Don't come on too strong. Be cool yet flirtatious. Subtle, yet sexy. Taking a deep breath, she held her hands over the keyboard for a minute, then plunged in. 'Ever get back to Elmhurst? I go back to see the parentals about once a year – I can do it in an hour in the MX5. Gx'

It had taken half an hour to compose, but Georgie was pleased with it. Subtle it certainly was, yet hidden in there was the suggestion that he was welcome to an Elmhurst-bound lift in her glamorous car anytime.

Ping. 'I get the train everywhere – and to Elmhurst to see the folks every fortnight. Morag books our tickets weeks in advance, so we can go Apex First. Great system – you ought to try it. D.'

Georgie was conscious of a rising sense of panic. She replied instantly, her fingers flying over the keys like the wind.

'So you don't even drive to work? Gx'

Ping. 'No. I get the train. But the choo-choo has its drawbacks – this morning a non-stopper rushed past so fast it would have taken my hair off if I had any left! Lucky my glasses are so heavy or they'd probably have gone too! Mind you, I'm hardly what you'd call thin either, so I was probably pretty safe! D.'

Georgie felt sick. It occurred to her that she wasn't the only one who had changed beyond all recognition since schooldays. If she herself had shed two stone and a pair of bottle-bottomed spectacles, the carefree, thick-thatched youth of fond memory sounded as if he had

picked them straight up and put them on. More than
this, he had apparently transmogrified into some sub-
urbanite who thought cars polluted the planet and
whose idea of a good time was golf, cats, the Rotary
Club and going Apex First with a policewoman called
Morag.

The king of her adolescent heart had turned into a
bigger square than Trafalgar. He'd be suggesting class
reunions next. And, Georgie suddenly thought in panic,
back-pedalling faster than a unicyclist in reverse, here
she was, flirting wildly with him. How the hell was she
going to get out of this one?

Ping. Oh God, another message from him. Georgie
opened it, heart sinking. 'Anyway, we've been so busy
chatting I've never told you the reason I was getting in
touch. I'm trying to get together an Elmhurst Class of
'89 reunion on July 31st. Fancy coming? D.'

I'd fancy the Elephant Man more, thought Georgie
as half devastated, half relieved, she typed a polite
refusal. The sound of Jenny giggling on the telephone
just across the desk from her hardly helped her mood.

Still, there were things to be thankful for. Finding
one's adolescent heartthrob had not so much feet of
clay than entire legs of it at least meant she wouldn't
wonder What Might Have Been With Dave Anderton
for the rest of her life. And, unlike poor old single
Jenny, even if she seemed perkier than usual, Georgie
at least had Tim to fall back on. Useless though he was,
he was better than nothing.

'I'm resigning,' Jenny told Georgie, as they left the

office that night. 'I've got a job as a commissioning editor on *Vogue*.'

'Congratulations. Wondered what the new clothes were about, I must say,' said Georgie, trying not to sound as jealous as she felt. 'Had enough of working with me, then?' she couldn't stop herself adding. As Jenny blushed fiercely.

To Georgie's amazement, Tim was at home when she got back to the flat. Even more amazingly, he seemed to be sorting out his clothes.

'Not tidying your wardrobe, surely?' Georgie said sarcastically. Not having seen much of them recently, she had forgotten quite how bad his clothes were.

'No. I'm leaving you.' Tim, sorting through a pile of socks, did not look up.

Georgie felt as if someone had hit her in the windpipe. This couldn't be right. *She* was in charge of this relationship.

'How – I mean, who . . .' she spluttered.

She was the one with the career wasn't she? *She* paid for everything – surely it was she who had the right to decide when everything ended. Men didn't leave *her*.

'Well, you obviously aren't in love with me any more. I found someone who is. Been seeing them for quite some time, in fact.'

'How, who . . . ?' Georgie's eyes were rolling like National Lottery Balls.

'Actually, I put an ad in the paper.' At least he had the grace to blush.

'You did *what*?' An *ad. Her* boyfriend. Like those tragic ones Jenny answered? Georgie felt her feet fizz with horror.

'It was for a piece about the new male singleton – that piece I couldn't tell you about. I had to put an ad in the lonely hearts column and see what happened if someone answered. But someone did answer. And it, um, suddenly became more than just a feature.'

'Who is she?' But Georgie's screeched demand dried in her throat. In front of her, on the bedroom floor, having fallen off the pile Tim was hurriedly stuffing in suitcases, was a pair of socks. With Scottie dogs on them.

Jessica Adams' first novel *Single White E-Mail* was an Australian and English bestseller and Fox Studios are currently adapting the book as a television comedy. Her second novel *Tom Dick and Debbie Harry* will be published in both countries. Jessica is also the astrologer for *Woman's Own* and *Cosmopolitan* (Australia) and the author of *The New Astrology For Women* (Harper-Collins) and *Handbag Horoscopes* (Penguin.) She is a Leo with the Moon in Aquarius, and Venus and Mars in Gemini.

Love on the Underground

Jessica Adams

When I turned twenty-one I left university and tried to get a job as Naomi Campbell. This was a bad idea, because I come from a long line of big bottoms. In fact, my Auntie Letitia is known as Lard Arse Letitia to the family.

She got that way because she used to be a security officer at King's Cross station. From 1971 through to 1985 she sat on a vinyl cushion eating jerk chicken with her fingers, watching black and white TV. As my Uncle Eddie always says, it had a terrible effect on her bottom. When Letitia came to my fifth birthday party wearing a suede skirt, all the kids sat underneath her and used her as a wigwam.

Did I get my own lard arse from Letitia's DNA, or from some weird kind of morphic resonance, transferred from her vinyl cushion to my bum? I'll never know. But I know one thing – you can't get a job as Naomi Campbell if you've got a lard arse. By the way, I learned what morphic resonance was at university. It's actually the *only* thing I learned at university.

When I graduated, I had to fill in a form for

the careers officer telling him if I liked people, if I enjoyed the outdoors and if I would consider myself ambitious.

When I took the form home my mother got to the ambitious bit and screamed, 'That's you! That's your personality, Angela! That's you!'

Well maybe. I suppose I was the first person from either side of my family to go to university – even if it was Leeds.

The Leeds bit didn't matter to Dad, though. It was enough for him to see me collect my scroll in an academic gown, even if the scroll did have my name spelled wrong, and even if it was for a BA, which a boyfriend of mine used to say stood for Bugger All. When I came down off the stage, with all the others, my dad jumped five seats to get to me, and cried all over the sleeve of my gown. 'You're getting us out of the Underground, Angela!' he sobbed. 'You're getting us out of the Underground!'

Of course, it was his family's fault that we all got into the Underground in the first place, if you know what I mean. My grandad Lee got off the boat from Jamaica in 1962 and started taking tickets at Paddington a week later, without even thinking if he liked people, enjoyed the outdoors or had ambitions. And after that, there was no going back.

My brother Viv is still a guard on the Hammersmith and City line, and even my sad Uncle Colin got a job as a cleaner at Willesden Junction. They gave it to him after he tried to throw himself under a train there one day. He was supposed to be going to the zoo at the time. But he's quite happy now.

Letitia's sister, my mother, got a Royal Doulton tea-set after doing the toilets at Brixton for ten years, and then there is my dad himself. He met my mother on the day his Curly Wurly got stuck in the chocolate machine on platform two. They gave him a refund, of course. London Underground has been very good to my family.

They even gave me a job yesterday. Not as Naomi Campbell, and not even as the tube's resident Lord Byron expert which, let's face it, is all my BA equipped me for. I am, however, about to become a Busker Buster. You get paid five quid an hour and they give you a free fluorescent green waistcoat.

The proper name for Busker Busters is Special Security Unit Four but it took about five minutes for this guy called Paul to rename it.

I quite fancy Paul. In a red-haired, computer-nerdy, weird-suede Hush Puppies kind of way. He's like me – he did a degree (his was in sociology, though, not Lord Byron) and then he lost the plot. We compared notes and found out that we'd both worked in The Body Shop, both gone travelling and been rejected as McDonald's managers – it was incredible. Paul also seems very appreciative of the family lard arse. Well I caught him looking at it, anyway, when we were supposed to be filing into a room for a slide show presentation.

The slide show was very interesting. It showed us the right way to arrest buskers ('Show sympathy and understanding for their point of view, then lightly touch them on the elbow and guide them on to the escalator.'). They didn't show the wrong way, though. Paul seemed to think this might be smashing their acoustic guitar over their head and telling them how much you hate 'Wonderwall'.

The other Busker Busters are a mixed bunch. Paul says he got the job because he speaks French and German, and half the buskers at Tottenham Court Road these days are tourists anyway. He thinks I might have been hired because of racial and gender sensitive issues among buskers. It's sad what sociology degrees do to some people. I think I might have been hired because my dad knows the guy who knows the guy in charge of Busker Busters. Plus if I need to immobilize someone with a guitar I can sit on them with my Letitia buttocks.

To prepare us for the job, they took us on a mini-tour of Oxford Circus tube, incognito. In Paul's sociology degree favour, I suppose I did notice they were giving all the Rasta musician guys to me. Well – I think they were Rasta guys. They were playing Bob Marley. But one of them was wearing a giant Tweety bird head and furry yellow suit, and the other one was dressed up as Sylvester the cat so for all I know it could have been the Spice Girls under there.

'And what would you do there, Angela?' the training officer said under his breath, as Tweety and Sylvester swung their hips in time to the tape on their sound system.

'Well I'd probably get someone dressed up as a giant dog to tackle the cat and then throw a blanket over the other one,' I said. 'Look. I don't know. Tell them to pick another song, everyone's heard "No Woman No Cry".'

Anyway. Then we all trooped off to look at one of those women who squat on the floor, begging with a baby. It wasn't exactly busking, but we all wanted to arrest her anyway.

And now it's Day One of my new job. A very emotional day for the family. Dad gave me his old London Underground red badge from the seventies for luck, and then Mum burst into tears all over her muesli. I guess she can see the slippery slope to Brixton toilets for me now, and after all the money she spent on course textbooks about Lord Byron, not to mention all the Lord Byron fridge magnets from the National Portrait Gallery, she can't stand it.

'It breaks my heart, Angela,' she said, as I went out the door in my brand new Busker Buster green fluorescent vest. But she did give me some jerk chicken to take in a little Tupperware container for my lunch. I have to say, I'm not into all the old Jamaican stuff. My brother is – he goes back to Kingston whenever he can afford it, and he's got every Lee Perry album since *Time Boom X De Devil Dead*. However, I make an exception for jerk chicken – Colonel Sanders, eat your heart out.

And now I'm here. New job. And new life too – for a while. And I get the feeling Paul might be part of it – but also for a while. Somehow, guys who wear glasses like the ones Paul's got on – you know what I mean, sort of pointy and like Brains from *Thunderbirds* – well, they never stick around for long, do they?

I wonder if Paul bought the glasses because he's trying to pull me? I don't remember him wearing them on the first day we met. We did ask each other what we did on the weekend, though, which is a fairly reasonable indicator of pullability – eligibility by both parties. He went clubbing he said. I watched *The Bill* on the couch with a blue Clarins face-mask on, but I didn't tell him that.

'Angela!'

What?

I mean, one minute you're thinking about date potential and what someone might look like naked, without their weird new Brainsy glasses, and the next minute someone actually wants you to do some work . . .

'Angela, if you and Paul take Tottenham Court Road, can you be back at Covent Garden for 11 a.m.?'

'Sure.'

Oh, this is good. It's just like school, except Paul and I aren't being asked to do back-to-back push and pull exercises in our vests, we're actually . . . well. It's almost like *The Bill*. All he and I need are big black lace-up shoes and a special theme song to clump along the street with.

'Come on then, Paul,' I say in a *Bill*esque kind of way.

We've got special passes with our photos on to get us around all the zones. If you actually enjoyed tube travel it would probably be your wildest fantasy come true. As it happens, though, both Paul and I discover we hate train travel.

'It's all the businessmen farting from South Ken to Sloane Square,' he says, as we sit side by side under the strip lighting on the train. 'They just sit there eating pork pies out of their wrappers reading *Loaded* and farting.'

'It's the wandering accordion players who get me,' I tell him. 'It's like being in some old episode of *'Allo 'Allo*. I hate people who give them money. Why do they give them money? They should be killed if they give them money.'

'I've got a new Toyota,' Paul says. 'You'll have to come out for a test drive one night.'

'Have some of my jerk chicken before it goes off,' I hear myself saying, handing him Mum's Tupperware container. God, it's like we're married already.

I think something is sinking in with Paul, too, because for a while he just sits there saying nothing, in an embarrassed yet slightly lustful way, while we watch a whole lot of Japanese tourists with Smythsons bags get on at Bond Street.

'What kind of music are you into?' he says, at last.

'Oh, you know. Morrissey.'

He tries not to look too gob-smacked by this but I

can tell he's not coping because his Evansy glasses are fogging up.

'Wot?' I say. 'Wot? Wot?'

'I'M SHOCKED!' he shouts, over the noise of the ker-chang, ker-chang of the train running over a few tube mice.

'WHY?' I shout back, but he's already shouting back the other way so he can't hear me.

'THE LIQUIDATOR!' he yells, 'THE ISRAEL-ITES! YOUNG, GIFTED AND BLACK! RIVERS OF BABYLON!' And I gather he's telling me his own taste in music here. Except I gather it's the cred version of 'Rivers of Babylon' he likes, not the Boney M one where they're wearing Bacofoil suits. Before we can go into it, though, we're at Tottenham Court Road already, so we have to get off, and shut up. Unless we shut up, we're not going to hear any buskers, after all.

'I can hear something already,' Paul says, lifting his head up as we climb the stairs. And I can too. A distant thwacking sound.

'It's reggae, mon,' I say, taking the piss. 'Your favour-ite. Could even be "Rivers of Babylon".'

But no, it isn't. It's Sylvester the cat and Tweety Pie, swinging from side to side with their bongo drums and guitars, and their little sound system in a box. They're playing something that sounds like 'Superfly' by Curtis Mayfield mixed through a cement mixer, then gargled by cows, but the tune is, Paul informs me, 'Hitter' by Garfeel Ruff ('Look out for the hitter, he's big and bad and sho'nuff black, he's gonna knock you down'). I don't know. All those blaxploitation soundtracks. They all sound the same to me.

We watch and listen for a while, trying to pretend to each other that we're sizing the situation up, when we're really just too paralysed with fear to do anything.

Then, at last, Paul, pushes his glasses up his nose and makes a move.

'Excuse me, but I'm going to have to ask you to stop,' he says to Tweety. But the bird doesn't move. In fact, he hasn't even put his bongo drums down. After that, I touch Sylvester the cat lightly on the elbow and ask him to move up the escalator. He's not moving either. Then, both Paul and I become aware of something that *is* moving behind us. It's a small crowd. I don't know who starts it first, but soon there's a slow hand-clap going on. And a few people are hissing.

Paul touches both Sylvester and Tweety lightly on the elbow simultaneously. Nothing doing.

'Boo!' says a guy in overalls. 'Boo! Hiss!'

'Come on now!' Paul addresses the crowd.

'Leave the cat in the hat alone!' says a strange woman.

'It isn't the Cat in the bloody Hat, it's Sylvester,' I tell her.

'Well leave them alone, what harm are they doing?' says an outspoken, possibly drunk, old guy. Is there some agency where they hire outspoken, possibly drunk, old guys to appear around London on a regular basis? I mean, is there?

And then, quick as a flash, Tweety is bending down

213

again, pushing the start button on the sound system. He's fast-forwarding it too. Maybe to some old Stevie Wonder thing – something to get the crowd on side anyway, I'll bet my life on it. It's just something in Tweety's eyes that's got me thinking that way – he looks manipulative.

'Move on sister,' Tweety says, taking his head off. He's got dreads and he looks like the drummer in my brother Viv's old band.

'No, you move on, or I'm fining you fifty quid,' I say.

'Fifty quid!' Sylvester shouts through his furry cat face. I'm not sure where his mouth actually is, either – behind one of the flared pink nostrils?

'Get the notebook,' Paul whispers to me.

What? Why me?

So I get it out.

'You do it,' he says, 'I'll get on the radio for local security.'

And I book them – to the sound of Tweety defiantly beating his bongos, and a crowd slow hand-clapping me. Then, in protest, Sylvester also takes his head off. He's a big guy, with a big, mean stare too – like one of those guys with ten-foot wide shoulders they hire to bounce people out of nightclubs in Dalston, Kingsland.

My heart is pounding. I can't believe it. I'm booking two guys in furry animal costumes, and I feel like I've just shot ten people in cold blood in an armed hold-up.

And time squeezes in weird ways after that – you know how unusual situations seem to make everything happen in a blurry kind of way? Well anyway. Suddenly it seems to be after lunch, and Paul and I are sitting in Tottenham Court Road staff HQ (you'd never know it's there, it's well hidden behind the stairwell) eating what's left of my mum's jerk chicken.

'You were great, Angela,' he says. 'I'm going to take you out to dinner.'

'You don't have to,' I say. But inside my underwear, I'm blushing.

'No really, I want to. Come on. Where do you want to go?'

'You decide.'

'African? Indian?'

'Harvey Nichols Fifth Floor Restaurant,' I say in the end. I knew someone who knew someone who thought she saw Morrissey eating salad there once.

We make it 8 p.m., to give both of us time to get home, get out of our fluorescent green waistcoats, and for me to have a bath and get rid of the sweat that seems to have taken over my body since the terrible Sylvester and Tweety crowd psychosis episode.

When I get home, Mum and Dad can't wait to hear about my day, but enough is enough, and I head straight for the bathroom, taking off Dad's London Underground badge and putting it in the fruit bowl on the table. Dad decides he's going to talk to me through the door anyway.

'Are you OK?' he yells over the sound of the bathwater running.

'Fine!' I yell back.

'You look stressed!' he shouts again.

'I'M NOT STRESSED!'

After that, he goes away. And even though I don't have time for any blue face-mask, half an hour later I at least feel vaguely human again.

I use my free tube pass to get to South Kensington, then I walk it to get some exercise and calm down. I know life isn't supposed to be like this when you've spent half your twenties having dating practice, but I still get nervous paralysis of the pantyhose. And as I walk, I keep thinking – Harvey Nichols Fifth Floor Restaurant with a guy. Not bad, Angela. Better than *The Bill* on the couch on Saturday night with a cushion.

He's already at the table when I sit down, and a waitress flaps around us until we order some wine (well he does, anyway) and then she goes away again.

'So,' he says.

I smile. I hate it when people do the 'So' thing. I always feel like I should say 'So' back, but then it all becomes like some kind of James Bond villain meeting.

'I was stressed out today,' I say.

'I thought we handled it fine!' he says. And I kind of let that one go.

'I just thought, when they started hand-clapping and all that, I'd better let you take over,' he says.

'Why?'

'Well they were obviously doing the hand-clapping

because I was – you know – a white guy arresting a couple of black guys.'

The waitress arrives with some wine at last, and I gulp the whole glass back as I try to sort this one out.

'Actually, Paul, the crowd was slow hand-clapping – though I don't know why that keeps on bothering us so much, kids do it at Sooty concerts when Sooty doesn't turn up on time – well they were slow hand clapping because they liked the music. Though god knows why, of course.'

He laughs.

'Yeah. You know, I love that music. Isaac Hayes. Sweet Sweetback. Curtis. They were murdering it.'

I shrug. 'I wouldn't know.'

'Oh yeah, you like the miserable white guy music. Have you seen Morrissey here by the way?'

'No, I haven't. I think someone made it up.'

We both order the pasta, which costs the same as two hours' salary for both of us at Tottenham Court Road today. And I suppose I should be nicer to Paul, because he's paying. But then he ruins everything.

'I scored some wicked ganja on the way here,' he says suddenly, just as I'm about to rip open a bread roll.

I smile. Along with people who say 'So' there's something about people telling me about their boring marijuana shopping that just makes my eyes glaze over.

'Do you like pot?' I use the word deliberately. To hell with ganja. He's white, for god's sake. He was born in Weston-super-Mare.

'You don't get high?'

'Why do you look so shocked at that?' I find myself saying.

He shrugs. 'Well, I don't know. I just thought –'

'Well unthink yourself.'

He goes to the loo after that, and I watch him head off the wrong way around the escalators, then back again, then I watch him get it wrong a third time as he traipses off towards the lift.

He's left his wallet on the table. And I know I shouldn't, but I can't help it. Will I be paying my own half of the bill tonight, or is this a man who has come prepared? Because if I'm paying my own half of the bill, then forget it, I'm out of here as soon as the bread rolls have disappeared.

Instead, though, I find two fifty-pound notes. So that's okay. I guess. But hidden behind them I see something that isn't quite okay. It's a photograph of a girl – maybe in her mid-twenties,. It looks like it was taken on a beach in Jamaica, and she's had her hair ironed so it isn't frizzy any more, and – yeah, she isn't wearing a bra. And she's signed it. 'To Paul with love, Lucy.' She's like Naomi Campbell's sister. Maybe her slightly uglier older sister, but still.

When he gets back, I get up.

'I'm leaving.'

'Why?'

'The main course hasn't arrived, I'll just fix you up for the rest.' And I throw him two ten-pound notes and get to the lift as fast I can. And although I have a horrible feeling he's going to chase me, he doesn't. Thank God. And as soon as I'm down on the Brompton Road, I find a taxi and jump in.

The best thing about taxis – and what you pay for, in my opinion – is the thinking time. And on the way back home, I do a lot of thinking. About the guy I used to date at university (the one who said Bachelor of Arts stood for Bugger All) who also specialized in serial black girlfriends. And I think about my brother Viv, and what ganja – god I hate that word – did to his brain, and why he started work on the Hammersmith and City line when he should have gone to university. Like me.

If I add up the taxi bill and the Harvey Nichols bill, it's about what I'll get paid for two more days' work as Busker Buster. So, even though it kills me the next morning, I drag myself out of bed at 6 a.m., and on to the tube, and over to Tottenham Court Road again.

I'm ready for Paul. That kind of thing doesn't scare me. Hey, I'm the woman who arrested Tweety and Sylvester the cat, all right?

But Paul's not there. Someone tells me he hasn't turned up, and they're putting on some guy called Rob in his place. Rob's nice. The first thing he tells me is that I've becoming a living legend in Busker Buster circles, and the second thing he tells me is that he's got tickets for Morrissey if I'm interested.

I tell him I'll stick the job out for another week after this, and I do – right up until the following Friday, when they send me to Oxford Circus, the hardest gig a Busker Buster can get – because my triumph at Tottenham Court Road has won me some kind of reputation, it seems.

And that's when I hear it. The sweet sound of Morrissey – floating down the tunnel to platform four. Someone's got a guitar that's way out of tune, but it's the first decent thing I've heard since I started. So much so that I'm tempted to quit right there and then, just so I won't have to can the guy.

With Rob right behind me (*Bill* style – clump, clump, black lace-ups, theme tune) I make my approach. And I'm just about to steel myself for some elbow-touching when I realize it's him again. Tweety. My fate. My nemesis. My karmic punishment.

He's not on the bongos this time (well thank God for that, Morrissey was never meant for a jungle beat). He's in charge of a saxophone instead, but I'd spot him anywhere – it's the hip movements. 'What happened to the cat?' I say.

Tweetie tilts his head quizzically.

'Take your thing off. What happened to Sylvester?'

'I don't know what you're talking about,' comes the reply.

And off comes the head, and it's Paul.

'I bought it off him,' he says.

'What?'

'I bought it off Tweety. After we arrested him.'

'Oh.'

'I wanted to serenade you,' he says.

'Oh. Thanks.'

His red hair is all sweaty and sticking up from the bird head, and his Brainsy glasses are starting to go misty.

'Are you going to touch me on the elbow and ask me to go?' he says, trying to make a joke of it.

'No, Rob is,' I hear myself saying..

And I leave them to it.

Patricia Scanlan has written eight No. 1 bestselling novels and is currently working on her ninth. She is a series editor with the Open Door literacy series and taught creative writing to transition-year students. She lives in Dublin.

Fairweather Friend

Patricia Scanlan

'Why do you bother going on holidays with Melissa Harris? She's such a cow. She only uses you, you know,' Denise Irvine said crossly as she forked chicken korma into her mouth and took a sip of white wine.

Sophie glowered at her sister. 'She's not *that* bad!' she snapped irritably, dipping a piece of nan bread into her tikka masala sauce.

'Oh come on, Sophie, she's a walking bitch and always has been. She drops you like a hot potato as soon as there's a bloke on the scene and then you don't see her for dust until she's ditched and needs a shoulder to cry on. You're too soft with her and always have been. It's time you told her where to get off. Remember last year you were supposed to go on holiday with her and then she dropped you at the last minute because she met Mister Wonderful, and took off to Ibiza with him?' Denise pronged a stuffed mushroom and ate it with relish.

Sophie looked at her younger sister with envy. Denise could eat and drink all round her and not put on an ounce. She'd be up two pounds at least on the scales after this pig out.

'What happened to Mister Wonderful anyway?' Denise topped up their wine glasses. 'I thought they were going back to Ibiza.'

'She found out that he was two-timing her. She's in bits, really she is, Denise. I've never seen her this bad,' Sophie said earnestly. 'She was crazy about Tony, really nuts about him. He was the love of her life.'

'Don't be daft, Sophie!' Denise scoffed. 'How could *he* be the love of her life? She's so passionately in love with herself, there's no room for anyone else.'

'Oh, leave her alone,' Sophie muttered.

'Well I would have told her where to get off, if she'd asked me to go on holidays with only a week's notice after her behaviour last year,' Denise retorted, helping herself to a portion of aloo saag.

It's all right for you, Sophie thought glumly, as she studied her bright-eyed, immaculately groomed, supremely confident younger sister.

Denise had friends to beat the band and men fell over themselves trying to get a date with her. She breezed through life with not a care in the world, the epitome of the nineties woman about town. She revelled in her busy career as a publicist in a large publishing company and, at the age of twenty-two, drove her own company car.

Sophie, two years older, drove an ancient Fiesta that she'd had for the last six years. She was a paediatric nurse and while she enjoyed her job, she felt that her life lacked the glamour and excitement of her sister's.

Her two closest friends had got married within six

months of each other and in the last two years she'd had no one to go abroad with. The idea of going on a singles holiday filled her with dread. Hence the acceptance of the offer of two weeks in Majorca with Melissa Harris.

Sophie sighed and took a slug of her Australian sauvignon. She'd known Melissa since her schooldays. Blonde, blue-eyed, bubbly, and indescribably self-centred.

Melissa was the centre of the universe in her own eyes, or, as Denise cruelly christened her, *The Queen of the Me, Me, Me, Planet*. An only child, spoilt by doting parents, Melissa swanned through life accepting adoration as her due.

In Sophie, she had the perfect handmaiden. It had been so from the moment in junior choir when Melissa decided that she preferred Sophie's little black velvet bow to the red ribbon that adorned her own golden ponytail.

Sophie had handed over the bow unquestioningly, mesmerized by the baby-blue eyes batting perfect long black lashes at her and thrilled beyond measure at the invitation to join Melissa's gang. Although the entire class aspired to be a member of Melissa's entourage, only the chosen few were given the honour.

The honour was withdrawn regularly according to Melissa's mood and whim, and Sophie would find herself on the outside of the golden circle until Melissa had need of her services again. This was the pattern of their friendship, through childhood, teens, and while

Melissa studied to become a beauty therapist and Sophie was a student nurse.

'Weeks could go by and Sophie wouldn't hear a peep from Melissa and then some crisis would occur and Melissa would arrive at Sophie and Denise's flat in search of TLC and sympathy, while she sobbed over her latest heartbreak and declared that 'All Men Were Bastards.'

Tony Jenkins was the most recent addition to the AMWB's list. He and Melissa had been scheduled to take Ibiza by storm again until Melissa had discovered him in a steamy clinch with a beautician colleague at a friend's engagement party. It seemed they were having a rip-roaring affair.

'I really loved him,' Melissa wept. 'I just don't understand what he sees in her, Sophie. She's an awful airhead and she's got cellulite! When I think of all the times I did electrolysis on her – she has a terrible hairy lip – I should have let the needle slip and scarred the fucking bitch for life.'

Sophie made a mental note *never* to have Melissa do electrolysis on her. Not that Melissa ever did beauty treatments for her, now that she was qualified. It had been a different kettle of fish when she'd been training and needed guinea pigs. Sophie had been manicured, pedicured and French polished, not to mention tweezed and waxed within an inch of her life. *That* had been painful!

'That tart is going to Ibiza with him. Can you *believe*

it?' Melissa was incandescent with rage, her usually flawless porcelain skin mottled red with temper. 'Soph, you simply have to come on holidays with me. I'm damned if Jayne' – the cellulite afflicted 'other woman' – 'is going to come into the salon sporting a tan and showing off photos of her and The Rat.

'We'll go somewhere and get the best tan ever and find the most gorgeous hunks to take care of us and our photos will make that fucker pea-green with jealousy. I'll make sure he gets to see them. But even if he comes crawling on his hands and knees, he's history, Soph. I'll go straight to the travel agent's tomorrow and book a holiday for us.'

Melissa assumed automatically that Sophie would drop everything and be thrilled to go on holiday with her.

'I don't know, it's very short notice. I wasn't planning to go abroad,' she'd protested. 'I'm a bit skint.'

'Don't be silly, Sophie. What do you mean short notice? You're not doing anything, are you? You weren't planning on going away, were you?' Melissa scowled. 'I'm skint too. When I found out about The Skunk and that two-faced so-called friend, I went out and blew a fortune on this gorgeous Frank Usher two-piece. It's to die for, Sophie, but my Visa card is having a nervous breakdown, so it will have to be a cheapie for me too. But who cares? We'll strut our stuff on the beach and we won't have to spend a penny,' Melissa retorted confidently, her eyes beginning to sparkle at the thought of her next conquest.

A fortnight in the sun would be nice, Sophie thought dreamily. Lazing on a lounger with a big fat blockbuster novel and a Piña Colada or a dressed Pimm's, while Melissa strutted her perfectly toned and sculptured stuff. Sophie would be quite content to lie on her lounger, her flabby bits not being at all suitable for strutting.

Two weeks later they were sitting in a bar at the airport waiting to board a TransAer flight to Majorca. They'd been delayed for three hours and Melissa was frothing at the mouth.

'This is bloody ridiculous. The plane hasn't even left Palma yet. We're going to be here for hours. That's a whole day wasted. It will be the middle of the night before we get to . . . Portal . . . Portal . . . wherever that place we're going to is.'

'Portal Nous,' Melissa murmured.

'I hope it's going to be a bit lively. It's three miles from Palma Nova. It was all I could get at such short notice,' Melissa fretted.

'It will be fine, Mel, stop panicking,' Sophie placated. 'Now, let's have coffee and a sandwich, I'm a bit peckish.'

Her nerves were frayed. Three hours of Melissa whingeing and moaning about their delayed flight and the devastating betrayal she'd suffered at the hands of The Unmentionable was doing her head in.

'Oh no, not coffee. Let's go and get pissed.' Melissa flung back her golden hair and uncoiled herself from the hard chair she'd been sitting on, quite aware that every male eye in the vicinity was upon her. She undulated towards the bar in her skin-tight white jeans and tightly fitting black halterneck.

Sophie's heart sank. If Melissa went on the sauce, she was in for a load of hassle. Melissa, unfortunately, could not drink, and always needed looking after when she was the worse for wear. Many were the times Sophie had hauled her into loos, or shoved her head out of taxi windows as she threw up all round her.

'Now, Melissa, go easy, you've already had three tequila slammers,' she warned.

'Oh quit it, Soph! You're not my mother!' Melissa snapped as she ordered another drink. 'Do you want one?' she asked ungraciously.

'OK, I'll have a Bud,' Sophie agreed. It might shut Melissa up for a while. Personally, she'd be happy enough to sit in the boarding area and read one of the six books she'd brought with her. She couldn't decide which to start with. The new Bridget Jones or *Memoirs of a Geisha*. She was so looking forward to getting into them.

Three hours later, Melissa was well and truly plastered and had upchucked twice. She was draped across a tall, dark, arty type who was waiting for a flight to Crete.

'We should shange our flight and go to Schrete . . .' she slurred gaily.

'Off you go,' muttered Sophie, utterly pissed off.

Two hours later they finally boarded their flight.

Melissa promptly fell asleep and snored loudly for the duration, her head lolling on Sophie's shoulder. Sophie couldn't believe her luck. She pulled Bridget Jones out of her travel bag and chuckled her way across France and Spain as Melissa's musical snores drowned out the roar of the jet engines.

Unfortunately a bumpy descent into Palma Airport revived both Melissa and her stomach and, for the third time that day, Sophie resisted the urge to drown her in a toilet bowl.

It took another hour to collect their luggage and find the coach that was to take them to their apartment. Sophie found it hard to keep her eyes open as the air-conditioned coach sped along the motorway towards their destination. She half-listened to the forced jolliness of the rep as she reminded her clients to use lots of sun factor and not to imbibe too much San Miguel.

Melissa, green-faced, once again found refuge in sleep.

By the time the coach pulled into the small, two-storey apartment block, Sophie was whacked. It didn't look ultra-modern, she noted as they stopped outside a building that had white flaking paint and two pots of dried-out wilting flowers at the entrance. She was too tired to care as a sullen receptionist took their passports and handed her the key to room 103. They were the only passengers to get off the coach, so at least the check-in was quick, Sophie thought wearily as they click-clacked their way down a tiled floor, dragging their luggage behind them.

'It's a bit kippy,' Melissa moaned as Sophie struggled to get the big black key to turn in the lock.

Basic, was how Sophie would have described it, she reflected as she surveyed a white-painted room with a shabby sofa and two chairs, a pine table and chairs, and an alcove that housed a two-ring cooker, sink and fridge.

The bedroom had a built-in wardrobe whose doors didn't close properly, two divans, and a small bedside locker each. The bathroom, decorated in mustard tiles, was not a place she'd spend too long in, she decided. It was 3 a.m., she was exhausted and Melissa's shrieks of dismay were the last thing she needed.

'Let's go to bed. You chose the apartment, Melissa. It's not my fault. I've had a long day. I don't want to hear any more about it. I've had enough, so zip it,' she exploded tetchily as she pulled off her T-shirt and jeans and dived into the nearest divan.

'There's no need to be like that,' Melissa sniffed huffily as she undressed. 'Can I have some of your bottled water to wash my teeth? My mouth tastes horrible.' Melissa, of course, would never be so organized as to have bottled water. That's what Sophies were for.

'Help yourself,' Sophie yawned as she pulled the white sheet over her and buried her head under the long thin pillow on the narrow divan. At least the sheets were crisp and clean, she thought drowsily. Minutes later she was fast asleep.

She awoke, she had no idea how much later, to high-pitched screeches emanating from a frantic Melissa in the other bed.

'Getawayfromme! Getawayfromme!'

Dazed, Sophie sat up, trying to remember where she was. Melissa was shrieking like a madwoman, arms and legs flailing in the dark. The unmistakable buzzzzz of a mosquito gave a clue to the cause of the drama.

'Oh for God's sake, Melissa, it's a mosquito. Spray some stuff on yourself and go to sleep,' she snarled, finding the light and snapping it on.

'I think it's a bat!' wailed Melissa.

'It's *not* a bat, it's a mosquito. Here.' She sprayed mosquito repellent over the distraught Melissa, then over herself, and switched off the light.

'You've got really grumpy, these days. You used to be much nicer,' Melissa said in her little girl voice.

Spears of guilt prodded Sophie. She was being a bit of a bitch. Melissa had a fear of insects. 'Sorry!' she apologized. 'PMT,' she fibbed.

'We're going to have a good holiday, aren't we?' Melissa asked anxiously.

'We're going to have a *great* holiday. You're going to get a MEGA tan and find a hunk for your photos, and The Skunk is going to be the sorriest idiot in the world.'

'Yes, he is an idiot, isn't he? But I'm not taking him back. Definitely not.'

'No, you're not. He's not worthy of you. There's a much nicer man waiting for you out there,' Sophie said kindly.

'Yes there is. A millionaire, possibly,' Melissa agreed. She always thought big. 'There's a marina around here somewhere, where the *crème de la crème* of the Mediterranean park their yachts.'

'Berth,' Sophie corrected sleepily.

'What?'

'Berth their yachts, not park,' Sophie explained.

'Oh! Right, I better remember that.' She leaned on her elbow and stared over at Sophie. 'You know Majorca is very "in". Don't forget Princess Di used to come here. The Spanish royal family come here and Michael Douglas brought Catherine Zeta Jones here. He has a huge villa in Deya. I've read about it in *Hello!* Maybe we should go there for a day. We'll hire a car.'

'Fine,' murmured Sophie, wishing Melissa would go back to sleep.

'Imagine, if I met a millionaire, I might even invite Tony and Jayne to the wedding,' she fantasized. 'That would really rub their noses in it. Wouldn't it, Soph?'

Silence.

'Sophie?'

But Sophie was asleep. A deep and dreamless sleep.

Sophie came to, to find sunlight dancing through the green shutters and Melissa standing on the patio, arms akimbo as she surveyed the scene in front of her.

'We can't possibly stay here, Sophie!' she declared, aghast. 'It's in the sticks. We don't even have a sea view, which I specifically asked for, and the swimming pool

– if you could *call* it a swimming pool – is no bigger than a *bath*!'

'Beggars can't be choosers, Mel, and after all it was a cancellation – we might not get anywhere else at such short notice.' Sophie scrambled out of bed and went to join her friend on the postage-stamp patio. The sun was shining. That was all that mattered!

She gazed around at the dry, barren scrubland that backed on to a scree-filled cliff dotted with pine trees. They were perched on a small hill. Below she could see other apartment blocks nestled among trees, and in the distance the glittering, silver blue sparkle of sunlight dancing on water.

'There's your sea view.' She grinned, stretching and breathing in the warm scented Mediterranean breeze.

'This is the pits! The pits!' Melissa moaned. 'And look at those kids jumping up and down in the pool. Horrible little beasties. Urrgh.' Melissa was not at all the maternal type.

'Well, it did say suitable for families, and it did say this was a quiet area in the brochure,' Sophie pointed out reasonably.

'I wonder, would they move us to Palma Nova if I kicked up a fuss?' Melissa asked hopefully.

'Let's give it a chance for a day or two until we get our bearings. It's only ten minutes by taxi to Palma Nova anyway; the rep told us last night when you were asleep.'

'Oh, OK then. But if it's dead quiet, were moving

and that's it,' Melissa declared as she marched back into the bedroom. 'Let's go and see what they serve for breakfast in that snack bar by the pool.'

'Yes, let's. I'm starving. And I'm dying for a cup of coffee. Then we can explore.' Sophie didn't care if the apartment wasn't exactly the Ritz. She was in Majorca, the sun was shining and the beach beckoned.

They breakfasted on fresh coffee, croissants, crusty white rolls and jam and fruit. Even Melissa had to admit that it was tasty.

'Let's go to the marina and see if we can nab a millionaire,' she suggested gaily. Her humour was improving by the minute.

Sophie heaved a mental sigh of relief. Maybe they *were* going to have a great holiday.

'*This* is where we're going to breakfast from now on,' Melissa announced joyfully an hour later as they strolled along the sea front cafés. A fifteen-minute walk from their apartment block had brought them to a completely different world. '*This* is where I was born to be.' Melissa was giddy with excitement.

Yachts filled with beautiful people bobbed up and down on the gentle waves. The chic designer boutiques oozed sophistication. There were no prices on display. It was that kind of place.

Melissa sashayed along in her tight white shorts and bikini top, black glass hiding her eyes, for all the world like a film star. Sophie in her denim shorts and black T-shirt felt lumpy and frumpy beside her.

'Let's go to the beach. It's getting hot. I'd like to go for a swim,' she ventured.

'Don't be silly, Soph. We have to do some serious strutting here!' Melissa smiled enticingly at a tanned, gigolo type in a cream Armani suit.

Gigolo smiled back.

'See,' Melissa whispered.

'Mel, you can strut – I'm going to the beach over there and I'm flopping.'

Gigolo was ogling Melissa from head to toe.

'See you on the beach. I'll get a lounger for you,' Sophie offered.

'Fine,' Melissa said snootily. 'If you want to miss the chance of a lifetime to go and slob out on a lounger, do it! I'm staying here.'

'Have fun,' Sophie said drily as Cream-Suited-Gigolo flashed a toothy grin at Melissa.

Melissa smiled demurely back and fluttered her eye-lashes.

Sophie left her to it.

The beach was a golden, curved crescent of paradise. Pine trees fringed the edge of the cliffs. White-crested wisps of waves lapped the shore.

Off the beaten track, it wasn't crowded like the big resort beaches with their serried rows of white loungers. This beach was a little jewel dotted with coconut umbrellas and delightful green loungers that could be hired for the day.

A small island lay about a mile offshore. There were no motor boats or hang gliders or pedalos in sight. It was a most peaceful place. Sophie chose two loungers, laid her towel on one, stripped to her black M&S bikini, lay down, closed her eyes and breathed deeply. She was in heaven. It was too relaxing even to read. A balmy little breeze whispered around her, the sea murmured its soothing, rhythmic lullaby. Sophie fell asleep.

Melissa joined her several hours later. She was on a high.

'Remember that guy?' she asked excitedly. 'He asked me would I like coffee. His name is Paulo and he's *absolutely* loaded! He's staying on a yacht with friends; they're cruising around the islands for a month. Imagine! He asked me out to dinner tonight. What will I wear, Sophie? It will have to be something ultra sophisticated. Do you think the little black silk dress I brought would be OK?'

'It will be fine.' Sophie tried to sound enthusiastic. Melissa hadn't wasted any time. It looked like Sophie would be dining alone tonight. Her heart sank. Just as well she had plenty of books to read.

'I'd better get some serious sunbathing done before tonight.' Melissa unhooked her bikini top and slathered on some Hawaiian Tropic. 'Sophie, it's great that we came to this place. I'd never have met anybody like Paulo in Palma Nova. That marina is mega posh.' She gave a positively beatific smile as she slid elegantly on to her lounger, stretched out and closed her eyes.

Sophie tried not to feel envious as she surveyed her friend. Melissa had everything. Looks, fabulous figure, bubbly personality. No wonder she was never manless for long. A deep sigh came from her toes as she looked at her own tummy that was not flat and taut like Melissa's but curved and rounded with a little soft, jelly sort of bulge, no matter how tight she held her muscles in. Her thighs were dimpled at the top, unlike Melissa's firm, toned, satiny-skinned ones. And there was no denying that she had thick ankles, Sophie thought glumly as she surveyed Melissa's shapely turned ankles and perfectly pedicured feet.

She felt disgruntled . . . and hungry.

'Will we have some lunch?' she asked.

'Oh God, no! I couldn't eat a thing, I'm so excited.' Melissa yawned. 'Besides, Paulo bought me a gorgeous cake with the coffee, earlier.'

'Well, I've had nothing to eat since breakfast. I'll just go and get something myself.' Sophie pulled on her sundress, grabbed her bag and flounced off.

'Enjoy it,' Melissa called airily after her. She hadn't even noticed that Sophie was annoyed.

Bitch! thought Sophie, simmering with resentment. Denise was right. Melissa was so self-centred she thought the world revolved around her. Barely their first day on holidays and Sophie would have to eat alone twice.

She climbed the curving wooden steps up the side of the cliff and tried not to pant. She was so unfit it was a disaster. Still there was nothing she could do about it now. She might as well treat herself to something tasty for lunch, she decided. Food was always a great comforter.

Besides, it was quite nice to sit at a shaded table outside the clifftop restaurant and tuck into deep-fried squid in batter with a crispy, crunchy side salad and sip ice-cold San Miguel beer.

It was her fifth day alone. She might as well have come on a singles holiday after all, Sophie reflected as she lay on the lounger in her favourite spot on the beach. Melissa had spent two days with Paulo after the first momentous dinner-date.

'You don't mind, lovie. He's such a pet. You should hear the gorgeous things he says to me and he's *such* a gentleman. He's really smitten, Soph,' Melissa twittered as she changed into yet another outfit for a shopping trip to Palma. That night she arrived back at the apartment, eyes aglow.

'You'll never guess, Soph? Paulo has asked me to go to Ibiza on the yacht. I'm so excited.'

'How long are you going for?' Sophie demanded. She was furious.

'Don't be like that, Soph,' Melissa muttered defensively. 'This is the chance of a lifetime. Paulo is just what I need after The Rat.'

'Look, Melissa, you asked me to come on holiday with you. So far we've had one breakfast together and I've been left to my own devices ever since. You're being really selfish and I don't think much of your behaviour,' Sophie exploded.

'No, *you're* being selfish!' Melissa rounded on her. 'This could be the best thing that's ever happened to me and if you were truly my friend you wouldn't be so mean.' She took her case from the wardrobe and began to pack. Sophie felt like thumping her. How typical of Melissa to turn the argument to her advantage.

They didn't speak for the rest of the night. The following morning Sophie kept her head under the pillow until she heard Melissa leave the apartment, dragging her case behind her.

So much for the gentleman, he didn't even come to collect the cow, she thought grumpily as she heard the click-clack of Melissa's white high heels fade away.

Surprisingly, once her anger and resentment had abated somewhat, Sophie had actually enjoyed herself. She spent her days on the beach, reading, swimming, watching the incredibly confident, affluent young Spaniards who congregated after school. It was an entertainment in itself. At night she took a taxi to Palma Nova, ate at one of the beach-side restaurants and then browsed around the myriad of shops before going home to sit on her patio with her book and an ice-cold Malibu. The days melted into one another and Sophie realized that being on holiday alone was not half as daunting as she'd imagined. It was a liberation of sorts to know that she was perfectly capable of enjoying herself alone.

She was enjoying the late afternoon rays, immersed in her crime novel, when a child's piercing scream rent the air. Sophie looked up to see a little Spanish girl of about four howling in pain as her elderly grandfather tried to comfort her. She had seen them come to the beach every afternoon and thought they were so sweet. The grandfather doted on the little girl and made magnificent sand castles to entertain her.

Sophie jumped up and hurried over. 'Can I help? I'm a nurse,' she said.

'Oh, thank you very much. Maria has been stung.' The man spoke perfect English.

Sophie soothed the little girl then turned to the grandfather. 'Could you get me some vinegar from the restaurant and I'll remove the sting and put some cream on it.' The old man spoke in rapid Spanish to a young student nearby who raced off up the steps towards the restaurant.

Sophie kept talking in calm, comforting tones to the little girl, who has stopped screaming but whimpered pitifully.

She squealed again as Sophie applied the vinegar and removed the sting, but once the balm of antiseptic cream had done its trick she was soon playing again, the incident forgotten.

The grandfather was effusive in his thanks. 'My daughter is pregnant and Maria's nanny had to return to Madrid as her mother is very ill. So I've been looking after her in the afternoons,' he explained. 'I am Juan Santander.' He held out his hand.

'Sophie Irvine,' Sophie recriprocated.

They chatted easily for a while. It was nice to have someone to talk to.

'Your friend has not come back?' Juan remarked. 'She was here with you just one day.'

How observant, Sophie thought.

'She went on a cruise to Ibiza.'

'Did you not want to go?' Juan enquired.

'I wasn't asked.' Sophie laughed.

'I see.' His eyes were kind. 'You will be here tomorrow?'

'Yes.'

'We will see you then.' Juan gathered up his grand-daughter's bits and pieces. 'Tomorrow.'

The following afternoon, Sophie smiled as she saw the pair make their descent down the steps. Maria raced over to proudly show off her bandage.

Juan winked. 'For such an injury a bandage was necessary. May we join you?'

'Please do,' Sophie invited.

'I wonder, would you consider something?' Juan asked. 'I told my daughter what had happened and that you were a nurse and that your friend had left you alone. We wondered if perhaps you would like to come and stay with us for a few days in our villa up in the hills? We have a pool and lovely grounds and it is most comfortable. My daughter is looking for someone to mind Maria and the new baby for at least six months. Maybe you might be interested in the position. If you spent a few days with us, you would know if it is something you would like.'

Sophie's eyes widened. It seemed a fantastic prop-osition. Leave dreary, humid, stuffy old London and spend six months in this paradise. It sounded like a dream.

To her amazement she heard herself say, 'I'd love to.'

'Excellent. Can you come today?'

'I'll just go up to the apartment and get my things.'

'We'll collect you. Just give me the address,' Juan instructed. 'We will pick you up in an hour, won't we, Maria?' He spoke in Spanish to his little granddaughter.

'Si, si.' The little girl hopped up and down with excitement.

'See you in an hour then.' Sophie couldn't believe how impulsive she was being. But this was the chance of a lifetime.

She had just packed her books when the door of the apartment burst open. Melissa appeared, red-eyed and on crutches.

'Thank God I'm here. That bastard was so callous. I broke my leg in Ibiza and he couldn't get rid of me quick enough. I even had to get a taxi at the marina. They let me off and then they sailed away. Can you believe it?' Melissa burst into tears. 'My luggage is in reception – can you collect it for me?' she sniffled.

'Sure.' Sophie's heart sank as she headed off to reception. Trust Melissa to do something dramatic and break her leg. She saw a big silver Mercedes drive up to the entrance. It was Juan and Maria. She couldn't really go with them now and leave Melissa.

She'd leave you, a little voice said. Sophie stood stock-still. What kind of a fool was she? Melissa wouldn't think twice about putting herself first. It was time Sophie did the same. For once in her life she was going to do something spontaneous. She lugged Melissa's case back to the apartment.

'Why is your bag packed? Where are you going?' Melissa demanded as Sophie hauled the case into the bedroom.

'To stay with friends,' she said jauntily.

'What friends? You don't have friends here,' Melissa snorted.

'Yes I do. Look out the window. See that silver car over at reception?'

Melissa's jaw dropped. 'Who are they?'

'Sorry I can't stay and explain, Mel. Have to go.'

'But you can't go!' Melissa was incredulous. 'You can't leave me! My leg is broken. I'm on crutches. How will I manage?'

'You'll be fine. We're on the ground floor. You can eat by the pool. You can sunbathe. The rep will bring you to the airport. No worries.' Sophie was enjoying herself.

'But you're a nurse. You have a duty to sick people!' Melissa raged. This wasn't the Sophie she knew. 'You can't leave me here on my own!' she fumed.

'Watch me,' Sophie drawled as she lifted her bag from the bed.

'Good-bye, Melissa. Enjoy the rest of your holiday. I know I'm going to. To tell you the truth it's the *best* holiday I ever had.'

A Year Later

'Did you hear about Sophie Irvine? She's engaged to some wealthy Spanish doctor she met when she was working in Majorca. They're getting married next month, Denise was telling me. Flying the whole family out to Majorca for the wedding!' Angie O'Neill told Melissa as they tidied up the salon after a very busy day.

Melissa's fingers curled and her lips tightened with envy. What a bitch that Sophie Irvine had turned out to be. Leaving her alone in that grotty little apartment with a broken leg. She hadn't seen her from that day to this. And now to hear that she was engaged to a rich Spanish doctor. Was there no justice in the world?

'Don't mention that girl's name to me. I thought she was a friend. Little did I know until she stabbed me in the back.'

'She stabbed you in the back!' Angie was astonished.

'Not literally, you idiot,' Melissa snapped. 'I invited her to go on holiday and then she met these people and left me in the lurch, on my own with a broken leg. Can you believe that?'

'*Really*? I'd never have thought it of Sophie. She sounds like a bit of a fairweather friend. Just as well you have me to go on holiday with this year,' Angie soothed. 'I wouldn't do anything like that.'

'I know, sweetie.' Melissa smiled. 'You'll love where we're going to. It has a marina full of yachts and rich people. It will be the best holiday ever.'

'I can't wait!' exclaimed Angie excitedly. 'Thanks for inviting me to come.'

'You're very welcome,' said Melissa graciously. 'Could you be a pet and finish off here? I've a thumping headache.'

'Oh! OK,' Angie murmured. Funny how Melissa always got a thumping headache on Friday evenings when the salon had to be cleaned.

'See you at the airport tomorrow.'

Melissa swanned out of the salon leaving her new best friend to tidy up. Angie would be an *excellent* holiday companion, she thought with satisfaction. Not like the soon-to-be-married Judas Irvine.

Clare Naylor was born in 1971 in Yorkshire. She studied English Literature at London University. A prizewinner in the *Vogue* Young Writer's Talent Contest in 1993 she has worked as a journalist and as an editorial assistant. She has written two novels, *Love: A User's Guide* and *Catching Alice* and has just finished her third novel. She has co-written and plans to produce an original screenplay *The Accidental Husband* and divides her time between London and New York.

Something Different

Clare Naylor

'It might help if you were in a car accident.' Tim had said to Anna. She looked at him with a squint of the eye. Wondering if she'd heard him correctly. 'If you were in a coma or something then I'd realize how much I loved you. How we're meant to be together forever and I'd be overcome with the urge to marry you.'

'So if I were to die you'd want me back?' Anna asked, unable to process the car accident revelation.

'Yeah, I really think I would.' Tim said as though this in itself were a declaration of the most romantic sort.

'But as it is you're leaving me? Think you can do better?' She continued picking the scab of their five-year relationship. She didn't want to be left with a shiny white scar but neither could she help herself from nudging away at the edges until a little bead of blood popped out.

'It's not that. It's just that if you have green beans every night for five years you get a bit bored. Kind of want something else.' Tim sat on her bed and continued to look as appealing as he always had despite having just revealed his true self, his soul, as a rotting, stinking

Freddy Krueger type of man. He was certainly not Julian Sands in *A Room With a View* as she'd once imagined. Though his hair was blond.

Too many green beans. Anna supposed she should be thankful that he hadn't said that life with her was like broad beans. That would have been unrecoverable from. Green beans could perhaps be fixed with something tiny from Agent Provocateur. Broad beans would have involved two months in the gym, a frontal lobotomy and a visit to a discreet man in Harley Street to prune the tip off her nose or whatever the prescribed treatment was to win back your man these days.

As it was she never made it to Agent Provocateur. She couldn't get away from her desk any lunchtime that week and so sadly by Friday she'd been rendered single. Cut adrift. Just like that. One evening in Pizza Express and many crumpled tissues down the line she'd ceased to be Anna'n'Tim and become any one of any number of casualties of that daunting statistic which dictates that there are about seventeen spare women for every man. So any woman with a man should consider herself blessed. The statistic which means that any old banker, no matter how dull his conversation or cheap his deodorant, can get a date any given night of the week and every woman, no matter how many A-levels or how immaculately highlighted her hair, has to stay at home on Friday nights hiding her Agent Provocateur under a bushel. Or a pair of Gap sweatpants, and watch comedy on BBC2. Anna was a Singleton. One of the

Bridget Jones generation. She'd have to start making friends with gay men so that when she reached thirty-three she'd have a donor for the child she knew she'd never have now because she clearly couldn't make a relationship work. Anna was alone.

'Poor you.' Laura poured Anna another glass of wine and fiddled with her wedding ring. 'But I know you'll be fine. You're still young, that Internet bloke at mine and Andrew's dinner party the other month really fancied you. Tim will realize that the grass isn't always greener. He'll be back,' Laura reassured. Though somewhere in her mind she too was less than certain. She'd read this really chilling article in the *Daily Mail* the other day about women who had careers and everything and whose tits hadn't even *begun* to sag and even they were forced to go to dating agencies, so bad was the man drought these days.

Anna dripped tears into her wine, 'Do you really think he will? I mean the grass isn't really greener, is it? We were happy, you know.'

She remembered the rosy Sunday six months ago when they'd driven to Kent and walked along the seafront and eaten Cornettos at a motorway service station on the way home. She forgot that she had spent every Sunday since cooking things out of the *River Café Cookbook* for when Tim came home hungry from golf. She'd forgotten that she'd had a crush on the man on her bus to work for the last six months. She'd put that down to hormonal flux. Not the fact that Tim had become as dull as a dishrag and was asleep by ten-thirty even on Saturday nights. Selective memory syndrome. Playing the Victim. She knew the phrases. She knew that their relationship had been as dead as a dodo but she was just so bloody paralysed by the fact that there was only one man for every twenty-seven women. (Last week's *Guardian*. Could have been a typo, but she chose the less scenic route of the pessimist.) And so Anna ignored the flags and the signposts and the big fluorescent landing strip to Liberation From The Wrong Boyfriend and instead took to her bed. And her diary, which became fat with clichés and sadness and quotes from bad slow songs. And her friend's kitchens where she cashed in her compassion chips that she'd been storing up throughout her relatively trouble-free five years with Tim.

'You're so skinny.' Lucy walked up the stairs to the beauty salon behind Anna.

'Misery. I've cried every day for the last two months. Doesn't leave much time for eating. Sometimes I think it'll be okay and I'll be halfway through nibbling a prawn ball and I remember that we've split up. That he doesn't love me any more, and I just want to spit the prawn ball out again.'

'I should break up more often. I look like a heifer even in my fat-girl jeans at the moment.' Lucy put her arm round Anna's shoulders to show she didn't mean it and ushered her into the warm face-cream scented

SOMETHING DIFFERENT

reception of the hottest, coolest salon in town. On the wall was a photo of Gwyneth Paltrow with, 'Thanks. Your bikini wax changed my life' scrawled across the bottom. Anna wished she were Gwyneth with a reputation for loving and leaving before the glow faded and the men discovered what went on between waxing sessions. The days you weren't on hot, Oscar-winning, pink-dress-wearing form. Gwyneth never stuck around long enough to become a plate of green beans. She was a spear of asparagus. Not in season long enough for a boy to tire of her. Anna had learned this if nothing else. Never take your eye off the ball. Never think that your dazzling wit is enough. Always keep up with your bikini wax.

Anna looked at the diagrams before her and hastily pointed to the one with the most hair. The heart-shaped one would have been cute if she didn't have a doctor's appointment booked for next Monday and the others were best left to Japanese porn stars. Anna looked apologetically at the disappointed beautician.

'Just the plain old triangle for me,' she mumbled as she lay back on the couch.

'I asked for the triangle and she gave me the one called Mohicana. Can you believe it? It's obscene. It's like going to the loo with a stranger. Just as well I don't have a boyfriend or he'd think I was a complete pervert.' Anna returned to the table from the Ladies and blew the froth off her cappuccino with a splutter somewhere between mirth and horror.

'You got the stripper wax.' Lucy grinned proudly.

'You'll be addicted in no time. It's incredibly erotic. Trust me.' Anna felt like the Country Mouse in Lucy's wake. 'Just don't waste it.'

But what was she meant to do with it, Anna wondered as she pulled on her pyjama bottoms that night. She hadn't kissed another man in five years. She'd had fantasies about Bus Man but she would never in a billion years have done anything other than run the rest of the way to work if he'd actually propositioned her. No, she'd been totally committed to Tim. And now she was totally committed to his memory. And to dreams of what could have been. And what still might be if everyone she knew was right. They all concurred that not only was the grass not greener out there in Eyes Met Across a Crowded All Bar One But She Didn't Look Nearly So Hot When I Was Sober In Her Flat Above A Shop In Fulham The Next Morning Land but that the grass was positively mud. Tim would be back with his tail between his legs and a diamond ring in his pocket in no time. Anna lived for the day. She vacillated between the country wedding and the impromptu Chelsea Registry Office job where she'd buy her shoes from Manolo Blahnik en route and call her parents from the mobile to invite them along. Either way it meant happily ever after etc. The fact that before Tim had mentioned his car accident fantasy and the whole green beans thing she'd never had a wedding dream in her life seemed irrelevant. She'd merely been oblivious to her heart's true desire. Which was to spend the rest of

every waking moment with a man who had once bought
her a bar of soap for Christmas. Who could discard
what had essentially (apart from the soap) been a brilliant friendship, relationship and all-round Good Thing
on the grounds that he hadn't sampled every sweetie
in the shop yet. That he might, on a good night with
a few pints inside him, be able to do better. But still
Anna longed for him. Yearned.

'Please God just let him come back before my fabulous bikini line grows back,' she mumbled as she
climbed into bed to fill her diary with more clichés
about love and marriage and how beautiful their children would be when Tim came to his senses.

Hope took a battering a few weeks later when she called
Tim about a book of hers he still had and hoped for a
warm, comforting chat full of reminiscences and the
drip drip of regret on his part. He was well. Yeah, fine.
Definitely had been the right thing for them and all
that. He was a bit busy at the moment but maybe they
could meet up in a few weeks for a beer or something.
Anna put the phone down and became catatonic with
grief. If there was a wall to hit she'd rushed headlong
into it and crumpled. This was rock bottom. The lowest.
The gutter of things. But in all the clichés she filled her
diary with it never occurred to her that after this
moment the only way was up.

Every other man looked wrong; told buttock-
clenchingly embarrassing jokes; or simply wasn't Tim.

And she looked. She learned to dress the new reduced Anna in up-for-it skirts and saucy boots, and discovered a flattering thing to do with her fringe. She looked at men in a way that suggested she might want to have sex with them even if she didn't really. And the list of men's mobile numbers scrawled on the back of her *Yellow Pages* beside the phone seemed to suggest that the statistics might have lied. That perhaps there were in fact seventeen men for every woman rather than the other way around. And one night after she'd been to a Pimms-on-the-lawn vibe with some work friends she began to suspect that there might even be twenty-seven men for every woman. Anna's success rate was high. Which in turn made her skin glow in a way that sparkly powder couldn't. Which led to more mobile numbers and a battery of excuses on her part. Because, sadly, whilst the statistics were wrong the clichés remained. Tim had been The One For Her. He had been the milk on her cornflakes. The only one who could make her truly happy.

And right up until the very last second she hadn't believed it could be true. She didn't even know what she was doing here in the office at eleven-thirty. The small drinks party had finished hours ago and the flotsam of conversation had drifted away along the corridors, out into the street to nearby restaurants and down into the tube station. Only Anna and someone from marketing called Simon remained behind. She picked at the white plastic cups, lifting their rims with her teeth until she had a small graveyard of cups on the desk beside her. Simon sat on the desk and folded a memo about the staff rounders game into ever smaller pieces.

And even as he leaned over to kiss her. As he broke off his sentence about how he'd lived in New Orleans for two years to bend down to kiss her on the swivel chair. Even as he did this she had no idea whether she fancied him or not, or how she got here. She wasn't even drunk. Her last cup of white wine had been at least an hour ago and yet her hands were touching the back of his head and she was kissing him. Still not sure why. And it was different. As she put her hand to his cheek it wasn't sharp like Tim's but soft, and his hair was shorter. And the earlobes weren't the familiar ones she'd fiddled with every lazy morning for as far back as her memory could take her. But though it wasn't Tim it wasn't bad. She knew the moves. Took his fingers in her mouth as his hand slipped under her T-shirt. Smelled his skin and didn't have to run from the room. In fact she wanted to stay. Anna was kissing Simon. She'd never kissed a Simon before. Hadn't kissed a man with black hair since she was seventeen. But it was all right.

The next morning as she sat in bed chewing her pen the clichés crowded her head. She picked up the ringing phone.

'Anna, it's Lucy. What happened last night? You stayed late.'

'Yeah, I did.' Anna lay back on the pillow ready for

a long one. 'He's nice. I mean, I don't know. It's different.' She thought about it and smiled. 'But it's not serious. I mean, I'm not ready for anything like that. I mean, I'm still heartbroken and stuff.'

'Just one thing. Did he smell nice?' Lucy asked. Anna thought back to the fluorescent lighting of the office. The way he'd kissed her in the lift on the way down to reception at midnight. The taste of him.

'Yeah. He did.' She smiled to herself.

After she'd put the phone down on Lucy. After Lucy had asked whether she'd made the most of her bikini wax. After Anna had told her that she hadn't but that she had come home with her bra in her handbag. After they'd made a lot of noise and laughed a lot, Anna picked up her pen. Reached for a cliché.

'Splitting up with Tim was the best thing that ever happened,' she scrawled.

Polly Samson was born in London in 1962. She has worked in publishing and as a journalist and has also written song lyrics. Her short stories have appeared in the *Observer* and the *Sunday Express* and have been read on BBC Radio Four and BBC Radio Scotland. A collection of her stories, *Lying in Bed* and a novel, *Out of the Picture*, are published by Virago.

The Itch

Polly Samson

He has his back to me while I tell him about my day: the fresh Cornish crab I bought at the fish shop for our supper, lunch with my mother at Peter Jones. 'It's got worse,' I say. 'Her hands shake so badly she spilt soup in her lap.' The hem of his jacket is down, the light catches a spidery thread hanging there and I wonder, has he always looked out of the window when I talk? There's nothing much to see outside. Just the lawn, still striped from his weekend mowing, and next door's cat asleep on the wall.

'Lucky for you the crab's already dead,' I point out as I chop purple shallots on a board. His hand strays across the table to last Saturday's *Telegraph Sport*.

'I hate the thought of them screaming,' I say.

'It's only air escaping,' he says, glancing at a racing page that I feel sure he must already have committed to heart.

I slice cleanly through tomatoes and wonder if it's possible that he no longer thinks about other times; that for all he cares to remember we might never have cooked together or bought live crabs from a Cornish fisherman. It's unfair really, isn't it? There are things that I would like to forget but I can't and then there are happy memories that I cling to, with a real effort, like squinting at a Picasso to see the face behind the abstraction.

The tomatoes then were from the little shop in the Cornish village and were more knobbly than the slippery supermarket ones I've just cut. The knives in the cottage were blunter too: seeds splurged from the gashes I made in the tomato skins and spilt on to the breadboard like spawn. We cobbled together our supper to the sound of a tinny transistor radio, Johnny Walker's hits from the seventies: 'Play that Funky Music', and Boney M, and songs about summer and love from *Grease*. We danced around each other in that unknown kitchen, lost in the moment, as though fate were our choreographer and Venus a puppeteer pulling our strings. Alan rubbed garlic on to toast, heaped the tomatoes on top and added swirls of olive oil. I swung washed green salad in a tea towel above my head, allowing drops to splatter violently in wet stripes against the window and walls and to fall on to us like rain; he pulled the cork from the wine and wiped debris from inside the neck with his finger. 'Mamma Mia, Here I go again . . .' We mimed the songs into stainless steel salt and pepper shakers: 'My, my, how can I resist you . . .' We leant towards each other until our shoulders touched, really, we did . . .

'Do you remember?' I say, but he's already dialling a number. He's standing with his back to me, the telephone cradled between his shoulder and ear, a file from the office scattering papers on to the dresser before him. 'Hello, so sorry I wasn't able to get back to you earlier today. Now, about those prices . . .'

I hum to myself. I remember.

How bright we were. Not just younger. Everything around us was more brilliantly coloured and we moved through life on lighter feet. Dancing indeed! Funny that I can remember more about our time in Portreath than I can about, say, last weekend. Was it roast beef or roast chicken? I have no idea. But I can picture us in that cottage right down to the jam jar of sea pinks on the table and if I stand here now and lick my hand it reminds me of Al's skin and him lying on the sand.

It was supposed to have been crab supper then too: a pair of them, the size of ornamental fans scuttered across the cottage floor on stiletto claws when the fisherman tipped them from his sack and I screamed at their lollypop eyes.

'Well, of course they're looking at you,' laughed Al, my boyfriend, as my husband Alan then was. 'How can you possibly expect them not to?'

Petroc the fisherman licked his cold-sores with a fat tongue, nodded his agreement. Up and down went his head while his eyes popped at me until I was more afraid of him than the crabs.

'Thank you, very much,' said my husband-to-be noticing my panic and ushering him away from where

I stood. He held open the door: 'Tell me, what do we owe you?'

One of the crabs lay half-heartedly inspecting its claw under the table, the other was manoeuvring itself along the skirting board, scraping and rattling like a clockwork toy. I tried to stop my hands shaking as I set water to boil in the large tin pan. The letting agent had pointed to it in the scullery, said it was what all the visitors used when they bought from the crabman who would surely come calling. He never missed a sale when the cottage was rented, apparently. 'Likes to grab an eyeful of the lady visitors, does old Petroc,' the agent had told Alan, jerking his thumb to where I stood looking out at the sea through the kitchen window.

I left Al to watch over the water while I walked down to the shop by the beach huts for salad. I took much longer than necessary; stopping to talk to a dog, reading the labels on bottles of sauce, choosing new shoelaces. The impending death of the crabs hung over me, pressing down on me like a lid; I wanted to be neither executioner nor accomplice. By the time I forced myself back into the kitchen, the pan was trembling as steam made a cymbal of the lid, clanging away and starting the crabs up again in clipping tangos across the stone flags. Al looked at me, his brows high, a question. 'No way,' I said, dumping the paper bags on to the work surface. 'I'm not doing it.' I had my hand on the door through to the other room, I could smell the blood and guts of the fishing boat, probably from the sack that

Petroc had left on the floor, and I thought how strange it was that I'd always known that smell as fear.

Al looked from the crabs on the floor to the boiling pan of water, back to the crabs, and then to me, still standing by the door. I couldn't tell if the brightness in his eyes was laughter or anger. I hadn't known him long enough, though he'd been fantasizing about eating fresh crab all the way down in the car. It wasn't until he spoke that I realized I had been holding my breath. 'I'm not really all that hungry,' he said, and I let out a sigh.

'There's tomatoes and stuff,' I said, 'and we can have some toast.'

Then he tuned the radio to Johnny Walker and that's when we danced, elated because our merciful hearts beat as one and our eyes were bright with the power of absolution.

There was the occasional click of shell on shell to remind us about the crabs which were safely back in the sack, coaxed there by Al and the fire shovel while I hid in the back room. We ate the tomatos on toast and salad by candlelight, sitting huddled together at a little blue painted table by the back door with the beach stretching into the shadows beyond the sandy patch of rough grass and the sea wall.

We mopped our plates clean of juice and oil with bread torn straight from the loaf and drank cold white wine from heavy tumblers because we couldn't find stem glasses. It was one of those meals that you know will be memorable even before the moment has passed.

I sat back and tried to stop my mind from wandering while Al cleared away the plates.

'Right, I think it's time,' he said, coming back from the kitchen with the sack. Together we clambered on to the wall and jumped down to the beach where the seaweed was strewn across the sand like rags. There was half a moon that night and I watched as Al became a silhouette, a shadow-dancer, halfway down the beach, tipping open the sack, holding it by its corners at arm's-length, to release the crabs. He had to shake it quite hard in the end as the crabs clung to the hessian, their pincers clipping and snapping like surgical instruments. The sack had become their comfort blanket. I stayed where I was as he finally managed to untangle them and I heard them fall on to the sand with two little thumps, like shoes on to a carpet, before they scuttled towards the glittering darkness that was the sea.

The crabs disappeared into the shadows long before they reached the water. I could see the marks they had left in the sand, like scars or stitches or lines of perforations to be torn apart. Al went back to the cottage for the remainder of the wine and then we sat on the damp sand, side by side, swigging from the bottle like teenagers.

I was leaning back on to my elbows and looking up at the stars and for a moment I felt entirely at peace in a way that I hadn't managed since I was a small child. But then Al, in all his innocence, touched me and the strength of his hands brought the blackness back, like old bruises made new. He pushed me on to my back, beside the stinking fisherman's sack. He pinned me there, with my skirt around my waist and the rough grittiness of the beach against my skin. He was using his knee to push my legs apart. I wanted to cry out. I wanted him to know about me without my having to tell him: I needed him to understand that gentleness and privacy were the only options. His fingers were rubbing me, but I knew I'd stay dry while I fought the panic that was knotting me up like old rope.

'No, stop.' I tried not to scream as the sound of the waves grew ever louder in my ears, except it wasn't the sea, it was his breathing.

'Ssh,' said Al then, his hand over my mouth. 'I can hear someone,' and rising from his knees he shouted, 'Who's there?'

There was the scrunch of boots on sand behind my head but on our side of the sea wall. 'Evening to you,' and then a rumble like laughter, muffled by a sleeve.

'The crabman,' whispered Al, as Petroc, hunched and snaily inside his oilskin, continued on his way to check his pots, his torch beam swaying before him but leaving us untouched by its light.

I could still hear the sea through the bedroom window and the light from the lamp outside was soft through the open curtains. Al's mood had changed between the beach and the cottage and he unwrapped me gently, as though I was made from bone china. He brushed the

sand from my legs as I pushed my shoulder blades deep
into the pillows which made my breasts rise towards
him; I pulled in my stomach so that – from the outside
at least – he would believe me perfect. The pillows
sighed beneath us as he leant over me, drawing himself
inside so tenderly that I could believe it was the first
time for us both and his brown eyes stayed open, warm
and liquid as malted milk, even at the end when his
breathing became more frightening.

'I didn't withdraw.' It was later, I don't know how
long, but he was stroking my face with soft fingers,
as we lay face to face, curled into one another like
babies.

I should have told him then. It doesn't matter.

'I love you,' he said, 'I hope you don't mind.'

Why would I mind?

There were things about me he didn't know then.
About the scars inside. About the things those men had
used, the meat reek of them, the smell of my own
blood, their eyes closing in on me, so many years ago
that for most of my life I could pretend it never happened. My therapist once told me – I think it was while
I was still in the hospital – that within seven years, not
a single cell of my body would remain that those men
had touched. I suppose she wanted to give me something to look forward to when she said that.

'I want to marry you,' Al said. I should have told
him. 'I want you to have my babies,' he said. Then I
knew it was wrong of me not to say and I started to
cry. The sea rushed to the shore, close enough that it

sounded like it was boiling on the stones. 'Marry me,' he said.

I always think there's something rather disgusting about preparing a crab; the juiciness, the trickle on your fingers from the wet brown meat you've scooped out, like scrapings from the inside of a skull, and after that, probing with a skewer into the fiddly places makes me think of bits of brain being pulled from an ear and I get a pain in my own, like when you stick a Q-tip in too far, or a hairpin. There was something on the radio the other day about how you can slice a brain any way you like but you won't find a morsel called memory.

I mix the meat with finely chopped shallots, tomatoes, cayenne, salt and pepper and spoon it back into the shell, packing it neatly like cement. Alan likes it like that and it really is the least I can do, though he's never as appreciative as I would like him to be.

There was a time. Candy-stripe sheets on a rented bed and Al's fingers following the lines of tears on my face. 'Nothing you tell me will change the way I feel,' he said and for a while I allowed him to believe that I was perfect. There was a time by the sea that Al was so dazzled by love that he couldn't see anything deeper than the blush on my skin.

I lie in bed, Al becomes Alan once more and the world fades.

'You do realize we'll have been married seven years next month?' I say.

'That's what it must be then,' he says. Perhaps he thinks that I no longer understand his sarcasm.

'Someone once told me that there's a scientific explanation for the seven-year itch,' I continue. 'Apparently it takes that long for each and every cell in the body to die and regenerate. Strange to think there's nothing of us left that set those crabs free on the night you asked me to marry you.'

He doesn't reply, instead he clicks off the bedside light. He likes to wait until he thinks I'm asleep before he starts on me. I shut my eyes, let my breathing deepen. It's not long before I feel Alan reach out and lift my nightdress, efficiently, like a surgeon. His fingers move across my stomach like calipers and I no longer bother to breathe in as his hands pass.

Alecia McKenzie was born in Kingston, Jamaica. After university in the United States, she worked for several media organizations including the *New York Times* Regional Newspaper Group, *The Wall Street Journal Europe* and InterPress Service. In 1992, her first book of short stories, *Satellite City,* was published, winning the regional Commonwealth Writers Prize for Best First Book the following year. Since then it has been translated into Dutch, Italian and Polish. Alecia is also the author of *When the Rain Stopped in Natland*, a novella. Her stories have appeared in literary magazines (*The Malahat Review, Deus Ex Machina, Kunapipi, The Journal of Caribbean Literatures*) as well as in anthologies such as *The Oxford Book of Caribbean Short Stories, The Penguin Book of Caribbean Short Stories, Das Paradies liegt vor dem Fenster* and others. The title of her forthcoming book is *Racconti Giamaicani*. She lives in London.

Morro

Alecia McKenzie

His mouth tasted of cane juice. His hands, too, when he touched her face smelled of sugarcane. She wondered drowsily whether he were a juice vendor, but his sculpted body said otherwise, and besides she hadn't seen any juice stalls here on Morro de São Paolo; back in Salvador she had seen quite a few, screaming with germs.

She pulled back from him, reluctantly, the realization hitting her that they were still in public, the object of amused glances from the few people already out on the beach before breakfast.

She had gone to lie on a beach chair in front of the pousada as soon as there'd been enough sunlight. And it had taken five minutes for him to approach and stand looking down at her. 'Where are you from,' he had asked in Portuguese. She had looked up at him and immediately quelled the brush-off that had risen in her mouth. Jesus, what did Brazilian men do to look like this? He was amber-coloured, with curly reddish hair and brown-green eyes. But that was nothing compared to the body—toned muscles emerging upwards and downwards from the skimpy bikini trunks. Her eyes swept from head to feet and noticed he had a crudely wrapped bandage around his right big toe.

'I'm from Jamaica,' she answered.

He put a hand over his heart. 'It's my dream to go there,' he said. 'Bob Marley.'

Oh Christ, everywhere she'd been in Bahia she'd got the same response. She'd seen Bob's face emblazoned on hundreds of T-shirts being sold in the streets of Pelourinho, and she'd been laughed at when she asked if they hadn't a T-shirt with Jorge Ben Jor on it.

She gave her muscled friend a broad smile. 'Jimmy Jallah,' she said.

His grin shone whitely in the morning sun. 'Yes, Jimmy Jallah, he lives here in Brazil.'

She nodded. She knew that. It was Jimmy who had invited her to Bahia the four times she'd been there to perform, but she didn't tell the young man that. 'Peter Tosh,' she said instead, and he did an enthusiastic thumbs-up sign.

'Shabba Ranks, Mr Lover Man,' he said. Now he sat down in the chair next to hers.

'Me, I like Ras Michael and the Sons of Negus,' she told him, reaching back into her youth.

His face went blank.

'And Jacob Miller. My God, he was a good singer, but he's dead now,' she continued.

Her new friend frowned slightly.

'Don Drummond, that was the best musician we ever had. He played trombone but he killed his girlfriend and died in Bellevue – that's a madhouse.'

He was losing interest so she had pity on him and asked, 'Do you like Ziggy Marley?'

His smile returned. '"Look Who's Dancing",' he said.

'Yes, that's my favourite too,' she agreed.

He looked long at her, one of his eyes slightly squinted, a movie-bad-guy gaze. 'I always wanted to kiss a Jamaican girl,' he said.

It was the 'girl' bit that did it. If he were sweet, or nearsighted, enough to call a tough-back forty-five-year-old woman like her a 'girl', he deserved a kiss. So she slowly sat up and bent towards him. But before she knew what was happening, there were tongue and teeth involved and waves of warm sea water were rushing through her head. He was good. If she'd been standing up she would've had to sit down.

A second after the kiss ended came the unwelcome thought that he had said he'd always wanted to kiss 'a Jamaican *girl*'. He probably hadn't meant *her* at all. Had she made a blasted fool of herself? But he was smiling at her as if he wanted to do it again. She shifted back in the chair and put on her shades.

'What is your name?' she asked, making her voice formal.

'Paolo,' he said, and she wondered whether it was an easy alias, derived from the name of this part of the island.

'What's yours?'

She gave him the second half of it. 'Marie.'

'Where did you learn Portuguese?'

'A friend.' Her face clouded momentarily as she thought of Antonio. But she made his image go blank. 'Besides, this is the fourth time I've been to Brazil.'

'Do you like it?'

'Of course, otherwise I wouldn't have come back.'

'You're the first Jamaican I've ever met.'

'Yes,' she said drily. 'We like to go to North America, not South.' But he didn't get it.

'Are you staying at this pousada?'

She looked towards the pastel orange-yellow walls of the Casa das Pedras guesthouse, and nodded.

'There's a party at the bar next door tonight? Do you want to come?'

'You mean they're going to have another party tonight? I couldn't sleep because of the loud music last night, and I thought this was supposed to be low season.'

'They have a party there every night,' Paolo said. He sounded impatient. 'Do you want to come? I can meet you here at ten o'clock.'

'Well, since I won't be able to sleep, I may as well go.'

'OK,' he said. 'I have to go to work now. *Ate logo.*' He squinted, smiled and walked off down the beach, limping slightly. She watched him through her shades and hoped, Jesus, hoped, that he was at least twenty-five. Make him please be older than my son.

She waited until he had mounted the steps that led from the beach up to the 'town' before rising from her chair. She wrapped the *canga* she'd bought in Salvador two days ago tightly round her waist and, satisfied that her not-as-firm-as-they-used-to-be thighs were hidden, she went back into the Casa das Pedras for breakfast. The buffet was impressive, with the heaps of fried and boiled plantains, slices of pineapple, papaya and melon, pots of cooked yam, and two platters with cakes made from rice and cornmeal. It was all a welcome change from the greasy meat dishes she'd had in Salvador, and for the first time in days, she ate her fill.

Paolo was punctual. She casually emerged from the pousada at quarter past ten and he was already there, wearing a light green short-sleeved shirt, washed-out blue jeans and brown leather sandals; the bandage was still on his toe. He said he had been waiting for ten minutes, she apologized, and they strolled down to the open-air bar where Bob Marley's 'Exodus' was already blaring. She hoped the DJ would play some Brazilian music because if she'd wanted reggae with her beach she would've gone to Negril. She had to admit though that this place was much nicer than Negril. In the two days she'd been on Morro, no one had tried to sell her yet another carving or offered her ganja.

'Do you smoke?' Paolo asked, after the bartender had brought them their drinks – a *caipirinha* for her and coke for him.

'No-o,' she said hesitantly. 'Smoke what?'

'What Jamaicans smoke. I have some, if you like.'

Jesus, it had to happen. 'No, I gave that up a long time ago,' she said. In truth, she had never smoked although nearly everyone in every band she'd sung with had been inseparable from their spliffs, or their rum bottles. But she had always said no. Always? Let's revise that. She had tried a spliff, a big hell-of-a-spliff, after Antonio had left, but it hadn't done a thing for her. Just made her think more about her troubles.

'You said you had to work today. What do you do here?'

'I'm building a house,' Paolo beamed. 'When it's finished I'll rent some rooms out to the tourists.'

A house? Was he married? 'How old are you?' she asked him.

'Twenty. I'm the oldest of nine. My mother and my brothers and sisters live in Porto Seguro. It's the most beautiful town in Bahia. Have you been there?'

'No. I've only been as far south as Ilheus. That's also nice.'

'Not as nice as Porto Seguro. If you're still here next weekend, I can take you. There's a bus from Valenca.'

So he didn't have a car. That wasn't a problem. She'd travelled from Salvador to Morro by bus and boat and had enjoyed it, especially the ferry from Cidade Baixa to Bomdespacho. On it, a mad-looking man in a torn T-shirt had suddenly started shrieking, making the other passengers uneasy. When he had everybody's attention, he opened a suitcase that had seen better times, set up a make-shift stage and proceeded to give a puppet show in which two quarrelling spouses con-tinuously screamed at each other. She had laughed along with the other spectators although she hadn't understood all the jokes.

Would she still be in Morro de São Paolo the following weekend? Things could be arranged. Her next concert was three weeks away, in Miami; maybe she could reorganize her flight so that she flew directly from Salvador to the States instead of going back to Kingston. A little sightseeing in Porto Seguro wouldn't hurt.

As they sipped their drinks and talked, the bar started filling up. Anne-Marie looked around; besides the jowly bartender with his long grey hair, she had to be the oldest person there. The perfect young brown and tanned bodies made her feel her full four-and-a-half decades.

The D J had now switched from Marley to Olodum, and the young people quickly took to the concrete dance floor. Anne-Marie smiled; before coming to Morro she had seen Olodum live in Salvador where their drumming had made even the most jaded tourists dance for hours on the Largo do Pelourinho. It was Jimmy who had taken her to the free outdoor concert and he had jumped up on the 'stage' – the steps of a museum – and sung along with Olodum's lead singer. Typical Jimmy. She smiled once more, tapping her fingers on the bar counter to the beat of the drums, and Paolo looked down and said, 'You have very beautiful hands.'

'*Obrigada*,' she said, thinking: you should talk. All of you is beautiful. And my son is three years older than you.

He was looking at her with one eye squinted again and she quickly decided to call it a night. 'It's past my bed-time,' she told him. 'I have to go.' She slipped from the stool and began walking away but he came after her and held her arm. 'Let's just dance once,' he suggested.

She used to be a good dancer. When she'd started performing publicly, she would dance while she sang, but for six years now a recurring back problem had made her leave all the moves to her back-up singers. She had no intention of going on the dance floor with Paolo and definitely not alongside those young girls who shook their hips faster than the eye could follow.

'No, I don't feel like dancing. I'm sleepy.'

He shrugged. 'OK, I'll walk back with you.'

There was no one on the patio of the pousada, and he accompanied her towards her room which was at the end of a paved track that led from the beach to the back of the guesthouse. She had asked for a room at the back hoping to be spared night-noise from the beach, but the two blue-eyed sisters who ran the pousada hadn't told her about the bar when she'd checked in.

A few steps from her door, Paolo stubbed his toe on one of the paving stones and cried out in pain. She peered closely at him, trying to see if he were pretending, but the grimace looked genuine.

'Come inside,' she said. 'Let me look at it.' In the light she saw that the bandage on his toe was soaked with blood.

'What's wrong with your toe, anyway?' she asked, as she pulled him into the bathroom.

'A snake bit me.'

'You're joking? Here, on Morro?'

'Yes. I stepped right on it. Up on the hill, near the waterfall.'

She decided not to ask any more questions, telling him instead to hold his foot under the shower while she took off the bandage. Afterwards, she got her first-aid travel kit and put Mercurochrome and a new bandage on his toe.

'*Obrigado*,' he said, breathing deeply. 'You're such a nice girl.'

'I'm forty-five,' she snapped, vexed for no reason. 'I could be your mother.'

'My mother is thirty-six,' he replied. 'But you look much younger, believe me.'

She sighed, unable to think of an appropriate retort; she hoped her son never talked about her in that way.

'Beautiful room,' Paolo said, taking in the wide bed with the mosquito netting, the granite floor, the mahogany chest and chair and the white hammock on the balcony, just visible through the French windows.

'Haven't you ever been inside the pousada?'

'Not in this room,' he answered, with a smile and squint.

She opened the windows after spreading mosquito repellent over her arms and face. She handed the little yellow bottle to him but he shook his head: 'They don't bite me.' He went to lie in the hammock. 'Come,' he said.

She took off her shoes and lay beside him. He kissed her, long and deep, to the sighing of the breeze, the pounding of the waves, the thumping of the music from the bar, and the buzzing of the mosquitoes. They were feasting on her legs. She had forgotten to put repellent there.

She came up for air. 'Let's go back inside,' she said. They walked in, holding hands; she closed the windows, and went to sit on the bed, lifting up the mosquito net so he could come under it as well. Later she would forget who took whose clothes off; she only knew that one minute she was clothed, and the next she wasn't. Nor was he. He was lying on her and she was trying to pull him closer. His hand was in her hair, his tongue in her mouth, his thighs between hers, and she wanted more. But he was slowing down, holding back. He whispered words that she didn't want to be bothered with; why did some men always want to talk during love-making? Antonio had been like that, too.

But the more she tried to weld her body to his, the more insistent the whispering became, until she was forced to pay attention. *Camisinha*? He wanted his shirt back? Was he cold? *Camisinha*. Condom! Yes, that was it. He wanted to put on a condom. How thoughtful.

'*Que quere voce*?' she asked, just to be sure.

He asked if she had a condom. He had forgotten to take one with him.

'It's OK,' she said. 'I can't get pregnant.' She couldn't think of the Portuguese word for hysterectomy.

She smiled at him and tried to pull his head down to hers, but he remained unbending. 'It's better with a *camisinha*,' he said. 'AIDS'

She sprang out of bed, almost pulling the mosquito net's fixture from the ceiling. 'Jesus Christ. Are you telling me you have AIDS?'

'No, no,' he said. 'But I don't want to get it. I mean, we just met. I don't know anything about you.'

She stared at him before her Kingston temper came blasting forth. 'Put on your clothes and take yourself out of my room,' she shouted. She said other things as well, perhaps even threw in a couple of 'rasses' which he wouldn't have understood anyway. But at her wrath he dressed and limped quickly out.

She immediately started packing, muttering to herself, vowing to catch the first boat in the morning from Morro to Valenca, and recalling a similar scene where a man had run away, but for other reasons.

Antonio da Cunha Olivera. She had loved the sound of his name. She met him in the first of the two months that she'd been the featured weekend performer at the Seventh Heaven in Montego Bay. Usually she hated performing on the North Coast before the sunburned tourists with their beer bellies and shorts, and some, the Europeans, in sandals and socks. She'd found that most of them had no taste for her kind of music, especially after being fed things like Lord Kitchener's 'My

Pussin' – a song about a 'pussy', or cat, he had lost.

But the Seventh Heaven Golf, Tennis and Beach Club was different, with its waterfront villas, acres of land and plants of every kind. There the clientele were the hip rich, and along with the calypso and mento songs, she could sing reggae hits from Toots, Desmond Dekker and the Melodians; most of the other hotels on the North Coast would've preferred to be hit by a hurricane rather than to allow reggae or worse, a Rastaman, through their doors. Still she always closed the show with a song she'd learned from her grandmother, and she'd found a way to voice the lyrics so that people listened:

> *If I had wings like a dove*
> *If I had wings like a dove*
> *I would fly, fly away*
> *Fly-ay-ay-ay away-ay-ay-ay*
> *And be-e-e-e at rest*
> *But since I have no wings*
> *But since I have no wings*
> *But since I have no wings*
> *I have to sing, sing, sing, sing*
> *If I had wings like a dove . . .*

The old men in the band loved the song, especially when they were full of rum, and they would put their hearts into the chorus, transcending their straw hats and floral shirts. She herself preferred a simple black or red close-fitting dress, something that went well with her cedar-coloured skin and short jet-black hair.

One night, as she was drinking lemonade at the bar after the show, he approached her.

'You have a lovely voice.'

'Thanks.' She flashed him a warm smile and hoped he would leave her alone. After being on stage, she found it difficult to have a normal conversation. The music was still in her head and spiritually she was somewhere else, back in childhood, listening to her grandmother sing 'If I had wings' at nine-night, the wake for her father.

'May I buy you another drink?'

'No thanks. I have to leave soon.'

'No encore?'

She smiled again, as the rush in her head began fading. 'Maybe tomorrow night.'

'Where can I buy your records?'

She looked at him fully for the first time. He was about her height, five feet ten inches, with curly dark-brown hair and a square face. She wouldn't have noticed him in a tourist crowd, but up close he exuded niceness.

'I don't have any out yet,' she told him. 'Next year, though, there'll probably be something.'

'OK, I shall look out for it. Would you write down your name for me, please?' He gave her a business card, the blank side turned up. She wrote: Anne-Marie Myrie, handed the card back and he gave her another, this time for her to keep. She looked at the name, more out of politeness than interest: Antonio da Cunha Olivera, director. The company's name was in Portuguese, but with a London post office box address.

'Please let me buy you another drink, just to show how much I liked your singing.'

Now if she refused it would seem like her mother hadn't taught her any manners.

'OK,' she said. 'A fruit punch.' She was going to drink that fast and leave because her feet were killing her in the high heels.

'When can I see you again?' he asked.

'I'm doing a show tomorrow then I go back to Kingston Monday morning. I have a class in the afternoon.'

'You're still in school?' He seemed taken aback.

'University. I'm twenty-one.' She laughed.

'Ah. What are you studying?'

'Theology. No, I'm just joking. Spanish language and lit.'

'And you sing on the weekends?'

'Yes. What do you do?'

'My company does import and export. We sell a few things to you and buy a few things from you.'

She didn't recall seeing any Portuguese products on the island, but she said nothing. In fact she didn't know much about Portugal except that they'd colonized a lot of countries and treated the people like shit. But she didn't say that either.

'Sorry, but I have to go,' she told him. 'Will you be at the next show?'

'I would love to, but I'm leaving your country

tomorrow afternoon because I must be in London on Monday.'

'Well, it was nice meeting you. Have a good trip,' she said. She knew he watched her all the way to the lobby, so she tried to walk jauntily in the blasted high heels. When she got to the front of the hotel, she quickly jumped into one of the go-carts and eased off her shoes, and the young driver, Trevor, drove her through the cool night air to the beachfront room that the hotel let her have for the weekend.

Antonio da Cunha Olivera was at the show the next night. Had he missed his flight or what? Postponed, he said, the business is not that urgent. He had put off returning for another five days and moreover he had rented a car. 'I'll drive you back to Kingston if you promise to give me a grand tour. Show me the places where the music comes from.'

At the end of the five days, he left for Lisbon or London, she wasn't quite sure which, and she went back to Seventh Heaven for another weekend stint. He had promised to come back at the end of the following month, and she tried not to think about it. But he kept his word. They made love on the first night of his return, and he taught her things that made her forget it was her first time. The next day she introduced him to her mother and grandmother, who both took an instant dislike to him. 'What you see in that white man?' her grandmother said in front of Antonio, and Anne-Marie hurriedly pulled him out of the house to spare his feelings. But Antonio was amused. 'She reminds me of my own grandmother,' he said.

'Does she live in Portugal?'

'She died three years ago.'

'Oh.'

'Grandmothers have a way of doing that.'

He spent the weekend with her at Seventh Heaven, applauded loudest when she sang, then left again for London. Over the next year, he came back to the island every month, spending five days or a week each time. And like a poor worker looking forward to her pay-cheque, she waited for his visits, living from month-end to month-end. He brought her jewellery and clothes and books on learning Portuguese. She taught him to speak patois and to dance. There was nothing about him she didn't like, except . . . except for the way he spoke about Africa and the way he constantly referred to 'doing business in the Third World'. Jamaica wasn't third-anything. Where did he get those words from anyway? But their time together was so short that she didn't want to waste it arguing.

After Seventh Heaven, she made sure she didn't have to sing at any hotels, weddings, parties or concerts dur-ing his visits. They stayed at a different place each time he came: one week at the Village in Negril, five days at Frenchman's Cove in Portland, a weekend at Paw-Paw Grove in the Blue Mountains.

Then the following December, after his visit, she missed a period and it frightened and elated her. She wrote to him at the London post office box saying she had a surprise and couldn't wait to see him, but he wasn't able to return to the island until the end of February, and by then she'd had the confirmation. When he came, she booked two nights at the Courtleigh Manor in Kingston so he could rest before they travelled to Mandeville.

It was in the bathtub at the Courtleigh, soaping each other, that she asked him, 'Do you notice anything?'

He smiled indulgently. 'You're letting your hair grow?'

'No, no. Look here,' she touched her abdomen.

'You've been eating too much of the chocolates I bring you.'

She laughed. 'I'm pregnant.' His face froze, and her laughter died.

'What do you mean?'

'I'm pregnant,' she repeated, staring at him, hoping to see joy.

'By me?'

'Who else?' her voice came out in a whisper. She felt cold.

He smiled lopsidedly. 'There must be doctors who do abortions here, no? How much do they cost? Shhh, shhh, what are you crying for?'

She got out of the tub and roughly towelled herself off. He did the same. 'Anne-Marie, listen. A baby would spoil everything. Don't worry, we'll find a doctor while I'm here. I'll pay for everything. You're too young to start having children.'

'My mother had me when she was twenty.'

'Yes, but that was in the old days. And what about your singing, and university and everything?'

When she wouldn't stop crying, he finally confessed: married with children . . . two . . . didn't want to leave his wife . . . couldn't live in a place like this . . . didn't know she thought the relationship was serious . . .

That last bit sparked her temper. She opened the door of the room and began throwing his things outside, in front of the people sitting around the pool. And when he ran out to pick up his suitcase and his Nikon camera, she slammed the door after him, locking him out, leaving him in the spotlight of curious, amused stares. The next morning there was an envelope with several hundred American dollars under her door. He hadn't even written a note.

The baby, Michael, was born in early September. Despite the accusations and recriminations ('Your father would turn in his grave if he could see you like this'), her mother and grandmother immediately took over, and Anne-Marie flung herself back into her singing as soon as she could. She'd only been wasting time at university anyway; her heart had never been in it. By the time Michael was six months old, she had an album out, recorded at Dynamic Sounds, and RJR and JBC competed to see who could play the title track 'Run Man Run' the most often. It had a fast dance beat and angry lyrics:

Run man run
Run till you tumble dung
Leave this woman here
Run back to the one over there
Leave your pickney behind
Push us out of you mind
Run man run . . .

She suspected that it was mostly women who bought the record, although men also liked it because it amused them to know that someone was singing of their exploits. She wondered if Antonio ever heard the song, if he knew where the music came from. She never forgave him, but the self-pity didn't last long because soon Isle Records came courting and she became one of the few women on their label. Back then the sound of the island came from men – singers and DJs; the one glowing exception to the rule had been Millie Small some years before with 'My Boy Lollipop'. But where was Millie now?

After a busy two years, Anne-Marie's music began taking her places, even to countries as far apart in location and feel as Germany and Brazil, eclipse and sunshine. Michael, meanwhile, grew up with two doting mothers . . . three, when she was at home.

All in all, it hadn't been a bad life and it was only lately that she'd started to feel dissatisfied, started to feel out of it. Maybe it was Michael's moving into his own apartment, or the hysterectomy, or the back problem. Or maybe it was seeing Patra on MTV. There was a new generation of singers who weren't afraid to bare buttocks and belly button, and Anne-Marie thought it was time to be moving on, doing something else. Except that on stage was the only place she felt whole, coherent.

She had talked to Jimmy Jallah about it when she arrived in Bahia for the music festival. Jimmy had been living for years now in Brazil, where he was a big star, although few people back home spoke about him any more; they thought he had betrayed his roots, not understanding that when someone as expansive as Jimmy is transplanted he has to grow new roots fast or let himself shrivel and drop. Jimmy had grown to love the Brazilian soil and he had suggested she changed countries instead of careers. He'd sent her to Morro to 'cool out' and think things over. She hadn't expected to meet Paolo.

By eight o'clock, the sun has warmed Morro, and it's hard to remain inside even for those who feel like hiding. Anne-Marie is more relaxed now, after having had a few hours sleep since the bar closed. Maybe she won't leave today after all. She takes from her suitcase a slender book of poems, *Crown Point*, and goes out to the beach chair. Let him see how little he has affected her.

He's already there, with three other boys doing capoeira near the water's edge. He's much better than the others, in spite of his 'snake bite'. She's aware that he's now showing off for her benefit, walking on his hands for minutes at a time, her neat bandage from last night moving in the air. The others try to do it too but don't have his stamina. On his hands, he walks over to her beach chair. '*Bom dia*,' he says upside down. '*Tudo bem?*' She puts on her shades and focuses on the book.

'I'm sorry about last night. But I don't see why you got so upset.'

She ignores him and he finally does a half-somersault and stands upright.

'It's always better to be protected,' he says.

She suppresses a bittersweet smile in the face of such reason. It's a lesson she should have learned a long time ago. But then there wouldn't have been Michael.

She looks at Paolo now. 'You're right. At my age I should know better than to take risks, and at your age you can't afford to.'

There is a pause, during which the sudden screams of a child being beaten breaks the calm of the beach. Paolo tenses and Anne-Marie looks toward the food-shack next to the Casa das Pedras guesthouse. On the two previous days, she has exchanged a few words with the woman who runs the shack, an easy-smiling mother of five – four girls and a boy. The harsh sounds of the strap make her flinch.

'I can't stand it when she does that,' Paolo says. 'It's her son, she's always beating him. I'll go talk to her.' He walks over to the shack and after a brief argument, the beach is quiet again.

'Have you seen the *quarta praia*?' he asks, when he returns.

'No, I've only walked up to the town and down to the *terceira praia*.'

Her pousada is on the 'second beach'; Morro has four different stretches of beach in all. The first one is the most developed while the fourth is supposed to be an unspoiled expanse of sand and palm trees.

'Let's go,' he says.

'Can you walk that far with your toe?'

'Yes. It's much better. *Obrigado.* Come.'

She wraps her *canga* around her, takes up her towel and leaves the book of poems on the chair for when she returns. It is a good hour's walk to the *quarta praia*, past guesthouses of every hue, past restaurants offering feijoada and moqueca as well as hamburgers and pizza, and past the little airstrip at the end of the *terceira praia* where rich tourists can take a five-seater back to Salvador when they get bored with sand and sea.

The fourth beach stretches empty except for a wood-and-thatch restaurant built high on logs for protection against the tide. It's closed and they walk on, going to the far end of the beach where they have only the palm trees for company. Anne-Marie is happy there's no one to see her do something she probably will regret later. She helps Paolo to spread her *canga* and towel on the sand and they both lie down. This time there is no talking. He hasn't forgotten the *camisinha*, and he makes Anne-Marie come in waves.

He wants her to stay until the following weekend and to go with him to Porto Seguro, but she feels like leaving Morro when her seven days have passed. She promises to return in a month, after the concert in Miami and a trip home. He carries her suitcase to the dock and they stand there for a long time kissing. She asks him to leave before she gets into the boat, but as he walks away, she calls out to him. 'Paolo, do you drink cane juice for breakfast?'

'Sometimes,' he says and waves, the watch she bought him yesterday glinting in the sun.

The boat is tiny, half the size of the one that brought her to Morro. It seems full to sinking point, but the 'captain' keeps accepting more people: a dark-skinned man with a briefcase, three blonde Germans with souvenir bands around their wrists, a haggard woman with a stunningly beautiful little girl who carries a violin without strings. Anne-Marie moves over to make room for the woman, whose hands have no fingernails. The boat feels dangerously low in the water now, and she can already see the headline in *The Gleaner*: 'Overcrowded Boat Sinks in Brazil – Old-Time Jamaican Singer Dead'.

Just before they push off, a rich-looking woman with long black hair, high cheekbones, and firm legs enters the boat with . . . her son? He is a smooth honey colour, and his lean face with its full lips could be on the cover of *GQ* magazine. He's wearing a white T-shirt, black shorts, white socks and expensive white Nike sneakers. The woman has on a denim jacket and matching shorts which show off the legs. They sit on the bow of the boat because there is no space anywhere else.

The way the woman looks at the young man makes it clear that he is not her son. He pops a mint into his mouth and apparently asks her if she wants one as well. When she nods yes, he puts it lingeringly on her tongue and her eyes eat up his face. His eyes are hidden behind designer dark glasses.

Anne-Marie tries not to stare at them but can't help it. Are they married, she wonders. What does he see in a woman who has to be at least fifteen years older than him? She knows what the woman sees in him. She has felt the same thing with Paolo. Last night, after they made love, she knew all at once and now can even put it into words. She has no intention of marrying or even living with Paolo until she dies of old age. No, but she will come back to Morro, bring him trinkets . . . and sleep with him, pulling his youth into her bloodstream for as long as he lets her. She looks again at the couple in the front of the boat, and the woman's eyes meet hers. Anne-Marie gives an almost imperceptible thumps-up sign, and the woman flicks back her hair and laughs, suddenly seeming like a young girl.

Adele Parks is 31 and married. She was born in North Yorkshire but has lived in London for most of her 'grown-up life' (using the term loosely). Her career is more colourful than a sartorially challenged chameleon. She has taught English in Italy, worked as an account manager in enormous advertising agencies in London, tiny ones in Botswana and, for a time, worked in the marketing department of a stonkingly huge management consultancy. Yet she never felt (for want of a better touchy feely term) fulfilled until she got the plot and admitted to herself that she had always wanted to write books. So, she did the slog, found an agent, who cut a deal. Now she's a full-time writer.

Flung

Adele Parks

Whilst standing in an endless line for tickets at Victoria Station, London, it hits me that, likely as not, right now Donald and Amelia will be deciding between beach or pool. The most exciting decision I have in front of me is cheap day return, versus an open ticket. I sigh and look down at my scruffy rucksack. Life's so unfair. I bet Amelia has a matching set of Louis Vuitton. Besides the emotional baggage I am travelling light. I'm wearing my bikini under my sun-dress and I've packed my toothbrush and a clean pair of knickers because I want to be wild and spontaneous (but clean).

> Hi, Bruv. How goes it? . . . Good, good . . . Me? Awful, since you ask. He's ditched me . . . Yes, I know Donald Drake *is* a stupid name. I admit that . . . Very funny. Yes. I'm sure that you've been saving up the Disney jokes since I met him, haven't you? My line's bleeping. I'll call you later.

My mobile phone is warm in my hand and if there is any truth to the theory that it emits brain-frying waves then I suspect my brain is well and truly frazzled. It has been attached to my head, more or less constantly, for four days.

Hi, Jenny . . . Oh, I'm OK. You heard. Who told you? . . . Michelle. Well, saves me putting an announcement in the paper . . . Devastated obviously. I mean single at thirty is bad . . . What? Yes, admittedly he has a stupid name. But he also has the cutest smile and up until ninety-six hours ago was the custodian of my heart! . . . Oh you were right . . . Yup. Amelia in Accounts. She seduced him with her dinky little embroidered slip dresses and *definitely* non-work-place-appropriate strappy sandals . . .

The woman in the queue behind me gives me a sympathetic smile-cum-grimace. I acknowledge her sympathy with a hound-dog expression that I've perfected over the last few days.

Yes I know it takes two to tango . . . I thought you said he was perfect for me . . . Oh, and now 'you never liked him'. Thanks . . . Yes, he is a bastard. It is bad . . . The added humiliation is that the once-in-a-lifetime holiday to the Caribbean, that we'd planned together, saved for together and booked together – left with him! And can you believe he offered to buy me out of the

holiday so that Amelia could go instead? ...
Exactly, a bastard.

I move up the queue. The guy in front of me is Italian.
He is communicating his desire for a one-way ticket
on the Gatwick Express by gesticulating madly. It puts
me in mind of the histrionics I displayed as Donald
tried to leave. I blush as I remember clinging to his
trouser legs begging him to reconsider. It was obvious
that a relaxed, new-millennium, adult approach to parting was not an available option. Sharing a bedroom
platonically was out of the question (although, argu-
ably, we had managed this successfully for the last six
months of our relationship). I wanted to tell him to
fuck off. To keep his money and crappy holiday.

I wanted to mean it.

But as I am an underpaid assistant in a small PR
agency, with barely a foot on the first rung of the cor-
porate ladder, decadent displays of passion are not practical. I'm waiting for his cheque to clear.

I pull myself out of my self-pity and tune back into
Jen, who is still chatting merrily on the mobile.

You're right, he was an arrogant, self-absorbed git
... he's never been that sensational in bed ... I
can't concede the point on flings though. Oh, Jen,
they waste time ... I'm sure that couple-
counselling does increase after the holiday period
... Yes, it could be seen as an advantage that I
have avoided that but ... What is my problem?

I was kidding, I don't really want to hear ... I don't see that a string of long-term relationships, which seamlessly transition into one another, is a problem ... Well, yes, Donald could be a wanker on occasion but ... Yes ... Yes, I suppose I would have married him if he'd suggested it ... It's not obscene. I know it's character building but I'm pretty happy with a lightweight character ... the thirties are *not* great years ... I haven't been freed from the insecurities that plagued my twenties ...

Then, as now, I had an overwhelming fear of dying alone, losing my battle against orange-peel thighs and under achieving at work.

... No I haven't tried the Clarins one. Does it really work? I'll give it a go. Look, got to ring off; I'm near the front of the queue. Yeah, love you too. Thanks ... Absolutely like a fish needs a bicycle.

I go for it, open return. It's the least I can do to honour my promise to my mum. After Donald did the dirty deed I dissed him to all my friends, ripped up his letters and photos and then climbed into the fridge to see if there was any comfort to be found. There wasn't. So I called my mum. I told her about my plans to spend a week alone; detoxing, sleeping, recuperating. She talked about more pebbles on beaches. I mumbled and sniffled, explaining that I'd seen a lovely dress in Pronuptia. She snapped and switched her wise words from 'fish in the sea' to 'cart before the horse'. She told me that it is a mistake to start choosing the children's names before I've drunk the second round on a first date. It's serious when your mum encourages you towards casual sex.

I am on a life-long search for Mr Pucker and historically I have not had time for flings. My CV is as follows: age fourteen to seventeen – exclusive to Dom. Age seventeen to nineteen – devoted to Ivan. Age nineteen to twenty-three – adored Paddy. Age twenty-three to twenty-six – attached to Giles. Age twenty-six to twenty-eight – passed time with Richard. Age twenty-eight to thirty and a half (and those six months are significant) – stayed with Donald. Over half my life wasted – that is if you consider my end goal; a small Tiffany blue box and a large white dress.

I check the timetable. If I leg it I'll make the 10.25 a.m.

Everyone agrees that I need a holiday, that I'll feel better with a tan, that I should have a holiday fling. I try to explain that I don't do 'fling', I do serial monogamy. All my friends have real boyfriends (i.e. not the breed that run away days before you are due on the runway) and therefore none of them are available for said holiday. Undeterred, I did visit the travel agent. I'd argued to myself that it's a huge planet, surely there's a destination where it's possible – even acceptable – to be single and still get a sun tan.

Apparently not.

For several excruciating minutes I discussed my travel plans with the woman behind the desk. She had big boobs, big bum, big hair and a big gob. I was feeling delicate. I noted that she had a huge diamond ring on her third finger, left hand. I didn't want to hate her because of this. So instead I hated her for making me admit, in public, that, yes, I would have to pay the supplement for a single room. Since it's July and I needed to depart immediately, my choices were limited. My financial state quickly reduced the choices from 'limited' to 'prohibitive'. I left the travel agent's more depressed than when I'd arrived. I walked in knowing I was sad, single and on the shelf. I left knowing that I'm also flat broke and flat-chested.

. . . Well you can't just mope at home . . .

I can.

. . . You'll never meet Mr Right whilst watching *Neighbours* omnibus . . .

Good point.

In the end I was more or less forced to promise I'd visit seedy clubs, shag anything that moves and adopt a policy never to turn down an invitation.

The Brighton train leaves from platform 14. I'm getting quite an expert at working my way around Britain's stations. This is because I'd thought the answer to my holiday destination dilemma lay in a series of day-trips. This week I have visited Bath, the Tower of London and Windsor Castle. All trips proved to be edifying and educational. That is if your idea of company is packs of school children – squalling and shrieking, it appears, is an international language – and if your idea of education is six-thousand-year histories potted into nine minutes of audiotape. My opportunities to buy souvenir tea-towels and key-rings have run into hundreds. My opportunities to flirt, fling or score, nil. Determined, I'm now trying Brighton.

I find an emptyish carriage and stare down a middle-aged woman and her son, who were keen to bag the last couple of seats facing the direction of travel. The seat's mine, it's a small victory but it cheers me. I pass the journey staring out of the window watching the houses and fields rush by. I think this is symbolic.

Jen, I said symbolic not 'some bollocks'. Anyway what are you up to? . . . A survey of the worlds's hundred sexiest men. Really? Who wins? . . . Well, that's stupid. OK, I admit there is something interesting about Robbie Williams, Brad Pitt and George Clooney. But they are all too 'bad boy' to seriously be considered for matrimony . . . Yes, Tom Cruise is marriage material but Nicole Kidman beat me to it by a hair's breath . . . River Phoenix and James Dean are dead . . . I don't think including 'a young Sean Connery' is fair . . . Prince William is jailbait . . . Why are you laughing? If it's not meant to be taken seriously then what's the point of it? . . . Well, it doesn't make me feel sexy. I'm too old to be doing it *sur la plage*. . . To be honest, I've never watched the sun set on any part of a humping anatomy . . . I just can't imagine it in Brighton. Jen, it's not that there's anything wrong with Brighton per se. But it's not the Caribbean, is it? It's not even Ibiza . . . Yes, I'm sure it's very trendy now and a great place for a holiday fling. Yes, I know I've promised. Yes, I'll keep a look out. I'll try. Jen got to go.

The train has just pulled up in East Croydon and my attention is caught by a group of blokes larking around on the platform. They are all in their mid-twenties therefore generally pretty spotty but their overall impression is buoyed up by an overwhelming aura of self-confidence. There are five of them, one's ugly and happy looking, two are average looking but clean and trendy enough to push their score up to a six or seven out of ten. One is a clear eight, with all-American good looks. He might be interesting. The fifth has his back to me. My carriage pulls up parallel to where they are standing. I am stuck between willing them into my carriage – which is empty except for an old couple with a flask and egg sandwiches and the disgruntled mother and son – and desperately wishing them to sit elsewhere. The motivation for these opposing wishes is the same. If they sit near the opportunities are ripe; this is 'fling alert'. They choose my carriage. I bury my head in my book.

'Is this seat taken?'

I look up. Eleven out of ten. The most sensational looking man *ever*, is smiling at me. He is literally breathtaking. He is tall with broad shoulders and slim hips. I wish he'd turn round so I can check out his bum. He has scruffy, long, dark, gypsy hair. It falls over his cobalt blue eyes. He smiles. The smile ignites his entire face and many other parts of my body. Too stunned to speak, it takes all my presence of mind to shake my head. He sits down next to me. His knee brushes mine and my knickers jump into my throat.

'Going far?'

It's a simple enough question. I do know the answer but my tongue is temporarily paralysed.

He stares at me strangely and then nods as if understanding something. He says slowly, 'Are. You. Going. All. The. Way?'

Now I am confused.

'To Brighton?'

I nod slowly.

'Where. Are. You. From?'

It's obvious from this that my stupid inability to answer his initial question has left him with the false impression that I am either deaf or foreign. Oh my God, how embarrassing. How do I put him straight? I think fast.

'Er Paris.' I volunteer, but I pronounce it, '*Oh Pari*'!

'*J'ai parles Français.*' He smiles.

Bugger, I don't. I failed my GCSE. Quick U-turn.

'But I em Swedeesh, not Paris.' I smile my newly acquired Swedish smile. He beams. And why wouldn't he? Show me a man who doesn't want to meet a Swede with a French education.

I soon discover flirting is fun. Flirting in Swedish is doubly so. During the course of the journey I leave behind my British reserve and throw myself into my new persona. Unaccountably my hair is blonder, my breasts bigger and my thighs thinner. Or at least they must be because Mick from Croydon obviously finds me a super-babe. Then again that could be because he is twenty-three.

A toy boy.

The idea is at once absurd and . . . attractive. I allow myself a few moments of respite from the particular breed of agony which is, 'I am no longer Donald's woman' as I drift away into a fantasy of something other than a few quick thrusts. If I remember correctly, younger men do go long enough to guarantee a freight train shudder, other than their own. My mum, my brother, Jen, Michelle and all my other friends are going to be so proud of me. Not only is this guy sex on legs, he's a toy boy and since I have spent the last forty-five minutes making up a fictional persona for myself, including a new nationality, even I concede this is not a relationship with a future. This is fling.

I consider that for the last three months I have beaten the living daylights out of my Boots loyalty card in an attempt to de-fuzz, de-scale, retone and tan every inch of my body, which, thinking about it, is a not-so-bad-in-the-right-light-all-things-considered body. I have treated my credit cards with the same lack of respect as I assembled a beautiful wardrobe of tiny, flirty, pretty dresses and shoes. And assuming that his entire cultural correspondence with Swedes is the same as mine – pornographic stereotypes – he won't be able to resist. I know I'm right when two just-past-adolescent girls climb on to the train. His mates swoop but Mick doesn't seem to notice. He's made the right choice. They may have concave stomachs and bodies so pierced they have more holes than my tea strainer but I bet neither of them knows the prank with the fingers and anus, nor the one where you put both balls in the mouth at once. I sit back, shocked at my own thoughts. But then it's not my fault I have such thoughts, it's my Swedish genes.

'Are you meeting anyone in Brighton?' asks Mick.

'I em alone.' I hope this makes me sound enigmatic rather than a loser. Mick grins again and I think I can safely assume that it's the right answer. So far I haven't said much so that he doesn't notice how phony my accent is. He, on the other hand, has chatted freely. Assuming I understand little, he and his friends have discussed me openly, the only precaution that they take is to speak quickly. I purposely misunderstand, interrupt in the wrong places and stare dumbly out of the window. I haven't had as much fun in ages.

'Check out the pert tits.'

Why thank you.

'Sensational.'

'Eesn't the view so?'

They stare at me, scared for a moment that I've understood.

'Sensational, the view.' I elaborate by waving at the

window and they sigh, relieved, nodding enthusiastically.

'Well if you don't want her, mate, just say the word
and I'll oblige.'

Excuse me!

'Forget it. She's gorgeous and I saw her first. Anyway
you're an ugly bastard and she wouldn't look at you.'

No, I wouldn't, but you Mick are certainly worth a
second glance.

It's very hot and Brighton is heaving. Mick's mates
walk all of two hundred yards from the station and
suggest stopping for a drink. Mick and I make our
excuses and tactically agree that we'll go on alone. I am
flying. Helga (my pseudo name for which I apologize,
it shows a lack of imagination) has lent me a new-found
confidence. I am open, misleading, worldly, guileless,
arch and alluring by turn. It's easy because Helga man-
ages to elicit cheap laughs by mispronouncing words
and appearing charmed by Kiss Me Quick hats and
bubble-gum machines. I can't remember a time when
I wasn't trying to get married. Therefore, my conversations with men are usually a thinly veiled attempt to
check out their suitability. I mentally tick the lists. Right
age and income bracket, territory, education, and evidence of ability to commit. Helga doesn't want to get
married therefore the deepest conversation Mick and I
have is what type of topping we prefer on our crêpes.
I'm in charge. I'm not trying to snare him. I can behave
just as I please.

We wander through The Lanes, the Pavilion and

along the pier. Simultaneously we are both overcome with an enormous hunger. There are dozens of grotty cafés that serve strong tea in huge mugs with greasy chips and fried sausage. Normally I'm squeamish about cholesterol and I only eat nutritionally balanced, calorie-restricted meals. I don't think this caution is very Swedish so I join Mick as he tucks into a gigantic fry-up.

Finally we make our way to the beach, which is pebbled rather than the white sands that I know Amelia will be treading. I don't hesitate but whip off my sundress. Mick nearly falls over, when for a moment, he thinks I've nothing but my birthday suit underneath. Even so, he doesn't look that disappointed with my bikini-clad bod. I can't believe I'm doing this. I'm normally so body conscious I bathe with the lights out.

'Stones are better than sand, eh?' My accent is wavering monstrously. It would probably be better if I kept my mouth shut. Well, most of the time.

'Sorry?' asks Mick. I'm delighted to note that he isn't quite able to concentrate on what I'm saying.

'Sand, it gets all where,' I elaborate. For the first time in a week I think I got a better deal than Amelia. If I know anything about Donald's performance on holiday, sand is all Amelia will be getting in her knickers. Mick grins and I hope he is thinking what I'm thinking. He is.

'You are driving me wild,' he confirms, sitting down next to me on the pebbles.

'Err, you want to go for er dive, er drive?' I ask.

'No. Well, come to think of it . . .'

Of course I am not oblivious to my *double entendre*. I smile encouragingly.

'I said you are driving me wild,' he shouts. I continue to look confused but only so he has to repeat himself again. Each time he does so he raises his voice and I like the attention we are attracting. This is excellent news. I don't think I ever drove anyone wild when I held a British passport. With Donald it was definitely a case of familiarity breeding complacency. Towards the end we had settled into a routine of fortnightly sex. Donald's desire communicated to me by switching off the bedroom light and twiddling my nipple as though it were a radio dial.

Not that I'm considering having sex with Mick. I mean, I've only just met him. It would be indecent. It would be too forward. It would be risky.

It would be fun.

As a Swede it's necessary to play the role to the full i.e. be a complete nymphet. I know I am pandering to stereotypes but it is a once-in-a-lifetime opportunity to behave like a hussy without endangering the reputation of British girls. It's almost a patriotic act when I turn to him and push my tongue down his throat. He kisses me back. His kisses are expert; fiery, centred, explorative. The kisses last all afternoon. They last an age because we have nothing to say to each other. As this is a fling I don't have to prove I'm intellectually stellar, I just have to be a tease. I run my hands up and down his body, checking out his taut muscles and lean waist.

'You are hard like a rock.' He blushes furiously and

I know that I'm being childish but it's the best fun I've had since, oh, I can't even remember when. Since I *was* a child, probably. His hands are dead still on my ribs, just millimetres from my breasts. My breasts are literally screaming for him to make his move. My nipples have stiffened and I hope to God that it's sweat that I can feel between my legs. I wonder if it breaks etiquette if I make a grab for his cock before he's even reached first base. I'm demented.

The sun starts to set but the beach is still pretty busy. We watch people round up their cross kids; tired and burnt they cry and argue with their siblings. Older couples are walking their dogs. They've already been back to their hotels, showered and changed into their pastel shirts and summer dresses. Whilst we watch them, they steadfastly try to avoid letting their gaze fall on us. I think they are afraid that our obvious lust and desire is infectious. I feel like shouting out and assuring them that it's not. I should know, I've been trying to catch a bit of this long enough.

I shiver.

'Are you cold?'

'Before you say I am hot?' I feign confusion. He smiles and rubs his hands up and down my arms. It feels soooooo good. His fingers pierce me and yet his strokes are a balm. He caresses my ribs. They haven't made an appearance for about fifteen years but are now sticking out everywhere. His fingers weave around my breasts (despite my best efforts to get them to stop off there), and up to my shoulders and neck, which he massages firmly. I close my eyes and therefore feel, rather than see, him kiss my ears, which causes the hairs on my body to stand to attention. His fingers trace a route back down the side of my breasts, across my waist and over my stomach. Past the edge of my tiny bikini and he wavers. Hesitating, hovering over all the areas that haven't got a suitable name. If he doesn't touch me soon I'm going to combust.

I want this man to take me, to pull me, to push into me. I want this man. How do I broach the subject? Not easy in a first language, being Helga helps.

'Now we take 'otel?'

'Are you sure you want this?'

Want this? I want him more than I've ever wanted a wedding list at John Lewis.

Oh my God. Oh my God. Oh my God. Yes it is me. Why do I sound different? . . . Yes. I am flung!! Well at least Helga is . . . You heard. Who told you? . . . Michelle. Saves me putting an announcement in the paper . . . Yes, Helga is a stupid name; I was under time pressure. The most amazing smile, sort of Robbie Williams. Eyes to die for, kind of put me in mind of George Clooney. The tightest butt, very Brad Pitt . . . His . . . Yes, huge! I seduced him with dinky little embroidered slip dresses and strappy sandals . . . Yes, I know it takes two to tango . . . sensational in bed and *sur la plage*. . . Well you can't just mope at home . . . I really concede the point on flings.

The thirties are great years . . . I'm freed from the insecurities that plagued my twenties . . . Sod the cellulite cream . . . After all, I am young, free and invited. No?

Helen Lederer began her career as a stand-up comic in the early eighties, surviving the Comedy Store and culminating in a sell-out show at the Edinburgh Festival. Probably best known for her performance as Catriona in BBC TV's *Absolutely Fabulous* she has also appeared in many other shows including *Harry Enfield's Television Programme*, *One Foot in the Grave*, *Happy Families*, *Girls on Top* and *Casualty*. She wrote and performed her own material for *Naked Video* for BBC2, *Life with Lederer* for Radio 4 and currently contributes a regular column for *Woman's Hour*. Apart from contributing occasionally to *She* magazine, the *Mail on Sunday* and the *Guardian*, Helen also wrote *Single Minding!* (Hodder & Stoughton) and is currently writing a novel for Penguin. She occasionally re-visits the world of stand-up, but from an older perspective.

Pull Me in the Pullman Carriage

Helen Lederer

Karen glared resentfully at a couple of girls wiggling their way up the Edgware Road towards her, their minuscule knickers outrageously visible through the chiffon of their summer dresses.

She pulled herself together. Just because it was Bank Holiday and most other people were having barbecues in strappy vests and shorts or sex with their partners somewhere conveniently close to the M25, didn't mean she had to curl up and die. Well not yet. Something would happen to her. It would. But then she remembered the last time Positive Thinking had brought a result.

She had noticed her friend's brother looking at her out of the corner of her eye in the car on the way back from Ikea. The more he looked at her, the more she had re-arranged her mouth to resemble what she thought was a Michele Pfeiffer pout with wide startled-looking eyes.

Then suddenly he said, 'Karen?'

'Mmmm?' She looked at him apparently casual.

'Do you know what you remind me of?'

'No,' replied Karen expectantly, opening her eyes wider and puckering her mouth like the clappers.

'A goldfish.'

'Thanks.'

Yes. She had good reason to be depressed. And last night with her flatmate hadn't helped.

'When was the last time you had sex?' Cora had wanted to know. She was only bothering to talk to her because her boyfriend was out experimenting with male company and beer, 'in case their own relationship got co-dependent', and also because Coventry was playing Munich.

Karen made the mistake of telling her.

Cora screamed incredulously. 'Five YEARS? – There's something wrong, Karen.' And then she offered, 'Have you thought about the Wrens?' after a few pitiful looks.

Instead Karen thought half-heartedly of the vibrator that had been left behind in the flat. But she knew that she couldn't bring herself to actually use it. In any case, Cora had told Karen not to, since they didn't know where it had been. Actually, Karen could well imagine where it had been, which was an even better reason to leave well alone.

No, she'd hang on for the real thing. Bank Holiday had to be got through with or without sex – and since it was without, she might as well catch a train.

'We all know about you and trains,' said Cora derisively.

Karen bitterly regretted a previous occasion where

after a few cranberry vodkas she had rashly confided that she always got turned on in a train. She couldn't exactly account for it, but it might have something to do with the regular vibrations which seemed to speak to her vagina and get it purring. Once, on a particularly long journey, she'd even had to find a loo to go in and give herself a seeing to before she exploded.

Instead of being impressed at this account of rather original sexual display, Cora had been disappointingly horrified.

'What, in the loo?' she'd asked, amazed. 'On public transport?'

'It wasn't public,' defended Karen. 'That's the point.'

'You're weird,' confirmed Cora.

'I'm not,' said Karen. 'Look at those male commuters – have a look at what they're doing to themselves under those tables. They're not tapping the Formica underneath I can assure you!'

But Karen could see this was not a subject to dwell on with Cora, so she justified the train journey as merely a necessary mode of transport to get her to her 'friendzzz' in the country for Bank Holiday – rather than any surrogate sexual playground of orgasmic possibilities. Perish the thought.

'Is that the friend whose brother thought you resembled a goldfish?' Cora needed to know.

'I can't remember,' said Karen. Cora really was a pain. She'd be buying a *Time Out* at the station to start auditioning for other flatmates as well.

* * *

319

'Great' said her friend Frances when Karen had invited herself over the night before, making out she wasn't desperate but could she come down the next day, please?

'As long as you don't mind sharing the bed,' Frances stipulated.

'No,' said Karen truthfully. 'Who've you got in mind?' she joked.

Frances didn't laugh because she'd been married to Brian for a few years and had therefore lost the art of repartee.

'You've met her before?' said Frances.

'Not that woman from Cornwall with the caring personality?' Karen asked.

'She's a homeopath – well, she's training to be anyway and –'

Karen cut her off, bored already. 'Anyone else?'

'Her kids.'

Great, thought Karen, *a homeopath from Cornwall and kids as well.*

Impulsively for a second she toyed with an alternative plan. Perhaps she could get herself booked on a last-minute 'water-sports' weekend. She'd seen it advertised on afternoon television: a group teamed up at a man-made lake and learned about being wet and cold with some sailing thrown in. But what if all the men were accountants? Or worse, what if there weren't any men at all? She could always do what that weekend Life Skills workshop had recommended – hang out in Hyde Park talking to trees. But to be honest she didn't want to attract any more unkind attention. Cora was enough.

No. She'd chosen the only course of action available. Even if Frances *was* married to Brian, at least it was a known quantity and she knew she'd hate it marginally less than staying in London.

The train was hot and crowded as she bumped herself along the carriage with her carrier bags of women's magazines and a rather phallic-looking brie baguette. Her overnight bag was lolling off her shoulder, which meant she had to raise her armpit to straighten it, which meant in turn that the faceless grey men at the tables might spot her armpit stubble or, worse, get a sniff. God, summer was a worry.

Oh, for the camouflage of winter, when velvet-tailored jackets hugged themselves tightly over unsightly body parts. But no. Her Ghost dress with matching cover-up cardi was falling off with the strain of her ill-thought-out baggage and smelly cheese.

This was getting increasingly annoying, as three carriages down she *still* couldn't find a seat. The only 'possible' was an aisle seat next to a man whose lap-top, phone and spread sheets had been staked so obviously across the table. She wasn't in the mood to squeeze in and balance her carriers on the two centimetres left. Nor was anyone else, which she could see was an effective use of the territorial imperative but, really, who gave a fuck. Obviously she would if she could, but not with him.

Finally Karen spotted a seat opposite a woman and baby. The seat next to them was piled high with baby bags, toys and general nappy paraphernalia, which explained why the whole area had been given a wide berth.

As Karen set about committing herself reluctantly to the seat, the woman smiled in a rather fixed way at her, clearly enjoying the sucking of the baby at her nipple. Karen really didn't know if she could stomach such a sight for long. But it was between 'lap-top' or 'breast'. Bank Holidays brought them all out, it seemed.

The woman's eyes seemed to glaze over as if in a sexual reverie, which looked ominous. Karen decided if the woman got near a climax she'd turn tail and go, carriers or no carriers. She'd sort of suck it and see, as it were, before moving on.

Karen distracted herself with the weekend ahead. Perhaps they'd do that drive again to the nearest Ikea where you bought small candles and tiny noticeboards and paper-clips, having looked at the garden furniture and decided against. Sensible in her case, given she had no garden. Or perhaps they'd stay in and have a take-away. A far cry from when they were at school. She remembered nostalgically how Frances and she had been allowed to go away together at eighteen and catch the ferry to Calais. If only their parents had known what had been in their minds they'd never have been allowed out of their rooms.

But then, in those days, if you wanted a snog you just went out looking for it. Why wasn't it possible now? She was just as keen to get one but somehow looking hopeful seemed to put men off once you turned thirty-five.

Or was it the fact that they'd both been virgins which seemed to open so many doors? Not theirs, per se, but did 'Virginity' offer more pleasure possibilities than the 'lone penetration' of the future? Karen pondered on these profundities as she watched the baby twitch and guzzle while the woman smiled unashamedly.

Her Life Skills weekend workshop had advised her that if she thought of those moments where things had gone really well, she could re-create the mood and make them happen again – more or less. Karen set to on an early memory involving a penis.

Here was one. She remembered Frances' sister had got them both tickets to a hockey club disco in Sidcup. A drink in one hand, she could remember looking around pleasantly at the men, none of the insecurity of the present day with, 'Do I look attractive, are they committed and does my breath smell?' tattooed across her waistband. It was simply, 'Here I am, in my nice white rosebud Biba cotton dress – take me I'm yours and we'll deal with the virginity factor later.'

She remembered how a real-life Wimbledon player who had been deseeded (as he was fast soon to become again) asked her if she'd like to go out for a walk. She did, and very soon found herself snogging him against a wall. She felt it was necessary to tell him about the virginity thing, since it was quite interesting to her and she assumed it might be of interest to him, but he didn't seem to be listening – a rummage around her breasts and a fingering up her pants seemed to be more pressing. After a lot of heavy breathing Karen knew she had to take action to prevent the usual cross and sulky riposte. This was the lot of an active virgin. She leaned down to oblige him but he'd already got there before her, waving it about as if to say, 'Ready!'

She had become quite efficient at seamlessly hoovering up, like a cat with a saucer of cream. A neatening up of housework really, thought Karen fondly.

Then she had reported in to Frances about exactly what had happened with the tennis player and received general approval before they were driven home by the unwitting sister.

As the train journey continued Karen busily went over other penis occasions and started to wonder how often Frances had similarly reported in to her? The thought suddenly struck her: had it just been Karen who'd gone round doing the 'plating', as it was then called. What had Frances been up to in the meantime?

She knew Frances liked to *talk* about it a lot and remembered when she first met Frances' husband Brian, he seemed to like it too. She found him staring at her mouth in a rather odd way. Eventually she asked him what was up and he replied, 'I'm just imagining that little mouth round all those dicks. Hope you don't mind.'

Well, she did, but as usual she didn't say.

'Tell him about the chewing gum,' Frances had instructed.

'No, I can't,' said Karen, 'I really can't.' Not sure if she liked being in the company of Frances and Brian together.

'Let me then,' begged Frances.

Karen had allowed the telling to go ahead, since at that point in her life talking about sex wasn't as painful as it had become. Talking about it now just reminded her how easy it had once been and would she ever remember how to do it again? 'Your hole will heal up at this rate!' Cora had cheerfully remarked recently.

Frances duly got into her stride about the chewing-gum incident, which had involved a tall Australian. He had been allowed to take Karen to a beer cellar near Charing Cross and it was here that he had suggested kissing Karen 'there', which was indeed a new one on her – so much so that she'd thought she'd misheard him at first. But when he dropped her back home, she soon realized she hadn't. They went into the play-room upstairs – which had been re-named the 'piano room' for obvious reasons. (They had cut out Formica flowers and stuck them over the piano since it was the late sixties and the room needed to reflect its time. Frances always liked using background information to embellish a scene.) A lie down together on the Mexican rug was followed by the usual routine of 'Hey, I'm a virgin but you can play with me' type of thing. Frances then described how, at bedtime, Karen couldn't get her knickers off. They were stuck and she simply couldn't think why. She pulled and she pulled, until she bent over and had a peek. The Australian was obviously partial to a bit of gum and, rather than break off proceedings with Karen, he had chosen to deposit the gum – perhaps as a personal signature, like the flag left on Everest. Karen, however, wasn't that impressed at the time since much scissor work was required to free her from her pants.

Brian had clearly enjoyed the gum story and insisted on a re-play of just exactly *where* the gum had been, and *when* did she discover it, and *how* did she remove it from her – you know . . .

Karen had started to get slightly uncomfortable then, about how much pleasure they both might be getting at her expense.

'Why don't you tell Brian about when we went camping in Brittany then?' suggested Karen. 'You know, when we had to go in the tent and you ended up with Robert and . . .'

'You ended up with Patrick,' finished Frances.

Brain had started to shift about in his chair stiffly.

'When was this then?' he asked.

'Oh,' Frances said airily, 'it was ages ago. I think it was more to do with Patrick and Karen though. Do you remember when you got in his tent and he came before you even got to lie down!'

'Yes,' said Karen, not sure whether to pursue how Frances and Robert's goings-on had all got a bit ugly because Robert had been one of the few blokes who *wasn't* keen on the virginity thing at all. Karen remembered having to find her torch – which wasn't easy because she had to slip about over Patrick before finding it in her rucksack and go and calm him down. Amazing what the offer of a plating can do to placate an ugly scene, she mused. Then they'd packed up and left the next morning without reference to it again.

Brain had changed the subject after that and suggested quite a strict game of Scrabble which didn't allow people's names. Which ruled out Dick, of course.

Karen was just beginning to doubt the real usefulness of going down to see her friend at all, when there was a commotion opposite. A woman was lurching down the carriage with a bottle heated up in a tumbler. She screamed when she got to Karen's section.

'What?' said Karen, nervously looking around, wondering what was wrong. 'What?' she asked again.

'My baby!' screamed the woman. 'My baby!'

She looked furiously at where the suckling woman was sitting – who, it had to be said, appeared to be on the brink of a massive orgasm judging by certain sounds and kicking movements of her legs against the table-top.

The new woman plucked the happy baby from a monstrously enlarged nipple and shrieked, 'She's mine!'

The first woman could no longer keep the orgasm at bay as it had been building for so long and roused herself with a 'Yeeees!' before sinking back into the seat with closed eyes, clearly spent.

'I *told* you,' said the new woman, now apparently

familiar with the situation, 'I *told* you I'd be a few minutes, but it's Bank Holiday – they're short-staffed.'

The baby had started to whimper without the succour, so the new woman shoved a teat from the now heated-up bottle in its mouth. Then the two women started to snuggle and admonish each other indulgently.

Karen's mouth had dropped open so much the two women turned to look at her with interest. 'This is too much,' thought Karen as she gathered up her bags, looking around for support from the neighbouring passengers. None was forthcoming. Apart from looking up at the louder phase of the orgasm, most of them had retreated back into their holiday reading and Game Boys.

'It has to be first class,' Karen decided, and began hobbling down through the corridors again. By now several people had got off and it was easier to find an empty compartment. Karen was shaking with disbelief and settled down to ring Frances on the mobile to tell all.

She was still looking at the mobile when a man came through and sat opposite. Karen felt very exposed since two people alone in a private compartment are somehow required to acknowledge each other. She looked up quickly to see who the offending interloper was and whether there would be any more trouble ahead.

Amazingly and miraculously, the interloper turned out to be a man of around her age, not particularly good-looking but not ugly either. Karen started to feel hot. Perhaps this was it. Positive thinking had worked.

This was a man on his own in her compartment. She made herself look directly at him since the Life Skills workshop had forced everyone to look each other in the eye for at least five minutes. This had been excruciating but was apparently crucial for bonding and sexual attraction. The man soon became aware of Karen using her new life skill and finally could stand it no longer. He asked her. 'Is that a Nokia?'

'Yup.'

'How do you find it?'

'OK. Well except I can't plug in addresses.'

'It's easy,' he said, keen to get rid of the staring eyes. Karen was just as keen to stop staring because it had produced tears and she didn't want him to think she was emotionally unstable. He moved a little closer to her and said, 'May I?'

'Of course,' Karen replied as if they were at a tea dance.

She was starting to get hot. Hot because she liked him. Hot because he was a man and hot because, well, it was summer and her Ghost outfit absorbed the heat.

'It's hot isn't it?' The man took off his jacket and Karen noticed some sweat marks under his arms. She found this exciting and mentally worked out how long she had before her stop. Was there time to either jump on him or at least get a firm promise of a date? She tried to look attractive while she weighed up her options.

'Do you know who you remind me of?' he said.

Oh no, she thought. *Here we go.*

'A goldfish?' she suggested, to get it out of the way.

'I wasn't thinking of a fish, no,' he said.

'Look, I know this is mad,' Karen ploughed in, realizing she had ten minutes left and simply had to jump in feet-first. 'But I, well I'd started wanting something to happen today and now it has, so I was wondering . . .'

The man looked very interested. 'Yes?' She could see his pupils starting to dilate, which was encouraging.

'And, well, I wonder, if you could just, well, could you kiss me, do you think?'

'Here?' he asked.

'Yeah, it's just a train thing,' said Karen, trying to be throw-away. 'It's just with the rocking motion of the train, I tend to vibrate . . .'

'Do you?' asked the man with even more interest.

'Well, I wondered if you could just, sort of test it for me, to see if I'm vibrating?'

Karen hoped this made sense to him because it didn't entirely to her but they were getting close. The man stood up awkwardly and slightly adjusted his trousers. He came over and cleared his throat, and then started very tentatively putting his tongue over her lips and then inserted it into her mouth.

It was so long since Karen had snogged anyone, she'd completely forgotten what to do. But she wasn't going to argue. She just sort of hung her mouth open to see where he was going next. Then he used his hands to prise off her cardi and pull down the straps of the Ghost shroud. People were getting off at the station and looking in with fascination. She realized that one breast had been taken out of her bra and was pointing straight at the window but she didn't care. Something was happening. She'd made it happen and it was happening now.

The train pulled out with many more curious people waving at their window. With some awkwardness he lamented that he lacked 'protection' but offered to lick her if that would appeal at all? She said it would and together they moved into an even more unusual position, with her legs up against the window while he set to.

Suddenly his mobile rang.

Oh no, don't stop now, Karen thought but couldn't really give this too much attention. He picked the phone up, breaking off only to say he'd missed the stop and that he was sorry. Then he resumed the action.

Then Karen's phone rang, which he deftly intercepted and said, 'It's for you,' holding it by her ear while he continued his work.

It was Frances.

'Was that your right breast I just saw winking at me through the window?' she demanded.

'Probably. Are we there already?' gasped Karen, raising her hip for a better angle.

'You *were*. I can still see the train in the distance. I forgot to tell you my brother was on the same train. He would have got you off in time. Mind you, he brought his friend down with him, who apparently went off to the loo and hasn't been seen since.' She sounded annoyed.

'Ooohhh,' managed Karen.

'Exactly,' agreed Frances. 'I was going to set you up with him. The least you can do is turn up. What am I going to say to the friend?'

The man paused to lick his lips.

'Ooohhh, sorry, can't think right now . . .'

Claire Calman switched to book publishing, editing and writing after several years in women's magazines. She has had a number of short stories published, as well as a novel, the bestselling *Love is a Four-Letter Word*. She is also a poet and broadcaster, and has frequently performed her own verse on radio, including Radio 4's *Woman's Hour*, *Loose Ends* and the comedy series *Five Squeezy Pieces*. Her second novel, *Lessons for a Sunday Father*, is due to be published in January 2001.

The Plain Truth

Claire Calman

Do you know what it's like to be ordinary? To be a plain Jane? Do you have any idea? Perhaps you do. Perhaps, like me, you're used to the way men's eyes slide over you without noticing, as if you're part of the wallpaper. If that's all you know, you expect it as your due, but watching – always – seeing how they look at other women, their eyes lighting up like a panther who's spotted the prey.

For me, it had never been any other way. I wasn't a pretty child. I've always tried to comfort myself with that. How much worse to be irresistible when you're six, only to watch your childish charms disappear one by one, your angel skin spotted, your flaxen hair dulled to mouse, your china-blue eyes faded to bruised grey. They used to take care to praise me, saying: 'Lisa's ever so good with her hands, isn't she?' 'What a neat little girl,' and 'Aren't you doing well at school?' But it was planned, painstaking praise; I could see it even then, embarrassed for them that they tried so hard, pretended for their sakes to be gratified, biting the inside of my lip when I saw the real thing – their spontaneous smiles at the sight of a truly pretty child, their Pavlovian delight.

If you're one of the blessed, the lucky ones, you'll have about as much understanding of all this as you would if I was speaking in Klingon. For you, attention is as normal as breathing, compliments an everyday occurrence as unappreciated as a bus turning up on time. Next time you're at a party, basking in the smiles and too-long looks, take a moment to look around. See, there, in earnest conversation with another woman, ably demonstrating the art of looking like she's having a great time, or in the kitchen thoughtfully washing up some glasses, you'll see one of us.

If you can fight the natural tendency for your gaze to sweep on – yes, the women do it too – take a good, long look. See how neatly she keeps her fingernails, buffed but without the arrogant look-at-me semaphore of shiny nail polish. Notice the hair, properly trimmed and tidy, but not fashionably cut. The clothes now, the skirt not quite the right length perhaps, the skirt of a woman ten or twenty years older; a maiden-aunt blouse with some silliness about the neckline or the buttons, a solitary piece of self-indulgence. Or she may be in no-nonsense jeans and shirt, showing how little she cares for all that dressing up and shallow flirting.

My two best friends, Alison and Jo, are also, well, *average*, shall I say? At least when we go out, there's none of that feeling like 'the other one' all the time. But I've got this other friend, Becks, who's a bit of a knockout. She's tall – five feet ten, I think – and her hair's all just pinned up any old how with bits hanging down, but the general effect is sort of soft and tousled and sexy. If you analyse her features one by one, there's nothing extraordinary about her. It's the whole picture though. I've watched her at parties, or even when she's just going into a sandwich shop. When she enters a room, she stops, pauses for a moment or two inside the door, almost as if she's arranged to meet someone. Then she does one small thing – pulls a strand of hair out of her eyes or reaches up to adjust one of her earrings. And I swear, she has no idea she's doing it. But it's like she expects people to turn around, to stop whatever unimportant thing they're engaged in and look at her. And they do. Especially the men.

And then I come in and everyone goes back to their conversations or their drinking. Sometimes I want to shout, to scream at the top of my voice and stamp my foot on the floor like a spoilt brat: 'Look at me! *Look at me*! I'm here. I'm not fucking invisible!' But I don't of course. I'm not bonkers or anything.

I went and had a free make-up lesson in a department store once, some special promotion it was. I was only in there for a pair of tights but the assistant talked me into it. It felt nice, having someone fuss over my face for half an hour, feeling the cool liquid foundation being sponged on, the flick of the blusher brush over my cheeks. Then, when it was finished, they showed me to the mirror with a flourish as if I were the ugly duckling about to see myself as the swan. I'm surprised they didn't have a trumpet fanfare on tape.

I didn't look like me. There was this horrible, creepy doll staring back at me from the mirror. She'd changed the outline of my mouth, drawn in a new one outside my own lips and filled in with this glossy lipstick – it looked as if I'd tried to swallow a pot of strawberry jam all in one go. It was disgusting. There was so much mascara on my lashes that I had an expression of permanent surprise – which was just as well because it masked my look of total shock. I could hardly speak. I murmured a quick thanks and said I'd think about the products, but must just nip to the ladies. The other shoppers must have thought I was wetting myself, the speed I dashed to the toilet. I scrubbed it all off and dried my face on those awful stiff paper towels, grateful for the roughness purging my skin, grateful for once to see my own familiar, plain face reappearing in the mirror.

And then, a couple of months ago, I saw the dress. It wasn't in the window waiting for me or any of that it-was-destiny twaddle that people say. I was in the nearly new shop, Jeanette's, looking for a mac and a decent jacket for autumn. But there wasn't much in my size. I'm a 12 and, frankly, it's the best thing about me. I'd like bigger boobs but I've enough to be going on with. Jeanette and I were trawling through the rails when she remembered that a woman had brought in some stuff but it hadn't been pressed or priced yet. Still, I go there quite a bit so she said I could have a rummage. I had a dig around, feeling for something tweedy in this big black sack, when my fingers touched velvet. Gave it a tug to pull it out, just to have a look, you see.

It was that crushed velvet, the colour a rich, dark green. I held it against myself in the mirror, turning away from the shop, guilty as a thief. Jeanette bobbed up by my left shoulder.

'Try it on. Go on. The colour's right for your complexion.' At least she hadn't laughed.

It was designed to be almost off the shoulder, so the velvet framed my collarbones and neck, making my skin look smooth and pearly. I felt different in it – more glamorous, of course, but not just that. For one moment, I suddenly knew how it might be to feel lovely and a shiver spun up my arms. I told myself I was a fraud, scowling to spoil the effect, bullying myself in my briskest, most no-nonsense voice.

It was a good fit, too, except the zip was broken. Jeanette let me have it cheap because she couldn't be bothered to fix it.

In the wardrobe, it hung for a month. I used to stroke it casually, as if it were my pet, when I reached in for a blouse or to hang up my skirt. But its presence embarrassed me. Where on earth did I think I was going to wear it?

Then, about three weeks ago, Becks rang up: she was going to a dinner-dance with her chap Tim and his brother Alec, but Alec's girlfriend had just broken her leg skiing. Did I want to come – so long as I understood it wasn't a double date or anything, but just so as not to waste the ticket. Well, who could refuse such a gracious invitation? Still, I was grateful.

The dinner was being held at that incredibly ugly hotel, you know, the big modern one on the edge of town with those silly white pillars at the front that look as if they've been pinched off a wedding cake. Becks had asked me to stay with her and said I could get ready at her place too, as it's on the right side of town. I took the dress in its protective zip-up cover and, in case I felt the need to chicken out, my good black skirt with the white silk blouse. I laid them out on her bed for inspection.

'You haven't been taken on as a waitress for the evening without telling me, have you?' Becks gestured at the blouse and skirt. 'No contest, babe. The velvet is *hot*.'

Once I had it on, Becks walked around me, nodding to herself like a judge at a horse show.

'Make-up? What've you got?'

She poked through the contents of my toilet bag.

'Is this it?'

I retrieved my lipstick from my handbag. 'And this.'

'I'll have to do you with mine.'

She bent over me in the bathroom where I sat perched on the edge of her bath, assessing her handiwork as if she were restoring some old painting that might turn out to be worth something after all.

'Your skin's fine – so just a little light foundation. Where's my blemish stick? That blusher's too pink –

go like this, see? Use a fat brush, that one's hopeless. Now, look down, look up – we'll use this grey shadow as liner . . .'

I reached up to pull my hair back into its clasp, but she stopped me.

'Try it loose. Oh, hang on. Head down.' She put some sort of gloopy stuff on her hands and scrunched it through my hair, then tweaked at bits of my fringe. 'Better.'

It felt odd wearing my hair loose, naked almost. Or it may just have been all the bare skin around my neck and shoulders. I tugged at the unfamiliarly low neckline.

'If you're going to wear it, you've gotta go for it,' Becks bossed me. 'It's no good looking apologetic. Shoulders back. Stick your tits out. Don't keep fiddling with it.'

'Sir, yes sir!' I gave her a crisp salute.

Of course, I had this daft fantasy that Tim's brother would take one look at me and swoon in adoration. Becks said I looked 'the biz' and I really thought I wasn't at all bad. Alec was polite and thanked me for being his escort but, frankly, I thought him rather boring. He talked a lot about his work and kept saying how everyone else in his office was a total tosser and didn't ask me anything about me or what I did.

It was one of those buffet affairs, where you have to stand in line for your food as if you were at a motorway service station, a bit of a cheek when you think how much the tickets were. I was helping myself to some salad when a man queue-barged and stood right next to me.

'There you are, darling. Could you just give me a little of that?'

I looked around behind me, but he gave me a look and then a smile before nodding at the salad again. He had dark brown eyes and very straight eyebrows. I tried not to stare and piled too much salad on to his plate. As I did so, he leant towards me, treating me to a heady whiff of maleness, a sort of spicy-woody smell, a touch of cigar smoke, and said, 'Sorry about that. Forgot the salad. They'd lynch you as soon as look at you if you jumped the queue here.'

'Rightio, *darling.*' I smiled.

During dinner I tried to keep an eye out for the salad-man, but he must have been on the other side of the room. I kept thinking about his eyes and the way he had looked at me. I hardly noticed the food – some kind of chicken thing with rice and rolls that had been left in the oven too long. We all danced; the band wasn't bad and in the breaks, they had a disco. Then, one of my favourites came on, a Gipsy Kings track. I can never keep still when I hear it. Becks and I rushed on to the floor and, maybe it was the dress or maybe it was the wine, but I really let go. My hair swung out around my bare shoulders, the velvet clung to me; there was only me and the music and I loved it.

When I went to sit down, I saw the man again. He was standing on the edge of the dance floor.

'Becks, Becks. Have I got food stuck in my teeth? That bloke's looking at me.'

'That's 'cause he fancies you, stupid.'

I smiled back. He raised his eyebrows and stood there, openly staring at me. As I watched, a woman came up and laid a hand on his arm and he went back to their table. Like most people there, he seemed to be with a group but he was definitely *with* this woman. Thing is, she was really attractive, the sort men like. She had blonde hair – OK, bottle-blonde, but still blonde. A bright red dress with a slit up one side. But there he was, sitting next to her, and sneaking glances at me.

A slow number came on and Tim and Becks smooched on to the dance floor. Alec nodded lazily towards the floor, a question.

I don't want you to think that I'm so desperate that I'll dance with anyone, even if they can barely be bothered to ask me, but I hate sitting at the side, grin fixed in place, showing everyone how much fun I'm having and I'm only not dancing because my shoes pinch a little so I'm taking a break, certainly not because no one's asked me, ignoring me, left over like the knobbly bone on the plate at the end of the chicken supreme.

We moved around dutifully in small circles, walking rather than dancing, Alec's hand on my waist, no more intimate than if he'd brushed against my elbow in the street. Looking past Alec, I saw the man, saw him manoeuvre his partner a little closer to us, then closer still. Then, like clockwork figures dancing to a preset pattern, the two couples rotated in synch. At every turn, his gaze met mine over his partner's shoulder. Unabashed, I looked back.

I went up to the bar to get some more wine. As I stood there, waiting, I caught his eye. His arm was resting along the back of the blonde woman's chair, his hand on her shoulder. She was talking to someone else on her right. And then – while he was looking straight at me – he started to stroke her shoulder. His fingers lightly swept over her skin; his thumb drew a line down her neck, tracing me a message. Beneath the velvet, my own skin shivered. I could feel his desire wash over me in a wave, felt myself flush with the knowledge. Embarrassed, I concentrated on my glass as it was refilled, focused on the coolness in my hand. I reached round to the back of my neck and held it with my cool palm.

Then Alec came up and said would I mind drinking up because we ought to be making a move soon. He had an early squash game before work and wasn't it all a bit of a drag anyway? As I walked back to our table, I half-turned, but the man was hidden behind a group of people, so I couldn't even nod goodbye. I wondered if he would notice that I had left.

'OK?' said Becks. 'Ready to slope off?'

That night, I lay awake on Becks' sofa-bed, my eyes open in the dark, reliving each moment. I rewound the evening like a video, redirecting it in my head, rewriting the script. He came up to me and I said something amusing, clever, he laughed with delight. He bent his head near mine and breathed in my scent. I felt the light pressure of his hand on my back, his touch on my arm. His fingers explored the boundary between velvet and skin over my shoulders, sliding beneath, questing for the soft swell of my breasts. He murmured into my hair, saying my name, his lips brushing my ear.

There was no way of finding out who he was, and nothing I could do. The dress went back in my wardrobe, entombed in its plastic cover, my hair clipped neatly back into its clasp.

And then, yesterday, I saw him. I had dashed into town for a bit of shopping and I popped into WH Smith's for a packet of coloured drawing pins. He was standing at the magazine racks. I couldn't just march up and say hello, so I loitered nearby, pretending to be looking at the books, hoping he'd see me. Then he picked out a magazine and moved towards the till. As I headed for the same till, he turned and looked me full in the face. I smiled and started to raise my hand in a discreet wave. But he yawned, half-covering his mouth, then he looked back down at his magazine.

I stood stock still, clutching my little box of drawing pins like a lifebelt, as if it were holding me up. There must be some mistake, I thought – he can't have seen me. I pushed myself forward to the other till, saw his eyes lazily travel around the room, slide over me once more, look down at the coins in his hand as he reached the head of the queue.

Afterwards, I went home and cleaned the flat, gave it a good going-over, letting the smell of bleach and pine cleanser fill my nostrils, scrubbing behind the taps with an old toothbrush, clearing out my old junk, dreary papers and clutter and silly things, bundling them into rubbish bags.

I felt better when I'd done it. Stood on my doorstep for a moment, looking at the black sacks as if they were a row of prize cabbages. They'll take them away tomorrow morning, the rubbish trucks grinding into my sleep. But now, tonight, all I can hear is the rain outside, pattering on the plastic, making it cling to its cargo – that terrible old pink lampshade, hundreds of hoarded paper bags, my magazines and, now cut to ribbons, the green velvet dress.

Yasmin Boland is one of those Australians who live by the maxim 'have laptop, will travel'. As such, she spends half the year in Bondi, Sydney, and the other half in – or en route to – London. Her writing career has spanned features editing for *Just 17* magazine to working as assistant producer for Channel 4's *The Word* to writing columns for *Playboy* and *Elle*. Her first novel *Carole King Is An Alien* (Penguin) was published in April 2000. She is currently working on her second novel.

Mr Charisma

Yasmin Boland

It was late Tuesday afternoon and I was hungry enough
to eat my own arm. I'd spent five humid hours hanging
around on a pavement (read: gutter) outside a dance
studio at the back of Hackney somewhere, waiting for
Ricky Martin to emerge.

He was (allegedly) inside, auditioning dancers for his
forthcoming UK tour. If so, he must have back-doored
it, because I never saw him. After my sustenance-free
sentry duty, I was finally homeward-bound, without
a photograph to speak of, and headed for my local
Costcutters mini-supermarket on a dinner-or-bust
mission.

Belle Clark hit me right between the eyes the moment
I walked into the shop. Metaphorically, of course. In
the violent exchange which followed, she was very much
the passive victim. She was at the counter waiting to
be served, looking like someone had hung a DO NOT
DISTURB sign off her nose. Her shoulders were so
hunched that her chest was concaving, but trying to
look incognito was pointless. Twelve years playing the
fiery Fran Adamson on *The Crescent* had made her

famous. Her sacking from the TV show, in a media blitz of accusations and denials, had made her legendary.

The scandal which led to her demise involved: a televised outdoor charity event, too many drinks and a security guard who ended up with a bloody nose (after Belle decked him, for trying to stop her from driving home under the influence). After being 'interviewed' (aka 'ritually humiliated') on one of those Friday night post-modernist-up-yer-own-ass-ist TV shows, she'd slammed the door of her high-security Clapham Common mansion in fury, refusing all further interview requests. She was unemployed but evidently not broke or stupid.

The more she refused the media's interview and photo opportunity requests, though, the more they (we) chased her.

So far she'd dodged our cameras.

Now here she was before me in a small grocery shop in South London; her bleached chignon in need of bobby pins, her pale yellow dress in need of a belt, her tights in need of a lycra infusion, handing over a tenner for an ill-concealed litre bottle of Jack Daniels.

I can't explain my actions or even say I know what came over me. What I do know is that I've spent the last twelve months of my so-called career trying to convince a man called Rod Wilson that *I uncategorically do not want to be a paparazza*. And yet, faced with Belle and her bottle of JD . . .

Before the guy behind the counter had a chance to put the bottle in its paper bag or Belle had a chance to notice me, I pulled my camera out of its case, lined up the shot and pressed the shutter button.

Now I had her attention.

My flash exploded, freeze-framing her over-plucked eyebrows, her bleeding red lipstick and saggy jowls. For a second, all I could hear were the clicks of my motor drive whizzing. Then Belle's guttural voice:

'Oi!'

I legged it out of there as fast as my mules would carry me.

The nastiest of my Belle shots adorned three columns of the front page of the London *Evening News* the next day. My boss, Rod, couldn't have been more delighted. He called me from the clattering fluoro-lit picture desk to his cubicle.

'Ru, baby, Ruby, aaaaaaangel, well done.' This was his version of a celebratory haka, saved for scoops and spoilers. 'Check her out. No wonder she won't appear in public any more.' He held the paper up for me, tapping at the first edition newsprint. My shot was what we called 'clean'; eyes-open-and-to-the-camera, unobstructed clarity. I agreed that, looking at Belle's craggy face, it was little wonder she now *'vonted to be alone'*. Twelve months out of the limelight had apparently done her grooming routine few favours.

'You did well, sweetie,' Rod went on.

'Thanks.' Did I really take those pictures?

He leaned across his desk towards me conspiratorially. 'Ru, love, there's something else you should know . . .'

'What's that?'

'Belle had an accident yesterday.'

'What?'

'After you left her in the shop. She went home, got pissed . . .'

She was buying a bottle of JD when I saw her.

'She fell down a flight of stairs. Her husband found her out cold. We've had a call from her lawyer . . .'

'Is she OK?'

'A sprained ankle. Minor bruising. No breakages.'

'God.'

'It's not a problem. The legal guys say there's no way she can hang anything on anybody. She's drunk all the time.'

'Thank God for that,' I said, not meaning it the way it sounded.

In the two years I'd been at the *News*, my rapidly rising star seemed inextricably linked to my apparent paparazzi prowess. Small and female, I didn't look much like your average snapper. My slight frame – a liability in a jostling crowd – was also my best asset; with my spiky blonde hair flattened under a headscarf, no make-up and my camera gear stored in a backpack, I could pass for a Scandinavian tourist on a busy London street.

Catching Belle unawares had been an aberration. Usually, Rod Wilson got the tip-offs from his shonky mates and I was sent to get the shots. So far I'd managed exclusives of 'Famous Female Popster Exiting Club In Tears', 'Ageing Lothario (Rock Star) Shopping For

Lingerie With His (Latest) Mistress' and 'Young Married Male Film Star Suspiciously Embracing Very Married Sky TV Presenter/Model/Whatever'.

Not to mention (please) 'Belle Clarke Getting Ready For A Boozy JD Bender'.

When I wasn't being clandestine, I was sent to wait by the red carpet with my milk crate at film premiers, first nights, major club openings and celeb weddings. I'd asked Rod to let me have a go on features, and the best he'd come up was a story headlined 'Get Out Ya Mugs!' The *News* had campaigned on behalf of a timid 22-year-old called Amy to get some bad-mouthed squatters evicted from her Golders Green flat. The cops were called after our first pictures appeared and a grateful Amy moved back into her rightful, if wrecked home, just a few days afterwards. Call me fussy, but photographing squatters using large bits of furniture to threaten petite home-owners didn't float my boat any more than celebrity-baiting.

'So anyway, Ru, tell me, you're going on holiday, aren't you?' He smiled. The more of his teeth I could see when he talked, the less I trusted him. 'Tomorrow, isn't it?'

'The day after . . .'

'But you deserve an all-expenses-paid holiday. Remind me where you're going . . . ?'

'To Tuscany.' My intention was to stay in a farmhouse – complete with swimming pool, patio, telescope and temperamental Fiat Uno – all owned by my aunt Liz. Liz had offered me the place after she got a last-minute booking cancellation. She knew I needed foreign solace, post-Patrick, but was suffering the usual cash-flow dramas.

'Tuscany?' he made it sound like a snake's hiss. 'The good news, Ru, is that I have a proposal for you. A very decent one.'

I narrowed my eyes into slits which I hoped said, 'Don't-mess-with-my-plans, Buddy.'

'I propose this place, Ruby.' He passed me a postcard with a shot of a very, very blue bay, surrounded by a Mediterranean-looking town or village. The swirly gold inscription said *Greetings From Malta*. The idyllic colours were deliciously unreal. The picture looked like it had been taken in 1955.

'Turn it over. It's from my sister-in-law Fiona. I just got a call from her. She's been on holiday there, renting an apartment in a place called Bencini Bay. She says she saw Johnny Rigg having a Cisk in the apartment next door to hers, last night.'

'Having a what?'

'A Cisk,' he said, pronouncing it *chisk*. It's the local Maltese lager.'

'Johnny Rigg?'

'Yes. The long lost Johnny Rigg. In Malta.'

'God. Do you think it's true?'

'Fiona's daughter reckons it was him, too. And she should know. Her bedroom's covered with Johnny Rigg posters. They saw him on the porch before he turned in.'

'I see.'

'So, as you're about to go on holiday anyway, Ru,

and as you did so well with Belle, I thought you could take your camera with you, and go to Malta instead.' He clasped his hands together, as though this was a done deal. 'It's a beautiful apartment, Ruby, practically five star. Rustic. You'll love it.'

'. . .'

'Ru, Fiona's coming back to England today, and you can rent the apartment she was in . . .'

'But . . .'

'. . . It's right next door.'

'You're joking, aren't you, Rod?' He could *not* be serious.

Then again.

'But, Rod, you know this celebrity thing . . .'

'Of course, we'll help you out financially.'

It's not just that I didn't want to miss out on Tuscany. The idea of spending my holiday chasing a movie star – who, on top of everything else, most likely wanted anonymity – sucked a very large and fat one.

'Rod . . . that's not a holiday. This movie-star-chasing thing . . .'

'Ruby, I'll be covering your costs . . .' Tabloid purulence oozed from his pores like coke from a detoxing addict. 'I'll throw in a per deum and only deduct five days from your annual holidays, whether or not you find Rigg.'

'I'm only taking seven days plus the weekend, Rod!'

'Sorry, Ru. I need you down there. Your flight's booked for tomorrow at midday, from Gatwick.'

* * *

I expected to fly into a barren island full of big fat Brits and Germans on package holidays, wearing Liam Gallagher hats and blow-up rubber duckies round their waists.

From the moment I stepped into the hot air outside Malta airport, though, the vibe was mellow. I was collected by a driver in a rusty yellow Mercedes whose ID card said he was called Joe Caruana and who ferried me under a bright blue sky into an open landscape. Pot-holed roads took us through shady avenues, past limestone churches with huge green domes and alongside shops with faded awnings. On the pavements, old women were gathered chatting and fanning themselves, while nearby, men stood around smoking like it was 1975.

We rounded a corner which revealed a glimmering coastline and horizon, then took a narrower road which led down to a bay, with colourful row boats bobbing on its still waters.

'Next right for Bencini Bay Road,' Joe called out in his singsong accent, as our tyres squealed around another corner and we pelted down a yet narrower street, swerving to avoid the odd stray cat and semi-naked child. As I watched sun dancing on the water through the cracks between the buildings, I felt marginally less murderous.

Having paid and tipped Joe, I followed Rod's instructions to 'walk down the gravelly path at the side of the building'.

And there it was.

My des res for the week.

I dropped my suitcases to have a proper look.

It was rustic, to be sure. But not the five-star luxury Rod promised me. Not at all. In fact, it was more like three-star or plain old home stay. And far, far superior. The exterior was white. The front porch was woven with bougainvillaea. The front door was thirty seconds walk to the glistening sea.

Inside was cool, in both senses of the word. There was a mini chandelier in the living room, a floor mosaic in creams, ochres and greens, and a woolly three-piece suite. The yellowing Laminex and PVC setting in the kitchen looked seventies authentic, and the TV hissed so loudly when I turned it on that I jumped. Even the phone line had an exotic dial tone.

Glory be to the *Evening News*.

I switched off my mobile and took off my shoes to enjoy the cool tiles. Leaving the front door open to the warm evening air, I felt a light sea breeze filter out a bit of the London pollution in my head.

What a place.

For a fashion shoot location.

For a study of the Maltese lifestyle caught in a fast narrowing time warp.

For a gal.

To be alone.

I allowed myself just one thought about Patrick McColl.

He would have loved this.

* * *

More or less housebound by my Evil Johnny Rigg Mission, at least for the first few dutiful hours, I showered, changed and repaired to the porch to admire the view while I contemplated my options. In the end I ate lunch out there, bread and a sticky white cheese bought from the shop across the road, and enjoyed the solitude and late afternoon sun.

For want of anything better to do, I spent a couple of hours writing a cathartic letter to Patrick McColl, which I knew I'd never send. I told him I still can't compose a letter which isn't angry, that I can't remember the 'good times', that I only have pointless thoughts about him making passionate love to Pippa behind my back, and sick questions about what she looks like, and if she's similar to, or very different from me. I told him I wonder if he'd seen my shot of Belle or if he still checks the *News* for my by-line.

Less than four months ago, Patrick came home and told me about Pippa. Our brittle, mature discussion shattered into a shrill screaming match in moments as it became apparent that this Pippa woman was more than 'just' a fling.

'How do you feel about her? Are you going to stay with her?' I screamed across our living room.

'I don't know, Ruby,' was his death knell response.

I found out last week that Pippa has moved in with him.

It never would have worked anyway. When he insisted we go to salsa classes together, I felt like we were turning into his ballroom-dancing parents.

When I found myself resisting the urge to call him a fucking bloody asshole c*nt, I sighed, re-read and shredded the letter.

As I pondered over my glass of duty-free white wine, Bencini Bay shimmered under a pale early evening sky, humidity glowing, a transparent half-moon rising and yellowy streetlights across water lighting up early. The smells of evening started. Someone was frying garlic nearby, making my mouth water, despite my snack. My holiday flat was wasn't set in the rolling hills of Tuscany, but if I could just find Johnny Rigg and be done with this unspeakable business, it would very seriously do.

I grabbed my camera and ambled down to the shore-line to a large rock, listening to the water licking my toes. I wanted to photograph this place, with or without Johnny Rigg in the frame. I had about ten minutes of light left before sundown.

I raised my camera. Then froze.

Two men were approaching. And one was Mr Movie Star himself, the multi-millionaire male Miramax muse, Johnny Rigg, was approaching, crunching down the path to the flats, rounding the corner.

He was wearing fly-eye shades, and his floppy hair had been shorn to a number two, but he was instantly recognizable.

Mr Charisma incarnate.

He hadn't spotted me. I zoomed in for maximum close-up and looked through my lens. I took a milli-second to admire the guy Johnny was with. He had curly sun-kissed hair and a big smile, and sounded like he was encouraging Johnny into something.

'But you'd better hurry, mate,' was all I heard him say.

Holding my breath, I started snapping, taking Johnny's picture twice, getting him clean from the waist up. Then I carried on clicking, panning slowly, from left to right, as if I was taking an innocent 180-degree-stick-together-later-panorama extravaganza. As I stood out there on the rock I was confused about a lot, but very sure on one thing: this wasn't why I'd become a photographer. Johnny Rigg kept walking towards the flats. As I lowered my camera, the blond guy started across the grass towards me.

'Hey. What are you up to?'

I almost lost my footing on the moss as my body prepared for fight or flight while simultaneously trying to look casual. 'Pardon?'

'Sorry,' he said, closer now, half-smiling, perhaps in amusement as I shakily headed off the rock to the sand. 'Sorry.' He put out a large tanned hand for me to balance on, which I accepted. 'Hi.'

'Hi.'

'What are you taking pictures of?' He was much taller than me and he had a London accent.

'These . . . apartments. They're gorgeous. I'm staying in that one.' I pointed.

'Yeah. They are gorgeous.' His skin was the colour of melted chocolate and he had heavy-lidded eyes.

'When did you arrive?' he asked, sizing me up. How good was his radar?

'I just got in today.' If I'd really been on my toes, I'd have adopted a Norwegian accent to complete my Demure Tourist disguise.

'Holiday?'

'Yeah.' I nodded sincerely.

'Right. Hi.' The sun made his face tawny. 'Sorry about . . . I was just . . .' He didn't finish his sentence as we watched Johnny Rigg disappear inside the flat. 'I'm Stu.'

'Hi, Stu.'

I listened to the evening.

'So, you're staying next door?' he asked.

I nodded again. 'Yep. I got in a few hours ago. From Gatwick.' We walked towards the flats and stood awkwardly between his porch and mine.

'Excellent.' His face softened and I could have hugged him. His eyes were acid blue. Johnny Rigg emerged from their flat carrying a large black backpack over one shoulder.

'I'm cutting it fine.' He looked at his watch.

'You'll get there,' Stu said. I looked from the movie star to his mate, my mouth open as I failed to think of something to say. The stillness was broken by the sound of a car horn honking.

'That'll be it, mate,' Stu said.

'Yeah.'

'I'll help you with your stuff.'

'Thanks.'

Inside me, a voice was reminding me why I was here. To stitch up Johnny Rigg. I'd got my shots but I didn't feel as victorious as might have been expected. This close up, Johnny Rigg looked more 'human' than plastic icon movie star. Moreover, his face exuded a funeral despair, as if an acting coach had commanded it.

Johnny turned and left, as if headed for the guillotine. Just as well I had my shots. The temptation to ask them where they were going was almost overwhelming. Stu looked at me. 'See you.' He disappeared round the corner with Johnny and I settled at the table on my front porch, to see what unfolded. I felt like a frog on a log, waiting. But I didn't want to just disappear inside my apartment. I furtively hit 'rewind' on my film.

When Stu returned a few moments later, he stood by my porch, giving me a moment to admire his laid-back air, the clear eyes, the fuzzy blond hair on his forearms and his big bare feet, sprinkled with sand.

'Enjoying the sunset?' he asked.

'Mmm . . .' The view in general, actually.

'Sorry about before. I was just . . .'

'Don't worry about it . . .'

'Are you busy?' he asked.

'Not really.' Smiling.

'. . . because I've got some *pastizzi* and a few Cisks. If you want one . . .'

'What's a *pastizzi*?' Had Johnny Rigg gone for good?

'A Maltese pastry, if you're hungry.'

I was and I'd be very happy to taste my first *pastizzi*. Not to mention inaugural Cisk. Even so, I was reluctant to dine with my prey. Or the friend of my prey. No matter how extremely cute he was. And I mean, extremely.

Stu returned from his flat with paper bags greasy with heat and two cans of Cisk. Snapping one can open, he offered it to me with a grin that flicked the switch on my internal combustion.

'Thanks,' I simpered as I accepted it, proving that it isn't only men who can't hang on to their hormones.

Johnny Rigg's disappearance from London had come suddenly and lasted far longer than anyone had expected. The son of a celebrity shoe designer and a pouting former model from the sixties, one minute he was the leading thirty-something man in enough films to hold his own festival, the next his wife, a make-up artist called Sally, was unfaithful to him, with her personal trainer, a former Gladiator (once known as Vlad, now called Brad). It was a classic Pash And Dash. After their tryst, Vlad/Brad apparently ran straight from Sally's arms to the nearest journo hack he could find, to do a tabloid tell-all, for a reportedly very large fee.

Less than two weeks after publication of Vlad/Brad's imaginatively titled 'My Two Nights Of Passion With Johnny Rigg's Wife', Johnny cancelled out of a string of promotional appearances for his latest blockbuster.

Then his agent pulled him out of a film commitment he was all but signed to.

Johnny Rigg was AWOL.

Stu pulled out a chair for me and passed me a diamond-shaped pastry. 'Welcome to Bencini Bay,' he smiled as he raised his glass.

'Thanks.'

His blue eyes seemed to relax. 'So what's your name?'

'Ruby.' In the candle's flickering, I noticed his broad, one could say noble, shoulders.

'Go on then, take a bite.' He motioned at my *pastizzi*.

I grinned and gulped my lager, then cracked the top off the crispy pastry, watching the steam funnel out. I made 'Mmmmm-ing' sounds and tried not to choke on my beer with confusion. 'This is extraordinary.'

'I love it here,' he agreed.

'It's incredibly beautiful.' I stopped chewing and we smiled. Then he stumped me. 'So, Ruby, what do you do? Do you live in London?'

I'd let my guard down without a pat alibi in reserve. 'Yeah. I'm ... a greeting-card writer.' What? 'You know, I write those little ditties in greeting cards. "Roses are red, violets are blue, I'm in Malta and so are you." That sort of thing.' He'd never fall for it.

'Excellent,' he laughed. 'I guess someone has to do it ...'

'Do you think it sounds like a strange job?'

'No. Not at all. I just never met anyone ...'

'You never met a greeting-card writer?'

'No, funnily enough.'

'Well, you have now.'

While he talked, I envisaged the *Evening News* headline that would hit the streets in a day or two, thanks to my shots: 'We Track Down Heart-Broken Superstar To Paradise Isle'. But where had Johnny Rigg gone?

As we chatted I could sense my camera at my elbow. Maybe it was too late. Perhaps I was already the tabloid shark I'd supposedly railed against becoming.

I knew my shots of Rigg could go towards buying me a pay rise at the *News*; and if I quit the *News* and sold it on the open market? A new car? A new car with a stereo and new tyres? A cheaper new car and new wardrobe? A lot of the camera gear I still needed to go into freelance?

'So, Ruby, let's hear one of your favourite greeting-card messages.'

'Pardon?'

'You must have a favourite.'

'Oh. OK. Let me think . . .' This evening was too balmy for straight thinking. 'All right. My favourite ever ditty – but it wasn't one of mine . . .'

'Go on then . . .'

'OK.' God. I cleared my throat. 'I love you, I love you, I love you almighty, I wish your pyjamas were next to my nightie. Don't get excited, don't get red. I mean on your clothes line, not in bed . . .'

Ground, please eat me.

What I'd recited was a poem my sister Melanie and I said as kids. When I'd found it printed on a greeting card, I'd stuck it to the kitchen pinboard at home. At Patrick's home. At what was now Patrick and Pippa's home.

Stu grinned rather generously at my pathetic effort as I felt myself blushing. 'You write them for a living?' he asked, sounding incredulous. 'OK. Another one . . .'

'Oh no, Stu, don't. I don't want to think about work.'

So we changed the subject and did the safe tourist

chat thing, about sunsets we'd known and places we'd seen. We treated ourselves to some duty-free Cointreau and we launched into a discussion about the ideal holiday.

My thoughts flitted between his travel tales and my not so Zen yen to touch his curls, to feel if they were as soft as they looked. By rights, I should have been on the phone to Rod hours ago, figuring out how to get my shots to the *News* picture desk for tomorrow's morning deadline. Instead I sat idly chatting, laughing at Stu's many crappy jokes, talking about home and panicking slightly as we figured out we had about one point five degrees of separation; his flatmate's ex-girlfriend used to work at my sister's old advertising agency.

'So how long are you here for, Stu?'

'The flat's rented to the end of the month. You?'

'Ten days.'

'Have you been here before?'

'Never. Have you?'

'A few times. My parents have a timeshare at the other end of the island.'

'Aha.'

'They're coming out tomorrow. I'm picking them up.'

'What about your mate?'

'What about him?'

And I couldn't resist any longer. I had my shots. 'Your mate Johnny Rigg . . .'

There was silence, then a raised eyebrow and a sheepish smirk.

'Are you two old friends?'

'We've known each other since we were five. Our mums used to model together.'

Cute. 'Where's he gone, if you don't mind me asking?'

'Back to London . . .'

Once he was back in London, my shots would be nigh on old news.

'I might as well tell you, Ruby, since you'll probably see him.' He paused. 'He's probably coming back in a few days. With his wife.'

'I thought . . . I read . . . Are they getting back together?'

'Maybe.'

'After . . . ?' The Vlad/Brad Fiasco.

'Maybe. The Press don't know he's here. He might actually get some privacy. He's put the apartment next door to ours on hold. If things go well, he'll take a villa on one of the islands . . .'

Then he changed the subject, and made me laugh for at least another hour as he told me about his job as a copywriter, about a long-standing offer he had from Johnny to go sky diving (Johnny had dared him a hundred pounds he wouldn't do it), about the craziest things some of Johnny's female fans had done over the years and about what he and Johnny used to get up to as kids, when their mums took them on modeling jobs. I could just picture Stu as a five-year-old with a curly blond mop, flirting with the make-up ladies and ankle-biting the photographers.

'Do you want another beer, or a glass of water?' he asked finally, as my face threatened to fall off from laughing more in one night than I had in the last few months. I watched him through the window of his apartment, as he poured two glasses of water and fired up a CD player. Maybe it hadn't been easy jollying his famous mate along through his marital crisis. He set the glasses next to my camera on the table, and grinned. The sound of '*Volare*' swelled. 'Want to dance?'

My body practically zinged all over at the thought, but he took my hand anyway, and pulled me to my feet and towards him. His body was warm and strong and he smelled just like the sea air. Blame the heat, or the Cisk, or even the *pastizzi*, but I surreptitiously threaded a few fingers through the damp curls at the nape of his neck, just to feel their texture. My fingers got tangled and as I looked at him in amused embarrassment, he took his opportunity and kissed me.

As the cicadas chirruped, I almost forgot I was kissing the best friend of my latest victim.

We stopped to draw breath and he moved me against the table, his arms around me, my body pressed into his. Then we kissed some more. After some time, things got a little bit hot and hectic and as we squirmed, we bumped the table and my camera and the glasses of water all smashed to the ground. The glasses shattered and my camera bounced open, exposing the rewound film canister. Stu scooped it up and handed it to me, his eyes heavy.

'Is it OK?'

I wiped away water droplets and clicked the camera shut. The Nikon was clearly more resilient than its owner. 'It's fine.' I cleared my throat. 'You know Stu, it's getting really late.'

'True.' He kissed my neck.

'What time do you have to get up to get your parents tomorrow?'

'God. I'd forgotten. Early.'

'I'm exhausted,' I added.

A girlfriend of mine says: 'If you like him, sleep with him. But if you really like him, wait.'

I always say, 'Don't even get to third base with a man if you're about to sell intrusive photographs of his famous best mate to a national newspaper.'

I had to go to bed.

Nine hours later, I awoke after a blissful sleep, cocooned in my cotton sheet, bathed in the sunshine sneaking in around the edge of the curtains.

The first thing I thought of was last night's zinging.

The first thing I saw, though, as I opened my eyes, was the damnable, damned and damning roll of Kodak on my bedside table. I lay awake, reliving the previous night. The main thing that irked me about selling the Johnny Rigg shots was that it would scupper any plans Johnny had of returning to Bencini Bay with his wife. Moreover, another successful paparazzi hit would be just one more reason for Rod Wilson to send me out celebrity-hunting.

I made coffee and watched the yellow and black film canister, feeling like it had eyes which were following me around the room.

Meeting Stu, and getting even a tiny insight into the life of one of my victims, was deeply unsettling, not to mention extremely inconvenient. Perhaps I'd call Rod at the *News*, tell him that Johnny Rigg was nowhere to be seen and demand to be taken off the paparazzi circuit. I didn't want to be doomed to this work, just because I had some hideous knack. Even going freelance and doing bar mitzvahs, weddings and baby portraits – at least to start with – would have to be a step up. My cheapish new car (with the good stereo and new tyres) didn't bear thinking about.

I showered then breakfasted on the porch, with the roll of Kodak in front of me. Finally, I picked it up and walked down to the water's edge.

My last paparazzi moment encapsulated it; I was exhilarated at finding Belle, devastated at the results of my hit. I jiggled the film about in my palm, willing it to fall into the glistening sea. Maybe Johnny Rigg could have brushed off a little papp shot of him on holidays as a mere annoyance. But if he was coming back here to reconcile with his wife, who was I to get in his way?

Gripping the film, I drew my hand back behind my head as far as I could then dropped it to my side again. Then I inhaled, drew it back again, and threw it forward, keeping my fist closed, just to see what it would feel like.

Finally, I put the film down on the rock and picked up the nearest heavy stone I could find, and pummelled and pounded the canister until I broke its seal.

I rose and stood, then I threw the roll of film as high and as far away from me as I could. It soared up, peaked then started tumbling down towards the water, glinting as it went, making a tiny splash as it broke the surface.

A gull squawked what sounded exactly like sincere congratulations.

As the ripples dispersed, I heard the gravel crunching on the path behind me. I turned to see Stu rounding the corner, accompanied by a tall, older man, and pushing a little old woman in a wheelchair. His parents. Stu saw me and waved. His mum smiled at me, shielding her eyes from the sun with a raised hand.

As I walked towards her, I searched her craggy face for recognition and found none, thank God.

Stu started to make introductions, but he needn't have bothered.

I knew his mum.

Her name was Belle Clarke.

Pauline McLynn grew up in the west of Ireland, and was educated there and at Trinity College Dublin, where she studied Modern English and History of Art. (She was a bad student, but had a wonderful time.) She then fell into acting as a career, and has many stage and screen credits to her name. In 1996 she won top television actress at The British Comedy Awards for her role as Mrs Doyle in *Father Ted*. She divides her time between Dublin and London, and sometimes visits her husband, Richard, in Kilkenny (he is a lovely man and she hopes to see more of him in the future). Her first novel *Something for the Weekend* was published in February 2000, and a follow-up *Better Than A Rest* is on the way.

The Sun, the Moon and the Stars

Pauline McLynn

Rosie Andrews leaned against the wall of the narrow corridor and sighed. The screams from the nearby dressing-room grew louder and louder. Some poor soul was getting an earful. Actually, anyone within earshot, and probably for a radius of half a mile, was getting an earful.

'*Red* grapes,' the voice shrieked. 'Don't you understand plain English? I said *red*! Not *green*!'

It was amazing that such a beautiful woman could make such an ugly sound, thought Rosie. Beverley Tremayne was fast approaching her sell-by date, of that there was little doubt, but she still had the vestiges of her most popular assets, and was still beloved of the nation, particularly for her early roles as doomed heroines in bodice-ripping television series. These had been her forte, as well as marrying and divorcing most of her leading men along the way.

'Dear Lord,' she continued, 'how am I to summon my muse when I am thwarted at every turn? It's just one damned annoyance piled on another. How will I rise above the mire? But I must,' she wailed, 'and I *will*! In spite of all of you and your petty meanness.'

Rosie hurried along around the corner. The old Victorian theatre was a warren of corridors and unexpected rooms. She hung a right by a generator and continued along a little-used walkway. The corridor darkened and curved to the left, leading to an unmarked door. She paused to catch her breath and calm her racing heart, her excitement hard to contain. She knocked lightly. 'Come,' growled a man's voice. Oh yes, she would. She opened the door of the room, but could see nothing, so she reached for the light switch. A hand slapped hers away. 'Don't you dare. You should know better than that by now.' Rosie gasped with anticipation; a new game? 'Take your clothes off,' the voice ordered, pulling her into the middle of the room. Rosie did as she was told.

Anthony Dubray was worried. This summer season had not turned out as expected. He had never finished a theatre run without having an affair with *someone*, but this one was nearing an end with no affair in sight. A trickle of sweat ran down his back. The air-conditioning system was as ancient as some of his chat-up lines, he thought, sourly. Or could it be that he was simply losing his charm or good looks? Or both? He shivered, in spite of the cloying heat. In the distance he could hear the sound of a raised female voice. He was obviously not the only one feeling the pressure.

The season had sounded like a wonderful idea when his agent had called, although he did not show that he cared even slightly for it.

'Darling, very exciting project for you. Sir Francis Birkin is mounting an ensemble company to perform some new short plays in rep for six weeks. There is talk that Channel 4 may be interested in taking some of these to television then. What do you think?'

'You know I hate repertory work,' he said loftily, 'chopping and changing parts from night to night. It's too much pressure for an artiste, and I really do think it's so *passé*. Could I not just wait for the telly version to come up?'

'Frankly, no. You're in from the beginning or you're out. And face it, Tony, work has been thin on the ground for you over the last while. They've got the best of the youngsters around signed up for the juve roles, and you'll be playing a few dads to them and some juicy character cameos. On top of all of that, this will get a lot of press attention.'

'Mmm, I'll think about it.'

'No, Anthony, you'll do it. I'll get them to bike the scripts and a contract over. Oh, and by the way, your ex-wife Beverley is involved, so that should add some spice. Congratulations, darling, you'll be just marvellous.'

'As always,' he sniffed, to a dead telephone line. The deal was done.

'Do hurry up, Dickie, the driver is looking daggers at the house. You know how impatient the working classes can get.'

'I'm going as fast as I can at my age, Oliver. You, as

a younger man cannot fully appreciate that, but in time you will, dear boy.'

Richard Hardwicke (seventy) stood in front of Oliver Dickens (sixty-eight). 'How do I look?'

'Divine, my dear, divine. And that hair-rinse was pure genius; you don't look a day over forty-five.'

In truth, both men could have passed for one hundred and forty-five. They took one last gaze into the hallway mirror, adjusted some bits of linen and silk, and wafted out to the waiting black cab.

'The Drewsbury Theatre, West End,' Oliver told the driver. 'Sit right back, Richard. You know there's precious little purchase on these seats, and we don't want you sliding about and perhaps hurting yourself.'

'At my age.'

'At your age. Now, checklist: scripts, yes; biographies for the programme, yes; signed pictures for the fans, yes; Earl Grey, yes; and a packet of your favourite shortbread.'

'Anything else?' asked Richard, teasingly.

'Um, no, not that I can think of.'

'Oh, come now, I think we both know that there is a little something I never leave for the theatre without.'

'No, Richard, I can't think of what that might be.'

Richard Hardwicke was aghast. 'You don't have it, do you?' He began to fidget, then to hyperventilate. 'We shall have to go back. I cannot face the theatrical world without it.'

'Without *what?*'

'My lucky Dresden cat, you fool. Dame Edith gave it me, and you know perfectly well that I cannot perform without it. We *must* turn back, Ollie.'

'And might this be the little fellow?' Oliver asked, innocently producing the ornament.

'Oliver Dickens, you are a wicked, *wicked* man. You ought be ashamed of frightening an old man so. Give me my treasure. *I* shall be curator of Diddums henceforth. Your wicked sense of humour precludes you from the job.' Richard Hardwicke cradled the little china cat in his arms, and attempted to stifle a theatrical sob. The only sound to emerge was a dry, hoarse honk.

'I was only teasing,' sulked Oliver.

'Oh, I forgive you, you foolish youngster. You and your silly pranks.'

The taxi driver took a particularly vicious left into Drewsbury Lane, throwing both men to the right. They were just untangling themselves when the cab jerked to a halt outside the theatre. A small knot of people stood in the portico.

'Oh my goodness, Ollie, it's a welcoming committee. I had hoped for a little breather before meeting everyone. I'm so nervous.'

'Well just don't soil yourself,' warned his partner, 'we don't have any changes with us.'

Richard Hardwicke and Oliver Dickens gathered their belongings and alighted with considerable aplomb from the car. Delighted chatter filled the air.

'Ah,' boomed Sir Francis Birkin, 'it's the two Dicks.'

* * *

Marcus O'Neill surveyed the rehearsal room and its assembled company as Sir Francis welcomed them and gave the initial, obligatory pep talk. His innards were heaving with terror, but his calm and beautiful exterior betrayed nothing. Two months ago, he had been sitting in a rented flat in Dublin wondering how he would pay his bills. He had just completed a hugely successful production of *The Plough and The Stars*, which had played at the Abbey Theatre, toured Ireland, and then, most crucially, wowed London audiences at the National. He had been paid well for the job, but he had also lived well for the duration, and so the O'Neill coffers were bare. Unbeknownst to him, as he fretted in Dublin, Sir Francis was putting together his own package in London, and Marcus O'Neill was top of his wish list.

'We need his youth and vision. He's wonderful with actors, by all accounts; well, the results speak for themselves. Let's hitch this season to this rising star. And of course, we catch him at the start of his career; so he'll be that little bit less expensive.'

Marcus had met everybody, however briefly, before this first read-through. Some of the actors had been chosen by Sir Francis, because he had worked with them before, or felt that they were box-office draws. But Marcus had insisted on informal one-to-one chats with all of them, to assess them and to make a personal welcoming contact. He pinched himself surreptitiously, to check that this was not a dream. There were faces in this room that dated from his childhood, stars from television and film. Perched by one corner of the huge table at which they sat was Alan Larkin, whose sitcom *Then as Now* had run for nine years on the BBC. Marcus could still hear him say his famous catchphrase 'Well now, Mary-Lou'. Opposite Alan was Beverley Tremayne, who had played havoc with his teenage hormones as she undressed every Sunday evening in *The Follies of Beckford*. She had deliberately distanced herself from the youngest female member of the cast, Elysha Bryant. If the young woman noticed, she gave no indication, but sat arm-in-arm with Ashley Hancock, with whom she had just starred in *The Tempest* at the RSC. They were both hanging on Sir Francis Birkin's every word. Anthony Dubray looked lustily in Elysha's direction. He, no doubt, would ply her with his I-was-just-pipped-to-the-post-for-James-Bond-by-Roger-Moore-but-of-course-I-was-far-too-young-anyway story by the coffee break. Marcus did not rate Anthony's chances of success there. Oliver Dickens was dispensing shortbread to Richard Hardwicke, and catching the young director's eye as often as possible for a flirty smile. Marcus could not resist a chortle; the man was old enough to be his father twice over.

Sir Francis was nearing the end of his speech.

'I will be pressing you to talk to the media throughout our short rehearsal period, a necessity in this day and age. And we'll be running our own aggressive publicity campaign over the coming weeks. Our tag-line is "Bringing home the Birkin", as this is my first theatrical venture in London for some time. Hammy, yes,' he acknowledged to the company's groans, 'but catchy too. Any questions? No? Good. Then I'll hand you over to Mr O'Neill, who will take over today's proceedings from here.'

There was a smattering of applause as Marcus rose to his feet.

'Welcome all,' he purred in his deep, Celtic tones. 'I'm delighted that you could all find availability to work on this project. I think we'll have a lot of fun with it, as well as doing some good, innovative work. The acting core has been introduced by Sir Francis, so I'd like to introduce our production staff. Many of you will know James Long, our designer, and Frank Williams, our lighting designer. To my right is Rosie Andrews, our stage director and her assistant Jonny Brewer. And last but by no means least is Greta Moore, our wardrobe supervisor. Obviously, this is a very daunting project, but I feel sure that it will be a very satisfying one also. Right, I think it's time to read the plays out loud, don't you? Let the games begin.'

Again, applause sounded in the room. Marcus's heart was pounding hard in his chest as he sat down. Only Rosie noticed his hands tremble. She was delighted; he was sensitive as well as gorgeous. She wondered how she would concentrate on her work with such a distraction close by.

Some hours later they all knew the scale of what they were attempting.

The company was mute with excitement and worry.

'Thank you all for your work today,' said Marcus. 'I don't know about the rest of you, but I could murder a pint right now. I'll be repairing to The Marquis of Denby next door, and you are all very welcome to join me. Rosie will give you your calls for tomorrow.' He turned his gaze to the elfin stage director, admiring her auburn hair and playful dark eyes, as he had on the day they had first met. 'You'll join me too, won't you?'

'Yes,' Rosie croaked, as a shiver ran up and down her spine. He was so handsome, yet oddly vulnerable. She looked forward to getting to know him better. Much better.

The first week sped by. The schedule was so hectic that the actors had no real time to develop or nurture rivalries; they were simply too busy nailing down their lines and moves. Richard Hardwicke did, however, have time to notice how much attention Oliver paid to Marcus O'Neill, notwithstanding that he was the director. Beverley Tremayne noticed how much attention Marcus paid to Elysha Bryant. Anthony Dubray noticed how much attention Elysha repaid Marcus. He also hit on the notion that his ex-wife had a different shaped chest now, and resolved on some detective work to prove his theory. Rosie Andrews noticed every detail of attention paid by or to Marcus O'Neill. She found it a torture, even if she was the centre, however briefly, of that attention.

And it didn't help that a lot of other things were

getting on Rosie's nerves. Alan Larkin took to calling her Mary-Lou, specifically so that he could use his sit-com catchphrase at every possible opportunity. Each time she corrected a line, or reminded him of a movement he would say 'Well now, Mary-Lou' in mock horror. Anthony Dubray put a lecherous arm round her shoulders or waist any time he wanted a prompt. Elysha Bryant arrived at rehearsals in ever-shortening skirts, as the weather got hotter. And the two Dicks began to whine about the air-conditioning, their billing on the poster and what dressing-room they would get.

The only one amongst the actors who might have been bearable was the young Ashley Hancock, but he too had his drawbacks. Or at least one major one: the man was a crashing bore. On their first evening in the pub, Rosie had been cornered by him and treated to a history of fishing, and Ashley's place in its role call of fame. She now knew of the thrill of the cast-off, the waiting, the waiting, the waiting and the waiting, the eventual hooking, reeling, landing and release of the poor unfortunate fish. If he even ate the sorry beggers, thought Rosie, the whole saga might at least have a potentially macabre twist. Ashley Hancock was a model actor and a pleasure to work with, but socially he was to be avoided at all costs.

'I'm having a lot of trouble with my diaphragm.'

Rosie's attention snapped back to the rehearsal room, and her eyes honed in on the speaker, Elysha Bryant, who was looking very worried. Rosie could not believe the audacity of the young actress; this was hardly the correct forum to be discussing her chosen method of contraception. Then she realized her mistake. Racy as the comment had seemed, it was in fact an actor 'talking technical'.

'I just don't feel that it's giving me full capacity. I need a lot of steam to reach the back wall of the theatre here when I'm crying out for help, and I'm not confident about it.'

Anthony Dubray rushed to the rescue. He stood in front of her and gripped her breasts. 'Don't breathe from *here*,' he said, giving said breasts a squeeze, 'breathe from *here*,' he was now clutching below her ribs. To underline his point, he repeated the exercise. 'Not *here*,' he reiterated, hands on Elysha's breasts, '*here*,' hands below ribs.

Marcus O'Neill cleared his throat while contemplating the floor. 'Yes, Anthony, thank you for that.'

Elysha Bryant looked into Anthony Dubray's eyes and echoed the director's words. She seemed genuinely grateful. Rosie turned to her assistant Jonny Brewer, who had buried his face in his script and was choking silently on his own laughter.

'Actors,' she whispered, 'what are they like? He obviously just wanted a quick grope, dirty old goat.'

With that, Beverley Tremayne ran to the middle of the rehearsal space and said, 'Anthony, could you show me exactly what you mean there? I fear I've been using the wrong organs altogether for my breathing.'

Anthony Dubray obliged, as Marcus O'Neill called a coffee break.

* * *

By Saturday afternoon, the company was exhausted but pleased with their first week's work. They decided to celebrate with a drink in The Marquis of Denby. On this occasion, although he paid plenty of attention to the actors, Marcus seemed to position himself easily within Rosie's reach, and would include her, wherever possible, in his conversation. Was it her imagination, or did he brush past her just a little more than was strictly necessary? Did he meet her eyes boldly, intensely, whenever she spoke? Whatever the answer, it was certainly thrilling and Rosie did not want it to end.

When it came time to leave, she began to assemble her many bags together in preparation for her trek to the tube.

'Rosie, you're going my way aren't you?' She looked up into Marcus O'Neill's piercing green eyes.

'Am I?' she asked.

'Don't you live southwards?'

'Em, yes, eh Vauxhall, actually.'

'Great. I'm headed towards Clapham Common, so you can share my car. It's one of the perks of being the director. Mind you, I think Sir Francis laid on the transport because he heard what a crap time-keeper I am, and he wanted me to be punctual for rehearsals.'

After a quick round of goodbyes, Rosie found herself nestled in the back seat of a Mercedes speeding towards the river. Marcus chatted excitedly about the rehearsals, and asked her opinion on various technical matters. She found it hard to put sentences together, and wanted to answer just 'yes' or 'no' so that she could gaze at him uninterrupted. London was bathed in a hazy light, and the hot weather meant rolling down the car windows. The breeze played with Marcus's already tousled curls, and Rosie had to fight an unbearable urge to reach out and steady them.

They arrived at her apartment all too quickly. Once again she began to gather her belongings, hoping that her exit from the Merc would not be too awkward with all the excess baggage.

Marcus turned to her and said, 'So this is it then.'

'Yes, this is me.'

He reached over to kiss her, and automatically she turned her cheek to him. His hand touched her face and brought it around to his. Then he kissed her full and long on the lips. It was so unexpected that Rosie pulled away slightly and gasped for breath. He was delicious. Her head swam. This couldn't be happening. Then she reached forward and they kissed again, this time with tongues entwined and searching. It was ferocious, passionate.

When they parted, he smiled and said, 'I'd better come in, don't you think?'

'Yes,' gasped Rosie. It was a word she would use a lot over the next twenty-four hours.

They had a tacit agreement that none of the company should know of their affair. It would not do to have any awkwardness about it, and the best way to see to that was to keep it a secret. And that's where the game-playing began. They would read each other's movements, second guess one another. They began to meet in unlikely places during the day to steal time together. The excitement reached a fever pitch, not least because the opening week was suddenly upon them.

The technical rehearsals were a nightmare. The two Dicks became increasingly cranky, and Rosie suspected that it was not entirely acting-related. Any time Marcus gave a direction to Oliver, Richard would shoot angry looks at both of them. Then he would complain loudly that he was not lit on stage.

'Everybody in the business with half a brain knows that Frank Williams couldn't light his way out of a paper bag,' he announced, well within earshot of the lighting designer. 'That's why he's known as The Prince of Darkness, for crying out loud.'

'God, but those two are a nightmare today,' Rosie remarked to Jonny.

'You missed the fireworks earlier,' her assistant said. 'I had to go in and break up some fisticuffs, no less. Wardrobe are still trying to get the blood out of Oliver's original costume.'

Rosie looked out on to the stage. Sure enough, Oliver Dickens was not in his intended attire. He was also swaying alarmingly. Then before her eyes he slumped into a dead faint. She rushed on stage, yelling at Jonny to call a doctor. When they made Oliver comfortable in his dressing-room, a weeping Richard Hardwicke admitted to hitting him so hard across the face earlier that he had dislodged one of Oliver's teeth.

'Now he's lost so much blood that he's fainted,' Richard wailed. 'And it's all your fault,' he cried, pointing at Marcus.

'Oh shut up, you silly old fool,' croaked a weak little voice. Oliver's hand wobbled into view and took hold of his partner's. 'Don't you know it's you that I love. The boy means nothing to me, even if he is a genius. Go now, everyone, I need to rest and I'll rejoin you as soon as I can. The show must go on.'

True to his word, after a brief snooze and a visit from the doctor, Oliver Dickens was back at work. Strangely enough, just in time for the press conference. 'I didn't need the quack,' he declared. 'Doctor Theatre was my cure.'

A bank of photographers snapped incessantly as journalists barked questions at the company. An American in the crowd called Beverley 'Beaverley' and the name stuck. Elysha was whisked away to pose draped across a coffee table on the set, with Ashley pouting in the background.

'Beaverley' sniffed in dismissal. 'She'll look like a giant human-shaped ashtray when that's printed,' she opined.

'Any romances in the company?' asked a tabloid hack.

For the briefest moment Rosie caught Marcus's eye, then they both looked away. No one else noticed.

Sir Francis laughed and said, 'How can you ask that when we have one of the most enduring romances under our very noses?' He gestured to Richard and Oliver, who preened on cue.

'Mr Dubray,' called another, 'any chance of a reconciliation between you and Miss Tremayne?' Rosie remembered that they had been married for five minutes during the seventies.

Anthony was delighted to be the centre of attention. 'That is entirely up to the beautiful and talented Miss Tremayne,' he replied chivalrously. He even surprised himself with his sensitivity.

But attention was quickly diverted when Alan Larkin used that very moment to plant his catchphrase 'Well now, Mary-Lou', and the media frenzy turned its spotlight on him.

'Damn comedians,' Anthony swore to himself. 'Can't bear to be ignored.'

He looked appraisingly at his ex-wife. Not looking too bad, for an old bird, he thought. She might do if there was no one else in the offing, so to speak.

From there on out, matters were a haze of previews, re-rehearsals, more previews, floral deliveries, a first first night (for there would be three in all, as the programme changed), much air-kissing, schmoozing, agent-hugging, TV executive toadying, more interviews, and the inevitable reviews. They were universally good, the box-office was strong and the company was well pleased with itself.

But as the final batch of plays opened, everyone began to get a kind of 'gate fever'. It was like the experience of prisoners when they know that release is upon them; so close and yet so far. Rosie was charged with organizing a last-night party, some drinks, food and music in the latest hot spot, a bar in Soho called The Sun. She hated every moment of it, because when that was over, so too was the season, and, she supposed, her relationship with Marcus.

He began to act differently towards her. The games had stopped, though he still spent most nights with her. And one day during that last week, he took her aside, 'to have a proper talk'. Rosie knew what to expect, and her heart was sore in her chest as he began.

'Rosie, you know that these last weeks have been a very special time for me. I have never felt so passionately about anyone. This has been a rollercoaster. I never believed that I could do some of the things that we have. The abandonment of it, and I suppose the, the . . .' he searched for a word, gesticulating with his long fingers as he did, 'the . . . *wantonness* of it, has over-whelmed me. But my feelings for you have changed over the weeks, and I can't do that any more. Do you understand? I feel something else now, something more profound. And I need to know if you feel it too. Do you? Can we move on, do you think?'

So there it was. She had heard similar speeches before, though perhaps none had been so lyrically obtuse. She blinked back some tears. He wanted to be friends, that hoary, old, deep and meaningful way of ditching someone. What a fool she had been. She really had thought that this was different, that this was *real*.

She was in agony as she fought for breath to reply. Because Rosie Andrews realized there and then that she had fallen in love with Marcus O'Neill.

'Yes, I understand,' she said, haltingly. 'I feel the same way too. Don't worry, everything will be fine, it'll be no trouble at all.' Then she ran away into the darkness of the theatre, and Marcus was sure he could hear her cry. He was bemused. What a strange way to react, he thought, I've just told her that I love her, and I didn't even get a kiss. Perhaps she needed time to come to terms with the situation. He decided to leave her be until she did. But then a terrible thought occurred to him – perhaps she could not return his love. Marcus pushed that to the back of his mind; he could not bear to live with that option.

London had been in the grip of a heatwave for two months and something had to give. On the last night of the season, a massive thunderstorm was forecast.

Sir Francis Birkin was delighted. 'We'll go out with a bang,' he declared to everyone.

The only bang Anthony Dubray longed for was from a different natural source than the one referred to by the company manager. On the half-hour call, he followed Rosie and Jonny into Beverley's dressing-room. It was not by design. They just happened to be ahead of him in the corridor and he had followed them without thinking. Jonny was carrying a large basket of red grapes for the diva and Rosie was distributing maps of how to get to The Sun later on. When the stage management team left, Anthony and his ex-wife sat in silence, looking at one another, perspiring gently in the clammy heat. Then Beverley stood up and let her flimsy robe fall open.

'I'm having trouble with my breathing again,' she said. 'Could you show me where that damned diaphragm of mine is?' They became a tangle of limbs and groans, and both of them began to wonder why they had ever separated in the first place.

As they reached Elysha Bryant's dressing-room, Jonny casually suggested that he would deliver the map. Rosie handed it to him, only half listening. But as the door closed and she heard the words 'Darling, I've been longing to see you all day', Rosie realized that her head had been firmly stuck in the clouds for far too long.

Richard Hardwicke and Oliver Dickens were washing one another in their shower when she called with their map to the festivities. Happy sounds of laughter and splashing filled the steamy little room. She made no noise to disturb them, but her mind reluctantly strayed to images of the many baths and showers she had taken with Marcus, and she fled the room as her tears began to flow unchecked.

Ten minutes later the first crack of thunder sounded and the old theatre groaned. Rosie sat miserably in a corner by the stage, silently bearing witness to the fact that it was not just the storm that was making the theatre moan so, but also the sounds of pleasure emanating from the many dressing-rooms below the performance area. Her broken heart ached and she wanted to die. She resolved to get very, very drunk later that evening.

The final performance was a triumph, and after the standing ovations, champagne toasts, and dressing for the party, Rosie found herself wedged into a corner of The Sun looking at Ashley Hancock's favourite fishing photographs. In fairness, they were moving a little in and out of Rosie's consciousness as the alcohol in her system took effect. She finally escaped him on the pretext of getting them both another drink from the bar.

On her way she encountered Alan Larkin who, predictably enough, arched an eyebrow and uttered, 'Well now, Mary-Lou.' Rosie trod heavily on his foot and apologized profusely for her clumsiness. She edged by Anthony and The Beaver, but they didn't notice, attached to one another as they were in an adolescent snog. She joined Jonny at the bar, and noticed that he was surreptitiously holding hands with Elysha Bryant.

Rosie felt that the black cloud of her misery could get no darker. And then it did. Marcus O'Neill had been scarce all evening, but now he made a grand entrance, with a beautiful blonde on his arm. Rosie let out an involuntary cry of anguish and bolted back the nearest drink she could find. It was a straight vodka, which seemed to burn straight through to her soul, as Marcus O'Neill had done for his own flippant pleasure. How could he do this? How could he be so cruel? Even if he was finished with her, and he had made it clear that he was, why make a statement like this? It was so unnecessary. She was hurt enough without having her nose rubbed in the squalor of it all. Something snapped in her brain and Rosie decided that she had had enough.

'Jonny, get me a pint, would you? There's something I have to do.' With that she hoisted herself on to the bar and called the company to attention.

And when they were all rapt, there, in The Sun, Rosie Andrews leaned over and mooned at the stars. As their shocked, upside-down faces became distinct between her legs, Rosie noticed one in particular coming forward to speak to her.

'Rosie,' said Marcus O'Neill, 'when you're done there, I'd like you to meet my sister.'

Victoria Routledge grew up in Cumbria and now lives in Balham, Gateway to the South. She worked in publishing for three years before her first novel, *Friends Like These*, was published; the second, *Kiss Him Goodbye*, is also published by Little, Brown. Victoria's own hair is the colour of a dunked ginger snap and she goes to a fantastic hairdresser called Caroline, who makes her hair look wonderful and always has great conversation.

The Shell of Venus

Victoria Routledge

Maura slipped her shades on as she pulled the front door shut and, as she locked it, she wondered nervously whether the dark glasses would just attract attention to her, particularly if she saw anyone she knew. That was why celebrities wore dark glasses, wasn't it, so people would say, 'Ooh, there's a celebrity! Is it that one out of *Coronation Street*?' An anti-disguise disguise. In the same way that Slimfast was a diet product disguised as a high-fat, ridiculously indulgent milkshake.

She hesitated for a moment, one hand on the door-keys still rooted in the lock, the other on her shoulder bag, then decided that on a sunny day in the middle of August it wasn't that odd to be wearing shades. No less odd than the enormous sun hat she had on to disguise her bright blonde hair, anyway.

It was the first time in nearly a week that she'd been outside. Ignoring the remnants of her hangover banging in her ears, Maura strode quickly across the street, flinching under the blast of sun on the small amount of skin she'd risked exposing, and slung her bag in the back of her Mini. Three crisp packets and a self-help tape skittered into the footwell, joining the clutter beneath both seats. She gave the tape an evil look. And much good you were, she thought. Three weeks of in-car brainwashing, and I still have about as much internal tranquillity as Conan the Barbarian.

With a quick check around, Maura slid into the car, with some difficulty, due to the diameter of her hat, feeling about in the back for the London A–Z. Normally she drove creatively on directional instinct, but today there were appointments to keep and she had to check where she was going, since her holiday transformation was decidedly not going to be taking place locally.

Everything was dark behind her Ray-Bans, and then the hat kept getting in the way, and then, as she tried to bend the brim back, Maura thought she could see her friend Daniella turning into the street, so in the end, she frisbeed the hat into the back and executed the fastest three-point-turn she had done since her driving test, screeching on to the main road while she rammed a tape into the machine.

'Holiday' by Madonna.

'Celebraa-aate,' sang Maura, and then grimaced to herself.

Once inside The Shell of Venus, Maura hovered nervously by the nail-varnish display. Beauty salons put her on edge, reminded her of all the delicate areas of feminine cultivation she tended to skip in favour of longer lie-ins and guilt-free evenings out on the razz. The same way some people dreaded hospitals for reasons of their own mortality she dreaded beauticians for reasons of her own cellulite. And also because Phil was forever telling her to stop biting her nails.

She had chosen a salon in North London because she didn't know anyone who lived there, and, more importantly, as far as she knew, neither did Phil. The Shell of Venus wasn't somewhere she'd been before: she had picked it out of the *Time Out Shopping Guide* on the basis of its nice warm towels.

The junior behind the reception desk seemed nice and warm too. So warm, in fact, that she put her emery board down almost immediately, and asked, 'Can I take your, um, coat?' refraining from the obvious question, 'And why *are* you wearing a fur-lined parka in this weather?'

Maura peeled off her anorak and handed it over. Hot, but necessary on the disguise front. Underneath, her arms looked very white and faintly clammy. She rubbed them self-consciously, until Miss Manicure ran her beautiful red nail down the appointments list and looked up with a big smile.

'Is it Maureen?'

'Maura. Sorry.'

'The all-day pre-holiday day?'

'That's it.'

'Lovely. We like to start off with the aromatherapy massage and sugar waxing, get you in the mood. Why don't you come through to the massage suite? Debbie's just cleaning herself up for you.'

Oh good, thought Maura. Get the walls scraped

down before the next customer, why don't you. Nice touch.

'You just take your things off and lie down there,' invited the receptionist in buttery tones, pointing to the massage table. Maura eyed it dubiously. The last time she had lain on a bed with paper towels on it, there had been serious metallic consequences for her internal organs. And the time before that had been . . .

Maura bit her lip and blinked quickly. Where was all the internal water *coming* from? She hadn't been able to wear mascara for weeks.

She made herself go through the memory. *The time before that* had been with Phil, who didn't see why simple female functions should spoil their not inconsiderable fun. He had taken messy female emissions in his stride along with everything else. Blocked pipes, broken expansion bottles, post-tequila projectile vomiting, he had dealt with the lot. A model boyfriend.

She bit her lip harder and squeezed her eyes into a squint to stop the tear sneaking out. Bloody hell. The arrogance of the man. Even randomly associating himself with her periods.

'Maura! I'm Debbie!'

She swung round, images of Phil all sweaty and glinty still hovering in the back of her mind, and saw a round-faced woman in white overalls bearing down on her with a big Australian grin. Maura shook herself and put on her co-operative client expression. This had been going on for weeks now. She had to get a grip. And if anyone could make her get a grip, surely this brisk au pair of a woman could. Maura looked at her strong brisk Australian hands. A grip like a gorilla.

'Hop up!' said Debbie, patting the paper towels.

She gave a weak smile. When she saw it in the mirrors lining the tiny room even she had to admit it was a pathetic imitation of her usual grin. A *Stars in Their Eyes* imitation.

Maura pulled off her things without looking at herself or Debbie and hoisted her protesting body on to the table. It was a relief to feel the towels (warm, as advertised!) settle on her back, and even more of a relief that Debbie didn't start talking until her strong brisk hands had massaged Maura into yielding semi-consciousness.

Phil began to subside into the background again. What kind of man wanted to have sex during her period anyway? Freak. And paper towels. What did he think it was, *Animal Hospital*?

Debbie soothed and smoothed all the crossness from her back. Small meteors spun in Maura's closed eyelids.

'I'm now putting some stones on your back to refresh your chakras,' said Debbie cheerfully.

Maura felt three round drops of coolness settle on her spine, and the clenched feelings she had been carrying in her lower intestine suddenly fell away, through her stomach, through the table, through to the floor. She almost leapt up in surprise, wanting to clutch them back. They had been quite reassuring.

'You're in for the full monty today then?'

'Oh, er, yes.' Maura was temporarily too distracted

by the unexpected lightness in her stomach to be shy. 'Waxing, fake tanning, highlights, the lot.'

'Going somewhere nice?'

'Er . . .' Maura debated with herself. What was the best thing to say? Yes? No? Come clean?

Before she could make up her mind she felt a stabbing pain in her coccyx that made her yelp out loud. When she twisted herself up on to one elbow to see if Debbie had ripped her spine out of her back like a half-eaten trout, Maura only saw Debbie applying her thumbs to a point currently marked out with four hot pebbles.

'You've a lot of tinsion in this area,' said Debbie. There was reproach in her voice, and disapproval very apparent in her fingers. 'Have you been aht on the lash much recently?'

'No!' Maura began defensively, but then as Debbie added another stone, changed that to, 'Oh God, yes, all right.' These days her body wasn't a temple so much as a lock-up garage – any old rubbish went in, and as long as the doors still shut she didn't care.

'Boyfriend trouble?'

'You could call it tha-aa-aa-aa-aa-aat!'

Debbie increased the pressure on her coccyx.

'Ah dear.'

Maura clenched her lips against the pain. What *did* you call your ex getting married on the spur of the moment to someone you'd never met? Or, to rewind a bit, what *did* you call finding out that your 'Blood Still Fresh Under The Nails' ex had announced his engagement while you were in Dublin on a training course – and you'd only found out because you were flicking through a day-old abandoned *Times* on the tube back from Heathrow?

That's 'Boyfriend Trouble'?

Right.

'Can you go easy on my spine, please?' asked Maura weakly. 'I need to walk out of this salon later.'

'Not until I've got all this *striss*' – Debbie gave her knots a fifth hot stone and a tweak – '*roight* out. OK?'

Maura sank her forehead back on to the warm towels. Even if beauticians did initially have to suffer femininity at its least attractive, there had to be some job satisfaction from watching the improvement emerge under your own hands – in fact, she would make a perfect case study, being well on for a total transformation. Maybe Debbie could start on her mind once her back was stress-free. Although that might take a little longer.

No one had met lovely, ideal Ruth, but that hadn't stopped all Maura's friends offering the usual range of advice, from 'It'll all be over by Christmas' (which is what she wanted to hear) to 'Sometimes love at first sight does happen, doesn't it? And you were always going on about how he wasn't really right for you, now, come on, weren't you?' Which she didn't want to hear at all.

She didn't want to hear, either, about how Ruth and Phil had met on the long weekend he'd taken in Cornwall to get over their final, messy break-up, or how, while she had been at their flat separating their CDs into His'n'Hers memories, each individual one of which had torn through her like labour pains, he had been wandering hand-in-hand over Bodmin Moor marvelling at lovely, practical Ruth's semi-professional rallying career, and no doubt laughing heartily at her range of camshaft quips.

But if Maura was being honest with herself, as she thought she might as well now all else had failed, things hadn't been going brilliantly with Phil in their last six months together. Her mother, who was Irish and given to dishing out lengthy proverbs during Maura's infrequent phone calls to Oughterard (infrequent mainly due to the exorbitant cost of suffering surreal extended metaphors long distance), had reminded her that Love was Like a Field of Kale, which needed Constant Hoeing and Tending or else All Would Go Rotten. Which was fine.

The way Maura saw it, if she and Phil were only talking about what kind of loo paper to get, and had slipped into the habit of wearing pyjamas all year round, then that was just letting the field lie fallow for a while, wasn't it? Things would get better as a direct result of doing precisely nothing. Wasn't that a direct extension of the Old Irish Relationship Field Metaphor?

Apparently not. Her mother hadn't mentioned the bit about your field getting repossessed by the tenant farmer and leased out to someone else. Someone with their own motorized combine-harvester.

'What are we doing first then?' enquired Debbie in

a brisk voice. Maura realized that all the stones had come off her back. 'Waxing or tanning?'

'Well, waxing, I'd have thought,' she replied, caught off-guard by a direct question, rather than a 'Going anywhere nice?' meaningless banter opener. 'Else won't you just wax my tan off?'

'Right answer!' There was an ominous clack of pebbles above her head. 'Like to make sure you're still awake!'

Still alive, more like.

Maura hoisted herself on to one elbow and heard all the discs in her back crack back into place. Debbie might have Hands from Hell, but she felt undeniably loosened up all over. Just thinking about Phil and Ruth's wedding for more than ten minutes without breaking out into a sweat was a step forward.

'Right-o, the full wax, is it?' Debbie was slopping a spatula round a basin full of warm cement while looking at the pale forest of hair on Maura's legs with some relish.

'Just the lower legs and, um, bikini line.' Not that there was any real point in the bikini wax, but presumably even German women had their pubes stripped back before wearing a bikini in public. And she was meant to be wearing one. Right at this very moment.

As Maura hoisted her knickers into the appropriate Brazilian position, she reflected bitterly that she'd never have guessed six months ago that having her pubic hair yanked out would be a preferable alternative to thinking about Phil and marriage in the same sentence.

* * *

Debbie waxed, smoothed, made small briskly consoling noises, and then anointed Maura's legs with fake tan, while Maura reclined like a slightly uncomfortable marrow and listened to the sinister whale music being pumped through the treatment room.

She thought of Cyprus. The lovely hotel. The beaches. The ancient ruins. It had been much easier to do it this way. Phil had always accused her of having the fighting spirit of a hedgehog. But, Maura bristled on the waxing table, she had her pride – what was left anyway. And, on balance, this apparently extravagant option was considerably cheaper than the mission to outdress every other woman in Chelsea Registry Office, including the bride. (No aisles for Ruth. Phil could never be doing with all that God malarky.)

Maura wondered mawkishly what Ruth would be wearing. Normally, with her boundless imagination and vast capacity for guilt-trips, Maura was very good at tormenting herself with this kind of speculation, but since she had no idea what Ruth looked like (except she would almost certainly be small – since Phil liked a girl he could tuck under his arm and carry home – and very practical, in a *Home Front/Top Gear* kind of way, since she was not, and blonde, because he was disturbingly specific about what he found sexy), she found herself thinking more about what Phil would be wearing tomorrow.

A David Beckham frock coat, probably.

Tomorrow.

Maura gulped. Water boiled up her throat.

'There! All done!' declared Debbie in the nick of time, with a final swipe at Maura's ankle. 'You can now move on to Stige Four in the Coiffure Suite!'

The Coiffure Suite, was, as Maura had correctly guessed as she shuffled through in her robe, the hairdressing salon bit of The Shell of Venus.

She arranged herself in the chair and flipped idly through an old issue of *Hair Now*, hoping that the stylist would be as content as Debbie had been with minimal conversation and a surprising reluctance to talk about the fabulous holiday she'd booked.

Her gaze fell on a hair-colouring feature called, predictably, 'Red Alert' and Maura wondered whether she should go the whole hog and turn ginger.

No, she thought, smacks too much of Ditched but Defiant.

Whereas *I* am Ditched, but . . .

But . . . ?

'Hello, Maura, I'm Carys, your stylist, and what are we doing today? Low maintenance holiday look?'

A weighted car slipmat was slung round her shoulders from behind.

Maura stared at their reflections in the mirror. Carys (small, dark, magazine definition of Petite) was already combing out the knots in her shoulder-length blonde hair. Maura had developed her own new style since Phil moved his life out of the flat: nervously twisting strands into knots before it dried, creating an attractive Crusty Mermaid effect.

As Carys combed and made hairdresser small talk about split ends, Maura's hair fell about her face in softer sheets, making her eyes, still fixed on her mirror image, look bigger and sadder and younger beneath, especially without her eyeliner. Debbie had whipped all her make-up off and thrown in a quick facial before her fake tan. With the emphasis on 'thrown in'. Maura's face was still tingling.

She looked choir-girlish.

I don't look like me, thought Maura unexpectedly, swiftly followed by, Why do bloody salons have mirrors all over the place? Just when you *really* don't want to see yourself?

'Going somewhere nice?' Tug, tug, tug.

'Um, yes, Cyprus.' Maura carried on flipping through *Hair Now*, feeling guilty. Normally she liked chatting to hairdressers, but this time she couldn't trust herself to stay on topic and there was precious little in her head that didn't relate in some way to Phil.

'Ooh, gorgeous. Self-catering or package?'

'Um, self-catering,' said Maura. A small stone of tension began to roll around again in her stomach. Debbie hadn't completely destoned her, then.

'Gorgeous food you can get out there. Markets, mainly. Been there before?'

'No, look, um, I . . .' Politeness won over irritation. Just. 'I'm a bit nervous about flying, actually, so I don't really want to talk about it.' She attempted a quick 'nervous but brave' smile.

There was a brief pause.

'No offence, but you've got a lot of split ends, if you don't mind me saying.' Carys held up a flaky strand in the mirror. 'Have you been suffering from stress recently?'

Maura felt like a pig being prodded in a pen. What were they? Beauticians or psychologists in here?

'Yes, I am stressed,' she said dangerously. 'My boyfriend, or rather, my ex-boyfriend, has had a whirlwind romance and is getting married tomorrow morning. He's only just got round to reclaiming his electric blanket from our ex-love-nest in Vauxhall, though by all accounts, his divan is hot enough to fry eggs on. I haven't even met his lovely new wifie-to-be, but I know I hate her. OK?'

Carys, to her credit, looked deeply sympathetic in the mirror.

Maura wished she could bite her tongue once in a while.

'Well, a half-hour with some olive oil would make all the difference,' suggested Carys tactfully.

'Um, right, so, all I want done today,' said Maura, feeling she should try to regain what little dignity she still had before the highlighting foils came out, 'is, basically –' how to phrase this? '– for you to give my hair a pre-holiday boost. Sort of as though I'd been in the sun for about a week?'

Carys picked up a hank of hair. 'You're very blonde already.' Pause. Faint impression of regret at the state of her hair. 'So maybe some highlights, not too many, bit of a trim to make it curl at the ends?'

'Excellent.' Maura swallowed. Her usual holiday look was: dried out by sun, greenish-tinged highlights due to chlorine/sea-salt, general lankness due to excessive external and internal application of dodgy cocktails. And she knew Carys knew. Hairdressers could pick these things up just by waving their hands over your head.

'Right, then, wonderful.' Carys dropped her grown-out fringe and patted her on the shoulders. 'Let me just get back to my other lady and I'll be right with you. Coffee?'

'Please.'

There seemed to be a fluttering noise somewhere very near her and when Maura looked down, she saw that *Hair Now* was trembling up and down like a butterfly in her old lady's shaky hands.

Maybe it's a *real* holiday I need, not highlights, she thought, trying not to meet her own gaze in the mirror.

When Carys came back, Maura was washed, towel-dried and floundering around in the sticky memory of her last holiday with Phil, cycling in the Aran Islands, wondering whether the seeds of her overthrow had really been sown by insisting on matching him Guinness for Guinness and being carried home on a donkey cart.

How embarrassing. Maura blushed for shame at the thought.

She didn't notice Carys start combing out her hair.

Well, said a distant voice (possibly her mother's), she

only had Phil's word for it that she'd been embarrassing.

As far as she knew, she'd been a grand laugh.

Maura glared at herself in the mirror, trying to identify which part of her face was making her look like someone else.

Since when had she allowed someone else to decide what was embarrassing for her?

Oh nag, nag, nag.

'It's almost too gorgeous here to go abroad at the moment, isn't it?' Carys' face was kind and enquiring in the mirror.

Maura blinked hard. If *she'd* been drinking it was only because *he* had no conversation.

'Yes, it's been lovely. I haven't . . . been out much in the sun though.'

Hadn't been out at all for a week, in case someone she knew saw her in Vauxhall when she was meant to be in Cyprus, sadly unable to make the wedding of the year due to 'prior holiday commitments'. Following which she would reappear, bronzed, sun-kissed and untouched by the finger of condemnation for not Being A Woman and going to the wedding. And that wasn't counting the vague references to holiday romances she could casually chuck into conversations later. After the bride and groom were safely in Montego Bay.

The Great Escape Plan.

Now, for some insinuating reason, seeming slightly stupid.

'Well, you wouldn't with your colouring,' observed Carys, snipping neat zig-zags into the nape of her neck.

'Gorgeous natural blonde hair, you've got. Now, my other lady's going for a complete transformation the other way.'

'Really?' Knowing her luck, Cyprus was probably hit this week by freak monsoons, and her carefully tanned legs and sun-bleached strands would give her away instead of protecting her from all those sympathetic glances and murmurs as she walked past.

'From Ava Gardner brunette to Jean Harlow blonde. Very brave. Surprise for her boyfriend.'

'Mmm.' How dumb to change for a man, thought Maura, and was struck by how dated the thought sounded in her head. It was the kind of thing she used to snap out with at college, when she had feminist principles, and couldn't actually afford leg-waxing that frequently.

That seemed like a whole personality away. Have I been changing for Phil, she wondered. Oh my God! Maura's grip on the magazine tightened. Has he moulded me into a boring-conversation-resistant model woman and then dumped me to fend for myself in a world where men like girls to talk about pop music and not the torque ratio on Lancia Integrale Evolutiones? Surely not. Surely he liked me the way I was?

Am?

Was?

Am?

Maura pondered her personality frantically while snowflakes of snipped hair fell round her face.

Accommodating, yes; personality contortionist, no.

But you're not as much fun as you used to be, observed one of the unnervingly mahogany models on the 'Red Alert' page.

Maura stared in the mirror. Three years ago I would not have given an electric blanket houseroom. I'd rather have died than admitted to needing one.

'Can't beat getting away, though,' observed Carys cheerily to no one in particular.

Maura felt a strange but exhilarating surge of reason sweep through her. It was so obvious!

She should go to Cyprus anyway!

As *well* as the makeover!

You only got the benefits from travelling if you actually went somewhere. Not to mention a lasting tan.

Exhilarating reason shoved reasonable reason out of the way. This was so much quicker than self-help tapes! Last-minute holidays were cheap, she could easily save a hundred quid in a week just by not being at home necking endless vodka cranberries while throwing all his left-behind possessions into dustbin liners, and wasn't it a long-term investment in her own self-esteem anyway?

She gleamed at the increasingly punky-looking choir-girl in the mirror, baring her sharp incisors to herself. The big stone that even Debbie's capable hands hadn't been able to roll from the pit of her stomach began to shift and gather speed up her spine.

And as for those made-up 'holiday romances' – well, it had worked for Phil . . .

Maura shivered pleasurably. She could flog his tool-kit, for a start.

Carys took this as an encouraging sign.

'When do you fly out?'

'This afternoon,' said Maura, staring drunkenly at the new her. 'As soon as I pick up my bags from home.'

'That's gorgeous!'

Carys swept the gown off Maura's shoulders and showed her the back of her haircut with a mirror. Tiny sun-streaked curls scattered around her ears, which Debbie had carefully tinted an attractive golden colour.

'You look like a different woman,' cooed Carys.

Maura smiled like a cat. 'Absolutely.' She dipped her head admiringly and the curls bounced like a shampoo advert. 'Thank you.'

'No problem,' beamed Carys, brushing strands off her overall. 'Will you excuse me? My other lady's due out from under the rollerball.'

Maura paid at the desk, leaving a healthy tip for Debbie and Carys, seeing as she was now in a holiday spending mood, and tucked a business card from the extended plastic hand by the nail-varnish display into her purse.

The receptionist offered her the sweaty parka back. Maura looked at it distractedly, recognized it as her own, and rolled it into a ball, which she squashed into her bag. No need for that, she thought, stretching her bare golden arms in front of her.

Just as the bell above the door was pinging her exit, Maura remembered her earrings were still in the Coiffure Suite.

Carys was shiftily combing out the freshly-washed

hair of her other lady without meeting her eyes. Even wet, Maura could see it was a vibrant platinum, almost as bright as her own. It didn't go all that well with the woman's eyebrows, which were still unarguably brunette.

Earring half in her ear, Maura stood fascinated by the scale of the transformation – beyond cosmetic – to walk in as one person and out as another, where even your own eyebrows would give you away every two weeks. What was the point? Did you get roots on an eyebrow tint?

And then the woman spoke, nervously, to the hairdresser's reflection in the mirror.

'Oh my God,' she croaked.

'It's gorgeous,' said Carys soothingly. 'He'll love it. Didn't you say he'd been dropping hints?'

'But my wedding! My dress is cream!' she wailed. 'I'll look like a white chocolate Magnum! Will it wash out by tomorrow afternoon?'

'Er, no,' admitted Carys.

Maura ran a hand through her fresh curls, put on her shades and drove straight to the airport.

Anna Maxted is 31 and lives in London with her two cats, Disco and Masha, and her husband Phil. Her first novel *Getting Over It*, was published this year (her sister loved it, her mother liked it, and her grandmother wrote her a stern e-mail saying 'it wasn't quite what I was hoping for'). Despite this, she is currently working on her second.

Man With A Tan

Anna Maxted

When you meet the man you're going to marry, you just know. Apparently. I suppose it's like walking into Whistles and just knowing you want the pink spangly halterneck top. You slink it on in the matchbox changing room and are instantly transformed into a sparkly, if curiously undernourished, sex goddess. It's only later in the cold light of your bedroom that you realize you look like a camp frankfurter brought to life in a mad experiment. Marriage can have a similar effect – though in this case your husband turns out to be the sausage.

Pardon me if that sounds harsh. I have nothing against buying spangly tops or tying the knot – either one ensures you oodles of attention and fuss, and if you look like a pig in a poke no one is going to mention it. Very nice. The reason I'm sceptical about the cupid's arrow theory is because, in my experience, love isn't as instant as a cup of Nescafé. It's a screamingly slow, foot-dragging process. I can only compare it to glaciers which move about one millimetre every thousand years.

When *I* met the man of my dreams I didn't notice

him. I was too busy posing in a deadly new pair of needle sharp stilettos. And when he brought himself to my attention – 'Ah, excuse me, but you're treading on my toe' – I *certainly* didn't think in terms of marriage. It would have been such a killjoy thought! Like binning the candyfloss and eating the stick. When the man of my dreams announced himself, my first thought was, 'So that's why the carpet feels lumpy.'

Maybe I'm cynical about happy ever after because I hail from a family as dysfunctional as The Simpsons without the exonerating factor of charm. (My partner, whose middle name is charm, can't quite get over it and avoids his in-laws like other people avoid ink clouds in swimming pools.) Ah yes. My partner. Wasn't that who you were waiting for? I have my eldest sister Gloria to credit for bringing us together. Thanks to her I live in a big sunny house where I don't have to lift a finger. And I can buy as many pink spangly tops as Whistles will sell me.

It all began on the second day of summer, the sky a weak lazy blue for the occasion.

'You know,' Gloria remarks to our dappy sister Denise while ogling a celebrity's over-pined home in *Hello!* magazine, 'I used to think that money didn't matter. But I want my three holidays a year!' I suggest she could earn it herself, but she blanks me. 'MC Magimix has his three holidays all right,' she drools. 'Oooh he's practically mahogany.'

I make a face at Robert, and say, 'What a shame,

he'll clash with his pine. I'll be making my own millions, won't you?'

Robert says, 'I'd rather be kept by a rich DJ personality, thanks,' and then Gloria tells us to shut it and get on with our work.

Robert and I giggle because Gloria – who doesn't know the meaning of the word 'tacky' – fancies her chances with Magimix. Gloria, who has a high squeaky voice and a bony nose, is the worst aspect of being employed by our family business which, I'll tell you now so you're not disillusioned later, is a contract cleaning firm. Dirty work and filthy pay. The one advantage is that I get to spend time with Robert – an old friend of mine employed by my mother and paid a pittance after he was sacked by Tesco. (He didn't change the doughnut oil in their bakery for a month and it went green.)

Gloria drops *Hello!* on the table, declares, 'I'm off to Prada, I need a new business suit. Page if you need me,' and sweeps from the room.

Denise snatches up the magazine, flicks to a page, and stares at it. She has yolk on her Laura Ashley cardigan from breakfast, but hasn't noticed. She squints, and her face wrinkles up like an old peach.

'What *are* you doing?' I say, trying to keep the irritation out of my voice. At least pretend to be working!

'Checking for dust,' she replies.

This bizarre response doesn't surprise me as Denise is away with the fairies and rarely makes sense. I glance at the clock. Twelve thousand miserable pounds per annum divided by 48 × 5 = fifty quid a week. I'm paid a tenner a day.

It's 3 p.m., so I say loudly, 'Denise, I've got a meeting with our accountant, it'll probably take hours, so I'll go straight home. And Robert is accompanying me to take the minutes.' I nod at Robert who smiles winningly and brandishes his notebook.

'Have a nice time,' says Denise absently.

We take advantage of her mental blip (so far it's lasted thirty-one years) and head straight for the pub where we spend today's tenners.

Robert shows me a fancy way of lighting a match that really impresses girls. I can't do it but he twirls a curl of my hair around his finger and says, 'You have other talents. You're a *sensational* liar.'

Sadly, when I stagger into work the next day in the grip of a vicious hangover, my stepmother proves him wrong. I know the game's up when I see her pacing the purple carpet in Christian Lacroix.

'Where've you bin!' she shrieks.

'Sorry, Edith,' I whisper, 'the car wouldn't start.'

She purses her mouth, and her bright red lipstick bleeds into her violent tan. She snaps, 'Don't lie, you've bin drinkin', I can smell it!' I stand still to avoid being sick. Her voice is so shrill my brain might shatter.

'Where is everyone?' I whisper.

'Brent Cross Shoppin' Centre,' she replies in a smug tone.

'Why?' I say.

'Because!' bellows Edith. 'Unlike you, yer sisters 'ave a brain in their 'eads!' That sounds right, one between two. 'Yesterday, when you was off drinkin',' Edith adds, 'Denise was proposishinin' clients!' I find this hard to believe, but suspect linguistic error rather than career change. 'And MC Magimix's agent got back to us, and said that Crispian – that's 'is real name, Crispian Bartholomew – it jus' so happens 'e *is* lookin' for a top-flight cleaning service, so we're goin' for interview and the girls are off buyin' new kit. 'E's seein' us at two.'

The curse of *Hello!* strikes again.

Happily, Edith decides I look too much of a state to stand trial and delegates me to another, less crucial client.

'Gloria doesn't want to be upstaged,' whispers Robert as I wave them off. How come *he* looks as fresh as a daisy that drank water and went to bed at 9 p.m.?

'Rob,' I say, 'you don't have to console me. I'm not so sad that I get off on scrubbing the toilets of minor celebrities, especially those with orange skin.'

Robert jumps into the Range Rover behind Denise. As they roar off, he shouts, 'Orangist!'

I smile into the silence that follows their departure. If it weren't for Robert my life would be pure drudgery. His teasing presence and filthy sense of humour promote it to impure drudgery, and make it just about bearable. An hour until I'm expected at my next job – cleaning the townhouse of Hattie Hayter, barrister. Time enough for a nap under my desk. I tootle back inside. The next thing I know, I am rudely awoken by an ear-piercing blast. I stumble out from under my desk, fumbling for the phone.

'Hello?'

I am nearly deafened by Edith yelling, 'Why int you at 'Attie 'Ayter's, you shoulda bin there ages ago!'

My brain is too fuddled to lie plausibly so I stammer, 'Oh.'

Edith growls under her breath then hisses, 'Git yer arse over 'ere, 'e only wants us to clean is 'ole aas –'

I interrupt. 'Pardon?' I squeak – I expect celebrities to be debauched but MC Magimix sounds disgusting!

Edith snaps, 'Just git over 'ere! Robert's gardenin', Gloria's goin' over the rates with Crispian an' chattin' about 'is job an all, an Denise is in 'is bedroom, she's bin tryin' to straighten' out 'is waterbed for the last 'arf hour, an I int doin no aaswork, so that leaves you, so ring 'Attie 'Ayter's an tell 'er you'll do 'er later, then git over 'ere!'

Never mind that I'm still over the limit, I scrawl down the address, brush my hair, crawl into my green Datsun and trundle off.

Hattie Hayter is understanding and when I offer to clean at half-rate she says, 'Don't be ridiculous.'

Twenty minutes later, I crunch up the tree-lined driveway leading to Crispian's white house and park the Datsun in a leafy corner. I expect a sign saying Magimix Towers and grey stone lions guarding the porch and for the doorbell to sing the initial notes of

'Heartbreaker' when you press it, but there are no signs, lions, or singing. I ring an ordinary buzzer and four seconds later the red door is flung open and I look into the stunning green contact lenses of MC himself.

'Wotcha!' says Magimix, but before I can reply, Gloria appears and says, 'There you are, did you remember your apron? Now, Mr Bartholomew – oh! [*simper*] Crispy, if you insist! how kind! – Crispy has a soiree tonight and he needs the house pristine, and if we do a satisfactory job, the account is ours. Come along now Ella, don't stand there – make use of those large capable hands. Hurry, time is money!'

Money and money, it's all she ever thinks about. I scowl at Gloria and smile at Crispian – 'Crispy' indeed – who steps aside to let me into the hallway.

'Ecstatic to meet you,' he says, and winks.

Gloria stares after him like a fox after a hen. Then she says, 'Start from the top of the house and work your way down. You've got three hours to do the best frigging job you've ever done in your life. I want him to be able to serve his soiree off the toilet seat.'

I bite back the response, 'I believe that's the norm in media circles,' and plod upstairs. I peer out of a stained-glass window and see Robert pulling up weeds in a flowerbed. I rap-rap and he looks up but can't see me. I fling open the window and sing, 'Woo-ooo!' He grins and blows me a kiss through mud-stained fingers. I shut the window, still smiling, look up and scream.

'Oh, sorry,' I gasp. 'I didn't see you.'

MC Magimix laughs and says, 'Am I that terrifying?'

He has an air of cool confidence and a voice as rich and creamy as a glass of Baileys.

I blush and say, 'I was just saying hi to my colleague.'

MC Magimix drawls, 'Live dangerously, sweetheart.' He looks close to a smile.

'Is that what you suggest?' I say.

He reveals white teeth and murmurs, 'I suggest your sister's an ogre and you're destined for better things.'

I can't resist a flirt and open my mouth to say, 'Crispian you are *so* right, but you needn't look so smug because by employing us you are propagating my misery,' but from downstairs Gloria's falsetto voice tinkles, 'Ell-ar! I do hope you're not chatting!'

I wince, excuse myself, rush to the top floor, and sweep it.

I give it some elbow and we get the Magimix account and Gloria is torn between elation and fury. She and Edith are thrilled because Crispy wants us to 'clean his 'ole aas' three times a week, but she and Edith are not thrilled because Crispy specified that he wanted *me* to clean it because I was 'a great scrubber'. If that's a compliment I'm not thrilled either.

'If you've got designs on Crispy, think again,' says Gloria, as she clambers into the Range Rover.

Robert – who has sat in grim glowering silence since Crispy's 'scrubber' remark – looks at me. 'You *are* kidding,' he says. 'Ella?'

'Don't be daft,' I reply, 'I passed him on the stairs and he leered at me and said hello. I bet he tries it on with everyone, the postman included. Anyway, what was I meant to do, blank him?'

I drive on to Hattie Hayter's with Robert. He spends the entire journey scraping the dirt from under his fingernails. He has nice hands.

'Too hard for gloves, are you?' I tease, but all he says is 'Ho ho,' in an unamused way. When we arrive at Hattie's he stalks into her garden without a backward glance. I feel anxious without knowing why.

I shrug, let myself in, and start gathering the army of coffee cups stationed about the house.

'Hello!' says Hattie, as I swish on the hot tap and squirt a squiddle of Fairy Liquid into the kitchen sink.

'Hattie!' I say, jumping.

'So,' she says, leaning against the doorframe, 'how was Radio Man? Ghastly?'

I shake my head. 'Not bad actually,' I say. 'Not as orange as I thought.'

Hattie draws up a chair. 'Indeed!' she exclaims. 'Do tell.'

Not much *to* tell. But Hattie's interested so we chat as I work. I would say that high-flying Hattie sees my mundane life as a diversion but she's sweeter than that. Every week, she demands instalments. So every week I tell her about Crispy who also likes to chat to me as I work, and Gloria, who is spending a fortune at Michaeljohn thrice weekly, and Robert, who can't stand Crispy, although Crispy is friendly and offers him tickets – offers all of us tickets – to his new club-night ('MC Magimix plays deep and funky house' –

admission £10, includes ONE FREE DRINK before midnight).

When Crispy offers, Robert says quickly, 'Thanks, mate, but I'm away that week, I'm visiting my gran in Seattle.'

Later in the car Gloria is triumphant and snatches away my ticket and says, 'Don't think you're going, he only asked you to be polite,' and I say narkily, 'I wouldn't go if you paid me, I loathe funky house, I prefer Beethoven.'

When I say this Robert gives me a strange look. His long-lashed brown eyes seem bigger than ever. For a second he is five years old.

Then he says shyly, 'We could go out tonight, Ella, if you like – you know, sex, drugs, and an ice-cream eating competition?'

He's been so offish that I seize on his invitation like a stray dog on a scrap of chicken, and he collects me on his second-hand moped and we go to Banners in Crouch End and drink vodka martinis and eat corn bread and ice cream and laugh and lean closer and closer. It's happened before but we've always pulled back.

Not tonight though. Suddenly we're kissing and half of me is thinking, 'This is *Robert!*' and the other half is thinking '*This* is Robert?!' and then we ditch the moped and get a taxi and because I still live at home and we don't fancy sneaking past Gloria and Edith we speed back to his Kilburn flat where we rip each other's clothes off in the hallway and it's all rather fairytale.

Making love to Robert knocks me sideways as do the beautiful things he says. It's wonderful but weird because I've known him for all this time and while I *saw* he was gorgeous and funny and clever he was so familiar to me I never thought of him in that way. And if I did I quashed it. But this warm summer night changes everything. It's as if my heart is re-wired in the heat of our passion. I am shyer and awestruck in his presence, it's like I'm born again and he feels the same.

He says he's always adored me but was scared to say, he's got peanuts but he'll get rich for me, he'll start his own business, we'll do it together and we'll live in a big sunny house – although he'd be happy with me in a damp hovel – and there'll be no more housework I won't lift a finger and he doesn't want to go to Seattle tomorrow but he can't disappoint his gran but he'll phone me every day.

So when he doesn't ring I am surprised to say the least.

I tell Hattie and she says 'Don't take any shit.'

I think, surely, there's got to be a reason, but I don't have his gran's number, and I can't believe he hasn't rung and three days pass and then I think, see if I care, the bloody bastard, and that'll teach me to sleep with my friends. Life is hellish enough but Gloria and Edith make it worse as they both have their knickers in a twist about MC Magimix's clubnight and keep snapping at me like a pair of crocodiles. Edith is hoping that Frank

Butcher will be there (she has no clue) and Gloria is planning to cop off with Crispy. Denise is excited because she's too dim to know any better.

I tell Hattie that I'm not going; I'll stay at home and watch Denise's vast collection of *Brookside* videos to make killing myself a more attractive proposition.

Hattie says, 'What nonsense!' and tells me I should get a grip and put on a frock and go to the club and dance to 'I Will Survive' or whatever they play in clubs these days.

'I've got nothing to wear and can't afford anything new,' I tell her.

Hattie says 'Wait' and disappears into a room and returns brandishing a skinny rib silver top and bootleg leather trousers. I gawp, and Hattie says, '*Not* mine, dear, my sister's. They'll fit you perfectly.'

I am doing my make up thinking spiteful anti-Robert thoughts, when the phone rings.

Gloria cries, 'Ella, why didn't you return to the office after Hattie's! The accounts need to be sorted before tomorrow morning, you'll have to work late tonight.'

'Oh,' I say.

'I'll pay you overtime,' she adds.

'Right,' I say.

She says edgily, 'You didn't have any plans?'

I tell her, 'No.' I put down the phone and consider doing the accounts. Truth is, they do need to be done before tomorrow. And I should have done them last week. Then I think, balls. My life is mush, I'm going to party!

There's a massive queue for the club but I march to the front and show my ticket and am ushered inside. I am a VIP and in a shallow nihilistic sort of way it feels *great*. It feels even greater when I totter to the bar to buy a drink and feel warm hands on my hips and spin round and see Crispy, smile fluorescent in the strobe lights. He shouts over the bass, 'Gloria said you weren't coming.' I shout back, 'I'm supposed to be working, if she sees me I'm toast.' Crispy takes my hand and snakes through the crush. Girls grab at his T-shirt and he unpicks them, leads me upstairs, opens a door and bows, and it's a room full of squashy red sofas and beautiful people.

'They won't find us here, sweetheart,' says Crispy. 'Might I fetch you a drink?'

I let Crispy 'fetch' me a drink. He does have a remarkable tan, but it is *not* orange. And he has great teeth and exquisite manners.

'Don't you have to DJ?' I say.

'Not till midnight,' he says. 'Don't think you'll escape from me that easily.'

I giggle and say, 'Aren't you embarrassed to be seen out with your cleaning lady?'

Crispy says solemnly, 'Not when she has the face of an angel.' I think, how naff but consider Gloria and smile anyway.

And after that we talk about the music business.

Crispy loves music but hates the business it's so false and backbiting but he shouldn't complain, he's done well out of it, but anyway, that's a yawn, what about *me*, why the hell am I cleaning loos for a living when I could be a model, and I say 'Well *you* employ me!' and he says, 'If I didn't I wouldn't get to see you,' and I turn pink and Crispy says, 'Sweetheart, do you really think I need my house cleaned three times a week?'

I'm flattered, I don't know what to say. And then he kisses me which solves the problem.

It feels good and it feels bad and best of all it spites my aching heart.

We don't stop kissing until midnight strikes and Crispy yells, 'Shit!'

He lifts my hand to his lips and kisses it and says, 'I'll call you!' and I think 'Yeah right,' but I am all of a flutter with alcohol and lust, and I am that dizzied up I take a cab straight to the office and sit there in leather trousers and silver top and do the accounts and fall into bed at 5 a.m. and when the alarm wakes me two hours later I rise like a zombie, wash my face, and sleepwalk into work.

Gloria is in a foul mood because Crispy arrived at the club at nine-fifty, disappeared at ten, and re-appeared at twelve-o-two but that was no sodding use because he was spinning discs and out of reach, but she can't take it out on me because when she snarls, 'Where are the accounts?!' I reply, 'On your desk,' and there's no quibbling with that.

I think I'm safe but I sneak out to get a sandwich

and when I return Gloria is sniffling and wiping her bony nose with a purple tissue and Denise is subdued and Edith grabs me by the wrist and yanks me into the corridor and hisses, 'What the 'ell are you playin' at!'

I twist out of her grasp and say, 'I beg your pardon!' and Edith says, 'You knew 'e was spoken for! 'E was Gloria's route to easy street! Don' come the innocent with me, jus' tell me why Crispy 'as called this office three times in the last arf hour askin' to speak to *you!*' Hm.

I tell my stepmother that last week while I was doing his bathroom Cripsy mentioned that he was looking for an Art Deco set of taps, and did I know anywhere. I said I did and I'd get back to him and that, of course, is why he's calling. I know Edith doesn't believe me and when I spin the same story to Gloria she shoots me the nastiest look I've ever seen apart from on a warthog with indigestion at London Zoo.

Then she says, 'Give me the number of the tap shop and *I'll* get back to Crispy for you.' I make up a number on the spot then excuse myself because I'm due at Hattie's. I want to call Crispy but I don't dare.

But in the end it doesn't matter because the next day Gloria and Edith go to Ascot and Denise goes to the dentist and I'm shuffling papers round the office and the phone rings and the receptionist is so excited she can hardly speak but I have a famous visitor and can she send him up?

I feel hot and I know it's not because of the summer sun it's lust and defiance and I check in the mirror that my nose isn't shiny and scrabble around Denise's dusty desk where I find a mint and I crunch it up and Crispy walks through the door holding the biggest bunch of lilies you ever saw and I can tell they're from a swanky florist and he says, 'Doesn't your sister *ever* pass on messages?' and drops the lilies on a chair.

He's wearing tight trousers and a tight T-shirt which is not the sort of get-up I go for on a man – Robert is a loose-fitted kind of bloke – but who cares about pale absent Robert when I have Crispy who is tanned and tantalizing, if tight-trousered. I feel briefly evil because four days ago Robert and I were forever and he so seemed to mean it. I believed him because I *know* Robert and he doesn't lie, and although Hattie might say 'If you and Robert were meant to be it would have happened sooner,' I think that some people *grow* to love one another and I don't think that sort of love is inferior to snap, bang love but then Robert isn't here and Crispy is.

Our office has lax security, by which I mean no cameras, so when Crispy bends me over a desk I don't worry about being caught, although the prude in me thinks that this isn't the most romantic position for a first bonk – I think of Robert wanting to gaze into my eyes but I banish the thought – although I do wonder because Crispy is so charming, I would have expected the missionary but the slut in me thinks just give it to me, baby, oh yes that feels good and it keeps feeling good until Robert walks in and walks right out again and I wriggle out from under Crispy and run after Robert but he's gone.

* * *

When Denise returns from the dentist she is surprised to see me crying in the road and when I tell her she says that of *course* Robert rang me from Seattle, he rang the office and our home, didn't Gloria tell me? Robert rang distraught to say his gran had had a stroke and he'd try and call when he could but it would be difficult. Denise says the third time he rang she took the call and wrote it all down but Gloria said *she'd* pass on Robert's message which was, 'I know you'll understand and wait for me.' When she tells me this my heart crumples like an old tissue.

I left Crispy to pull up his tight trousers and I ran home and called Robert to explain but he couldn't forgive me. He couldn't forgive that casual lust, it was too cruel, it changed me for him, irreparably. I wasn't the woman he thought I was. I cried and begged but I understood because five days is hardly much time to wait for love, not when you've waited for seven years, so what was left for me but to do the thing that would most spite Gloria?

If you don't believe in happy ever after, Crispy isn't a bad person to be with. He's sweet if self-satisfied, but our sex life isn't up to much. Whenever he tries it on I see Robert walking in and the pain on his face takes me back all those years to when he first tapped me on the shoulder and said, 'Ah, excuse me, but you're treading on my toe.'

Sheila O'Flanagan was born in Dublin and has worked for the past twenty years in financial services as a foreign exchange and bond dealer. She also lectured students for professional examinations while writing in her spare time.

Following the huge success of *Suddenly Single*, her first novel to be published simultaneously in the UK and Ireland, and which was both a *Sunday Times* top five bestseller while spending 11 weeks at No. 1 in Ireland, she decided to throw in the financial services towel to concentrate on writing – something that she has always wanted to do.

Now she lives in Clontarf, Dublin with her partner and cat.

Storm Clouds

Sheila O'Flanagan

I hadn't intended to go to France in July with Cleo and
Frankie. And I certainly hadn't intended to go to France
with Cleo, Frankie and twenty adolescent schoolgirls.
I'd had other plans – specifically, an all-inclusive resort
in Barbados with Mike, my husband, for an uninterrupted fortnight of sun and sand and sex.

Which would have been a pretty amazing holiday,
actually, because somehow we didn't have time for sex
in our marriage any more. We didn't seem to have time
for anything other than falling, exhausted, into bed and
dropping off to sleep immediately. In fact it was Mike
who used to fall, exhausted, into bed while I lay beside
him listening to his snores and wondering why he'd
married me in the first place.

I don't know how it happened. I thought we loved
each other. And love was supposed to conquer everything, even twelve-hour working days with no time to
phone, or cancelled nights out because Mike was
involved in some urgent project or other in the graphic
art company where he worked. I tried to be understanding – after all I was a trained aromatherapist and I was

supposed to understand stress – but I simply ended up more and more stressed myself. So I started to grumble at him and then he'd moan at me and it all just got worse and worse.

Shortly before we were due to go to Barbados things came to a head. We had an argument about something really stupid, like him leaving wet soap in the sink, and I screamed and yelled at him that he treated me like his goddamned slave and that he was only in the house when it suited and that I wasn't putting up with it any more.

'Don't, then,' he said calmly. He was always calm. It drove me nuts.

I looked at him in shock.

'If you hate me that much,' said Mike, 'then leave.'

'What?'

'Leave,' said Mike. 'I make you unhappy. I don't care about you. I don't bring you flowers. Honestly, Paula, if that's how you value love . . .'

'It's not,' I said fiercely. 'It's not about flowers it's about – everything!'

He shrugged. He was always like that when we had an argument. He'd be calm and reasonable and he wouldn't argue back. Suddenly, I saw our lives stretching forward like this forever. Mike with his dreams. Me with mine. And neither of us giving an inch because I was tired of being the one that always tried to make things better.

'OK,' I said. 'I will leave. I'll leave and I'll have a better life and I won't even think about you any more.'

'Fine,' said Mike.

And I left.

People who talk about divorce as being the scourge of modern society are talking about people like Mike and me. They'd say we should have sat down and worked things out, but there wasn't any point. He wouldn't listen and I was tired of trying. I had to get out before I went crazy.

'Of course you did,' said Cleo loyally.

We sat in the kitchen of the house she shared with Frankie and Kevin. Cleo, Frankie and I had gone to school together. We'd shared the house in Harold's Cross together too, before I married Mike. Kevin had taken the spare room when I left. He'd been our platonic male friend through our teenage years and he was still our platonic male friend.

I pulled the kitchen chair closer to the window so that the evening sun could warm the back of my shoulders. I'd felt cold ever since I'd left Mike.

'I'm always the one who compromises,' I told her.

'I know.' She pushed her long, curly, blonde hair out of her eyes. 'I told you that before.'

'I know you told me,' I said miserably. 'I just didn't want to believe you. And we were supposed to be going to Barbados.'

And then I started to cry and the tears rolled down my cheeks and plopped on to my short, sugar-pink skirt.

Which was when Cleo suggested that I go on the Adventure Holiday of a Lifetime with them and the twenty girls to the South of France.

Cleo was my best friend and a teacher. Every year she took a group of her pupils away on a sports holiday. Every year she told me about it. Every year it sounded like a nightmare.

'I couldn't go with you,' I said. 'I hate kids.'

Cleo laughed. 'Nobody said you had to like them. You don't even have to have that much to do with them. Just supervise them, that sort of thing. It's easy, Paula.'

'But I don't do sports, Cleo!' I wailed.

'Oh, come on, Paula.' She grinned at me. 'You can swim, can't you?'

'Not well,' I said. 'And I know this kind of holiday, it's all abseiling down the side of mountains and canoeing in freezing cold rivers. I was supposed to go to Barbados, remember? To do nothing but lie in the sun and drink cocktails.'

She laughed. 'We do windsurfing and yachting,' she told me. 'Absolutely no abseiling. A little canoeing but on the sea. And the sea is beautiful even if you fall in. It's summer, it'll be warm!'

'Surely there isn't room for another person,' I said.

'That's just the point,' Cleo said. 'There is. Frankie and I have been tearing our hair out because we desperately need another person. Carol Dunphy was meant to be coming but she dislocated her shoulder and she really doesn't feel up to it.'

I grimaced. 'Why am I the only one of your friends who doesn't go around abusing their bodies?' I asked. 'When will you and Carol and Frankie cop on to the fact that your body is a temple and should be treated with care!'

She roared with laughter. 'You're priceless, Paula,' she said. 'You're a member of the gym, aren't you?'

'Not with any great enthusiasm.' I crumpled up the mauve wrapping of the chocolate bar I'd just finished. I was comfort eating. Even with eating huge quantities of chocolate and not going to the gym I'd lost weight in the last couple of weeks.

'Besides.' She smiled. 'Having a professional masseuse will be very useful, don't you think? When we come back battle-weary and sore you'll be able to give us rub-downs.'

'Massage is not a rub-down,' I said crossly. 'And my massages are always restful experiences. I don't see how I can feel restful if I've spent the day rescuing drowning kids.'

'It's not like that at all,' she promised me. 'The place we're staying has trained people to look after them all day. We organize them, of course, but they go out on the water with professional staff. All we do is make sure they don't run off with an instructor or something. I promise you, Paula, you can sit on the beach with a good book and just glance in our direction from time to time. The only time you have to do anything is to shepherd them on and off the plane and the coach. Easy.'

I didn't really want to go. I wanted to stay at home and be miserable about the fact that I was twenty-eight years old and my marriage had disappeared down the toilet and that I had once loved Mike with all of my heart.

But I said yes all the same.

Emily Harris forgot her ID to go with the group passport which caused a panic at the airport. Dawn Purcell dropped an open can of Coke in the middle of the departures area and sprayed everyone within a few feet with the sickly, brown liquid. Treasa Dolan arrived with a face so perfectly made-up that she looked at least twenty and threw Cleo into a fit of worrying about how she was going to keep her under control on the mixed camp-site.

She hadn't told me about the camp-site part until a week before we left. I'd fondly imagined that we'd be staying in apartments but Cleo grinned and told me that the Hirondelles resort was made up of tents.

'But the adults aren't in tents, surely?' I asked in horror.

'Bigger tents,' she told me. 'Nice tents. With camp-beds and all facilities.'

'What facilities?' I demanded.

'A fridge,' she told me baldly.

I would have pulled out there and then but it was too late – if I'd backed out the whole trip would have been in jeopardy. But I muttered blackly under my breath as I trudged into town and bought myself a sleeping-bag. I'd never needed one before. I thought roughing it was staying in a three-star hotel.

The flight to Perpignon was relatively uneventful. I sat in my seat near the window and missed Mike so much that I wanted to be sick. But teachers couldn't be sick. Teachers were supposed to be concerned with their charges. All I was concerned about was Mike and how, right now, we should have been lounging in the all-inclusive resort on the beach, watching the sun set into the Caribbean Sea.

Cop on, Paula, I told myself fiercely, they're about five hours behind us in the Caribbean. You'd only be having breakfast.

It was early evening by the time we arrived at the resort and there was a slight haze over the sky, but the air was warm and the entrance to the camp-site was alive with brightly coloured bougainvillaea.

The girls jumped from the coach with great enthusiasm while I practised sounding adult and mature by saying, 'Helen Wallace, don't push!' And was rewarded by the lanky fifteen-year-old responding with, 'Sorry, Miss.'

Cleo, Frankie and I installed ourselves in our tent once we'd sorted out the children. 'I thought you said it was luxurious,' I said to Cleo as I stood in the middle of it and looked around.

'In comparison to the girls' it is,' she pointed out.

'Yes, but –' I shrugged helplessly. You're either a

camping person or you're not. I couldn't see that the small fridge and electric light made up for the fact that the plastic groundsheet was covered in sand and that the camp-beds looked decidedly utilitarian.

'You'll be fine.' Frankie grinned at me. 'And we'll go down town later and stock up the fridge with some booze.'

'What about the girls?' I asked.

'They can't come,' she said solemnly.

'One of us will stay,' said Cleo, 'while the others go and get some drink.'

I looked around the tent again. I thought of Barbados. I ached for Mike. Why, I asked myself, why should I suddenly start to care again when I knew it was all over? I said I'd get the drink.

I couldn't identify the noise when I woke up the following morning. It was a dull, thudding sound which seemed to echo around the tent. I sat up gingerly in the camp-bed and looked around me in bewilderment.

In the bed opposite, Cleo rolled over and opened one eye.

'It's raining,' she said.

'Raining?'

'You know, wet stuff.'

'Shut up,' I said. 'How can it be raining? It was lovely last night.'

'Happens sometimes,' she told me. 'But it usually goes after a few hours.'

I shivered and snuggled down into my sleeping-bag. 'Wake me when it stops.'

She laughed. 'You'll have to get up in ten minutes. It's breakfast time.'

I squinted at my watch. 'But it's only a quarter-past seven!'

'Yes,' she said. 'Remember the rota from last night? We're half-seven breakfast this morning.'

'Oh, God!' I groaned. 'And I probably have to queue for the shower.'

'Most people don't bother with the shower in the mornings,' Cleo advised. 'There isn't time. Anyway, you're going to be in the sea all day. Or,' she said benignly, 'in your case, sitting on the beach. A splash at the sink will do you.'

I groaned again. But Cleo was right, there wasn't time. As I contemplated getting out of the sleeping-bag, Frankie – who had a little room of her own in the same tent – put her head round the flap and told us it was time to get up. And that Greenhills College were already queuing for breakfast so if we didn't get up there soon those boys would have eaten everything – remember last year? So we'd better get a move on. Oh, and by the way, it was drizzling.

It was heavy drizzle. I felt my dark hair begin to frizz as I hurried along the sandy pathway from our tent to the open-air cafeteria.

The girls hadn't been any more enthusiastic than me about getting out of bed and I'd been very cranky with my lot shouting things like, 'Come on, come on, you know you're meant to be at the cafeteria before half-past,' while at the same time struggling to hold back the yawns. I was utterly amazed to see that Treasa Dolan had found time to complete a basic make-up which left her looking quite stunning at that hour of the morning while dressed in her jogging pants and sweatshirt.

'Is it too wet to go out sailing?' asked Emma Johnson.

Cleo withered her with a look. 'You'll be on the water,' she told Emma. 'You can't get much wetter than that.'

'But what if it's squally?' said Denise O'Halloran.

'It's a drizzle,' said Frankie.

'It might be a squally drizzle,' objected Denise.

I yawned again. I liked to ease myself into the day. A refreshing shower. A breakfast of fruit and yoghurt. Some time to do my make-up. I didn't just leap out of bed and into a crowd of people.

I closed my eyes and did some deep breathing. Anna Boland tripped over my outstretched leg and almost broke her jaw on the ceramic tiled floor.

It was too wet to sit on the beach with my book. And, despite Frankie's scathing dismissal of squally drizzle, it had become too rough to allow the children out in the boats. One or two hardy souls suggested that they could swim or body-board near the beach but the staff at Hirondelles said no. They couldn't be responsible in this sort of weather.

Cleo and Frankie decided that the thing to do would

be to bring everyone on a trip to the nearby town of Cap d'Agde. They normally did a trip to Cap d'Agde anyway, it would just be sooner rather than later. The girls piled in to the coach. I took my rain-jacket (thankful that I'd actually brought one) from the tent and slung it over my head.

The rain was coming down harder now and the clouds had descended almost to the level of the pine trees either side of the road.

'It's like Connemara,' said Aisling Ward gloomily as she peered through the steamy window of the coach. 'Only wetter.'

'I wish we could have gone out on the boats,' said Emily wistfully. 'I'm dying to go out on the boats.'

The coach swished its way along the country road. To our right, the sea churned in angry green and white. I shuddered at the thought of being out in a boat.

I wondered what it was like at home. We'd left Dublin bathed in warm sunlight, in the middle of a virtual heatwave. I imagined Mike sitting on the balcony of our apartment, sipping a glass of wine in the late-evening sun. Mike liked wine, it was his hobby. He went to tastings and lectured me from time to time on acidity and fruitiness and tannin and then I'd just take the glass and knock back the drink and he'd call me a philistine. But he used to laugh when he said it.

It stopped raining briefly while we walked around Cap d'Agde but, pretty as the town no doubt was in blazing Mediterranean sunshine, it was dull and gloomy that afternoon. The tables outside the pavement cafés were deserted, their chairs tipped against them to stop puddles forming on the seats. The local ice-cream seller looked miserable in his hut surrounded by huge wafers and pictures of ice-cream sundaes while water dripped from the green and white striped canopy above. The few people who were out on the streets hurried along, heads bowed.

Cleo decided that we should bring the children to the local swimming-pool so that they'd at least manage to have a swim. After all, she pointed out, they're here to swim.

They loved it. I bobbed around out of reach of the people who enjoyed pulling you underwater by your ankles and wondered what Mike was doing now.

We took the long way back to the camp. The girls took it in turn to sing Spice Girl songs over the bus microphone. None of them could sing. I had a headache. Cleo broke up a fight between Sharon and Emily. Frankie confiscated a packet of cigarettes from Treasa. The bus swung into the reception area of the camp-site and parked in the middle of a deep, wide puddle. We all got soaked as we jumped off.

When we got back to the tents, though, we stopped and looked in horror. The incessant rain had forged channels through the sandy surface on which they'd been set up. Small rivers ran through some of the channels while in front of some tents great pools of water had built up. The camp attendants were frantically digging holes at the side of the channels to divert the water from the tents.

'Oh, my God!' Cleo looked at us. 'What a mess.'

'We couldn't do anything about it.' The organizer came up to us. 'The rain was so heavy and at first we didn't realize . . .' His voice trailed off as Cleo strode into our luxurious tent and I followed her. The groundsheet was a sodden mess. So were her clothes which she'd neatly stowed beneath her camp-bed. I'd stowed some of mine under my bed too, but the slope of the floor had kept the water away from them and they were merely damp.

'Shit!' Frankie looked in at us. 'My stuff is soaking. So is everyone's!'

We walked out of the tent and surveyed the rest of the site. The girls were rushing into their tents – when not prevented by the puddles outside the entrances – and emerging shrieking that their clothes were ruined.

'My Prada suit is destroyed!' Treasa looked distraught. I would have been distraught too if I'd had a Prada suit.

'Prada!' Cleo looked at her as though she were mad. 'If you've brought a Prada suit on a camping holiday, Treasa, you deserve to have it destroyed.'

Nuala Gilmore, small, dark and elfin ran up to us. 'Isn't it a laugh!' she said. 'We're going to have to share clothes.'

'I'm not sharing with you,' said Treasa dismissively.

'I wouldn't be seen dead in the stuff you ponce about in!'

'Girls, girls!' Cleo pushed her fingers through her hair. 'Come on, let's help to clear up.'

We helped but it wasn't easy. It was still raining, the water still ran through the camp-site, we were wet and tired and cold. At one point I looked up at everyone digging trenches and felt, surreally, as though I was in a refugee camp. I suddenly realized how dreadful it would be. If one of these tents was your home, I thought, and not just yours but home to a number of families and it rained like this – I shuddered at the thought and applied myself to digging trenches with renewed vigour. I only swore when I broke a nail.

Eventually we diverted the rainwater, sent the wet clothes to the local laundry and changed into dry (or less wet) clothes. The girls, amazingly, thought it was all a bit of a laugh.

'Couldn't we go to a hotel?' I begged. 'I really need a hot bath.'

Cleo laughed. 'It'll be gorgeous tomorrow,' she promised. 'And you'll forget about today. Go and have a shower, Paula. They'll be really hot right now.'

I took her advice. The showers *were* really hot but it's very difficult to feel at ease under the spray of water when there's a pigeon roosting in the rafters above. I was beginning to feel as though I was in my own personal nightmare. Where there were no aromatherapy oils, or perfumed candles to ease the strain. Where just keeping clean was an effort in itself.

But, I thought, at least it would be dry tomorrow.

* * *

It wasn't. Or the day after that. Or the day after that. But whenever the rain eased even a little the girls went out on the boats and did their body-boarding and played beach-games. So did I. Actually, it was more fun than I'd expected. And the girls were fun too. They reminded me of myself when I'd been fifteen – hopeful, expectant, scared. And then they discovered that I did manicures as well as massages and suddenly I was booked up to do their nails for the on-site disco each evening.

'You're enjoying yourself,' Cleo told me one night as we played cards in the tent after the kids had gone to bed. 'You might even get to like camping.'

'You must be joking!' I shook my head. 'I hate this bloody tent. It smells of damp and it's full of wet sand and it's cold all the time.'

Cleo laughed. 'Poor Paula.'

'You can laugh,' I said bitterly. 'Your hair hasn't turned into basic frizz because of the damp. And you weren't meant to be in Barbados!'

'You miss him, don't you?' she asked.

'No.' I bit my lip.

'Why don't you phone him?' suggested Frankie. 'You owe it to yourself, Paula. A second chance, maybe?'

I shook my head. 'He has his second chance,' I said bitterly. 'And it's at being on his own again. Why would he want anything else?'

Amazingly, on the next day, the clouds lifted completely. I'd grown so accustomed to hearing the sound of the rain drumming against the roof of the tent that I couldn't figure out what the difference was when I woke up at seven the following morning. And then I realized that it was the lack of noise that had woken me. That, and possibly the sound of the birds chirping happily in the trees.

The sunlight gave everything a changed perspective. The trees swayed gently against a bright blue sky. The green and red tents looked bright and cheerful in the glare of the sun. The top layer of sand had dried to a shade of pale gold. And the kids hurried out of the tents before they were even called.

Later that afternoon, when everyone else was out on the boats, I walked up the narrow country road to the collection of shops and cafés. It was growing warmer, the scent of multi-coloured flowers filled the air and, suddenly, I felt almost happy. But there was an empty space inside which ached for Mike. I knew that I still loved him. It was simply that I wasn't sure whether I liked him.

I sat down at one of the pavement tables and ordered a coffee. It came in a huge bright yellow cup with a tiny pot of hot milk and two oblongs of sugar, served by a pretty, gamine waitress who smiled cheerfully as she sat it down in front of me.

As a child I used to love unwrapping sugar cubes. But I didn't take sugar any more. I sipped the coffee and leaned back in the wicker chair. I felt almost human again. Away from the kids and the tents and the incessant bustle of the camp-site I felt as though I was back in the real world. An adult world. And I wanted Mike to share it with me.

Cleo and Frankie had thought that coming to France would make me forget about him. Certainly, whenever I was herding children on and off coaches or making sure that they were where they were meant to be, I hadn't the time to think about him. The day that we'd used black refuse-sacks as raincoats because we had nothing waterproof left to wear, I'd actually been glad he wasn't around to see the state I was in!

But I missed him. I wished I hadn't walked out on him. I wished we'd had the belief in ourselves to work things out. I wished I knew where it had all gone wrong.

'Hello, Paula.'

At first I thought I was hallucinating. I'd been thinking about him, after all, and I have a powerful imagination. I blinked and blinked again.

'Mike?' I looked at him in amazement.

He sat down opposite me. His straw-coloured hair flopped over his eyes. His face was pale. He looked tired. The gamine waitress who'd served me earlier rushed out to take his order.

'Having a good time?' he asked.

I knew that I wasn't wearing any make-up. That my hair was a complete mess, destroyed by the rain and the sea and the sand. And that I was wearing one of Frankie's oldest T-shirts because I'd lent my last dry one to Anna Boland who'd wanted to wear green today and her green one had been ruined in the flood.

'The weather's been dreadful,' I said.

He grinned and looked less tired. 'I heard. Storm clouds all along the Mediterranean bringing heavy and persistent rain. According to Sky Weather.'

'How did you know where I was?' I asked. 'What are you doing here?'

'I rang Cleo's. Kevin told me.'

I looked cautiously at him. 'Why did you ring Cleo's?'

'To find out where you were, of course.'

'Why?'

His look at me was equally cautious. 'Because I miss you, Paula. Because I think I was mad to tell you to leave and because you never should have left. Because I love you.'

My coffee was going cold in the cup in front of me. The gamine waitress was watching us through the window of the café.

'Words are easy.' I tried to keep the wobble out of my voice.

'I know.' He sighed. 'I got caught up, Paula. In earning enough to help us buy a house. In feeling that it was important. In thinking that the prospect of a partnership with Jimmy was more important to me than how I felt about you. And I was wrong.'

'I was a nag,' I told him. 'I complained all the time. Maybe I should have tried to understand more.'

'I don't want to go home without you,' said Mike.

'You wanted me to leave,' I said.

He reached over and took my hand. 'I never wanted you to leave,' he told me. 'I was angry.'

'I didn't want to go,' I said.

'Come home, Paula,' said Mike.

'There's still three days of the holiday to go,' I told him.

'Why don't you leave the kids with Cleo and Frankie and we'll book into a hotel somewhere?' he suggested. 'Where we can stay in bed all day and I'll even give you a massage.'

It sounded like heaven. All I'd dreamed about for the last week was a hotel room with clean sheets and room-service!

I smiled ruefully. 'I can't do that. I have to stay with the kids.'

He nodded. 'I don't want to leave you, Paula. Even if you're in a tent and I'm in the hotel.'

I made a face at him. 'You don't know how much I long to be in a hotel.'

He smiled at me and suddenly he was the old Mike again. The Mike I'd loved and had married. It was as though the last few months had slipped away. 'When I heard you were on a camp-site . . . !'

'I love you,' I said.

He leaned across the table and kissed me on the lips. And then we both got up, still kissing. I opened my eyes. The gamine waitress was smiling in delight.

And the touch of the sun was deliciously hot on my shoulders again.

Rosalyn Chissick started her writing career as a feature writer on *Just Seventeen*. Published in *Elle*, *Company*, the *Independent on Sunday*, *The Guardian* and *The Sunday Times*, she was Contributing Editor for *New Woman*. In 1995 she gave it up to concentrate on writing fiction. Her first novel *Catching Shellfish between the Tides* (Sceptre) won prizes including the 1995 Armagh Writers' International Short Story Award and the 1996 Waterstones and Terrence Higgins Trust Short Story Competition (published in *It Must Be Love*, Penguin Books, 1997). She has also won prizes for her poetry which she performs in venues as diverse as Glastonbury Festival and the Dalai Lama's Temple in Northern India. Her second novel, *Colourbook* (Sceptre), comes out in paperback in summer 2000.

This story is for Ludwig.

Caravan

Rosalyn Chissick

The ticket collector does not look at Tara as she speaks.

'The ringmaster, you say? You want to speak to the ringmaster.'

She looks at Tara then and sees that she is wearing an anorak, plimsolls, silver combs in her hair.

'His caravan is the third on the right.' She waves her arm into the distance. 'You can wait for him there, if you like.'

Waiting for him in his caravan. Counting the drops on the walls. Perfect rust-coloured marbles. The walls are splashed grey metal. Thin, beige carpet. A pot and mug in oily water in the sink. The wind whistles under the door and this could be him, tramping through the mud, boots negotiating beer cans, broken bottles and carrier bags.

Tara stands up, sits down. The footsteps hiss away. Boots on metal steps, one, two. The bang of a door. Laughter. Voices. A woman leaning back in a chair perhaps, showing white teeth.

Tara is sitting on his bed; she is feeling the shiny satin of his sleeping bag under her fingers. She is looking at the picture of a woman by his bed. Her eyes follow Tara around the room. She imagines the ringmaster making coffee in the morning under those slanting brown eyes.

When he comes in, she will say: 'I saw you performing tonight. I was in the second row. I thought at one point – when an elephant was balancing on two legs and you were talking to it, so close – you looked up and saw me.'

It is after midnight. The moon looks like a broken toy in the sky, its angles too sharp. On a shelf, a book about boats. Black and white pictures of cabins and hulls, flat seas rising up like water walls.

When the ringmaster returns to his caravan, morning is criss-crossing the hills in lemon lines and there is a woman on his bed, asleep. Her hair has fallen across her face so he cannot see her, only the dark green of her anorak. He wonders how he knows her.

Plimsolls, bare legs, the shifting grey of her skirt. Her hair is an orange fire on his pillow. He sits in the chair and he watches her. The way her body shudders when she breathes.

The ringmaster smokes a cigarette, blowing smoke into the air between them. Five a.m. She is hunched into a ball now; one arm flung out towards him. He lights another cigarette, stays sitting very still so that when she wakes and stretches her arms and wonders, for a moment, where she is, seeing the photograph of a woman with slanting brown eyes and then the book about the sea – she does not know – the metal walls – he is looking at her, has been looking at her and she does not know for how long or what he has seen and she wraps her arms around herself, drawing in her knees.

'How long?'

'Long?'

'Have you been watching me?'

He leans back in his chair, looks at his watch.

'How long?' she asks.

'An hour.'

'An hour?'

'Or more.'

And he is smiling. Looking at her. He will not look away.

'Look away,' she says.

'Why?'

'Because you are embarrassing me.'

'You are on my bed,' he says, 'in my caravan.'

And he carries on looking. His eyes are green. A pale, almost translucent green.

'I saw you performing last night,' she says. 'I saw you juggle flames and eat razors. I saw you make coins appear from behind a boy's ear.'

He is looking at her again.

'You were in the second row,' he says.

'Yes.'

'I remember now.'

'I thought at one point,' she says ' – when an elephant was balancing on two legs and you were talking to it, so close –'

'I looked up,' he says, 'and I saw you.'

She does not know his name.

'Jake.'

'Jake?'

'My father's and my grandfather's name.'

'What is your favourite colour?'

'Green.'

'Do you tell the truth?'

'Usually.'

She says: 'Don't you want to ask me anything?'

'No,' he says, 'there is time.'

Outside the field is coming to life. Footsteps, voices, the clanking sound of pails. She can smell the beginnings of a fire.

He says: 'You are coming with us, aren't you?'

Who is there to leave? An old aunt, a cousin with runaway fingers, neighbours who gossip and rearrange the world.

'An old aunt?' he says.

'Yes,' she says. 'My mother's sister and her son. I have lived with them for most of my life.'

And now she is sitting with him in her aunt's red lounge and the clock is ticking. There is the clatter of china cups on saucers, the scrape of a knife against a plate. His mouth is filled, crumbs on his lips and dotting the front of his blue T-shirt.

'You want to take my niece with you.'

'She wants to go.'

Hooded eyes, he thinks. And a face that looks as if it has been fashioned out of crêpe paper – one snag and it will all pull away.

'You want to go?'

Tara says: 'It is a calling.'

Nuns get a calling and hermits and priests. A small insistent voice inside their ear: this is the way, this is the way. This is her calling: to be with him.

'A calling?' The aunt snorts.

'Yes,' says Tara. 'This is what I'm meant to do.'

Then they are walking up the stairs to the attic and Jake is filling all the space in the hall and Tara is saying: 'Wait outside.'

'Why?'

'Because of the mess. I don't want you to see.'

But while she is rummaging through her things and selecting and discarding – a book, a box of matches, a piece of polished stone – he comes and stands behind her. She feels him before she sees him, passes him a pair of jeans, T-shirts, shorts. He folds them into the rucksack. A notebook, a towel, a jar of face cream. The paperback book by her bed, her pillowcase, a small pile of letters.

Tara's aunt stands in the doorway.

'My watch,' she says. 'I want you to have it.'

Tara takes the watch. It is light and cold. The face is white and smooth, sculptured gold hands, one tiny diamond. She fastens it around her wrist.

'Hurry,' says Jake.

They run through the streets. Her rucksack is on his back, her hand in his hand.

'Quick,' he says. 'Quick.'

Darting across roads and around corners. They collide with a metal dustbin and its lid spins across the pavement, clatters in the kerb. Running through the streets that she knows: the painted doors, the trees arching and bending, the corner shop where a woman is standing in the doorway.

The big top has been taken down, animals in cages, wooden boxes on trailers. A line of caravans and cars. Without make-up and sequins the women flicking ash out of car windows and the men leaning back in car seats look ordinary. Passing them on roads or seeing them in lay-bys or service stations, you would see ordinary-looking people in jeans and jumpers with tiredness around their eyes.

'Where did you find her?'

Jake says: 'She found me.'

A woman leans out of a window, winds her fingers round Tara's arm. She has tiny green eyes and pink-painted lips.

'What can you do?' she says.

The circus drives for hours. Flamenco guitars on the radio. Hot air blows through the windows like a hairdrier on full power. In the early afternoon, they pull off the road to share sandwiches and nut-brown coffee. Cigarette after cigarette.

The woman with green eyes pulls Tara's hand into her lap. Holds it there, pressing her palms with light sticky fingers.

'I'm Pearl,' she says. 'I can read you. But not now,' she says, 'not here.'

It is late when the line of caravans and cars pulls off the road again. The sky is speckled with stars. The animals are fed: bales of hay and oats, sacks of vegetables and bananas. Then the fires begin. Flaring into the blackness.

Tara watches Jake wrap potatoes in silver foil then poke them into his fire. She drinks tea from a plastic beaker. Pearl comes to sit with them, peeling her nail polish off in strips.

When she stands, shaking the shiny polish curls from her dress, Pearl leans towards Jake and whispers into his ear.

'You can't frighten me,' he says.

But Pearl is laughing. A big, rippling sound that catches in her throat.

The night feels huge around Tara, nothing familiar except the bristled side of Jake's face and the way his fingers are tearing a blade of grass over and over. She falls asleep in her clothes. Wakes to find she is on his bed with his sleeping-bag over her legs. He is in the armchair, legs stretched out in front of him, a brown wool blanket falling off his chest.

She reaches for him because she has fallen asleep in her clothes again and woken to see him looking at her. She reaches for him because he is sprawling in the armchair and the blanket he has wrapped around himself has fallen to the floor.

'No,' he says.

He stands quickly. His hair is tangled, his shirt creased and falling out of his jeans.

He walks. Through the fields, between the caravans, along the lanes.

Tara waits for him, listening to the wind in the trees and the soft jangle of the animals' chains.

Sharing his bedroom, his shower, his kitchen. Imagining what he feels like up close, the things the woman in the photograph knows.

In the morning she asks him, sitting at the table, spreading jam on toast.

'The woman in the picture – did you love her?'

'Yes.'

'Is she the reason?'

'Yes,' he says. 'And no.'

The next day Tara follows Pearl between the caravans and back to her trailer. There is an empty whisky bottle outside the door, two beer cans, a bin bag spewing crisp packets and banana skins.

Standing by the door in the glare of the morning sun, Pearl pulls her dressing gown around her. The hem is black.

Walking up the steps, she leaves the door open wide. There are clothes everywhere. Stockings, dresses, blouses and scarves. There are glasses everywhere too, winking from chairs and shelves. The air smells of perfume and smoke. Ashtrays crammed with butts smeared lipstick pink.

'How long have you known Jake?' Tara asks.

Pearl says: 'Forever.'

'And the woman in the picture?'

'The one by his bed?'

'Yes, did you know her too?'

'Yes,' Pearl says. 'Her name was Alice.'

Alice. Now Tara has a name for her.

'What was she like?'

Pearl is sitting by her dressing table, smoking a cigarette.

'I don't want to talk about her.'

'What about her and Jake?'

'No. I will read you,' she says. 'Give me your hand.'

Pearl tells Tara: 'You will work with lions.'

And Pearl tells her: 'You will have a child.'

And Pearl tells her: 'Jake will never love you.'

Squeezing Tara's hand tight in the cramped, dirty trailer.

'You can't know that. How can you know?'

'It is here,' says Pearl. 'All I'm doing is reading. Jake will never love you.'

'Because of Alice?'

'No,' says Pearl. 'Not her.'

'Come,' Pearl says, 'come now.'

Pearl takes Tara into the lion's cage and stands with her on the straw.

'My mother worked with the lions,' Pearl says. 'Big cats rolled over at her feet. When a lion was sick my mother spent the night with it in the cage. Once I saw her asleep with her face on a lion's chest.

'She trained me. Seven years old, walking around the ring behind her, snaking my whip. Less than half the size of a lion and I could get it to do what I wanted. Would you like to touch one?' asks Pearl.

The lion is several feet away but there is heat all around him. Tara steps forward and the lion stays very still so that she can stretch out her hand, slowly, stiffly, into the heat and touch, for a moment, the tangled thickness of his mane.

Tara can feel the rumble of the lion's breath and the red drum of his heart.

'Will you teach me?'

'Yes,' says Pearl, 'and in return you shall tell me secrets.'

First the lion has to get to know Tara: her smell, her voice, the way that she moves.

Tara feeds the lion chunks of meat, watches teeth shredding.

'Don't turn your back,' says Pearl. 'And never look away.'

Pearl is measuring Tara for a costume. Deft fingers and tape whizzing over breasts and hips. The mound of Tara's belly, the distance between her thighs and the ground.

'What colour?'

'Green,' says Tara.

Sequins like fish scales, netting, lace, a plume of feathers.

Pearl lends Tara fishnet stockings, stilettos, a lipstick.

Numbers on a scrap of paper. A mouth filled with pins.

Jake and Tara are eating pasta. Slurping tomato ribbons into their mouths. A candle drips wax on to the tablecloth.

Tara says: 'It's an anniversary.'

She stands up.

'Two weeks since I fell asleep in your caravan. One week until I go into a ring with a lion.'

Jake says: 'I don't like you in Pearl's clothes.'

Says: 'You look better when you try less.'

Says: 'Why are you trying to be like Pearl?'

'Because people notice her,' says Tara. 'Even you.'

Kneeling on the plastic-covered bench, she presses her nose against the window and looks out at the night.

'So many stars,' she says. 'Like a huge dot-to-dot

puzzle. I feel as if I could join them all up,' she says, 'and make a picture.'

He comes to kneel beside her. Both of them wedged now on the small bench, his arm against her arm, his leg against her leg, hair twisting, tickling her cheek. Tara is learning not to feel him, to know he is sitting beside her on the bench, but to put her mind and all her feelings into a corner of herself –

but he is running a finger up her back, slowly, tracing the bumps of her spine and she is counting to a hundred – twenty-two, twenty-three – because she does not want to misread –

thirty-four, thirty-five – she can feel him on every part of her – forty-nine forty-nine – even though it is just her back, just her back and her lips now against his lips.

And the fingers she has watched hold pens and knives, tie boot laces and lock doors, those fingers brown with the sun, graze-lines like map references all over his palms – after two weeks of imagining.

When it is over, he pulls away from her with an intake of breath. Cool air now along that side of her body. The rasp of the sheets as she kicks her legs under them, watching the pale brown curve of his back.

'Where are you going?'

He shrugs his shoulders. 'Get some sleep.'

'I don't want to sleep.'

Jake turns to face Tara but he is not looking at her, not even looking through her, but away somewhere and she says: 'Are you sorry we did that?'

'No,' his says. His hand is in her hair now. 'Please don't worry, everything is fine.'

He is out walking and she is alone. The candle shadows on the walls look like misshapen heads. Two a.m. The sheet feels cold. And there is the picture of a woman and Tara wants to rip it, tear and tear it to shreds. She turns the woman to face the wall but Tara can feel her still as if she were here in the room. Tara takes the photograph and wraps it in newspaper, hides it at the back of a drawer crammed with brushes and empty jars.

Jake does not ask where the picture is. Tara takes this as a good sign, curling up next to him on the bed. On the radio, a play about a woman in love with one of her father's friends. She contrives to meet him, turns up at his office without an umbrella in the rain.

'How did you meet?'
'Who?'
'You and Alice?'
'Who told you her name?'
Jake moves his arm from beneath Tara's head and she falls back against the wall.
'How did you meet?'
He will not talk and although he sleeps with her in the bed, his long body stretched out beside her in the darkness, and although she feels him fidget and sigh and jump – his body jumps in his sleep like a cat on a chase – he does not reach for her, not even in his dreaming.

Some nights when he is sleeping but she cannot sleep because he is too close and too far, she slides into the gap between them, curls into his warmth, places her arm across his chest.

Some nights he is not sleeping. Lies very still, feeling the heat of her body. He wants to tell her things. But he cannot find the words, although he chases them like Chinese dragons around his head.

In the middle of a night that is irritable and hot, Jake moves towards Tara and keeps moving. Hands, mouth, legs. They make love in their sleep, although neither of them is sleeping.

In the morning their bodies are still wound around each other, but when he wakes he jumps away from her.

They pretend it did not happen. Not that night or any of the nights that follow.

'Are you and Jake lovers?'

Tara is standing on a chair and Pearl is hemming her costume.

When Tara says 'yes', Pearl's hands stop moving, pressing, for a moment, a pin into Tara's leg so that Tara has to say her name 'Pearl' over and over before Pearl starts moving again, her fingers thick now and clumsy.

'He comes to see me,' says Pearl. 'If you're wondering where he goes.'

Tara's aunt's watch has disappeared. It is not in its usual place under the bed. Tara gets down onto her knees and pushes her head and arms into the dust and fluff.

'It's gone.'

Jake pulls the bed out from against the wall. They search behind the curtains, under the carpet, through all Tara's books and clothes. It is not there.

'I saw it just a few days ago,' says Tara. 'I remember putting it back in the box.'

'It has disappeared,' agrees Jake. 'Like my photo of Alice.'

That night Tara cannot find her stage costume, although she searches for it for hours. It is missing the next day and the next so that Tara cannot perform for three evenings, watching Pearl from the sidelines.

Tara's silver hair combs disappear. Then her rucksack. Then her letters.

'True possessions are like boomerangs,' says Pearl. 'They always return to their owners.'

Tara is waiting for Jake in their caravan. Counting the drops on the walls, she feels as if she is wandering with him, outside wandering and all that is left on the bed is a set of clothes.

She puts on a jumper and steps out on to the grass. It is a wet night. The leaves are shining.

Walking between the caravans. Tara hears Sonia the

fire-eater snoring. Then the warmth of a cat against her legs. Pearl's cat. Tara runs her hand over the cat's fur; she feels her bones, the throb of her breath. The yellow-green of her eyes in the dark, then she is gone.

There is a light on in Pearl's trailer. Music on the radio. Smoke curling out of the window and into the night.

Pearl's silhouette against the curtain. A man in a coat with mussed-up hair. He kisses Pearl's neck, kisses down to her breasts. She curls an arm around him.

'Stay tonight.'

The man's hands are inside Pearl's clothes.

She steps away and Tara can hear his breath in the stillness.

'Until four,' says Jake.

'Five,' says Pearl.

'Five,' says Jake, reaching for Pearl again.

Jake says: 'I'm sorry I can't explain,' he says, 'about Pearl and me.'

'Pearl and you,' she says. 'All the time.'

'And Alice?' Tara asks. 'Who is Alice?'

'I can't tell you that,' Jake says. 'Not now.'

He says: 'I never meant to hurt you.'

And Tara says: 'I know,' although she does not know anything.

When Tara wakes and finds Jake is not there beside her, she curls into the darkness. She knows where he is now. Knows where to find him, where to go.

Tara makes buttered toast and sits at the table but she cannot eat. Looking out of the window. She can hear the movement of the wind, the low rustling echo of the trees. A spider on the ceiling lets out a thin silky thread and Tara watches it drop down from its web on to the back of a chair.

'They're gone.' Sonia's voice is ringing out now into the morning.

Tara does not move, but inside her T-shirt, inside her skin something is crawling along her spine.

'They've taken his car and her trailer,' Sonia is shouting. 'Jake and Pearl.'

Pearl and Jake.

Outside the air feels cool. Tara's tongue is thick. The sky is so blue it hurts just to look at it.

'They were lovers,' she says at last, voice so low she can barely be heard.

Tara looks at Sonia: heart-shaped face, blonde hair that is curling around her neck.

'Jake is Pearl's brother,' Sonia is saying.

'Pearl's brother?'

Tara is a parrot, repeating words, not understanding. The air is so sharp and clear it is hard for her to breathe.

'What about Alice?' she asks. 'Who was she?'

'Alice was their mother. She trained lions,' says Sonia. 'Like them, she ran away.'

469

Tiffanie Darke first put pen to paper when she stopped being a waitress and became Food and Drink Editor of the *Daily Telegraph*. One glance at the outrageous shenanigans going on in restaurants of the rich and famous convinced her she had to write a novel about it and the result was *Marrow* – a gloriously wicked tale of caviar, tantrums and impossibly handsome chefs. She is now 27 and Features Editor of the *Express* whilst working on her second novel. This story is for Charlotte – and all the girls who've been there and done that.

The Seven Steps from Shag to Spouse

Tiffanie Darke

Preliminary: The Pull

Charlotte sat in the corner under the plastic palm tree. The music around her thumped and roared and the occupants of the bar were already swaying. Julia was having trouble fighting her way back to the table without spilling their drinks.

'Here you go – now that should cheer you up.'

'What is it?' asked Charlotte, eyeing the fizzing concoction suspiciously.

'That, my dear, is a TVR, and if that doesn't give you wings tonight, nothing will.'

'A TVR?'

'Yup – tequila, vodka, Red Bull. Now shut up, down it, and FLIRT!'

Julia picked up her glass, gulped half of it down, squealed, then surprised herself by finding the Steps' song was worth standing up and dancing to after all.

Charlotte watched as a couple of the men near their table turned round to watch her hips moving in her silver dress. Julia was tall, blonde and gorgeous – she also, annoyingly, only had so much as to look at a sun-lounger to go a deep shade of golden brown. Charlotte looked down at her own pale legs – not half as exposed as Julia's – and sighed. Not that she cared much. Julia had dragged her to Majorca for the week to 'get the shags in' but this was something Julia had more fun with than Charlotte. It had been four months now since Charlotte had moved out of Dominic's, and apart from one disastrous Friday night in the pub after work, Charlotte had failed to be interested in anyone.

'You've got to get back on that horse!' Julia lectured, but frankly Charlotte couldn't see why. What was it all for anyway? You gave them your heart then they let you down. Christ, she had even said she would marry Dom – and she would have done – but somehow it had all gone wrong.

'All right, love?' boomed someone uncomfortably close to Charlotte's ear. 'Can I get you another drink?'

Charlotte turned round to confront the English voice behind her. A tall, mildly handsome boy in a white T-shirt and jeans was leaning over her. Charlotte was about to turn him down when she caught Julia's eye, hesitated, and replied:

'Um, yes, thank you.'

'What you having then?' he asked, clearly delighted not to have been knocked back.

'It's called a TVR.'

'A TVR?! Right then,' he said, thinking, she must mean business. When he got back from the bar he introduced himself as Dave. Charlotte noticed he had kind eyes, and a fringe that flopped over his face in quite a cute way. But she didn't want to talk to him, so she drank her TVR while he told her about a beach he and his mates had been to that day. By her third drink, however, she had changed her mind, and found herself regaling him with the tale of their scooter crash, and by the fourth she had accepted his offer to dance. By the fifth, (they were in a different bar now and Julia seemed perfectly happy chatting up the barman who was taking a very healthy interest in her cleavage), she had discovered Dave had very soft skin on his forearms. And rather delicious lips. After her sixth she couldn't remember a thing.

Step One: The Shag

The sun streamed through the window and on to the bed, filtering through the slats of the blinds and painting the two naked bodies with yellow and black stripes.

One stirred, nudging the other as it did so. Charlotte opened her eyes. White, scratchy sheets, an upturned glass on a side table she didn't recognize and the torn purple foil of a condom packet greeted her gaze. A throbbing in her head warned her not to move. The arm around her waist tightened its grip and she tried to remember. Not a thing. Slowly, Charlotte rolled over and looked at the boy. He had dark hair and strong shoulders. He opened his eyes and smiled at her.

'Morning, gorgeous,' he muttered into her hair.

'Morning,' said Charlotte, thinking, what the hell is

his name. Inwardly she began to giggle – she was still drunk, and she thought it was hilarious she was lying in bed with a total stranger in a room somewhere in Majorca, God only knows where. She couldn't help it – she began to laugh.

'What is it?' he asked, concerned that he may have just slept with a lunatic.

'I'm sorry,' said Charlotte eventually, when she managed to control her hysterics, 'but I don't know your name!'

Now he laughed too. 'Dave – and yours is Charlotte, by the way.'

He made her some foreign tea and brought her a slice of melon in bed and they kissed some more. Charlotte got up, put on her black dress and platform shoes and left, promising she'd meet him later in the same bar. In fact she didn't even know the bar he was talking about. She spent all morning screaming with laughter with Julia by the pool, who was snuggled up on her sun lounger with the Spanish barman called Carlos she'd picked up the night before.

Step Two: The Regular Shag

Two nights later, across the floor of a nightclub, she saw him again. At least she thought it was him, but she wasn't sure until he came up and said 'Hi' with that look in his eyes. Charlotte smiled back at him coyly, and he asked her if she would like another TVR.

'Not on your life, it's taken me two days to recover

from the other night.' Then she noticed his disappoint-
ment and felt flattered, and said 'OK, I'll have a pina
colada then.'

The next morning they actually had a sober conversation, and discovered they both came from the same
town – Bournemouth. Then they discovered they had
mates in common and drank in the same pubs. Charlotte wasn't sure if this was a good thing – he was her
holiday fling, she didn't want him rearing his guilt-
provoking face back home. But they ended up in bed
together the next night as well, and Charlotte began to
feel relaxed, lethargic even. In a nice way.

Step Three: The Monogamous Shag

The Night Jar had its legendary end-of-summer party
two days after Charlotte and Julia got back from
Majorca, but this time Charlotte took extra care with
her make-up. She dragged Julia along too – who
claimed to still be in mourning for Carlos (his parting
words were 'You are amazing, you English women,' but
he had resisted Julia's entreaties to follow her back to
England). Still, Julia seemed to get over it with her first
vodka, lime and soda. Dave was there, as he had said
he would be, and Charlotte felt surprised at how her
tummy jolted when she saw him. As soon as he caught
sight of her he came over, and they spent the next hour
flirting with each other, as if they'd only just met. They
left early.

They were getting on well in bed together too – as

they learned more about each other's bodies the sex got better. After a while, they came together. The mechanical procedures that Charlotte had undertaken in her last few months with Dominic seemed like a different sport. If that had seemed like a school cross-country run, then this felt like snowboarding. It was exciting – and addictive. She didn't know much about him, didn't know whether she even liked him, but this – she knew she wanted this. She found herself agreeing to a date the following weekend.

'So, you two an item then?' asked Julia, trying on Charlotte's new trousers for the date.

'Nah, don't be silly, the last thing I want is another boyfriend. We're just sleeping together.'

'But neither of you is sleeping with anyone else?' asked Julia slyly, watching in the mirror as a look passed across Charlotte's face.

'Well, I'm not.' She paused as she digested this new possibility. 'Why, do you think he is?'

'Could be,' said Julia. 'You never know – if you're not "seeing each other", there's no reason why not.'

'No – I 'spose not.'

Charlotte was alarmed. She knew she shouldn't mind, but she thought if he was sleeping with someone else at the same time as he was seeing her she might mind rather a lot. All these games, she didn't understand them, it had been too long since she had last played.

Step Four: Boyfriend and Girlfriend

The Italian was small and naff – the candles were stuck in Chianti bottles and the windows were half-covered in matted blinds, but the moment they walked in Charlotte knew she loved it. Dave held her by the hand and squeezed it as the manager came bounding across the room and kissed Dave rapturously on either cheek.

'Mama mia, Dave, ees been so long, why you no come here no more? Is good to see you again! And this lovely laydee – she your sister no?'

'No, Marco, this is Charlotte, my girlfriend.'

The word shot through Charlotte like a lance – girlfriend?! She didn't recall that being agreed. But she said nothing. They ate their meatballs and spaghetti in the candlelight and wallowed in each other's gaze. Conversation seemed unnecessary, and by the time she was in his arms in the back of a taxi she thought she quite liked the sound of it.

Step Five: I Love You

The next few months took Charlotte completely by surprise. She had never expected – least of all wanted – to be back on the romantic merry-go-round, but this boy! He just made her feel so damned happy. The exuberance, the fun, the chemistry between them: it was quite fantastic, and she just couldn't leave it alone. After the deathly, stultefyingly depressing last months with Dominic, then the misery of the break-up and the aftermath of adjusting to single life again this – this thing with Dave – felt like living again. It was winter now, and bitterly cold, but the way Charlotte felt inside she could just as well have been in the Caribbean. She was having fun.

She bounced down the concrete steps to the beach where Dave was standing by the seashore, his back to her, the wind whipping his scarf out at the cold green sea.

'Hello, handsome,' she called, bounding across the empty sand. He spun round, just in time to catch her in his arms as she leapt towards him. 'How you doing?'

Dave looked at her strangely, his eyes clouded, his face earnest.

'Charlotte – I need to tell you something.'

Charlotte's heart stopped. Panic scampered through her body. His face looked different, the gravity frightened her.

'What?' she replied, too quickly.

He smiled at her distress, and pulled her towards him. 'Don't look so scared. It's just there's something I've wanted to say to you for a long time. It's important, and I want to say it now.'

Charlotte was frozen. No, please God, no! Please don't let him finish it now. Her fingernails bit into her palms. Not now she'd fallen for him. *Please no*!

'Charlotte – I don't know how it happened, but I'm absolutely sure of it . . .' Dave paused and swallowed. 'You, girl – I've fallen completely and utterly in love with you.'

Cupping her chin in his hands, his eyes melting before her, he declared: 'Charlotte of Majorca, I love you.'

It took three long seconds for Charlotte to unfreeze. A tingle ran up and down through her body, from her toes to hair to her toes again and the tears popped into her eyes.

'Oh my God, Dave, oh – I think I love you too!'

Step Six: Living Together

Charlotte's room in Julia's flat was way too small for all her stuff, but initially it had seemed like a small price to pay for sharing with her best mate. When Dominic had kicked her out of his flat it had been about the only place she could go, and she had been very grateful for it. But Julia's lifestyle – basically nocturnal as it revolved entirely around the Bournemouth nightclub where she worked – was beginning to interfere with Charlotte's day job. She would be woken up at five or six almost every morning by Julia stumbling into the flat, bottle of vodka in one hand, random man in the other.

And Charlotte was not best pleased that all the clothes Julia had offered to keep in her wardrobe were now so trashed by Julia's constant abuse, that the only place they were fit for was Oxfam. Plus Julia was definitely being rather cool with her now – either because she felt Charlotte was crowding her space or, as was more likely, suspected Charlotte, she was holding the

Dave thing against her – in the way good girlfriends do when they've retrieved a mate from a broken relationship only to watch them embark on another.

Despite her protestations, Charlotte thought Julia was probably a little jealous her holiday romance had lasted, whereas Julia's hadn't. She and Carlos had spent the winter writing to each other, and there had even been talk of her going back there to work in the summer, but that didn't make up for the fact that Julia had no resident boyfriend.

So with Dave not wildly welcome at the flat, Charlotte had taken to spending more and more time at his – a two-bedroom place he shared over the other side of town with his brother, Neil. But Neil was moving out – he had a new job working for a record company up in London – and Dave needed a new flatmate to help pay the mortgage. Neither had spoken about it, but both knew the question was hanging in the air.

The problem was Charlotte had such terrible recollections of living with Dom. The way he used to go on about her not picking the towels up off the floor, how she always had to explain where she was going, how every Sunday she ended up cooking lunch for him and all his mates while they watched football on the telly. It was his flat and one of the most emancipating things about their break-up was having her own space again, however small her room was. Still, the situation was ridiculous.

Charlotte snuggled up to Dave in his big, soft bed,

pulling his duvet around them against the February cold.

'Do you know I can't remember the last time I spent a night at Julia's,' she mused.

'I can. It was Tuesday last week.'

'Oh yeah, I'd run out of knickers!' remembered Charlotte.

'Just how I like it. But I missed you terribly,' grumbled Dave, nuzzling her hair.

'You know, babe, I've been thinking,' she said, leaving a significant pause.

'Yeah, so have I,' he eventually replied, throwing her a half-smile.

'It does seem to make sense, doesn't it?'

'Yup – and you know what? I think, for the sake of appearances, we should make it official.'

Charlotte sat bolt upright in bed in shock.

Step Seven: The Betrothal

Charlotte glanced over at the suit bag on the empty seat next to her. The ivory silk was just visible through the window at the top of the bag, winking at her in such a significant way. Instinctively she reached out with her hand and smoothed the dress underneath its cover. It looked so beautiful on her, she thought for the millionth time since her first fitting. The most beautiful dress she had ever worn.

'Ladies and gentlemen, we will shortly be arriving at Las Palmas. We would like to wish you a pleasant stay in Majorca and look forward to seeing you on the return flight.'

An involuntary flutter scampered through Charlotte's body. She was so excited – not least because she was going to see Julia again. She had missed her since she had moved out, and now Julia had spent all summer in Majorca working in Carlos's bar their friendship had been confined to phone calls. Quickly, willing the plane down on to the runway, Charlotte pulled the seatbelt tight round her waist. Airplane seats were so uncomfortable, designed to scrunch your back and crush your legs so that when you got up you could barely stand. Charlotte suspected this was deliberate, to stop you wandering up and down the aisle tripping over the drinks trolleys. And the seats were even more cramped on these cheap pack-'em-in-tight flights. Still, it was all she could afford now Dave had 'officially' entered her as joint holder of the mortgage.

It was the take-off and landing Charlotte really hated. The luggage racks would rattle, the seats shudder, the window-panes vibrate. Still, it was all worth it, she was so looking forward to sun, sea and sand again, and as for the idea of a wedding on the beach, well, Charlotte thought it was wonderful. So romantic. Lucky, lucky Julia and Carlos. She looked across at the dress again, this time a little mournfully. Well, at least she got to be the bridesmaid.

Karen Moline is the author of the million-dollar best-selling novels *Belladonna* (Little Brown/Warner) and *Lunch* (Pan Macmillan), a film critic for BBC World Service Radio, 'Two on One' film columnist at the on-line magazine www.nerve.com, and a former inter-viewer for *The Big Breakfast* on Channel 4. She is also a freelance entertainment journalist who has written about Hollywood and pop culture for dozens of maga-zines and newspapers in the US, UK and Australia, including *Tatler, Vogue, Harper's Bazaar, W, Elle, Premiere, Company, New York*, the *Financial Times*, and the London *Evening Standard*. She lives in Manhattan, where she's writing her next two novels, *Game Over, You Win*, and *Remember Your Location*.

Lip Service

Karen Moline

'Oysters.'

'What?' Ginevra asked Sean.

'That's how I met her. At an oyster festival. And you know what – I hadn't planned on going to an oyster festival.'

'It's not the sort of thing you normally plan, is it,' Parker said, rolling his eyes as he helped himself to another beer.

'Oysters, yes. Festival, no,' his friend Gil said.

'I was walking home and it was just there. A whole lot of noise and a whole lot of people,' Sean explained. 'On Division Street. They blocked it off.'

'I've never been to an oyster festival,' Rachel said.

'Me neither,' said Ginevra. 'And I don't think I ever want to. Oysters don't do it for me. Although my parents ate them whenever they could and kept trying to entice me, every single time. They're too squishy.'

'I don't like the colour, either,' Rachel said with a shudder. 'Or the consistency. Yuck.'

'If you swallow them fast, you don't really notice.

485

The squishiness, I mean,' Gil said brightly. 'Helps them go down, as a matter a fact.'

'A lot you know about squishy things going down, I am sure,' Parker said snidely.

'Oysters are an acquired taste for only the most refined of tasters,' Gil retorted.

'Talking about yourself again?' Parker said, swallowing a mouthful of beer and licking his lips. 'Ha. You wish.'

'Oooh, he's getting all hot and bothered now,' Rachel teased.

'It was hot,' Sean said.

'When was hot?' Ginevra asked him.

'When I met her,' he replied. 'At the oyster festival.'

'Was it the heat that's made you look so off?' Ginevra added, looking at him closely with a slight frown. 'Or a few off oysters?'

'No, the oysters weren't off.'

'Not your usual punk self, pal,' Parker said.

'Just punky,' Rachel said, always trying to be the pragmatist and smooth things over.

'Come to think of it, you do look kinda peaky,' Gil told him.

'But it's not like we've seen you for the last few months. You did tell us you were going off to parts unknown on one of your usual assignments. But you've never come back looking like this. Something's eating you, obviously,' Parker said.

'He's eating the oysters, remember,' Ginevra said.

'Yes, but what month was it?' Gil wondered. 'You

can't eat oysters in months without an R in them. Everyone knows that.'

'You think everyone knows everything,' Ginevra said with a wink. 'When they don't.'

'Well, everyone should know everything about when to eat oysters. Whether they like them or not,' Gil said, a little defensively. 'It's one of those all-important lessons that will sustain you through life.'

'Through somebody's oyster-eating life, you mean,' Rachel said. 'I doubt that all the starving people in Bangladesh think that when to eat oysters is an all-important life lesson.'

'Oh, you always have to get so real and be a bore, don't you,' Parker complained. 'We're just talking about oysters, for cripes' sake.'

'It was September,' Sean said, not wanting to hear another verbal spat between Rachel and Parker, who seemed less and less a couple in love than a couple about to tear each other to shreds . . . and that was not something he could think about without an involuntary shudder. 'Labor Day weekend. That's why there was a festival, I guess. And it was hot. Really, really hot.'

'You said that already,' Gil said. 'But I do remember that weekend. That heat.'

'What he means is, *she* was really, really hot,' Parker said. 'The *she* he met. He met *she*. At the infamous Labor Day oyster festival.'

'It was one of those perfect cloudless summer days,' Sean said with a sudden smile so sweet he almost looked like his old self, the one that wasn't pale and drawn and so thin his jeans were practically falling off his slim hips. 'Hard to believe that there would ever be fall, or blasts of wind off the lake or snow and slush and freezing cold. Just heat, and sun, and blue, blue sky. The softest touch of a breeze. The kind of day that made you happy to be alive.'

'Not even the slightest hint of snowballs and sleet and frozen toes,' Rachel said, shuddering at the thought of another Chicago winter.

'Not even the slightest hint, no,' Sean replied. 'I almost wish there had been. It felt like May, like all of summer and the things that were meant to grow were yet to come. It was so weird. There was a bandstand at one end and a band playing an Irish folk-song, and all these people dancing and the tables where they were selling the oysters and the smell . . . The damp sea smell. You know: pungent. And briny.'

'Stinky, you mean,' Ginevra said.

'Combined with the smell of the Guinness. They were the sponsors of the festival, you see,' Sean explained. 'So it was heat and oysters and seaweed and stout.'

'Yum. Appetizing,' Parker said. 'Think I'll have another brewski.'

'So I was minding my own business, listening to the music, standing in a line to get my oysters, just because I could, you know,' Sean said. 'Sort of randomly looking around at the crowd. And that's when I saw her.'

'Your eyes locked,' Ginevra said.

'Across a crowded room,' said Rachel.

'It wasn't a room, silly,' Parker told her. 'It was out-doors. So your eyes locked across a crowded Division Street.'

'She was standing there. Eating oysters,' Sean said. 'Yes, our eyes locked. I've never seen anyone eat oysters like that. I've never seen anyone *look* like that.'

'What do you mean?' Gil asked.

'I'll bet it was her lips,' Parker said, licking his. 'Here comes the kissable lips part.'

'Yes, they were kissable,' Sean said. 'Absurdly, brightly, perfectly pink. I stood there and I saw her, and all I could think was: how do her lips stay so perfectly pink when she is slurping down all those oysters? I swore they almost got pinker each time she ate another one.'

'Pink and grey,' Parker said sarcastically. 'Just my colours.'

'Oh who cares about the colours,' Rachel said. 'I think that is so romantic.'

'It was,' Sean said. 'She saw me looking at her, and then I couldn't tear my eyes away.'

'What did she look like?' Rachel asked breathlessly.

'Like anyone else, that was the thing,' Sean said. 'Nice-looking, but not someone who'd take your breath away at first glance. Medium height; not too thin, not too fat. Long straight brown hair, pulled back in a ponytail. Cut-offs and a white T-shirt.'

'And pink, pink lips,' Parker said.

'Nothing like that has ever happened to me before,' Sean said, nodding. 'Ever. I couldn't move; I couldn't breathe; it felt as if all my senses had gone slack except for sight.'

'Sort of like when Tony sees Maria at the gym dance in *West Side Story*,' Ginevra said.

'And everything gets all fuzzy and the dancers are still there but sort of blobs of moving colour in the background,' Rachel said.

'And they have that dance. Tony and Maria.'

'I liked her dress. That frothy white thing. With the sash.'

'And to think that only a few minutes before she'd been busy holding hands with Chino.'

'I like the song where they have the fake marriage,' Rachel added, looking dreamy. '"One Hand, One Heart"; that's what it is.'

'You have the attention span of a gnat, you know,' Parker told her sternly. 'Would you let Sean finish his story? I believe we're up to the point where the fair damsel was holding oysters in her hand. Slurping them down with perfectly pink lips.'

'All I wanted to do was kiss her,' Sean said.

'Even with her oyster breath,' Gil said with a laugh.

'Can you imagine?' Parker asked. 'You have to be eating a lot of oysters too, not to notice it. Then your breath would be the same and it wouldn't matter.'

'But you hadn't gotten your oysters yet,' Ginevra said to Sean. 'You were still waiting in line, right?'

'Yes, but I wasn't hungry any more. All I had was this overwhelming urge to touch this woman and kiss her. Right then. I had to do it.'

'You didn't know anything about her,' Gil said.

'No.'

'Never seen her before in your life.'

'No.'

'Never felt possessed to kiss an oyster-slurping creature before.'

'No. And that's what she was. A creature.'

'Not a woman,' Gil said softly.

'No,' said Sean, after a long, uncomfortable moment. 'A creature. A presence.'

'You mean like a mermaid?' Ginevra asked him.

'Do you think mermaids like oysters?' Rachel said, trying to lighten the dark gloom that had suddenly settled in the room. 'I mean, why wouldn't they?'

'I bet they like pearls even better,' Ginevra said, smiling at Rachel.

'She was wearing pearls,' Sean said

'Your mermaid,' Gil said.

'Yes.'

'Does the mermaid have a name?'

'Maria?' Parker offered breezily. '"One Hand, One Heart".'

'She said her name was Amanda,' Sean said. 'Amanda Walker.'

'When did she tell you that?' Ginevra asked. 'When she finally stopped eating?'

'Slurping, you mean,' Parker said.

'Yes.'

'So who made the first move, you or Amanda?' Gil asked.

'She did, I think. Except the weirdest thing was, it was as if she hadn't moved at all. I mean, I have no recollection of her walking or moving toward me,' Sean said, staring intently at his shoelaces. 'I blinked, and she was just there. Right next to me. Smiling.'

'With her perfectly pink lips,' Parker said. 'This is getting freaky.'

'Did you kiss her then?' Gil asked softly.

'Yes,' Sean said, closing his eyes, only for a moment, so the muscles in his face relaxed and, again, he almost looked like his old self.

'Hey, pal, it almost looks like you are kissing her still,' Gil said a minute later.

'But I'm not,' Sean replied, that troubled look clouding his eyes again. 'I never am going to kiss her again. Never.'

'I don't like where this is going,' Rachel said. 'She didn't hurt you, did she?'

'Food poisoning, maybe?' Parker asked.

'But wait a minute, you're still at the oyster festival,' Gil said.

'And there she is, a woman-mermaid-creature-whatever. In your face. Kissing you.'

'With her oyster breath,' Parker said. 'Laughing because you didn't care about her breath at all.'

'But she didn't smell of oysters,' Sean said. 'Not a whiff.'

'That doesn't make any sense,' Gil said. 'But of course none of this is making any sense.'

'You know, she could probably patent a breath freshener and make a fortune. Instant Oyster Stink-Away Breath Freshener,' Parker said, laughing at his own absurdity.

'You really have to get a life, you know,' Rachel said. 'It's always money with you. So boring.'

'But I want to know what happened after you kissed,' Ginevra said.

'I don't remember,' Sean said. 'All I know is somehow we were back at my place. In my bed.'

'As in naked, in bed?' Parker said, his eyes lighting up.

'Yes, but I have no memory of how we got there. Did we walk? Did we get a cab? Did she have a car? I've tried and tried, but I just can't remember. All I know is that somehow, in what seemed like another blink of an eye, we ended up in my bed.'

'And obviously she was worth it.'

'For a while there, she was. She was unbelievable.'

'There's something you're not telling us,' Gil said. 'Something important. Something that has nothing to do with oysters.'

'Or oyster breath,' Parker said. 'Or oyster breath freshener.'

'No.'

'Well, are you going to tell us?'

'If it's something embarrassing, you don't have to say anything, you know,' Ginevra said quickly.

'No, I want all of you to know,' Sean said, turning his head slowly to look at all of them. 'Someone has to believe me. I don't believe it myself. Or I wouldn't, if it hadn't happened to me.'

'I'm glad I don't like oysters,' Ginevra muttered under her breath.

'Well, as I said, for a while she was worth it,' Sean said, sighing deeply. 'She was fantastic. Funny. Charming. Adorable. Had a great job, at Grey Advertising. And, as you've already figured out, completely amazing in bed. She did things to me that . . . I mean . . . when she did them I thought I was going to die of pleasure. Really. Sometimes I lay there, afterward, in her arms, listening to her breathing as she slept, thinking, if I did die now at least I will go to my grave happy. A happy, entirely satiated sexual glutton.'

'In the pink, you might say,' Gil said, chuckling.

'Did her lips stay pink in bed too?' Parker asked.

'You really are disgustingly rude,' Ginevra chided him.

'No, it's a fair question, after all,' Sean said soberly. 'And yes, they did stay pink. That was one of the odd things. One of the *many* odd things. Like she'd had the perfectly pink lipstick tattooed on, or something. Even though she hadn't.'

'But this isn't really about indelibly pink lips,' Ginevra says. 'There was something wrong with her, wasn't there. Something you couldn't put your finger on, at first.'

'Exactly,' Sean says, looking at Ginevra curiously, wondering how she could have known that already. 'Even early on, when sometimes I'd get a feeling that something about her was not quite right. It wasn't anything she did, it was how she would make me feel sometimes. That I was there, only because she allowed me to be. That even when we lay awake at night, talking, you know, as lovers do, about everything and nothing, she wasn't listening. Not *really*. She was there, and yet *not*. She'd gotten what she wanted, and that was enough for her. All the rest was lip service.'

'Indelibly pink lip service,' Parker joked.

'Exactly,' Sean said ruefully. 'But I started to wonder if she was real. I mean, who she said she was. We'd talk, and do things, and see each other practically every night, but I had no idea, after nearly six weeks, what made her tick. There were few clues in her apartment. It was perfectly nice, but . . .'

'But it didn't have the girlie touches,' Ginevra said. 'The photos and the knick-knacks and the mess in the bathroom. No personality.'

'Exactly,' Sean said. 'She was compulsively neat. Everything tucked away in boxes. No frills. Not like any other woman's apartment I'd ever been in. It felt like she'd hired someone to put it together for her, that the details were totally unimportant. Sometimes I'd sneak over to her building at lunchtime and hide, watching and waiting for her to come out, with her colleagues, for lunch or for a walk or something, just so I could reassure myself that I wasn't dreaming. That she was a normal person who went to a normal office and had a normal job.'

'As if advertising is a normal job,' Gil said, jokingly.

'You know what I mean,' Sean went on. 'She'd come out with her friends or her colleagues, and she never saw me. Sometimes I thought she really did know I was there and was looking through me just so I'd know what an untrustworthy bastard I was.'

'I don't blame you,' Ginevra said. 'Not if you felt in your gut that something was *off*.'

'It was,' Sean said. 'You all know how completely tone-deaf I am, but whenever we were apart, I found I was always whistling or singing that stupid folk-song the Irish band had been playing when we met. Like I was bewitched or something, and it was *her* song. *Her* reminder to me.'

'Her reminder of what?' Gil asked.

'That I no longer had any will of my own. I couldn't think straight, I couldn't eat, I couldn't do anything except think of her. And sing that stupid song. Even though I hadn't been paying attention to it at all that day.'

'What are the lyrics?' Ginevra asked him.

'"If your arms were around me, you know I'd never leave,"' he sang tunelessly. '"You know I'd never leave."'

'That's profound,' Parker said, trying to joke.

'Isn't it just?' Sean said ruefully. 'About as profound as a dog's bark. I mean, dogs would bark when they saw her coming.'

'A lot of dogs bark at strangers,' Ginevra said.

'No, these dogs would be across the street, and barking. Or down the street and around the corner and barking. At *her*.'

'You mean these dogs wouldn't have been close

enough to feel threatened?' Gil said. 'Or even to smell her.'

'But they still barked,' Ginevra said, looking at Gil. 'How odd.'

'Very. She'd laugh and say dogs hated her. She preferred cats. "I have my familiar," she'd joke.'

'What was her cat's name?' Ginevra asked. 'My friend Mrs Modeus jokes about her familiars, too. She has a cat she named Pandora, because it's always causing trouble.'

'I'll bet Miss Amanda Walker calls her cat Lucifer,' Rachel said.

'How about Pluto?' Gil offered.

'Nixon?' Parker suggested.

'Who on earth would ever want to call a kitty Nixon?' Gil wondered. 'Then you'd have to say "Nixon, Nixon" every time you wanted to feed the poor thing. And hear that name. No way.'

'Her cat's name was Brenda,' Sean said.

'Which is a very sweet name for a kitty,' said Rachel. 'Maybe she couldn't be all bad if she had a cat named Brenda.'

'You'd think,' Sean said. 'As much as she doted on that cat, though, she hated dogs. Not just 'cause of the barking. Said she always had, ever since she was little.' He paused. 'Except I could never imagine her as a little girl. Being chased by some poor dumb pooch as she went door-to-door in her nice quiet suburban neighbourhood, selling Girl Scout cookies. She seemed to have sprung from some other place, fully formed. That's what I thought the first time we were walking down the street and some dogs on the far corner started barking at her. Baring their teeth, ready to pounce. She called them devil dogs.'

'Devil dogs. You mean like Ring-Dings?' Parker asked.

'Of course he doesn't mean Ring-Dings,' Rachel sniped. 'All you ever talk about is what you can put in your mouth.'

'Well, I'd rather think about junk food than oysters or spawn of the devil any day.'

'What did you say?' Sean asked Parker, panic-stricken. 'What do you mean, "spawn of the devil"?'

'I don't know,' Parker replied, shrugging. 'It just sort of seems to fit. You mentioning her devil dogs, and all. And being "sprung from some other place," as I believe you just put it. Maybe she was just that. The devil's daughter. A *succubus*.'

'But that is exactly what she was,' Sean said in a voice so low everyone strained forward to hear him. 'A succubus. Who came to me in the night. And when she did, she wouldn't stop doing whatever until she had sucked me dry.'

'You mean, um, *literally*? Can you give her my number?' Parker asked after a long, uncomfortable moment, trying to joke again, and failing miserably.

'Thanks, sweetie,' Rachel said tartly to him. 'I really appreciate that.'

'You know I'm only kidding,' Parker told her as he leaned over to try to kiss her.

'No, I don't,' she said, pushing him away. 'You can't help yourself, can you? From saying stupid things like that. Especially in front of an audience.'

'No, of course he can't,' Gil quickly interjected. 'Which is why we all dote on him just the way he is. The dirty dog.'

'Devil dog, you mean,' Ginevra said. 'Hopeless Ring-Ding.'

'I like Drake's Cakes, too,' Gil said. 'He's the drake, and you're the duck.'

'Duck, duck, and who's the silly goose?' Parker asked.

'Sean is, without a doubt,' Gil said quickly, trying to dispel the odd tension that had infected them all, waiting yet dreading to hear what Sean was going to say next.

'But what was it that she wanted?' Gil asked.

'Normally I'd be the last man to complain if a woman wanted to suck me dry, as it were,' Sean went on, glancing briefly at Parker. 'And there's not a man alive who'd ever turn down or get tired of what she liked to do to me. But it wasn't about sex. Sex was merely the means for her to get what she wanted. And what she wanted was to absorb my very *essence*. That's what she meant to suck out of me. That's what *fed* her.'

'Are you sure?' Ginevra asked quietly.

'Yes,' Sean said. 'I've tried and tried to figure it out, why I started feeling so odd. So not myself. So *thin*, even though I was forcing myself to eat all the time. And the more I started to protest, the more she was into me. Literally. Until I realized that if I didn't get away, she would have me waste away to nothing.'

'And then what?' Parker asked, frowning.

'And then she'd find someone else,' Sean said, his tone so matter-of-fact that his friends found it hard to dispute his unbelievable story. 'I knew she was already looking. I caught her at it, at a party. When she was dancing. It was dark in the room, and smoky, and everyone else was dancing. I stood by the wall, leaning on it for support actually, and wondering how to get out of this mess. Nobody paid any attention to me. And then I saw her.' He swallowed hard, then continued. 'It was Amanda, yet not. It was as if she had transformed herself into what she really was – a sort of elongated form, all sinewy and boneless. Like Brenda, her cat. Her eyes glinted in the darkness and I caught her, her lips glowing all pink and her eyes sparkling, searching. Ready to wrap her tentacles around some poor guy and do to him what she'd done to me.'

'What did you do?' Ginevra asked quietly.

'I got out of there. Went home. Packed a couple of suitcases. Got in the car, and drove. Drove till I couldn't keep my eyes open, then slept at a truck stop. Got up, and kept driving. Called the magazine on Monday and said there was a family emergency, and I would check in soon. When I did, they asked me to go to Arizona, to do a story there.'

'Why didn't you call me?' Gil asked. 'You know I would have done anything to help.'

'I know, and I'm sorry,' Sean said. 'I couldn't tell you the truth, not then. I didn't think you would believe me. So I asked Roger, one of the guys at work to get my mail and stuff, and leave a message telling you I was away, on an undercover assignment.'

'I remember,' Gil said. 'It wasn't the first time you'd disappeared.'

'Exactly. And then, after about two months, I called Grey Advertising and asked for her. The receptionist told me that no one named Amanda Walker was there. Never had been. No one named Amanda Walker had *ever* worked there.'

'What about her apartment?' Parker asked.

'I asked Roger to go there and check the names on the buzzers,' Sean replied. 'Some couple was living in her apartment. They said they'd been living there for over two years.'

'Well,' Gil said. 'That is some story.'

'You believe me, don't you?' Sean asked, a pleading note in his voice.

'I believe you,' Ginevra said, biting her lip. 'I'm just glad you got away.'

'So am I,' Rachel added, shuddering.

'Me, too,' said Parker. 'But I wonder where she went.'

'I don't know,' Sean said, closing his eyes. 'I hope it's far, far away. But I still see her, those pink lips curved into a smile, when I'm dreaming. And sometimes when I'm walking home, out of the corner of my eye, I think I see her turning a corner. Hurrying away. Off to suck the life out of her next victim. And I wonder if I'm ever going to be free of her.'

'Well,' Parker said. 'I guess this means you won't want to join me for dinner tonight.'

'And what exactly were you planning on eating?' Gil asked him.

'You know,' Parker replied, a wicked glint in his eyes. 'Oysters.'

Chris Manby grew up in Gloucester and published her first story in *Just Seventeen* at the age of fourteen. Her first three wickedly funny romantic comedies, *Flatmates*, *Second Prize* and *Deep Heat* are available in Coronet paperback, and a fourth novel, *Lizzie Jordan's Secret Life*, will be published in August 2000. She lives in south-west London and lists her proudest moment as being dribbled on by Sir Robin Day.

Saving Amsterdam

Chris Manby

There are some advantages to being single, Lisa told herself. She didn't have to see the new *Star Wars* movie, for a start. She didn't have to pretend to play badly at *Goldeneye* on the Nintendo 64 in case she beat him and sent him into a strop. She didn't have to smell his socks or iron his shirts and get shouted at when she left the slightest crease somewhere that would never be seen. She didn't have to put up with his tedious friends, or baby-sit the younger members of his family while he went ahead and had fun in the name of work. In short, she didn't have to do anything she didn't want to any more.

And she knew that she should have been happy by now. I mean, she told herself, it had been six months since he did the deed; ending their relationship and an entire life mapped out in Hallmark card moments with just a few simple words.

'I don't think I love you any more.'

Lisa stared at him as if she'd misheard. Any second now, she told herself, he's going to break into a big smile and take me into his arms and hug me. Perhaps, that particularly mad bone inside her cried, he's playing a last cruel joke before he asks you to marry him. But he didn't break into a smile. And he didn't ask her to marry him. He really did want to finish their relationship and he wanted her out of their shared flat as quickly as humanly possible. He'd help her pack, he said, seeing as he was such a kind and thoughtful bloke. Would she like him to drive her back to stay with her parents? Later her best friend would point out that the newly christened 'Bastard Ex' had made sure that Lisa finished his VAT return before he finished with her.

The shit. She didn't see it coming. Not at all. She had believed him when he said that his unassailable miserableness was something to do with extra pressure at the office. Only that afternoon she had spent a fortune stocking up the fridge with his favourite foods so that they wouldn't have to leave the house all weekend if he didn't want to. She only wanted to make his life easier. He repaid her kind efforts with twenty-four hours' notice to quit.

She thought she would die from the misery. But some of her friends even muttered 'a lucky escape' to describe the agony that followed.

Six months on, she was, as they had predicted, getting through whole weeks without crying. Of course she was. And sometimes she would catch herself laughing in a strangely unfamiliar carefree way as though he had never been in her life and scraped the surface of her heart into mince with his carelessness. Sometimes she was the old Lisa. The Lisa who would have been sick with hilarity at the idea that she would ever iron a man's shirts and claim to enjoy doing it. The Lisa who would have had little time for a girl who could no longer walk down certain streets in London because, even if she wasn't likely to bump into the man who had left her broken-hearted, she was sure to see something that would remind her of him.

That was the worst part of being alone. Towards the end, he hadn't been so much in her life that he left such a gaping hole when he finally went anyway. Perhaps subconsciously sensing that his love for her was on the wane, Lisa had been seeing more of her old friends in any case. But there were certain things that would always be inextricably linked to the best times with the beloved. Certain things that would take her back to the happy times at the beginning of their relationship when he still opened car doors for her and helped her to put on her coat. Things that would make it seem impossible that he had spent their last few months together sitting in front of the TV like a vivisectionist's monkey with half its brain cut out while she lugged the shopping home from the supermarket on foot.

Yep, on a good day Lisa was well-versed in the reasons why she was better off without him. Towards the end, the man in the corner shop had known (and cared) more about her wild dreams and ambitions. But in the words of the song, there was always something there to remind her of the halcyon days when that hadn't been the case. Stupid things.

Red wine, for example. The bouquet of a fine Merlot

reminded her of his first fumbling attempts to seduce her. Chicken korma reminded her of evenings in his flat watching *Friends* and really wanting Rachel and Ross to be happy together because didn't everyone deserve to be as happy as Lisa and her loved one were back then? Certain songs could destroy her with their echoes of a happier past. Hearing 'Wonderwall' could actually take her knees out from under her and had done so on a particularly embarrassing occasion in Wimbledon's Central Court shopping mall. But there were also the stupid tunes that they had jived around the kitchen to; imitating each other's dancefloor styles and pulling goofy faces. Funny how he could only ever dance in time while he was doing an impression of her . . .

Well, that was then. Now Lisa had moved on to vodka tonics, become a vegetarian, stopped watching *Friends* and could no longer listen to 'Bewitched'. That wasn't too much of an inconvenience. The real pain was the constriction she felt around her heart when the tube sailed past Sloane Square. She hadn't walked down the King's Road since the night he said he no longer loved her. It was as though she might see the ghosts of them peering in through the window of a jeweller's shop. He was always looking at watches – though he was still unable to get anywhere on time if it mattered to Lisa. She had harboured a wild fantasy that one day he might spend a couple of minutes measuring up the diamonds for her left hand instead of the latest Breitling.

So, the King's Road was out of bounds too. At least until her mashed-up heart was a little less scabby. Perhaps in ten years' time she might once again brave the hallowed halls of Peter Jones. But as for Amsterdam . . . Amsterdam, she would never be able to go back to. Because, if there was a defining moment in their relationship it was a weekend spent in Amsterdam, December '96. Bright but cold. Frost crystals glittered the pavements. The trees along the canals wore little white lights in their bold bare branches. She thought she had met her soul mate. They were *in love*.

When she closed her eyes, Lisa could almost feel the icy tip of his nose as he kissed her on a dainty bridge somewhere near Dam Square. She remembered feeding him french fries and mayonnaise in a tiny café under the disapproving eye of some old matron; she remembered laughing with him at the dull brown pictures from Van Gogh's potato period in the Van Gogh museum; talking to each other in pidgin Dutch; learning the words for bedroom and whipped cream . . . He had loved her then, hadn't he? Looking back, with the sound of their last argument ringing in her ears, it was difficult to tell. Before the end, she had suggested that they go to Amsterdam to celebrate their anniversary. Now she knew she would never go back.

Shame her boss didn't quite understand the new world map of the recently broken-hearted.

Schiphol Airport, Amsterdam. Just twenty minutes to go before Lisa was due to make a presentation to her company's new Dutch clients. Lisa yanked the blue Samsonite trolley case off the luggage carousel and in doing so nearly managed to pull her arm from its socket. She thought she'd travelled a lot lighter than that. With one eye on her watch, as if constantly checking the time might stop it from passing so quickly, she hurtled through the arrivals lounge. A small gang of men leaned against the barrier to separate new arrivals from over-eager loved ones. Lisa scanned the drivers' hand-scrawled boards for her own name and, locating it with bionic long-distance vision, hurled her bag over the barrier towards her own driver before following the bag with a pretty spectacular vault.

They made it to the bleak out-of-town offices of the H & P Advertising Agency with two minutes to go. Lisa clipped her way into the building on executive heels, praying that she looked efficient and enthusiastic rather than plain (or should that be plane) manic. Her plan had been to arrive a whole two hours earlier. Where but at Heathrow could a girl find fog to ground a scheduled flight at the beginning of June, for God's sake?

A round-faced assistant showed Lisa straight to the conference room. She tossed her jacket on the back of a chair, grinned her biggest grin and opened her case to get out her notes. But she couldn't find them. Instead she found three pairs of stars-and-stripes boxer shorts.

Back at her hotel – The American (that irony was not lost on her) – Lisa finally let go the tears that made her feel as though her eyes must be bulging cartoon-style throughout the rest of the abortive meeting. She said what she could without the notes and her carefully drawn story-boards but she couldn't remember the deal-clinching figures. She had her lap-top in her hand luggage but the battery in that had run down and no one could find her the right kind of adaptor to use with Dutch plug sockets.

'Don't worry. Anyone could pick up the wrong case,' said the super-cool MD, but Lisa knew that kind of mistake had never happened to him, nor was it ever likely to.

'Imagine how the bloke who did get your case will feel when he pulls out *your* knickers at some high-level meeting,' said Jane when Lisa called the London office to check for messages and voicemail.

That was no comfort either. Lisa had packed the grungiest pants imaginable. So grungy that the thought almost made her ready to resign her own case to history forever. Even if he had handed it in, how would she be able to face claiming such disgraceful luggage?

'What else was in your case?' Jane asked in a further attempt to make light of the disaster. 'Vibrator?'

'Worse,' said Lisa. 'How about a self-help guide to finding your ideal man?'

'Sheesh,' said Jane. 'You're never going to be able to get that bag back.'

It was hot in the hotel room. Lisa leaned her forehead against the cool glass of the window and looked out into the square below. It was still light at seven o'clock. A beautiful summer night. Tourists milled about in search of somewhere to spend the evening. Café proprietors drew attention to their menus. Hot and bothered culture lovers were tempted from their museum tours by the prospect of a long cool beer.

Lisa had a sudden unwelcome flashback to the french fries and mayonnaise. Her bedroom window was almost opposite the café where the BE had licked her fingers clean and whispered promises for the night ahead. As if on cue, a young couple chose a seat in full view of Lisa's depressing hotel room and snuggled close. Lisa suddenly felt very sorry for the middle-aged woman who had once been subjected to a similar display and drew her curtains on the scene.

She had three more nights of this. A room with a view of the place where she had once been so happy. Miserable memories and not even a pair of clean knickers to do her wallowing in. She had phoned the airline but no one had handed in her case. The receptionist at the hotel promised to let her know if it turned up there instead. In the meantime, Lisa didn't have anything to wear but her best boardroom suit. It had been crumpled by the plane journey, sweated in on her race to the first meeting, and, even as she inspected part of the hem that was starting to come down, she somehow managed to spill half a cup of coffee on her skirt.

She ripped the skirt off immediately but within seconds the scalding heat had coloured her legs lobster red. Lisa cried again as she tried to rinse the stain out in the inadequate bathroom basin. Pale blue linen. Dark brown coffee. She rinsed without a hope.

Lisa sat on the edge of the bath and squeezed her eyes tightly shut. Maybe she would wake up. Maybe she would open her eyes and find herself back in her own little bedroom, ready to start the day with an entirely unmistakeable bag. But when she did open her eyes, the stranger's case was still in the corner of the room and the stain on her skirt was starting to dry in the shape of the British Isles.

Lisa ran her fingers over the Samsonite impostor.

What if the owner of this case had a pair of jeans or something in exactly her size? She could put on clothes from this case and go shopping. It wasn't quite eight.

Lisa opened the case and took a better look. The three pairs of stars-and-stripes boxer shorts were exactly where they had been when she opened the case in the H & P office. Gingerly taking each pair by the waist-band, she made a neat little pile on the bed and began to investigate further. She guessed by the careful folding that the stuff in this case was clean, at least. She pulled out a T-shirt, a bright souvenir from a Thai beach full-moon party. So the owner of this case had travelled. Or he knew a man who had. Ralph Lauren Polo socks. Not too impoverished either, by the look of things. Lisa admired his smart leather toiletries case. Took a deep sniff of his aftershave. Jean Paul Gaultier for Men. Nice. Different. Her ex had never liked it.

Beneath the wash-bag – bingo. Lisa nodded with approval when she pulled out a pair of battered 501s. Whoever owned this case must have a pretty neat backside. And long legs. Tall. Slim. Beautifully scented. He could be her ideal man.

But there was no point getting quite so attached to someone she would never meet. For all the identifying evidence in his Samsonite, the idiot hadn't taken the time to fill out his name and address on the luggage tag. Lisa resolved to leave the bag with the airline staff when she went to catch her flight home and zipped it shut again. Minus the jeans.

Combined with her neat black court shoes and her smart suit jacket, the look was a bit Farah Fawcett Majors, but at least Lisa was fully clothed once more. By the time she got to the lobby, she had convinced herself that she almost looked stylish in a very retro way.

She waited behind a man with spiked blond hair at the desk to hand her keys in. The concierge was taking her time with him. Lisa had been appraising his neat bottom for a couple of minutes before she realized that she was idly gazing at the backside she had been fantasizing about as she rifled through the poor man's case.

At the same time, the concierge noticed that Lisa was standing behind the stranger and with incredibly unwelcome efficiency, announced: 'Well, this is Miss Glover, right here.'

Lisa was pulling an expression that wouldn't have looked out of place on a halibut when the stranger turned to her with a milk-steaming smile.

'I think I got your case,' he said.

'I think so,' said Lisa.

'Are those my jeans?' he asked.

Right then, Lisa knew there was no God. What benign celestial being would have allowed her worst knickers and her well-thumbed copy of 'How to attract true love into your life through meditation and positive affirmations' to fall into such divine-looking hands. And then to be caught wearing his trousers?

The stranger was still grinning at her.

'Mark Law,' he introduced himself. 'And I do believe I'm wearing your knickers.'

After that, it would have been rude not to agree to go for a drink with him. Feeling only slightly less self-conscious in her own clothes, Lisa joined him downstairs in the hotel bar. Scanning the room for him, she was surprised to feel a long forgotten shiver of expectation when she caught sight of his face. He smiled at her as though he had chosen her to be his companion, not as though she was a random nutter who had somehow picked up his bag. When he told her she looked much better in her own clothes, she coloured to match her pink jumper.

'Pink suits you,' he told her.

She went two shades short of cerise.

They ordered martinis and talked about work. He

was American. In Europe to drum up funds for his new Internet venture. She told him about the disastrous meeting at H & P. He told her about the receptionist's face when he arrived at his own hotel and opened his case to reveal a pile of women's clothes when searching for his letter of reservation.

'Is this your first time in Amsterdam?' he asked.

Lisa had been laughing at his impression of the shocked matron at the hotel. Now she felt the cloud passing across her face. 'No,' she said quietly. 'This isn't my first time.'

'Then you can show me around,' he said.

And before she could explain that there were too many places in the town that she really didn't want to have to go back to, Mark had spread his map out on the table.

'I'm leaving for Switzerland tomorrow morning so I've got to get the best bits done tonight. Are you into art?' he asked her. 'Some of the museums are open late. We should see the *Night Watch*,' he announced.

Lisa started to pull a face. 'You know, that picture is . . .'

'One of the great works of the seventeenth century.'

Lisa shrugged. That was true. It was one of her favourites. But it was also one of the great works of art she had seen with the BE. She remembered all too vividly standing in front of the painting with his arm slung round her shoulders in the way that she loved. He had kissed her in front of that picture. In fact, she didn't think there was a single significant work of art in Amsterdam that he hadn't kissed her in front of.

'You don't mind seeing it again?' Mark asked. 'If we hurry we'll catch the museum before it closes, then we can go and get something to eat. If you want to.'

He fixed her with a grin that told her he wasn't often refused.

Fifteen minutes later, they stood before the famous painting. They stood close together, whispering in the reverential quiet of the gallery. Mark drew Lisa's attention to the little girl stepping through the soldiers.

She was suddenly aware of his hand on the small of her back.

'Rembrandt had such an eye for light and shadow,' she said, turning towards him to whisper in his ear. But her lips didn't meet with Mark's ear. They met with his own smiling mouth and brushed against his lips ever so slightly. Lisa pulled backwards and stumbled, which only had the effect of making Mark take her further into his arms.

'Do you think we look as though we've known each other for a long time?' he asked her as he held her close.

Lisa didn't know what to say. Or where to look. His face was so close to hers that she could no longer focus on his individual features.

'I think we look like we're lovers,' he told her.

She felt her most important organs melt.

* * *

Van Gogh didn't stand a chance. The museum tour was over. Back in her hotel room, Lisa fumbled for a light switch.

'Leave the light on,' Mark breathed hotly. 'I mean, I've already seen your knickers.'

Sex with her ex had become perfunctory. Always starting and finishing in exactly the same way. It worked perfectly, she had told herself. But there had been no surprises for a very long time.

Now, with Mark, Lisa felt a prickle creep up the back of her neck like ghostly fingers. She felt the hot seeping sensation as blood coloured her breasts blush pink with arousal. She felt the inside of her thighs become hyper-sensitive to his touch. His fingertips seemed so hot on her legs that she expected to see burn-marks wherever he laid them upon her. And meanwhile his tongue was in her mouth. His thigh was between hers, easing them apart. She wondered if she was getting giddy through lack of oxygen or the rising heat between their bodies. He took her hand and placed it on his penis. Carefully, he wrapped her fingers around the shaft and encouraged her to stroke the hard length of him.

She came before he did. She tightened her thighs round his waist, squeezing hard as he too reached a climax. She felt at once frightened and triumphant as she watched him come. The unfamiliar expression of a new lover . . . A new lover. She could hardly bear to think . . .

With his body still pinning hers to the soft white sheets, Lisa began to cry. The tears ran across her cheeks and down the side of her neck and on to his hand, still tangled in her soft brown hair.

Mark eased himself up on to his elbows and looked down at the tear-tracks glittering on her face.

'Did we do something we shouldn't have done?' he asked.

She wasn't sure. She wanted to say 'no' to reassure him and herself. At the same time she wanted to nod 'yes' and burst into disappointed tears. Lisa turned the bedside lamp off in an attempt to hide.

'Do you wanna talk about it?'

This time she did nod. In the dark, she felt she could tell him almost everything. If he couldn't clearly see her lips moving, perhaps he wouldn't connect her so inextricably with the story she was about to tell. Perhaps it didn't matter anyway if he thought she was sad or a nutter. They would probably never see each other again.

'The last time I came to this city,' she began, 'I was with someone I really loved.'

And out it spilled. And Mark listened. Never interrupting. He just stroked her hair and listened as she told him about the plans she had made for her and her beloved. The shock of the ending. The numbness that had been with her since. The red wine she could no longer drink, the curry she'd had to abandon, the television she couldn't watch, the music to which she could no longer listen.

'You've got to make new memories,' he told her when she finished. 'That's the only way to save the things you love for yourself.'

'I know that now,' she told him. 'And I feel like you've helped me save Amsterdam.'

'I'll make it my mission to help you save the world,' he said.

Lisa knew that he would be gone when she woke up. Mark's onward flight to Switzerland left Schiphol at 8 a.m. It was three minutes past now. Was he still taxi-ing down the runway? Hearing a plane pass high overhead Lisa pushed her hair back from her eyes and gazed up at the blank ceiling of her hotel room. There was still a faint scent of his aftershave about the pillows. When she put her hand to her chin, it felt sore where his stubble had rubbed at her pale skin as they kissed.

'Idiotic,' she told herself. Six months of careful, heart-healing celibacy blown on a mad night with a stranger. But there wasn't time to think about it now. Lisa had another meeting at nine-thirty.

She opened her case. On top of her own clothes was a pair of crumpled stars-and-stripes boxer shorts and a note on hotel notepaper.

Lisa expected a 'thanks for everything' at most. A sweet gesture but no contact number. Instead she found not only a number but another hotel address.

'Your mission,' he had written, 'should you choose to accept it. Next weekend. Save Paris.'

Daisy Waugh has published a novel, *What is the Matter With Mary Jane*, and a book about her time living and teaching in Kenya, *A Small Town in Africa* (both published by Heinemann). She has written for most national newspapers and magazines. She has contributed regular columns to various papers in various guises: a restaurant reviewer, an agony aunt, a Los Angeles adventurer. She has worked as a radio presenter and a TV presenter and is currently working on a new novel, *The New You Survival Kit*. She has a small daughter called Panda.

A Form of Release

Daisy Waugh

Cocà di Cocà woke up to the sound of her own sweet voice on the radio that morning, singing the song that had once been the nation's anthem. It was the song that had scooped her from nineteen years of innocent obscurity. The song which Danny wrote for her, which she stole from him, which would forever make the name Cocà di Cocà synonymous with a short and irrelevant moment in British history.

At the time the song was playing (late April, early May 1985) Cocà used to wear a lacy beret which sent the adolescents wild. For a month or two she couldn't climb out of a taxi without being mobbed. She couldn't cross the road. She couldn't buy her own lavatory paper.

> *Oh! Sasha dooo*
> *Sasha doo Sasha daa*
> *The ja-ja jolting in your heart*
> *Has me a gaga from my start – Sasha!*
> *Oh! Sasha daa-doo-daa*

A lifetime later she lay alone in her king-size Ethiopian silver bed while the song on the radio invaded her dreams. She was in the assembly hall of her old school again and Danny was there, elegant and loose-limbed as ever, standing beside her on the stage, just as it should have been, just as it had been that beautiful July night, the night of the Fifth-Form Leavers' Disco. He was looking across at her and they were both singing – he was grinning at her with so much mischief and love – and then the voice of the DJ broke in and Danny was saying, in an idiotic American accent: *Ooo, remember that? What a fab song. 8.17. Traffic news coming up . . . not looking good out there is it Jerry?*

Cocà di Cocà hadn't woken up to the sound of her own success in years. She could have taken it either way; as a happy reminder of how sweet things had been, or a cruel reminder of how much she had lost. It came to the same thing anyway. Cocà di Cocà woke in a council flat in South Kensington with a stream of tears trickling down her cheeks.

Today was the first day of her relaunch. The first day of her second relaunch, to be more precise. And this time she was doing it on her own; no record company, no public relations adviser. And most definitely, no manager.

So 'relaunch' was rather a grandiose way to describe it. Cocà di Cocà's second relaunch consisted of a single interview. A charming girl called Annabel something, from the Saturday *Express* magazine, had called her up quite out of the blue, inviting her to feature in the first of what promised to be a weekly series of glittering celebrity interviews, for which, in exchange for a lovely full-page colour picture, the celebrity was required to reminisce, *in situ*, about their days at school.

'It's going to be amazing,' the charming girl had explained, 'because, if you think about it, *school* is really the last place you'd ever expect to find a celebrity!'

Cocà said she thought the series sounded like a great idea and accepted the invitation at once. 'But I must insist – and, Annabel, you may know from your clippings that I always insist on this when I'm interviewed – but I must bring along my own make-up artist.'

Annabel said the budget didn't stretch to a make-up artist. 'If you want to bring your own, then of course – But we won't be able to pay for it.'

Cocà di Cocà hummed and hawed a while, backtracked, and a date was fixed.

It was from a desert of misery, inactivity and regret that the Saturday *Express* interview came along so it gave Cocà something to focus on. It also stirred a lot of old memories. She was lying in bed a few nights later, reflecting on her life's mistakes, when it occurred to her that she had so much to tell readers it couldn't possibly be fitted into a single page. She decided to write an autobiography and she climbed out of bed to begin it there and then.

The Sasha-Doo Girl, she wrote (because that rang bells with everybody) *an autobiography by Cocà di Cocà*

And she would dedicate it to Danny. *An Apology,*

she thought. *To Danny. An Apology to Danny After All These Years.* Or – *To Danny. I still love you. After all these years.*

Wording of the dedication kept her up until morning. But she felt better than she had in months. It was wonderful to have a project again.

Readers may already have guessed that at thirty-four years old, Cocà di Cocà was what might be described as washed up. A minor industry joke. Soon after the first hit single, for reasons that she never fully understood, and which were possibly never fully understandable, her record company went cold on her. The day before her second single was due to be released they sent a motorbike delivery man to her flat with a meanly worded letter severing all contact with her.

'Such is life in the nefarious world of show-biz,' her manager Charlie had said blithely. 'We'll get you a better contract somewhere else. Stop fussing and come to bed.'

But soon after that Charlie's boss Lionel decided, quite accurately, that Charlie's drug addiction was affecting his judgement, and fired him.

Charlie and Cocà spent the late eighties growing prematurely jowly together. They went to a lot of parties and took a lot of cocaine. They were on toilet-cubicle terms with some of the biggest names in the industry but still nobody wanted to work with them. Charlie might have set up on his own except, by the time he thought of it, he and Cocà had spent every penny he had ever earned. He was ruined. In the winter of 1989 there was a flurry of publicity when the Sasha-Doo Girl and her former manager, known to the industry as Gorgeous Charlie, checked into a drying-out clinic together.

THE SASHA-DOO GIRL
AN AUTOBIOGRAPHY BY
COCÀ DI COCÀ
page 43

At nineteen years old Cocà di Cocà (or Melanie, as I was called before Charlie came along) had the world at her feet. I was fearless and carefree and, though I say it who shouldn't, I was as pretty as a peach. I drank and, yes, I took drugs. Life was one big party!

Danny and I had known each other since we were five but we didn't fall in love until our last year at school. Danny had always been so clever and quiet and sort of smallish. But then during the summer holiday of '81 he had his growth spurt. I remember clocking him that first day of term. I couldn't take my eyes off him. Suddenly he had these broad shoulders and lovely long legs and that curly brown fringe falling over his blue eyes – I thought I was going to faint! He looked so gentle and self-possessed, as though he were thinking about something so important – like love, I suppose. I felt a lump in my throat. Something about his quiet *savoir-faire*, if you know what

I mean, suddenly made me feel ever so lonely.

He glanced across at me just as I was ogling him and I blushed! Me! I made the *boys* blush! And that, if you can believe it, was the beginning of a very very special friendship. We set up the band – or rather Danny did. After we left school I would have happily chucked in the whole business. It was Danny who persevered. He wrote the songs, organized the gigs. He was forever bugging me about rehearsals! And when we performed, because we were so very much in love, there was a sort of magic to our act which, I'm told, made everybody who watched us feel like life was beautiful. If only Charlie hadn't barged in and bust us up when he did we could have been so happy together. We could have made it on our own terms. Danny and Me. Like Sonny and Cher (only not quite!) At the top of the charts forever . . .

The first time Gorgeous Charlie set eyes on Melanie, or Cocà di Cocà as she was to be called from then on, she was wriggling her lovely hips in time to Danny's song, on a drab little platform in the corner of a pub in Earl's Court. Gorgeous Charlie, of the golden tan, the sunstreaked hair and the real Rolex (no longer) happened to have been in urgent search of new talent that night, due to the fact that a week earlier Lionel, the head of the company, had given him what amounted in the world of pop to a Very Formal Warning. Gorgeous Charlie hadn't been justifying his gorgeous salary of late and Lionel's patience had run out. Lionel wanted results. Lionel wanted a new sensation. He wanted a stunning kid with wiggly hips and white teeth and a tight arse and a lovely grin. And if Gorgeous Charlie wanted to keep his job then he had better be listening, because Lionel wanted her standing in front of his desk by first thing Friday morning.

It was late Thursday evening when Charlie stumbled into that Earl's Court pub. She was the thirty-third white-toothed girl he'd seen in four days, and the girls were beginning to merge. His secretary had kept a record of their bust sizes, hair length, smile widths, agent contact numbers etc etc, but then at six-thirty that evening, just as Charlie was about to call one or other of them in, the secretary admitted that the list had been 'temporarily mislaid'. Whatever. A sensation-free Friday and a salary-free future loomed . . .

Until Melanie. Half-past ten on a Thursday night and, frankly, she was no worse than the best of them. Nice wiggly hips, tall and blonde, with big blue eyes and a delicate upturned nose. Yes. An ideal woman, thought Charlie. She looked like a bit like a Barbie Doll. She was the one.

THE SASHA-DOO GIRL
AN AUTOBIOGRAPHY BY
COCÀ DI COCÀ
page 82

It was horrible the way Charlie and Lionel split us up. During the first few meetings Charlie didn't give us even a single hint as to what they were actually up to. It was only on our fourth visit to the offices that Danny was quietly pulled aside . . .

'Danny old boy,' said fat Lionel from behind his fat shiny desk. 'Won't you sit down?'

Danny knew. He'd always known. He just didn't want to – 'Have you got a toilet, sir?'

'I think you're an exceptionally talented young man.'

'Oh!'

'I think you're – a remarkable performer – an extraordinary performer – and a good song writer, too.'

'Oh!'

'However I don't think your interests are best served performing beside Melanie. Have you thought about that?'

'Well –'

'I think you are a much more – complicated – personality. You are, as I say, an exceptionally talented young man and to get the best out of both of you – you're not going to like this Danny, my dear – But I see you as a solo artist. A sort of Bob Dylan for the eighties. I'm going to split you up . . .'

'That's –'

'To be frank, I see your solo career as having a little bit more depth, a little more longevity than our lovely friend Melanie's –' He allowed himself a conspiratorial smile. 'Now, what I want you to do is to go home and get cracking on some new material. I want you to write until your knuckles are raw! Do you understand me?'

'Do I? . . . *Me?*'

'I want you to close the curtains, lock the door, take the phone off the hook. I want you to live like a hermit for six months, Danny. And in six months I'm going to get you back in here and we're going to work out what we want to put on your album. How does that sound?'

'Cr – we – I mean. Fucking Hell!'

Lionel chuckled. 'But first of all I'd very much like to purchase the song you and Melanie were singing for us this afternoon. Will that be all right with you?'

'Of course! My God! Of course!'

'Excellent . . . I expect to be seeing a good deal of you in the future, my boy. I have big plans for you.'

THE SASHA-DOO GIRL
AN AUTOBIOGRAPHY BY
COCÀ DI COCÀ
page 84

. . . sign here please.' – I never did find out exactly what went on in there but the song he sold that day was the song that sent the nation crazy five months later. He sold it for £220!

Danny obviously realized pretty quickly he'd been duped, which is why he acted so weirdly when he came to say goodbye. I remember I was in the process of analysing a video Charlie had made of one of my dance routines and he put a hand on my shoulder and stood behind me just watching the screen.

After a while he said, 'It's really good, Mel.'

He sounded so peculiar. I turned to look at him and there were tears in his eyes. I'd never seen him cry before. 'I think I'm going to head off,' he said. 'Just been talking to Lionel . . .'

He said Lionel wanted him to concentrate on his writing for a while. He said, 'Lionel says he thinks it would be better for both our careers if we just – didn't see each other for a couple of months. He says I've got to write.'

'Write what?' I said. I suppose I sounded stupid but I *knew* him. Danny wasn't a writer. Danny was a born performer. Like me.

'Just writing stuff,' he said. 'Whatever happens, Mel, I'll be thinking of you. I love you. Always. You won't forget me, will you?'

'Don't be an idiot,' I said. 'We're going to be seeing each other again in a couple of weeks! Once all the fuss has died down.' But I couldn't look at him. At the bottom of my heart – and this is what still gets to me – I understood. I understood exactly what Danny was saying. He had been sent on his way.

It was the last time I ever saw him.

Cocà di Cocà married Gorgeous Charlie shortly after they left the drying-out clinic. She had hoped, quite unreasonably, that Danny would read about it first and somehow come to reclaim her. But the occasion excited

barely a whisper of media interest and they were married at the Chelsea Registry Office without incident.
Charlie, drug free and bursting with enthusiasm for his
one and only client, attempted to stage a relaunch off
the back of it. It was humiliating. Cocà was persuaded
by Charlie (no longer creditworthy) to take out a
twenty-thousand-pound loan to pay for the celebrity-
studded party. They hired a room at the Café Royal,
and organized for all the waiters to be dressed in Sasha-
Doo Girl berets which had been specially made for the
occasion. Not a single celebrity or member of the press
bothered to turn up. (And neither, Cocà couldn't help
noticing, did Danny, to whom she had sent an invitation via his parent's old address.)

Cocà and Charlie never really recovered. She sold
everything but the Ethiopian bed to repay the loan and
made the first of many visits to her local DSS. Poor
old Charlie took to dealing in cocaine.

> *Oh! Sasha dooo*
> *Sasha doo Sasha daa*
> *The ja-ja jolting in your heart*
> *Has me a gaga from my start – Sasha!*
> *Oh! Sasha daa-doo-daa*

So, Cocà di Cocà, awoken by the sound of her failure,
wiped the tears away and dragged her skinny body out
of bed. Her head ached. She'd been up until four writing
her memoirs and it was apparent from evidence on the
desk that she'd polished off two-and-a-half bottles of

wine in the process. She was meant to be meeting Anna-bel from the Saturday *Express* in two hours' time – and she looked disgusting. A large spot had developed between her eyebrows while she was sleeping, her long blonde hair looked like a wig, and her skin was yellow and waxy.

The telephone rang. But it was only Gorgeous Charlie, her devastatingly attractive ex-manager, ex-husband, ex-human being; Cocà di Cocà's last remaining stalker and her only remaining friend. It was always Charlie. He was currently going through a clean phase, which meant he never slept. She let it ring.

'Cocà? It's me. Come on, pick up the bloody phone. I know you're there. Did you hear it? Did you? I know you're there. For Christ's sake, you stupid cow, you've just been on the *radio!*'

She picked up. 'Leave me alone, Charlie. I've got a meeting.'

'A meeting!' He laughed incredulously. 'Who with?'

And though she'd sworn she wouldn't tell him, she'd absolutely promised herself she was *not* going to let him ruin everything again – she just couldn't resist it.

'Come on, Cocà! The dentist? The doctor? The hair-dresser? Who with?'

'The Press!'

'The Press?' There was panic in his voice. 'The *Press!* What the fuck is that supposed to mean?' And then, immediately, 'Well, it's fantastic. It's perfect timing. They will have heard the song. I think we can work it to our advantage. What we need to do now is –'

And perhaps it was because the tears were still damp on her skinny cheeks, or because she was so lonely, or because she felt sorry for him, or perhaps it was simply the force of fifteen years' habit, but Cocà di Cocà told him – the time, the place, exactly what she had said to the journalist, exactly what the journalist had said to her. He told Cocà she'd done it all completely wrong and that he'd meet her up at the school to repair the damage. As he hung up she was still begging him to stay away.

Charlie called her mobile three times while she drove from South Kensington to the old school in Ealing. The fourth time he called she switched the machine to divert and tried to concentrate on the ordeal ahead ... *The last time she'd been at the school had been the night of the Fifth-Form disco. She had been sixteen. She had been in love. She had been with Danny* ... (Charlie was right, of course. The journalist might well have heard her song on the radio that morning. So perhaps Cocà could ask her for advice about the autobiography. Perhaps the nice girl knew of a friendly publisher.) ... *And she and Danny had sung the song that had vaulted her to stardom. She and Danny had stood on the stage in the old assembly hall and Danny had gazed across at her and she had never felt so beautiful or so alive* ... (And then of course the *Express* had – what? One million readers? Seven million? Who knew? Who knew where all this might lead?) It was another chance. One last chance to make something of herself.

She parked her dirty old car in the teacher's car park (virtually empty; it was a Saturday), pulled out a mirror and added a squeeze more to the thick layer of beige that already smothered her cheeks.

'Cola de Coco? Is it you?' A pretty girl in a bright red trouser-suit was grinning vacuously at Cocà's window. Cocà clambered out of the car as quickly as she could. She had not wanted the journalist to see it.

'Perfect timing!' said the girl. 'I'm Annabel! Are you ready? I think it's going to be great fun, don't you? Goodness! You look fabulous! Shall we go in?' Cocà smiled. 'The – er – photographer's setting up lights in the main hall. And I think the headmaster's hanging around in there too.' She giggled. 'He's *very* excited. Says he remembers you well. Apparently you were quite a naughty girl!'

Cocà wasn't listening. She looked across to the familiar building and her mouth, already dry from last night's wine, felt suddenly as if glue had set inside it.

'. . . I thought,' said Annabel 'that we could start with a tour of your old form room . . . Is that all right?'

Cocà nodded mutely. She needed to set the charm offensive into motion, but as she stepped through the door that led into the main corridor she reeled. It was the smell, of course. It reminded her so much of the past – which was only Danny. She moaned, a long, low, private moan – the first sound she had made.

'Are you OK. . . Colo? Are you OK?'

Cocà leant against the old drinks machine to steady herself. 'I'm so sorry,' she said. 'It's . . .' she hesitated.

Confession time. The moment she had been waiting for. He would read it. He would forgive her. He would – They would – 'It's a bloke I knew here. A bloke I disappointed . . . badly –'

Annabel said, 'Oh. While we're at it. Could you be sweet and sign this –' Cocà took the paper that was held out to her – 'Sorry about that. It's such a bore, isn't it? Wretched paperwork. Drives me insane! – Just *there*. . . Super! Thank you! Right. Let's get this show on the road!'

Annabel's mobile rang. She moved away and when she returned she looked quite flushed. She said, 'D'you know what, Colon? I think we're going to give the old form room a miss! I've been told there's a devastatingly attractive man in the assembly hall demanding to talk to you!'

'Already . . . Christ . . . I *told* him – who's he talking to in there? You mustn't believe a word he says! And I said –' Cocà stopped. There, distinctly, from the old assembly hall, growing steadily louder as it echoed down the corridor towards her – she could hear music.

> *Oh! Sasha dooo*
> *Sasha doo Sasha daa . . .*

Annabel grinned. 'Do you want to lead the way?'

Cocà mumbled something unintelligible, walked a couple of jerky steps towards the hall and then suddenly broke into a run.

'I think,' said Annabel, as she puffed to keep up with

her, 'this is the moment when I come sort of semi-clean. Because as you are about to realize, I am not actually from the Saturday *Express* magazine but from a fab new TV show called –'

As Cocà burst through the double doors into the darkened hall the old school stage exploded into light – and it was just as it had been in July . . . *Sasha doo Sasha daa*. . . the long loose limbs, the broad shoulders (broader now) the long dark curly hair . . . A familiar figure stood before her, a figure which had dominated her dreams for fifteen years, as irresistible as ever. With a smile he beckoned her to join him and she crossed the hall towards him like an automaton. She was oblivious to everything, the camera man, the sound man, the red-suited television presenter who'd called herself Annabel, the headmaster. All she saw was Danny.

The ja-ja jolting in your heart . . .

He was singing for her again. Just for her. For Melanie. She climbed up on to the stage and stood before him, waiting.

Has me a gaga from my start – Sasha!
Oh! Sasha daa-doo-daa.

The cameraman was lodged between them as the song came to its end. There was a moment's silence while the old lovers gazed at one another. His eyes were shining. He looked wonderful; lean and handsome and wildly happy. 'Hello, Cocà,' he muttered. 'Remember me?' He stretched across to stroke her cheek. 'I've been thinking about this moment for fifteen years.'

'Danny!' She stumbled clumsily round the camera into Danny's arms.

Suddenly, inexplicably, the auditorium burst into life. Light flooded the hall and one thousand members of a studio audience broke into raucous laughter.

Danny quickly disentangled himself, as instructed during the rehearsal, so that Annabel could step into the space between them. 'Welcome!' said Annabel. 'Everyone give Danny a big cheer! Didn't he do well?'

Cocà had been summoned to the school, she explained, to take part in an amazing, new peak-time television show in which – 'How can I put this?' she said. 'Old friends are given the opportunity to right old wrongs. To sort of start again. This,' she said, 'is really about *young love*. . . and –' she looked at the audience expectantly –

'REVENGE!!!!' they screamed.

'That's right!'

Annabel grinned. 'Danny's a computer operator from Swindon and he's mad about music, aren't you, Danny? He also happens to be one of Britain's Angriest Fellas! So tell us what happened, Danny!'

'Well, basically, Annabel,' said Danny . . .

Seven days after the show was broadcast Cocà di Cocà was hiding out in her South Kensington council flat, pretending to listen to Charlie as he wittered over the telephone about Phase B of her re-relaunch. 'We need to have a complete rethink about your image,' he was saying. Beside her the radio played a familiar old tune:

> *Oh! Sasha dooo,*

Danny sang

> *Sasha doo Sasha daa*
> *The ja-ja jolting in your heart*
> *Has me a gaga –*

She switched it off.

Helen Simpson has published two collections of short stories, *Four Bare Legs in a Bed* and *Dear George* (both available in Vintage paperback), and a suspense novella, *Flesh and Grass* (which appeared with Ruth Rendell's *The Strawberry Tree* under the general title *Unguarded Hours*). She also wrote the libretto for the jazz opera *Good Friday, 1663*, which appeared on Channel 4, and the lyrics for Kate and Mike Westbrook's jazz suite *Bar Utopia* (on CD/ASC). She has won the Somerset Maugham award and the *Sunday Times* Young Writer of the Year award, and was one of Granta's 20 Best of Young British Novelists. Her third collection of stories, *Hey Yeah Right Get a Life*, will be published by Jonathan Cape this October. Helen Simpson lives in London.

Hurrah for the Hols

Helen Simpson

These were the dogdays all right, these last flyblown days of August. Her maternal goodwill was worn threadbare. This was the nadir of Dorrie's year, all this holiday flesh needing to be tended and shameless bad temper on display.

She was sitting at a table in the unshaded barbecue area by the pool over a cup of terrible coffee. And yet it was supposed to be the annual high-water mark, their summer fortnight, particularly this year when they had rejected camping or self-catering in favour of splashing out on a room in this value-for-money family hotel.

'You really are a stupid little boy. You're really pushing your luck,' said the man at the next table to one of the three children sitting with him. 'I want to see that burger finished *now*. Can't you for once in your whole life . . .'

His voice was quiet and venomous. What was he doing here alone with his children? It must be the same as Max was doing with their three now, playing crazy golf to give her some time to herself. This man's wife was probably just round the corner over just such another cup of coffee. Was she too feeling panic at not making good use of that precious commodity, solitude?

'If you don't do what I say right now there'll be no ice cream. No swimming. No puppet show. I mean it.'

The small boy beside him started to cry into his burger, wailing and complaining that his teeth hurt.

'And don't think you're going to get round me like that,' snarled the man. 'I'm not your *mother*, remember!'

All over the place, if you listened, you could hear the steady exasperated undertone of the unglamorously leisure-clad parents teasing their tempestuous, ego-maniacal little people into, for example, eating that sandwich up 'or I tell you what, and you're being very silly, but you won't be going to the Treasure Island club tonight and *I mean it*.' It stuck in her throat, the bread of the weeping child. The parents said nothing to each other, except the names of sandwich fillings. She and Max were the same, they couldn't talk over, under or round the children and so it turned them sour and obdurate in each other's company. They held each other at night in bed but again could say or do nothing for fear of their children beside them, sleeping like larks, like clean-limbed breathing fruit.

She sipped and grimaced and watched the snail's progress of the combine harvester on the adjacent cliff. There was a splash as someone jumped into the pool, and a flapping over wasps and a dragging round of high chairs to plastic tables, and howls, hoots, groaning and broken-hearted sobbing, the steady cacophony which underscores family life en masse. At least sitting here alone she had been noticing the individual elements of the composition, she realized with surprise and some pleasure. When she was with her brood she noticed nothing of the outside world, they drank up all her powers of observation.

Here they came now, off the crazy golf course, tear-stained, drooping, scowling. Here comes the big bore, and here come the three little bores. Stifle your yawns. Smile. On holiday Max became a confederate saying things like, 'They never stop' and 'That child is a canni-bal'. Their constant crystalline quacking, demanding a response, returning indefatigable and gnat-like, drove him mad. There must be something better than this squabbly nuclear family unit, she thought, these awful hobbling five- and six-legged races all around her.

She could see they were fighting. She saw Martin hit Robin, and Robin clout him back. It was like being on holiday with Punch and Judy – lots of biffing and shrieking and fights over sausages. What a lumpen moping tearful spiritless mummy she had become, packing and unpacking for everybody endlessly, sigh-ing. Better sigh, though, than do as she'd done earlier that day, on the beach when, exasperated by their demands, on and on, all afternoon, she'd stood up and held out her hands to them.

'Here, have some fingers,' she'd snarled, pretending to snap them off one by one. 'Have a leg. Have an ear. Nice?' And they had laughed uproariously, jumping on her and pinning her to the rug, sawing at her limbs, tugging her ears, uprooting her fingers and toes. Such a figure she cut on the beach these days, slumped round-shouldered in the middle of the family encampment of towels, impatience on a monument growling at the sea. Or was it Mother Courage of the sand dunes, the slack-muscled white body hidden under various cover-ups, headgear, dark glasses, crouched amidst the contents of her cart, the buckets, wasp spray, suncream, foreign legion hats with neck-protective flaps, plastic football, beach cricket kit, gaggle of plastic jelly sandals, spare dry swimsuits, emergency pants. If she lumbered off for a paddle all hell broke loose.

'Did you have a nice time?' she said weakly as they reached her table.

Martin was shrieking about some injustice, his father's face was black as thunder. Robin sprinted to her lap, then Maxine and Martin jumped on her jealously, staking their claim like settlers in some virgin colony.

'She's not your long-lost uncle, your mother,' said Max, unable to get near her. 'You only saw her half an hour ago.'

Things got worse before they got better. There was a terrible scene later on. It was in the large room by the bar, the Family Room, where at six o'clock a holiday student surf fanatic led all the young children in a song and dance session while their parents sagged against the walls and watched.

> *And a little bit of this*
> *And a little bit of that*
> *And shake your bum*
> *Just like your mum*

sang the children, roaring with laughter as they mimed the actions. After this, glassy lollipops were handed out, and then the surfer started to organize a conga. The children lined up, each holding the waist of the one in front, many of them with the lollipops still in their mouths, sticks stuck outwards.

'That's dangerous,' mumured Dorrie. 'If they fell . . .' And she and other mothers discreetly coaxed the sweets from the mouths of their nearest offspring with earnest promises that these would be returned immediately the dance had finished. Then she glanced across the room and saw Martin in the line, lollipop stick clamped between his teeth. Max just beyond him, sipping from his first bottle of beer, caught her eye; she, without thinking as hard as she might have done, indicated to him the lollipop peril, miming and pointing.

The conga had started, the music was blasting out, and yet when Max wrenched the stick from between Martin's clenched teeth the boy's screams were louder even than the very loudly amplified Birdy Song. Martin broke out of the line and fought his father for the lollipop. Max, looking furious, teeth bared inside his dark beard, was a figure both ridiculous and distressing, like a giant Captain Haddock wrestling with a hysterical diminutive Tintin. Their battle carried on out in the hall, where Max dragged Martin just as the conga was weaving past, with screaming and shouting and terrible fury between them. They were hating each other.

Dorrie edged up to them, horror struck, and the next thing was that Max was shouting at *her*. All right, it was their first day, they were all tired from the journey, but this was dreadful. The other parents, following the conga, filtered past interestedly watching this scene.

'Don't, don't, don't,' said Dorrie several times, but softly. The other two children joined them, sobbing.

At last she got them all past reception and up the stairs.

'I don't like you, Daddy,' wailed Martin through tears.

'I know you don't, Martin,' huffed Max, storming off ahead.

Really, he was very like Martin, or Martin was very like him – both prone to explosions of aggressive self-defensiveness – although of course Martin was six, whereas Max was forty. Because Max did this, she had to do the opposite in order to redress the balance, even though doing so made her look weak and ineffective. He sometimes pointed this out, her apparent ineffectiveness. But what would he rather? That she scream at them like a fishwife? Hit them? Vent her temper or ignore them, like a man? Let them get hurt? Let them eat rubbish? Let them watch junk? Just try doing it all the time before you criticize, not only for a few hours or days, she reflected, as she reined herself in and wiped tears from blubbing faces and assisted with the comprehensive nose-blowing that was needed in the wake of such a storm.

At least he didn't hit them when he lost his temper. She had a friend whose husband did, and then justified it with talk of them having to learn, which she, Dorrie, could not have borne. She really would much rather be on her own with them, it was much easier like that. Like a skilful stage manager she had learned how to create times of sweetness and light with the three of them; she could now coax and balance the various jostling elements into some sort of precarious harmony. It was an art, like feeding and building a good log fire, an achievement. Then in Max would clump, straightways seizing the bellows or the poker, and the whole lot would collapse in ruins.

'I'll get them to bed, Max,' she said. 'Why don't you go for a swim or something?'

'I'll wait for you in the bar,' he said frostily. 'Remember they stop serving dinner at eight.'

'Yes.'

'Don't forget to turn the listening service on.'

'No.'

'I know when I'm not wanted.'

She choked down her reply, and gently closed the door behind him.

'Now then,' she said, smiling at their doleful, tear-smeared faces. 'What's up? You look as though you've swallowed a jellyfish!'

They looked at her, goggling with relief, and laughed uncertainly.

'*Two* jellyfish!' she said, with vaudeville mirth.

They laughed harder.

'And an *octopus*!' she added.

They fell on the floor, they were laughing so hard.

The second day was an improvement on the first, although, as Dorrie said to herself, that would not have been difficult. They turned away from the glare of the packed beach towards leafy broken shade, walking inland along a lane whose hedges were candy-striped with pink and white bindweed. A large dragonfly with marcasite body and pearlized wings appeared in the air before them and stopped them in their tracks. Then they struck off across a path through fields where sudden clouds of midges swept by without touching them. When they reached a stream overarched by hawthorn trees the children clamoured to take off their sandals and dip their feet in the water.

'This is the place for our picnic,' said Dorrie, who had brought supplies along in a rucksack, and now set about distributing sandwiches and fruit and bottles of water.

'We can't walk across the strand today,' said Max, consulting his copy of the Tide Tables as he munched away at a ham roll. 'Low tide was earlier this morning, then not again till nine tonight. Fat lot of good that is. But tomorrow looks possible.'

He had heard about an island not far from here which, once a day, for a short time only, became part of the mainland. When the tide was out you could walk across the strand to the island and visit the ancient cell of the hermit who had lived centuries before in the heart of its little woods.

'There doesn't seem to be any logic to it,' said Dorrie, looking over his shoulder at the week's chart. 'No pattern to the tides, no gradual waxing and waning as with the moon. I thought the tides were supposed to be governed by the moon, but they're all over the place.'

The children sat by them, each with a bag of crisps, nibbling away busily like rodents.

'There *is* a pattern, though,' said Max. 'When there's a new moon or an old moon, the tides are at their highest and also at their lowest. It's all very extreme at those times of the month, when the earth, moon and sun are directly in line.'

Martin, having finished his own bag of crisps, was now busily capturing ants from the grass and dropping them into his sister's bag.

'Don't do that,' said Dorrie.

'And when the moon's at right angles to the sun, that's when you get neap tides,' continued Max. 'Less extreme, less dramatic. What the hell's the matter *now*?'

Maxine had been trying to pull her bag of crisps away from Martin, who had suddenly let go, with the result that Maxine's crisps had flown into the air and over the grass, where Martin was now rolling on them and crushing them into salty fragments.

'Stop it!' called Dorrie.

'Get up this minute!' shouted Max.

'Why should I, it's a free country,' gabbled Martin,

rolling back and forth, enjoying the noise and drama.

'My crisps!' sobbed Maxine. 'They're all squashed!'

'What's your problem?' said Martin with spiteful pleasure, getting up as his father approached, and brushing yellow crumbs from his shorts. 'You threw them away, so that means you didn't want them.'

'I *didn't* throw them away!' screamed Maxine.

'Liar, I saw you,' goaded Martin. 'I saw you throw them in the air. Little liar.'

Maxine howled, scarlet in the face, struggling with her mother, who was trying to hold her, while Martin ran off out of range, dancing on the spot and fleering and taunting.

'Why is he such a poisonous little tick?' said Max, though without his usual fury.

On their way back to the hotel they passed a camp-site, and stopped by the gate to read its painted sign.

'Families and mixed couples only,' Maxine read aloud. 'What does that mean, Mum? What are mixed couples? Mum? Mum?'

'I'm not sure,' said Dorrie. She was reminded of her parents' description of looking for somewhere to rent when they first came to London, with the signs up in the windows reading 'No Blacks, No Irish' and her father with his Dublin accent having to keep quiet for a change and let her mother do the talking.

'Why do you suppose they want mixed couples only?' she murmured to Max. 'Why would they worry about gayness?'

'I don't think it's that,' said Max. 'I think it's more to put off the eighteen–thirty element; you know, bikers and boozing and gangs getting into fights.'

'You twenty years ago,' said Dorrie.

'Martin in ten years' time,' said Max.

'What's a couple?' persisted Maxine. 'What's a couple, Dad?'

'A couple here means a man and a woman,' said Max.

'Oo–a–ooh!' exclaimed Martin, giving Maxine a lewd nudge in the ribs and rolling his eyes.

'A husband and wife,' said Dorrie deflatingly.

'So a couple's like a family,' said Maxine.

'Yes,' said Dorrie.

'No,' said Max. 'A couple is *not* like a family. That's far too easy, just two people. It doesn't qualify.'

Dorrie was laughing now, and put her arms round his waist, her head on his shoulder. He kissed the top of her head and stroked her hair. The three children stood round looking at them with big smug smiles, beaming with satisfaction.

'Come in for a hug,' said Dorrie, holding out her arm to them, and they all five stood rocking by the side of the road locked into an untidy squawking clump.

'You're looking well,' said Max, gazing at her that evening across the mackerel paté and the bud vase holding the miniature yellow carnations. 'You've caught the sun. It suits you.'

'It was a good walk today,' said Dorrie, suddenly shy.

'They're lovely but they're very tiring,' said Max, draining his glass of beer. 'Exhausting. You should be more selfish.'

How can I, thought Dorrie, until you are less so? It's a seesaw. But she kept quiet. He went on to talk about the timberyard, how it was doing all right but they couldn't afford to rest on their laurels with all these small businesses going down all round them.

'We're a team,' declared Max, grandiose, pouring another glass for them both.

'Ye-es,' said Dorrie. 'But it's a bit unbalanced, don't you think, the teamwork, at the moment?'

'Are you saying I don't work hard enough?' demanded Max.

'Of course not,' said Dorrie. 'You work too hard. Don't be silly. No, I meant, you do all the work that gets somewhere and gives you something to show for the effort and pulls in money, but the work I do doesn't seem to get anywhere, it doesn't show, it somehow doesn't count even though it needs doing of course.'

'I don't see what you're driving at,' said Max, starting to look less cheerful.

'I don't know,' said Dorrie. 'At the moment I feel sub. Sub something.'

'Suburban?' suggested Max.

'Subordinate?' said Dorrie. 'No.'

'Submerged, then. How about submerged?'

'That's nearer. Still not quite . . . I know! Subdued. Though submerged is growing on me. Submerged is accurate too. That time at Marks, all my twenties, half

554

my thirties, it's like a dream. I've almost forgotten what it used to be like.'

And she tried to explain to Max her feeling about this encroaching blandness, adaptability, passivity, the need for one of them at least to embrace these qualities, even if this made them shudder, if the family was going to work.

'We all have to knuckle down,' he said. 'Sooner or later.'

'It's just it seems, some of us more than others.'

'If we want to join in at all,' opined Max. 'Life. It's called growing up.'

'It doesn't feel like growing up,' she muttered from her side of the fence. Rather it felt like being freeze-dried and vacuum-packed. Knuckled down was putting it mildly.

'Well, as I said, whatever you're feeling like, you're looking well,' said Max; and that made them both feel better.

'Lovely, in fact,' he added, leaning across to touch her face meaningly.

After dinner, sitting in the Family Room drinking coffee, they found themselves drawn into a quiz game provided by the hotel as the adult equivalent of the children's conga. The quizmaster was a sparky woman in emerald green jacket and pleats. She split them into groups and bossed them through an unnecessary microphone.

'What's the other name for kiwifruit?' she demanded,

and echoes bounced off the ceiling. The groups whispered and giggled and scribbled on their scoresheets.

'What flag is all one colour?' she asked. 'Here's a clue, somewhere not very nice. Ooh, I hope no one from there is in this room!'

'Birmingham?' suggested Max.

'Very funny, the bearded gentleman,' said the woman. 'Now we're out of Miscellaneous and on to the Human Body. Let's see how much you all know about the body, you jolly well should considering your age. And the one who's paying for the holiday will certainly be hoping to know a bit more about the human body of the opposite sex or else they'll have wasted their money, won't they?'

Dorrie's mouth fell open, she nearly dropped her drink, but nobody else batted an eyelid.

'And we've quite enough children here thank you very much while we're on the subject so let's hope you all know what you're up to,' continued the woman, arching a roguish eyebrow. 'Right. Now. Where are the cervical nerves?'

'And where's your sense of humour?' Max whispered into Dorrie's ear, observing her gape rudely at the woman.

In bed that night surrounded by their sleeping children, they held each other and started to kiss with increasing warmth. He grabbed shamelessly between her legs, her body answered with an enthusiastic twist, a backward arch, and soon he was inside her. There must be no noise, and she had pulled the sheet up to their necks. Within a couple of minutes they were both almost there, together, when there came a noise from Martin's bed.

'Mum,' he said sleepily, and flicked his lamp on. 'Mum, I'm thirsty.'

Max froze where he was and dropped his head and swore beneath his breath. Martin got out of bed and padded over towards them.

'Did you *hear* me, Mum?' he asked crossly. 'I want some water. *Now.*'

Dorrie was aware of her hot red face looking up from under Max's, and heard herself say, 'In a minute, dear. Go back to bed now, there's a good boy.' Martin paused to stare at them, then stumbled over back towards his bed.

'Do you think he's been traumatized?' she whispered to Max, mortified, cheated of the concentrated pleasure which had been seconds away, the achievement of it, the being made whole.

'Do I think *he's* been traumatized?' growled Max incredulously, rolling off her.

'Where's your sense of humour, then?' she murmured in his ear, but he pulled away and turned his back on her. She didn't blame him.

Their third day's adventure was planned by Max. They were going to cross the strand and explore the hermit's island. Today the tide was out at a reasonable time of the morning and the sun was up too. They stood and gazed across the shining sands at the exposed island, which was now, for an hour or so only, part of the mainland.

'It's further than I thought,' said Dorrie. 'It looks well over a mile. Maybe two.'

'Half a mile at most,' said Max heartily. 'Let's get going, remember we're racing the tide. Come on you lot, shoes and socks in the boot.'

'I think they should wear their plastic sandals,' said Dorrie. 'I can see stones. Weed.'

'Nonsense,' said Max. 'Lovely sand, skipping across the golden sand. Don't fuss, don't spoil it all with fussing.'

'Skippety skip,' sang Robin.

'I still think . . .' said Dorrie.

'Give us a break,' said Max.

'I'm not wearing my jellies,' said Martin. 'No way.'

'No way,' echoed Maxine.

When they started walking they were less downright, but by then it was too late. The gleaming silver-pink sand was knotted with wormcasts which made the children shudder, and studded with pebbles, and sharp-edged broken shells, which made them wince and squawk.

'Come on,' called Max, striding ahead on his prime-of-life leathery soles. 'We've got to keep moving if we're going to be there and back in time. Or we'll be cut off.'

Dorrie helped the children round the weeds, through ankle-deep seawater rivulets blue as the sky above, clucking, and lifting, and choking down irritation at the thought of the plastic sandals back in the boot.

'You were right, Mum,' groaned Martin mournfully. 'I wish I'd worn them.'

'So do I,' said Maxine, picking her way like a cross hen.

'So do I,' wept Robin, who was walking on tiptoe, as though that might spare his soft pink feet the worm-casts, and slowing them all down considerably.

'Come on,' yelled Max, a couple of hundred yards ahead.

'We can't,' yelled Dorrie, who was by now carrying Robin across her front. It felt desperate, like the retreat from Moscow or something. Trust Max to engineer a stressful seaside event, trust Max to inject a penitential flavour into the day. They were by now half a mile out; it would be mad to go on and dismal to turn back. The sun was strong but muffled by haze, and the sky glared with the blanched fluorescence of a shaving light.

'What's all the fuss about?' said Max, having unwill-ingly rejoined them.

'I think we'll have to turn back,' said Dorrie. 'Look at the time. Even if we make it to the island we won't be able to explore, we'll have to turn round and come straight back and even then we'd be cutting it fine. Why don't you go alone, darling, you're quicker on your own.'

'You always have to spoil it, don't you,' said Max, furious as a child. 'You never want anything I plan to work.'

'Their feet hurt,' pleaded Dorrie. 'Don't let's quarrel in front of them.'

'Robin, you'll come with me, won't you,' said Max, squatting down beside his son. 'I'll give you a piggyback.'

'Max,' said Dorrie, 'it's nearly midday, it's not safe. Why don't you go ahead with the camera and take photos so we'll all be able to see the hermit's house when the film's developed.'

'Robin?' said Max.

'I don't know what to choose,' said Robin, looking from his father to his mother and back again. He was out of his depth.

Dorrie felt anger bulge up as big as a whale surfacing, but breathed it down and said again, 'Take the camera, darling, that way we'll all see the secret island,' and hung the camera round his neck. She made herself kiss him on the cheek. He looked at her suspiciously. The children brightened. She forced herself to hug him. The children cheered.

'All right,' he said at last, and set off across the wet sand, running simple and free as a Red Indian.

'I didn't know what to say, Mum,' said Robin, spreading his hands helplessly. 'Daddy said go on go with me not Mummy. You said no. I felt splitted in half.'

'It's all right,' said Dorrie. 'Now everybody's happy. Look at that seagull.'

Above them, floating on a thermal, was a big, white, cruel-beaked bird. Seagulls were always larger than you expected, and had a chilly fierce look to them, without gaiety. She could barely speak for rage, but did not assign it much importance, so used was she by now to this business of ebb and flow. Who else, she wondered, could be living at such a pitch of passion as she in the midst of this crew; so uncontrolled, so undefended?

Having poked around the hermit's mossy cell and raced the tide back, white-toothed wavelets snapping at his heels, Max was in a good mood for the rest of the day, and they all benefited. He felt he had achieved something. He *had* achieved something. He had conquered the island, he had patterned it with his footprints, he had written his name on the sandy floor of the hermit's very cell with his big toe. Next week he would show them the photographs to prove it.

When the sun was low in the sky and the children were asleep, Max suggested to Dorrie that she should go for a walk on her own, just down to the beach below the hotel.

'It'll do you good,' he said.

He was going to sit by the bedroom's picture window in the half-dark with a beer, and would probably be able to make out her figure if the light didn't go too fast.

'Are you sure you'll be all right?' she said.

'Go on,' he snorted. 'Before I change my mind.'

She walked down barefoot through the hotel gardens, across trim tough seaside turf bordered by white-painted palisades and recently watered fuchsia bushes.

Then she turned on to the low cliff path which zig-zagged down to the beach and felt the longer grass brush against her legs, spiky marram grass softly spangled in the dusk with pale flowers, sea pinks and thrift and white sea campion.

Robin had had trouble getting to sleep that evening. Stay here, he had demanded tearfully, his hand on her arm; don't go. I won't go, she had said; close your eyes. She had stroked his temple with the side of her little finger. Gradually he had allowed himself to be lowered down, a rung at a time, towards the dark surface of sleep. He had given a tiny groan as she moved to get up, but he was too far gone to climb back. She had sat by him for a little longer, creaking with fatigue, looking at his quiet face, his still hand on her arm, savouring the deep romance and boredom of it.

There were no buildings now between her and the beach except for this last snug cottage to her left shedding light from its windows. She paused to look up at it. It must surely house an ideal family, sheltered and enclosed but with a view of the bay too. The father was reading his children a story, perhaps, while the mother brushed their hair. Where did this cosy picture come from? Certainly not from her own childhood. She turned away and carried on down to the beach.

It was lovely to stand barefoot, bare-legged indeed, invisible in the deep dusk, a great generous moon in the sky and her feet at the edge of the Atlantic. She looked out over the broad bosom of the sea and it was like an old engraving, beautiful and melancholy, and the noise it made was a sighing, a rhythmic sigh-ing.

As sailors' ghosts looked back on their drowned selves, dismantled, broken up, sighing like the sea for the collarbone lost somewhere around the equator, the metatarsals scattered across the Indian Ocean, so she wondered whether there could ever be a reassembly of such scattered drowned bodies, a watery *danse macabre* on the wreckers' rocks beneath a full moon. Was it possible to reclaim the scattered-to-the-winds self? She was less afraid of death, or understood it a shade more, purely through coming near it each time she had had a baby; but apart from that, this puzzle was to do with the loss of self that went with the process, or rather the awareness of her individuality as a troublesome excrescence, an obsoletism. What she wanted to know was, was this temporary, like National Service used to be, or was it for good?

She was filled with excitement at standing by the edge of the sea alone under the sky, so that she took great clear breaths of air and looked at the dimming horizon, opening her eyes wider as if that might help her to see more. It filled her with courage and made her want to sing, something Irish or Scottish, sad and wild and expressive of this, this wild salt air, out here, and of how it was thrilling, being alive and not dead.

When she turned back across the beach, away from the water, it was dark. The orange lights of the hotel up on the hill lengthened on the wet black sand like pillars of flame. She reached the edge of the beach, where it met the rocks and turf above, and started to climb back. A bat bounced silently past her ear as she crossed the little bridge over the stream, and then she felt the dust of the earth path beneath her feet again. As she walked on, hugging herself against the fresh chill of the dark, she looked at the cottages built on the hills around the bay, their windows yellow lozenges of enclosed warmth in the night.

Now she was walking back past the house she had envied on the way down, the house which was so secure and self-sufficient with its warm lit windows and snug family within. And from this house came the wailing of a child, a desolate hopeless noise. It was coming from this very house. On and on it went, the wailing, steady and miserable, following her up the path. Her throat tightened and her eyes prickled, she called herself every sort of fool as she trudged on; and she physically ached to pick up and hold the weeping child, and tell it there there, there there, then smooth it down and stroke its hand until it slept. The comfortless noise continued, not a baby's crying but the sobbing of a child. No child should be left to cry like that, she thought, ambushed by pity, by memory; and – in a rage – people aren't bloody well nice enough to their children!

Don't be so soft, came the advice; crying never did any harm, you can't allow them to run the show or where will that land you? Let them take themselves to hell, those hard hearts who leave their children to cry themselves to sleep alone, and in hell they will have to listen to the sound of a child crying and know that they can never comfort it. That was what Dorrie was thinking as she climbed back up the hill.

Sarah Ingham was a journalist, has done stints as a political researcher and now writes full-time, often to Father Christmas to send her Aussie surfies. Her first novel *Parallel Turns* (Coronet) was published in December 1999; her second, *Kissing Frogs*, is out in summer 2000.

No Worries

Sarah Ingham

Molly's last night in had been three months ago and twelve thousand miles away. Thursday, September 25th, London. An evening of sobbing and daydreams about napalm.

'You mustn't get like your coffee. Bitter.' Deborah had told her on the Wednesday, in a pull-yourself-together voice. 'This is all very awkward for Angus and me. We don't want to take sides.'

'You've taken sides,' insisted Molly.

If Deborah hadn't been her best friend, Molly would have hated her for several years, not just from that Wednesday. Henna-spiked Debs at teacher training college had gradually morphed into blonde-bobbed Deborah, then into Mrs Angus Sneem. She was now a high-maintenance size eight. Her Mercedes convertible seemed permanently stuck on the double yellow lines outside Prada, but she never got a parking ticket.

'How many more times must one go through this?' Since her marriage, Deborah had been keen on one and my. My architect, my Pilates, my charity work kept her busy. 'Angus is Ben's oldest friend . . .'

'And where Aberdeen goes, you go. Like Siamese twins.'

Deborah looked down my surgically sculpted nose, roughly the same vintage as my capped teeth. My tits were newer. My huge sapphire ring reassured her that she'd done well. If well meant a rich ugly husband known as Aberdeen. He was lumbering, red-faced and often on grass.

'Tell me, Debs, Deborah, why can't you let him out of your sight?'

'So, you're suddenly the expert when it comes to marriage?' Her fury could've stopped a buffalo stampede. 'Funny that. Considering how yours fell apart.' She gave Molly's homely, tatty kitchen a what-a-dump once-over. 'Perhaps you should ask Candy for lessons about how to make a place comfortable. And how to cook.'

'Debs and Aberdeen and Ben and Candy. How cosy. You'd better go. And start praying that you're never, ever in my situation.'

'I wouldn't be so dumb.'

'Enjoy the party.'

Molly hadn't had a summer. May to September had somehow vanished. Ben told her on their anniversary in May – Chelsea Flower Show week. The papers were full of pictures of a gameshow hostess, focusing on her canyon cleavage rather than the rose named after her. Instead of celebrating at a restaurant, instead of ordering asparagus, Ben said he'd met someone else, he was moving out. Sorry. He hadn't sounded sorry. He looked smug. Clever me, I've scored the most glorious bit of totty.

Was 'someone else' the new receptionist at the practice? Poppy? Daisy? Young, as pretty as her name, who still lived with her parents in the Kent suburbs.

'Candy?' Molly stared. 'No one's called Candy. Short for Candida? As in vaginal thrush?'

No short for Candice, as in Candice Bergen. Ben's sigh suggested he almost pitied Molly. The world couldn't really blame him for dumping someone so thick.

The evenings lengthened and grew warmer. In Molly's Hammersmith terrace, neighbours' gardens were full of barbecue smells and laughter. She slumped indoors, staring at her wedding photos – handsome Ben the healer – touching the clothes he'd left in the wardrobe and sleeping on his side of the bed. She was too wretched to eat, the rings loosened on her fingers.

Almost as shocked by Ben's departure as she was, Molly's colleagues became worried about her as the weeks passed. Even winning the staff-room Derby sweepstake failed to provoke her heart-warmingly beautiful smile. She didn't join in the scrutiny of the Royals' Ascot hats. Doesn't the Queen look marvellous?

Who gives a shit?

The Head gave her a reluctant talking-to after he found Molly in tears and Year Two in uproar around her, the pets liberated from their cages and being daubed with poster paint. He'd arrived just in time to stop Gary Cray, the world's most evil six-year-old, lynching Jemima the Gerbil.

Molly's friends assured her Ben would tire of Candy, the teenager from Sidcup. Molly and Ben's friends sounded cagey. They assured her they didn't want to take sides. Her probing about Candy embarrassed them. She's very different from you, Molly.

'You've met her?' She suddenly realized they'd all met her. It hurt. She pictured the party – Pimms and pretty dresses – held on the night she'd been burying catshit in the garden. She guessed they all had Ben's new mobile number too. He'd changed it after her last tiresome tearful call.

The longest day brought a new New Age Traveller Menace, according to the *Daily Mail*. Light filled the land. Barren winter entered Molly's soul. Receptionist? Deborah laughed uneasily. No. Candy was Ben's patient.

'To be brutal, she could be Liz Hurley's twin.' And Candy was about to make multi-millions when her Internet business went public. 'E-baby. You know. Site for mothers. She's always in the business pages. The E-baby Babe. Are you OK?'

Molly wasn't. She rushed to Deborah's spa-like bathroom to throw up.

She didn't watch Wimbledon that night. She gathered up every bit of Ben's stuff and put it in the spare room, which she'd always imagined would be the nursery one day. Perhaps she would have checked E-baby. Two summers ago, she'd stood with Ben in the crush around an outside court. No strawberries. Their onerous mort-gage meant scrimping and struggle. But, they'd agreed, it was worthwhile. An investment in their future.

Ben visited for three minutes to collect his post, which Molly had refused to forward to the practice. He looked fit, tanned, happy. A pink badge fluttered from his new blazer. 'Gay pride? Course not. Henley. Regatta. Rowing.' Had she seen his black tie?

'Why?'

'Er, Glyndebourne. *La Traviata*.'

Molly froze. She'd never even got him to a subtitled film. Glyndebourne? Last year they'd shared a tent at a Somme-like Glastonbury. Ben had still been working for the NHS. She'd been unhappy about his switch to private practice, which had been encouraged by Angus, whose City salary was often mistaken for a telephone number.

Term ended, with another defeat for England in the Test Match. The whole world seemed to be enjoying a glorious summer. Sun-soaked day followed balmy night. The papers reported record temperatures. *Corfu? Cor Phew! Hotter Than Greece!!!* Molly stayed inside with her lonely misery and torment for company, the sunshine filtered through layers of grime on the windows. She couldn't stop shivering. She huddled, bundled up in layers of clothes as if it were November.

Molly's friends became fed up with her apathetic weeping punctuated by Ben-the-Bastard rants. They built up a mental identikit of Candy and privately thought that Ben had traded up so stratospherically that he'd never come back. The news that he was sharing Candy's huge riverside loft in Chelsea seemed conclusive proof that Molly's cause was lost. It was time she moved on.

'I don't want to move on. I want to stay put. In my old life. With Ben.'

No, she didn't want to go to the beach. 'When we rented the cottage in Dorset . . .' Or to the Proms. 'We went last year, bet he doesn't expect Candy to stand in the arena . . .'

Ben and Molly's friends had become Ben and Candy's friends. They stopped calling her. Ben's family never spoke to her. Molly was Trotsky after a Stalinist re-write of history. Her marriage had never existed. She'd never existed. She'd been purged. Deleted.

'You're getting too thin,' Ben said on another collect-the-mail visit during Cowes week. The radio announced there'd been a collision in the Solent. His new cream linen suit couldn't hide the weight he'd put on. Fat and happy, Molly supposed. 'Get pretty again. Go on holiday.'

'Who with?'

'Viv?'

'She's filming.' Molly didn't need him to remind her that her movie-director sister was the successful daughter. Her mother did it often enough. The mother who told her to show some moral fibre, have some self-respect and put things behind her.

'Your parents? They're off to France.' Ben headed for the stairs.

'I'm thirty-one. I'm not going on holiday with my parents.' She saw herself in the back of the Rover, people wondering if she were special needs. Poor parents, the burden. Route squabbles, map fusses and toll grumbles. She tore up to the bedroom, where Ben was rummaging in the wardrobe. 'How do you know about France?'

'George came to see me. Where's my squash racquet?'

'Dad saw you? Why?' Outraged by his daughter's treatment, had her father threatened to shoot Ben?

'His back. He wanted a referral to another specialist.'

'What?' Visions of Ben being beaten to a pulp with a golf-club were replaced by another sick-making sense of betrayal. 'Are you and Candy going away?'

'Tomorrow. St Tropez, then Portofino.'

'How nice. Walking?' Last August they'd hiked in the Lake District.

'Driving. I've got a new car.'

Molly went to the window. Parked in the dusty street was a gleaming open-topped silver Porsche. Trembling, she clutched the sill for support. 'Well done, Ben. You've got away with fucking up my life, haven't you? Even my family's on your side.'

'Don't get moody. By the way, I want a divorce. You can petition for adultery. Candy doesn't mind being cited. We'll have to sell this place. Shall you talk to the estate agents or shall I?'

'Fuck you. Fuck you both. Just fuck off.'

He went. Molly rushed out into the street. If you think you look like something out of *L'Oumo Vogue*, you're very wrong, because actually, you bastard, you look more like the Pilsbury Dough Boy ... Ben sped off, the Porsche's engine drowned her out.

Molly called her parents. How could they? Treachery. Traitors. What a victory for Candy. What had about family loyalty? Going behind her back ...

'Your father's back is more important,' Molly's mother interrupted her. 'Do you want him in a wheel-chair? What would happen to our golf? Stop being so selfish. Do try and get a grip. Please.' *The Archers*' theme tune started, the line went dead.

Throughout muggy August, Molly shrivelled to nothing like the flowers in her neglected garden. The curtains stayed closed. She resigned from school, saying she'd be supply teaching from now on. She couldn't face going out, she avoided everyone. A failure like her couldn't inflict herself on a world full of golden couples, tanned more golden from their holidays. A loser like her didn't deserve a place in the sun.

Bank Holiday brought the Carnival, police uniforms jigging alongside sequinned, feathered head-dresses. And news of the party. A joint celebration of their birthdays, being held on Candy's decked terrace for three hundred of their closest friends.

September 25th was Molly's forty-third consecutive night in. Utter loneliness overwhelmed her. Dreams of napalming the Porsche with Ben and Candy inside it brought no relief. In the bath, she idly watched her engagement and wedding rings float off her skinny finger into the water then she tried to drown herself.

Viv suggested Molly came to LA immediately. 'Sell up. Give your solicitor power of attorney. Stay here.'

Selling the rings bought Molly a round-the-world ticket. First stop, 'the land of the free and the home of the brave'. Puzzled, she echoed the travel agent, then slowly smiled. Seeing that smile, he promised he'd try and get her an up-grade.

Viv's Californian friends talked empowerment psycho-babble but actually never once made Molly feel useless for feeling useless. They catapulted her into chi, soul alignment and medicine wheels. Deep down, she knew the vast profit from her house sale did her more good than the macrobiotic diet. By December she wanted to move on, hastened by a reluctance to stick around for Christmas with a smitten Viv and her brand-new partner, Aussie Alice. Alice's tenants had upped and offed, how d'you like that? Alice's new tenant, Molly headed across the Pacific to Sydney. She needed a summer.

'You wanted a latte, right? Shit. Sorry.'

'Cappuccino's fine . . .' pleaded Molly.

'I'll change it. No worries.' A sunbleached blond in his mid-twenties, the waiter seemed so laid-back that his only worry could be whether the surf was up. 'Say, are you Molly, the English teacher? I mean, the teacher from England. Dad told me about you.'

'Felice? The maths . . . ?' Molly had expected a four-foot cube like his father, Aldo, the café's owner. Male teaching staff she knew back home were more Jude the Obscure than Jude Law. She gazed into a gaze as blue and big as the ocean.

'Friends call me Phil. You're not panic-shopping like everyone else?' He looked round the deserted café. 'I told Dad it wasn't worth opening.'

'Aren't you meant to be away? Up in Wordsworth?'

'Byron,' corrected Phil. 'Mate's van died. Thought I'd better do the old man a favour. Let him have a rest. Enjoying your stay? Been to the beach?'

'Bondi. Coogee. Manly. Balmoral. Tamarama. Bronte. Bondi again.'

Molly had arrived a week ago. She slept with the blinds open, letting the southern sun wake her up. She'd go out on to the balcony and look across the harbour at the bridge and Opera House and the mini-Manhattan of skyscrapers. She felt like a desert flower after the rains with all the water, warmth and dazzling light around her. She'd have breakfast at the café next door, then explore and sight-see. Every afternoon she lay on some sand and listened to the breakers.

Had she been to the northern beaches? She should. But it was Christmas Eve, she must have plans. Shopping?

Molly had done her shopping. Half-bottles of champagne, a stack of books, a new bikini and a panetone.

That afternoon at Avalon beach, she watched Phil surf. Molly realized she was staring a bit too hard at a body that was one hundred per cent pure Australian beefcake. When he dropped her outside the flat, they talked for hours until he had to leave to go to Midnight Mass with his mother. He'd promised the old lady . . . Pity.

Pity, Molly agreed.

On Christmas afternoon, Phil came round as Molly knew he would. As they kissed and kissed, the phone rang twice. Later that evening, she got out of bed to open another bottle and to check the messages. Her parents calling again, worried about her spending Christmas alone . . .

It was Ben. 'Happy Christmas, darling. I've been a bastard. A stupid, stupid bastard, but we can try again. Can't we? Come home.'

Molly gazed out at the harbour, glowing gold in the setting sun. Wasn't she home?

'It's Debs. Happy Christmas.' Molly heard prolonged sobbing. 'Mine isn't. Happy. Angus has left me. And guess who for? Candy. Please call.'

Phil wrapped his arms around her. 'You OK?'

Molly smiled. No worries.

Amy Jenkins is the creator of the BBC 2 television series *This Life*. She has written and produced a feature film, *Elephant Juice*, for Hal-Miramax and has written and directed two short films. Her first novel, *Honeymoon*, is published 4th May 2000.

Re: The World

Amy Jenkins

I am a beautiful woman. My hair is dark and sleek, my face reminiscent of Marilyn Monroe, my body a collection of long luscious curves like some modish ergonomic furniture design. I have to dress cautiously or I stop traffic.

Nor am I just a pretty face. I have a masters in psychology and I am studying for my doctorate. I am an only child. My mother died of a rare tropical disease when I was thirteen. My father is a brain surgeon. He works although he doesn't need to work because we have money in the family. We are rich.

But don't hate me. Please don't hate me. If you saw me in the street, you might think I couldn't fail to be happy, you might think I'm one of those girls who 'has it all'. Or you might know better.

You might also think that men were queuing around the block for me. And there you'd be right. There is a motley bunch who line up along the railings outside my house. They are getting quite weather beaten and when it's really windy they have to cling to the railings like the nannies in *Mary Poppins* – for fear of being blown away. I am quite used to them by now. Otherwise, it is only the very brash and very handsome who approach. I do not want to spend the rest of my life with the very brash and the very handsome.

Of course, I dated when I was at university. I had a love affair with a man who fell off a cliff in Cornwall during the summer break. After that I concentrated on my studies. It wasn't a conscious decision to forgo, but I always found reasons to not go out with men. I was what you might call picky.

One day I decided it was time to find myself someone to love. This is the story of how I did that and how I found the only man in Europe who wouldn't want me. The only man in the Western hemisphere. The only man on the planet.

He took photographs of me. I don't usually let magazines take photographs of me. I refused to go into modelling when the pressure was on, when I was fifteen. But on this occasion it was different. A collection of designer dresses was to be auctioned for charity. And one of the dresses had belonged to my mother.

We met on the rocky bed of the Thames at low tide. It was grey and very windy. I said I didn't usually wear this kind of dress. But it was for charity.

One knee on the pebbles, he said. I don't usually take this kind of photograph. But it's for charity.

The dress blew up around my ears. My legs. Did I mention my legs? Sometimes I think my legs have a life of their own. Sometimes I eat a lot of cake to see if they'll notice me. It doesn't work. My legs just go on doing their own beautifully defined thing. I beat the dress down again with my hands.

I like your shoes, he said.

You like my shoes? I said. That's it? My shoes?

I tell you, that's the first man who's ever liked me for my shoes. I bought them in a junk shop when I was a student. Very high, very pale yellow and very strappy. They went with the gown.

Are you married? I said.

No, he said. But I could be. Are you good with children and dogs?

Dogs? I said.

But he had to go. He was in a hurry. He had more important matters to attend to, a plane to catch. I caught hold of his foot at the top of the ladder as it was about to disappear over the embankment. He turned to look at me strung out below.

My shoes, I said again. I had taken them off for ease of climbing. I waved them, trying to revive the subject. He wouldn't be drawn. He was gone.

I called the magazine editor to get his number. It wasn't that he was handsome really. He had the looks of a man who gets a long way with women by sheer force of will. Small, muscular, like a terrier. I left him a message. I said I hadn't met anyone like him ever in my life before. Some time later, two months later, he called.

What have you been up to? he said.

Oh, this and that, I said. The usual. What have you been up to?

I walked for thirty days through the mountains to photograph a tribe who've never seen a white man, he said.

There's not much you can say to that.

I'll be in London on the 20th, he said.

There's not much you can say to that either.

So he came to London and made me come within two minutes of being in my bed. His tongue was brave and confident.

Do you always come so quickly? he said.

Does it always take you so long? I said. He looked at me quizzically.

Two minutes, he said.

Two months, I said.

He didn't answer. I like your breasts, he said. You have beautiful breasts.

My breasts and my shoes. It was like that with him. Parts.

We made love. We lay awake and talked about life. Have you had women all over the world? I said.

He said an Afghan woman had come to his room in the middle of the night and risked being stoned to death. I imagined him with her. I wondered if Afghan women shaved their legs.

We slept for an hour and woke simultaneously and came into each other's arms, experienced the divine.

It's strange, he said.

What? I said.

It feels right, he said. I fell in love.

Over breakfast the next morning he told me about a man in Kosovo who had his ear cut off and fed to a dog. Then he had to go. He was in a hurry. He had important matters to attend to, a plane to catch. He hurried away with not a glance at the queue of rain-soaked men outside my front door. They watched him go, disconsolate.

He sent me passionate e-mails. Re: I want you. He said he dreamt about me intensely. Occasionally he would call me from airports. Out of breath, with two minutes to spare.

I was glowing. People said I was lit up. I caused a seven car pile-up walking down the Cromwell Road. I was obliged to go out in purdah like my Afghan woman friend who may or may not have shaved her legs.

Hours, days, weeks went by.

I've been thinking about the Afghan woman, I suddenly said when he called. The one who came to your room in the middle of the night. What happened to her? I said.

It all went wrong, he said.

Did you make love to her? I said.

Yes, he said.

And then? I said.

She wanted to marry me to escape the country.

And you wouldn't save her? I said. After you'd had her?

I'll be in London on the 3rd, he said.

When he came we danced together. Where were you today? I said.

At a meeting of the charity board, he said. In Stockholm.

Was it boring? I said.

The desire to see you was almost unbearable, he said. He took my shirt off and we slow danced like that.

Women have all the power, he said.

How's that? I said.

Only women know what's going on, he said.

They do terrible things to the women in Afghanistan, I said. My friend again. With the hairy legs.

They do, he said.

Because they think women have all the power, I said.

I hadn't thought of that, he said.

You hadn't thought of that? I said.

I just take photos, he said. His face clicked shut like the closing of the aperture. I took more clothes off to try to make it open again and let the light in. You could have any man you wanted, he observed.

Any man? I said. Do you promise me?

At breakfast he said that a woman on death row was due to be hung in five hours and forty minutes' time. Then he had to go. He was in a hurry. He had important matters to attend to, a plane to catch.

Does she shave her legs on death row?

He's an angel, I told people.

Angels are in heaven, people said. Not manifest.

Well then, I said, a hero.

Ditto, they said.

He's my hero, I said. I told the guys out by the railings. They were happy for me even though their clothes were torn to rags by the elements.

He called from the airport. I'll be in London on the 12th, he said.

We danced again.

Who was the last woman before me? I said.

I was in love with an evangelical Christian in the Bible Belt, he said. God told her not to sleep with me.

Do you like women who like you? I said.

What do you mean? he said.

It's a simple question. Maybe you only like women who don't like you.

What are you talking about? he said.

I love you, I said.

When he came he made a sound like he was dying. That's the first time you ever made a noise like that, I said.

Over breakfast, he told me about a doctor who was forced to amputate the limbs of thieves in football stadiums. Then he had to go. He was in a hurry. He had important matters to attend to, a plane to catch.

He didn't tell me when I would see him again. I never did see him again.

I'm walking for thirty days to photograph the building of a school for the tribe who'd never seen a white man, he said.

What do they want with a school? I said.

He didn't answer.

When will I see you? I said.

It's not enough, he said hopefully, is it? But I refused to comply.

I'll call you, he said. He lied about that. He wrote me a letter at Christmas.

Unfortunately I find it's impossible, he said. He enclosed a gift of a carved wooden knife. Unfortunately we are forced to amputate.

I read the letter out to the guys by the railings. Greetings for the coming year, he wrote. The guys raised their eyebrows. That's it, I said, end of letter. No love, no kisses, no regrets. That was when I noticed their clothes, ripped and torn like my heart. Am I not the most beautiful thing you've ever seen? I asked them.

Yes, they said. Did that make you think he'd love you? What made you think that? Then they asked me what he'd done to deserve my love.

He liked my shoes, I said.

But you're one in a million, they said.

One in a million, I said.

What is War Child?

"War Child was founded on a fundamental goal: to advance of the cause of peace through investing hope in the lives of children caught up in the horrors of war"

Bill Leeson (founder)

War Child is an international group of independent organisations dedicated to alleviating the suffering of children and young people affected by war and bringing this plight to the world's attention.

War Child UK focuses its attention on the provision of emergency aid and, in the longer term, the use of communications technology and the provision of education to improve the lives of war affected children.

What does War Child do?

War Child takes public money and donations and turns it into aid for the world's children. To give you just a few examples, in the six years since War Child was founded we have air-freighted emergency food to southern Sudan, provided vocational training for young people in Rwanda and provided clinical music therapy for young people in Bosnia traumatised by their experiences of war.

Without the support of the public, War Child would not and could not exist. Simple as that. Child rights means adult responsibility and we all bear that burden. So don't turn your back, help in whatever way you can.

Here's how you can help:

Post your cheques or postal orders (payable to War Child) to:

> War Child
> FREEPOST LON9980
> London
> NW5 3ZY
> UK

Or ring the credit card hotline (office hours): 020 7428 7598. We accept Visa, Mastercard, Switch and American Express. Or donate with your Charities Aid Foundation card

If you want to organise a fundraising event, or wish to give by Legacy or Covenant, please contact the office for more information on 020 7916 9276.

Thank you!